Alphonso Gentle

ELIGAH BOYKIN

ISBN: 978-1-64606-733-6   (Paperback Edition)
ISBN: 978-1-64606-734-3   (Hardcover Edition)
ISBN: 978-1-64606-732-9   (E-book Edition)

Some characters and events in this book are fictitious. Any similarity to real persons, living or dead, is coincidental and not intended by the author.

Book Ordering Information

Phone Number: 347-901-4929 or 347-901-4920
Email: info@globalsummithouse.com
Global Summit House
www.globalsummithouse.com

Printed in the United States of America

CONTENTS

DEDICATION

The present volume you now hold in your hands has traveled a rocky road. The energy of the piece first came bustling off the playground of Hutchinson Elementary School where my gang of friends played baseball. Here also is where Billy Ryan held his own with a bloody nose, closing his eyes against all comers. I fondly remember how we practiced kickboxing across the dusty, warped, slatted floor of the Hutchinson Music Room whenever our teacher would be called away from her piano to the Office.

The heat of creation then moves on to Joy Junior High School where I presented Miss Temple with my first novel. That work was filled with derivative James Bond and The Man From U.N.C.L.E. spy thriller antics and the dubious wisdom of my baseball friends about Human Sexuality. The great Pierre Rener ended up patiently listening to me reading the first few chapters of my literary efforts at Cass Tech High School and I picked up things from him that would later prove to be invaluable. Finally, I encountered Kevin Ransom while substitute teaching and attending classes for a Master's Degree at Wayne State University. He helped me procure enough unemployment money to bang out on a Hewlett Packard computer the story that is now yours to enjoy.

The people I have to thank for this current book reaching the public are legion. People I have never met or who barely know me would be surprised at how they have influenced and inspired me. Once again I thank Jerry Cleveland, Meghan Brown, Mary Riley, Clarita Mays, Sue Milus, Lynne Perry, Pat Rau, Bill Kux, Nick Meyers, Greg Brown, Frank English, David Rambeau, James

Wheeler, Dennis Galffey, Mike Mehall, Lester Johnson and Todd Erickson for their encouragement and support.

I would also like to thank Sean Connery, the Pope of the Action Adventure Hero. I learned much from his example over the years. He could be could be seen demonstrating the belief that inside every man there is a hero struggling to get out.

I am justly proud of ALPHONSO GENTLE and its odyssey to print. I would put it up against THE CATCHER IN THE RYE and the adventures of Holden Caulfield any day. That being said, since you have put your money where my print is, hold on tight to your ticket stub. You are now about to enter the world of ALPHONSO GENTLE.

-- Eligah Boykin Jr.

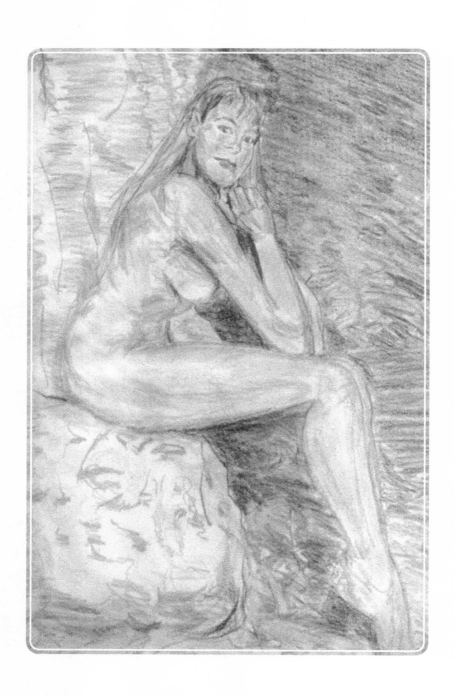

DIMENSIONS OF DAPHNE

Nothing like looking up at the bottom of some white man's shoe to make you feel like a roach. The face of Victor Baseheart loomed behind the sole of that shoe. He was all gritted teeth and red cleft chin. You would have thought he was Kirk Douglas in 'THE VIKINGS' the way he kept kicking me in the ribs and stomach.

"Where is she!" Victor roared at me. "What have you done with her?"

Every time I opened my mouth he would kick me again. I rolled and clutched at my privates. I drew up into a fetal position to protect myself. Whenever I caught my breath and attempted to scuffle to my feet, I would feel his hands clamp down on me like a vise. Between him slamming my head against the garbage cans racked out back behind Tony Ghetto's building and me kissing the flagstones of that gritty alley we were in, I was at a loss to find the time to answer his questions.

Funny the thoughts that can go through your mind when you are being served up an ass whopping with all the trimmings. The face of Daphne Wellington blinked in and out of my vision while the filtered sunlight flickered red through my eyelids. I could hear the haughty tone of her voice as clear as an echo from yesterday...

"That's sounds rich, coming from you, Mister High and Mighty. What gives you such a high vantage point on the missteps of us mere mortals?"

"I don't know, just calling them like I see them."

"I don't think you looking at the whole picture, Alphonso. People aren't as lily-livered as you make them out to be-"

"I didn't say that - "

"That's what you're implying. Besides," Daphne pouted at me with those gorgeous lips of hers, "I could wrap you around my finger any day of the week."

"Make me forget my own name, huh?"

"You better believe it, Mister!"

We chuckled quietly in each other's arms.

"Thanks for the vote of confidence."

"Thanks for scoring the human race so low on your scorecard!"

Daphne left me no doubt that she was speaking from experience. You know, that thing about wrapping turkeys around her fingers. Now as fine as she was, I was sure she found herself compelled to do that many a time, and baste them too. There never occurred such an event with the Gentle Man, however. The woman has not been born who can make me go gobble-gobble.

Check it out.

Daphne Wellington possessed that kind of supermodel beauty that made the average yahoo think not in his lifetime. She was so fine it was downright demoralizing. As a matter of fact, the first time I lined her up in my sights she was sitting next to a baby grand piano with a scowl on her face.

The jazz singer Diana Krall came to mind. There she was busting out in all her glory, that honey blonde hair spilling down to her slim waist college girl style. She dressed to the nines too. You know how some women just have that kind of look. It is no problem for them to look like the covers of fashion magazines or music CDs, and every time they move a camera in your head goes click.

Daphne was definitely calling up the file marked 'ALL FOR YOU' and, let's face it, gents, 'THE LOOK OF LOVE' on top of that. The only problem was that cold glare on her face. Honeys! They literally kill themselves with diets and cosmetics to get that magnetic wave going on where they can draw dudes to them like bees to nectar, and then get that faraway look in their eyes like that was the farthest thing from their mind!

Please...

Now tell me I am wrong.

Beyond that are the women who grow hard and cold turning so many dudes down with designs on them. Like I said, you can see their faces start to set into a mask of studied disinterest. That is for the dudes they just can't be nice to, the ones that won't take no for an answer. The ones who tag along when they are not wanted around and give them little gifts that are not asked for or appreciated. The ones who are so smitten they are sick with that puppy love.

All they need is a leash, brother!

Hey, it's all mellow with the Gentle Man. I'm just keeping it real. Anyway, so she's sitting there by the baby grand doing the sternness to me while she keeps those lyrically long legs defensively crossed away from me. The lights run a highlighted finger down her nylon thigh past the tapering calf and beyond the ankles to those big feet all strapped in to show her toes. No doubt about it, brothers, she's living sculpture in motion. Poof! I can see it all so clearly in my mind's eye. The bust of her I have just completed and the moist clay is still wet!

Now that really is a tragedy. The nudes I could do of her in terra cotta and charcoal, the scenes she could model in watercolor, acrylic and oil; just like this little vignette here. The trouble is, you can see the way her mind is set in her face she is not having it. So be it. It is time for your old neighborhood Gentle Man to walk on by. Let it never be said that yours truly forced greatness on anyone!

So I stroll on by with a civil smile before I bust out laughing with delight. See-it really is a shame, here she is with a whole lot of that Diana Krall working for her with a hint of that movie star Lauren Bacall in her attitude and it is all going to waste. Nothing I can do about it. I am sorry to inform you that the Gentle Man is not a social worker.

The other thing is that I don't want to hear how rare and scarce these precious specimens of beauty are to the experience of Man. Bump that junk! There is nothing so overwhelmingly abundant as good looking sights and sounds. After all, by now it should be common consensus that the beauty of Life resides in the Soul of Man.

"-and another thing," Daphne horns in while I'm pontificating, "if you and I and all mankind are the ultimate source of all the goodness and the beauty in the world, how can you be so down on all of us?"

"-because ya got pah-tent-shull! But Lordy, it can be so sadly wasted! You got it all in here-"

"Eep! Stop tickling me, Alphonso! Stop! I mean it now-"

"-but you got tah - got tah let it all flow out there-"

"You better stop!" Daphne punched and rubbed her knuckles into my shoulder. "I'm warning you, Mister-"

"- until - until all of it envelopes everything everywhere!"

"That's better! You better draw back - if you know what's good for you. What? You want a piece of me?"

"Yeah, and seconds!"

I could feel Daphne shoulders shake with laughter in the palms of my hands, that daffy brazen grin spread wide across her face shattering into chuckling smithereens.

There was no time to enlist new recruits. The main reason I was swooping down into the cut at this affair was all about business. I was returning a set of photo references to the hostess Mona. I kept telling her that with that Afro on jam and the loss of a few more pounds I would have her posing nude for me in no time. Luckily I saw her slap coming and dodged it.

I gave Mona a kiss on the cheek once I gave back her pix and headed for the door. Out the corner of my eye I could see Daphne sidle down the bench in front of the baby grand to tickle the keys. She started singing a little something to herself under her breath, but hey! That's no fun! You know what I'm saying?

That's why I'm over there in a flash, bumping her hip with mine as I slide down the bench and take over the piano. She frowns with a kind of startled annoyance, but guess what? I can frown right back too! I kind of recognize the tune she's pitter-pattering and pick up where she's left off.

"Excuse me? Do I KNOW you?"

"You will now, momma." I flash her my business card with practiced precision. "Gentle. Alphonso Gentle."

Doggone child, that double-oh-seven style! She's holding my card before she even knows it has happened.

"Aren't you Danny's friend?" She squints at my card.

"Yeah, he told you about me?" I said, riffing out of what she was playing into some Scott Joplin Mister Mannard had been teaching me. "What have you heard, baby?"

She narrows her eyes like she's measuring me with calipers.

"Unfortunately for you, yes. That's Scott Joplin, isn't it?"

"Uh huh. What did Danny have to say about me?"

"He told me to steer clear of a guy named Alphonso who was all smiles and teeth. That I should stay away from you because the first thing you would try to do is hit on me."

"Make you own observation, sweetheart." Damn that Danny! "Am I only smiles and teeth? Besides introduce myself to you, have I done anything to embarrass you?"

"I don't know yet." Daphne put her elbow on the baby grand and cocked her head back at me on her fingertips. "The jury's still out on that one."

"Call those suckers back in and acquit me. You know, I noticed you have a nice, soft voice. Do a set of pipes go with that?"

I ripple down the keyboard and beckon her to the side of the piano.

"What do you think?" Daphne crossed those fabulous legs again and I was greatly moved. "Do you think I might have what it takes?"

"Insufficient data. I know you know this one-" I riffed off into a rendition of 'What's Love Got To Do With It?'.

"Yeah, I know it. I didn't think a 'with it' fellow like you would be into 'old school', Mister Gentle."

"Stand over there, honey. I want to see what you're into now."

She took a spot next to the piano with the poise of a professional singer. Everyone gathered around the baby grand. Just like my brothers and sister used to do at my mama's house during the holidays to sing Marvin Gaye and Luther Van Dross. Daphne's voice rang out on the wing with the exhilaration of a mountain bluebird soaring free of its perch. Kind of freaky, really, sort of like switching channels from IFC to MTV. One minute she was in one mode and the next minute she was someplace else with a swiftness that was altogether unsettling and frightening. She went from baby grand wallflower through a warp in time and space to Diva almost without time for preparation to expect a transition. This startling appearance of a new Daphne created a rift in our perception of her. I was carrying this picture in my head of her and suddenly it seemed like she ripped it in half and I was trying to match the torn edges together.

Daphne's performance was classic textbook and of course with white people that is often the problem. Many can get the techniques and mechanics spot on perfect, but oftentimes the ghost in the machine is gone. That final revelation of self is withheld for no apparent reason and that can keep them out of the winner's circle. I guess it's a cultural thing. I have heard some white musicians play jazz and the music is straight out of a Hollywood movie. I will turn around and hear black musicians play jazz and it has this living, organic intensity that plumbs the depths of the soul in the backwoods of Georgia. Everybody has their preferences, but it's really apples and oranges when all is said and done. One thing is for sure, Daphne was definitely headed for Hollywood with no stops in between for passengers.

We would join in with her on the chorus lines and push her up through her atmospheric covering into free space where riding on our thrust she could navigate more effortlessly in cruise control. She finally landed without turbulence, her eyes glistening to welcome applause and hands outstretched to shake hers and clap her on the back. I was one of them to get the Diva's handshake, but then it was time for the Gentle Man to go.

There were canvases to stretch and frame and I knew Daphne and I would meet again some time were it meant to be. Right now, there was a project I was getting ready for my nephew. I needed him to rub crushed pastel colors into Arches' watercolor paper for the needed ground to a series of drawings.

I turned one more time to view Daphne at the risk of being turned into a pillar of salt. There she was where I had lifted her onto the piano, but from where I was standing right now it was all looking different. She crossed her legs and there it was again, that certain aura of glamour and that Hollywood thing beckoning to me. Just for a moment, she was like some famous photograph from the past. She was doing the movie star moment and I felt like Harry Truman walking away from Lauren Bacall.

"Why didn't you stay for the rest of the party?" Daphne asked, clicking my glass of wine with her own.

"Is this you, too?"

"Don't try to change the subject, Alphonso. Why didn't you ask for my phone number or something?"

"Would you have given it to me?"

"No,"

"There's your answer. What's going on here? What's with all the hair?" I snapped my fingers a couple of times, trying to recall the scene. "Wait a minute! Don't tell me, you're playing Rapunzel! Am I right?"

"Yeh," Daphne sat on the couch in her party gown and crossed her legs under her. "-but all that hair isn't mine."

"I can see that."

"We took one of the gym ropes and shredded the fibers and combed it out with one of those curry combs you use on horses."

I nodded to myself. No doubt about it. Even back then, Daphne was a beauty who stood out.

"Did you dye your hair red? Was the rope dyed red when you combed all the fibers loose?"

"Yeah," Daphne was sipping from her long stemmed glass, silently measuring me. "I wore the rope sort of like a fall. Back here, want to see?"

She turned her head to show me where she attached it, but there was plenty of time for that. I was in no hurry. I just wanted to make sure I got all the details. I went on to the next photograph of our highness.

"Don't tell me this is you playing 'Sleeping Beauty'!"

"Yeah, that's me. What makes you so surprised?"

"I don't know, talk about 'old school'! Yeah, that's you all right."

"What did you expect? I was in high school for crying out loud."

"Right. High School. Don't hide behind that lame excuse."

Daphne leaned a shoulder against the wall next to her photograph.

"Excuse me? I have done nothing I should feel ashamed or guilty about." Daphne folded her arms in defiance. "As a matter of fact, I am quite proud of my theatrical accomplishments. Have you got some kind of problem with that?"

"Oh wow!" I counted all the little people collected around her until I came to seven. "Do not tell me you even played 'Snow White'!"

"I wasn't the only one! We traded up on all the parts. We toured the schools."

"Don't worry, I won't tell nobody. Your secret is safe with me."

"What in the world are you talking about, Alphonso?"

"You shouldn't have to ask. Rap on 'Rapunzel'! Do that double duty 'Sleeping Beauty'! Cop them Z's! When you're 'Snow White', you're right, huh?"

"What's the matter? My acting career isn't 'fly' enough for you, Alphonso?"

"Naw." I chuckled confidentially. "We all come from some place. But you got to admit you got an awful lot of white bread on both sides of the baloney."

"Yeah? Seems like it's your baloney, if you ask me!"

"Yow! Mama Too Tight!"

"Yeah, right. Whatever."

"Over here, girl. Come on, woman, and get yo' whoppin'."

"Hmmn, I don't recall I invited you over here for corporal punishment."

"Come over here before I take one of these trophies and conk you over the head with it."

Daphne held up her silk green purse as though she were going to bean me with it.

"Take your best shot, mister."

I snatched up one of her trophies playfully and took aim at her. Daphne dropped her purse and shrieked.

"Be careful with that, Alphonso! Not that one! That's my Ballroom trophy."

"Your what?"

"You heard me. That's my trophy for Ballroom Dancing!"

"I'll make you dance, little Miss Muffet. Get yo' hind on over here."

"Oooo, daddy! I loves it when you talk like that to me."

After taking up her purse from the carpet, she headed my way. I snatched it from her and gently whacked her behind. I grasped her firmly by the wrist and led her back over to the couch. "What kind of dancing did you have to do for this one, honey?"

"Some kind of a waltz or maybe it was the rumba. C'mon, let's go a few steps and it should come back to me."

I circled her waist with my arms and swung her away from the couch again.

"Did you get what you really want, Alphonso?" Daphne smirked, poking me in the ribs.

"Yeah. I would have to say yeah. At least I never lied to nobody."

"About what?"

"About what it is that I really want."

"Never? Not even one itsy-bitsy-teensy-weensy time?"

"Welllll-naw-"

"Aw, come off it, Alphonso-"

"I mean not really-"

"Not even once?"

She turned her face to me and her striking beauty focused on me like a spotlight. When a female that fine looks you straight in the eye, you feel like you'll never get to heaven unless you give them the truth. So now I start to waffle just a little.

"I mean-look here, baby, I'm as human as the next dude, but-"

"See?" Daphne slaps her thigh triumphantly. "What I tell you?"

"Whoa. What's up with you, 'dere?"

"What's the matter, Alphonso? Afraid I'll keep my panties on unless you 'fess up? Strange, isn't it, how much truth matters when the nookey's on the line?"

"Sounds like you're quoting the master. You might as well write this one down too, while you're takin' notes, girlfriend. Truth cannot be paid in pussy."

Daphne mouthed those last six words to herself. After making an effort to find the sense in them, she at length shook her head, a quizzical expression forming across her brow.

"That sounds awfully cryptic, Alphonso."

"All I'm sayin'is you really want to see some lyin', just hold back on the lovin'. That's one thing that will make people lie their heads off. Dudes and honeys become walking billboards of lies for that."

"Okay, I'll bite. If you can't ransom love for truth, then what do you have to do to get it?"

"You give people what they really want."

"Hmmnn, how do you know what someone really wants?"

"When you find out how, I'll start taking notes."

"I thought you said you knew what you really wanted."

"No doubt."

"Are you going to tell me, Alphonso?"

"You keep doin' that, you'll just cause me to lie some more."

"Tell me, Alphonso!"

"What I really want I'm holding in my arms right now."

"Liar! That's a line if ever I heard one."

"You're the one at fault."

"No, really Alphonso, I'm serious about this."

"No doubt. When it comes to the truth, most people are."

"Stop playing with me, Alphonso. You say you know what you really want, then spit it out and tell me."

"Hey lady, don't mistake me for Suckertease. I'm not here to out philosophize you, mama. I'm really just a very simple dude."

"Oh boy, here it comes-"

"No, straight up. The aim of my game is to get beautiful women naked. I rub their bodies like the lamp of Aladdin and make a wish for ecstasy."

"That's all you want, Alphonso?"

"That's all I want."

"Sounds awfully shallow to me, Alphonso-"

"I never claimed to be no 'Mr. Deep'."

"-besides being a bunch of malarkey!"

"That's the other thing."

"What other thing?"

"When you tell people what you really want, the first thing they will usually try to do is convince you that you don't really want that at all."

"Oh, come on, Alphonso. All you want in Life is to see beautiful women naked?"

"That's all that matters to me."

Daphne tried to burn a hole through me with her best stony glare, but I would not be moved. When I would not give an inch, she flinched and broke up chuckling.

"That's right, and don't feel a lick of guilt about it, neither."

"I'll bet. Oh, here come the teeth and smiles, now. Let's say you get me naked, Alphonso, and mind you that's a big 'if'; what happens after that? Are we done when it comes to that point? What about me when you have got what you want? Once you've scanned my barcode and partook of the contents, where do you go from there, Alphonso? Do you save my box tops and coupons so you can get so much off on the next model?"

"I never lied to you, Daphne."

"What's that supposed to mean?"

"I never pretended to be anything other than what I am."

"Right. 'Said the spider to the fly.' "

"That's butterfly in your case," Daphne barely heard me mumble.

"What's that?"

"Butterfly. 'Said the spider to the butterfly.' Don't play yourself cheap, Daphne."

"That's ironic coming from you, Alphonso. What exactly do you think you've been doing all this time to me?"

"What you invited me here to do. You called me over to have a conversation with you. I accepted your invitation. Now we're doing that someplace where you feel most comfortable. I thought that was how you wanted it."

Daphne turned her head away from me. I didn't catch everything she said, but I remember hearing her tell me this:

"This is what you wanted, Alphonso. I just wanted to talk to you someplace where I knew you couldn't talk all that balderdash." Daphne turned her face back towards me and it was set in an angry scowl. "I know what I do not want. I don't just want to be an object of fantasy in your imagination."

Reminds me of the time Miguel Jimenez came up to the fourth floor while I was finishing up a painting. That was my last year at the University Academy of Fine Arts. He flashed all these pictures of him at the party after the Fashion Show he attended. Some of them showed him dressed as I usually encountered him as a student at the Academy. The others showed him with his hair about his shoulders, wearing lipstick and a dress. He seemed quite proud of those photographs. I shrugged my shoulders. Who am I to judge another man and his bliss?

I'll never forget what he said to me.

"You know Alphonso, I don't know why I'm like this really. Sometimes, I feel as though a whole other person is trying to break through my wrapper and jump out of my skin. She is my true self and she is a female."

While Miguel explained this to me, I gently gave him back his pictures. I listened to him and did not interrupt as a sign of respect. After that, he waited for me to say something. I suppose it was my time to share. I didn't know exactly how to put it; since there was no intention on my part to reveal how I was just a bitch at heart. Something humorous flashed into my mind, which I thought might be appropriate, so I just said that.

"I know what you mean, Miguel. To tell you the truth, I have always wanted to fuck everything that walks, crawls or flies. I don't know why I'm like that."

Miguel probably did not realize that I was paraphrasing a line from a Clint Eastwood movie. But I could imagine the exclamation on his face when he saw the movie and thought to himself, 'Alphonso said something almost word for word like that!' I love sowing the seeds of delayed reactions like that. I knew that one day Miguel would come up to me and tell me to my face: "What you said to me in the Academy, Alphonso! You heard Clint Eastwood say that! That's where you got that from!"

Yeah, chuckle, chuckle, and chuckle.

"I don't know what you're talking about, Daphne. Holding an honored place in my very fertile imagination is a grand place to be."

"There you go again-"

"What?"

"All that hype and self promotion. Just dispense with all the hooey, Alphonso."

"What are you talking about? I came right out and told you what I wanted with the greatest respect for your feelings. I didn't beat around the bush and talk your ear off with a lot of useless intellectualization. I explained myself and my intentions in such a manner as you would not feel the need or occasion to take offense."

"Jeez Alphonso, it all comes so trippingly off your tongue. Know what you sound like?"

"No, darling-" I blew a strand of hair away from her ear. "What do I sound like?"

"You sound like you're giving testimony in some Court of Law or something."

"That's right, dear. I'm defending myself in the Court of Love."

"Jeez Alphonso, don't you ever give that stuff a rest?"

The Gentle Man was not born to harbor the anger of the world. When you pursue that which you love, there are many who will ascribe hidden agendas to your cause. I was not born to explain why so much unhappiness exists in the world. I do not know why people place so much importance to giving over all their energy and attention to anger and hate and the violence needed to dim and extinguish the divine creative spark that exists within us all. I am not a philosopher, and these concerns are not within the domain of interests that inspire the Gentle Man.

I know what I love and I know what I want to love and that is enough for me.

But what clay can match the malleability of the female form, what canvas can encompass the orbits of that encircling splendor? What plaster cast can truly form a mold to the living dimensions of Daphne?

I do not know, but trust the Gentle Man to endeavor to solve this mystery.

The majority of males on this planet hunt women as though they were prey on a game preserve. I have never been above a playful game of wits with anyone, and that includes the ladies I have encountered. But the Gentle Man never goes where he is not invited, and comes only where he can enrich, not invade and be the interloper. I do not know why death and disaster stimulates the creative energies and mind of Western Man, or why he is so willing to jump at the opportunity to dissect a cadaver and draw out its contents on parchment when the newborn child would easily give him at least eighteen years worth of the study of developing Life. These issues are beyond the range of my understanding.

All I know is to go where my imagination takes me and to serve the energy of Life.

There is one other thing that I know. When one is invited into the bedroom of a beautiful woman, it is no place to make a declaration of War. I kissed Daphne upon a bare shoulder and took care not to ruffle her party gown. I arose from the white sheets we were cuddling upon while talking and the mattress sprang back as my weight left it.

"Perhaps this wasn't the best thing to do," I said as I bent over and laced my shoes back up. "I've tried to be straightforward with you, Daphne. Am I right?"

"You sound different, Alphonso-"

"Am I right, Daphne?"

Even now, reclining on her bed with her silk green gown on and strips of pink chiffon all about her breasts and bare back, I was fighting the urge to pull my sketch book out of my jacket pocket and do some preliminary sketches of her in those gleaming dancing shoes. I could imagine what she would say. The standard rap about how I was just taking advantage of her to create my Art. I turned slowly and opened the door to her bedroom. This was a beautiful opportunity I was letting go down the drain, but it was best to keep things on the up and up.

"You don't have to go right now, Alphonso," she said with bowed head.

"What?"

"I said you don't have to go."

"No, you wanted to talk to me somewhere you felt the most comfortable. I think we've had a good talk myself. Let's call a time out and think about some of the things we've both said."

"We can still talk, Alphonso,"

"Daphne, think about what you want out of this relationship. I'm really looking for someone I can share creative reason with, and use as a source of inspiration for my Art. She has to be willing to do what

I tell her without any lip and help me make the most of the ideas that go off like popcorn inside my head."

"What you want is a slave."

When she said this I almost busted out laughing, but the glint in her eye told me she was serious to the bone.

"You would think like that. That's got to be uppermost in my mind, right? How I'm going to turn the tables after all these centuries. That would be a switch, wouldn't it? An' you're figuring that I'm figuring it would serve you right, is that what's on your mind?"

"There you go again, Alphonso. What makes you so above it all?"

"I don't know, Daphne. I'm just not angry at the world the way you are."

Daphne twisted a lock of hair about her fingers and narrowed her eyes at me even more.

"I think you are."

"Look Daphne, you want to find somebody to help you shake your fist at the world, go right ahead. At least you'll be with somebody you find compatible. Life's too short to be angry all the time."

"I'm not angry all the time."

"That's the way you seem with me, honey."

"We were just talking," Daphne's tone started to soften when she said this.

"Daphne, let me hip you to something. I have never made love to a woman I didn't draw and sketch in the nude first. You would have been the exception!"

"We're not making love,"

"All the more reason for me to go. I should have all your clothes off by now and we should be takin' care of business."

"You think you're such big stuff, Alphonso."

"-an' evidently you don't! Take it easy, Daphne."

"You don't have to go!"

I headed for the door to her apartment. I was thinking how I was going to stretch the rest of those canvases, when she intercepted me.

She pressed her back against the doorjamb and lifted her chin with stiff pride.

"I invited you here. The least you could do is kiss me good night."

"For real?"

She seemed slightly amazed when I said this.

"That would be the polite thing to do, don't you think?"

"Yeah, I guess you've got a point there. Okay. But remember, I'm just doing what you want me to do. Hold on a second-"

I was going to give her a firm smooch on the lips, but she wanted so much more. The next thing I knew, our tongues were floating in each other mouths and we were half twisted around towards the bedroom again. Daphne was the one who pressed me back with the palms of her hands this time.

"Whoa there, tiger," Daphne exclaimed, "let me catch my breath! Let's not let things move too fast around here."

"All right. You've got my card, don't you?'

"Uh-huh." Daphne's face fell a little. "Don't tell me you still have to go."

"Yeah, baby, I really do. Unless you want to help me stretch some canvas for some paintings tonight."

"Nooo, why don't you just stay here?"

"Look, I'll be at my studio all this week. Stop by anytime in the evening and we'll talk some more, you dig?"

"Oh. Maybe. If I can find the time."

"Yeah, well," I kissed her firm on the lips the way we should have the first time. "You take care, hear? Come by and see me in my studio, okay? You invited me, so now I'm inviting you."

"You know, you really don't have to go, Alphonso," She whispered into my shirt.

But you see, I really did have to go. Otherwise, I would never get done all those beautiful charcoal drawings of her and all the rest that was burning a hole in my imagination. I just knew that once she had me wrapped around her finger, I would forsake all that for the treasure she had promised me with that last burning kiss.

The days passed and the image of Daphne all but slipped into a fading dissolve from my mind. There was much to do before my big opening at the gallery. Lugging my particleboard paintings up four flights of stairs when the service elevator stalled was getting old real quick to Danny. Every time we turned the corner on another landing, angling one of my five by ten foot masterpieces up the stairs, he would flash a pained complaint with a whine of annoyance.

"Mannn, the reason nobody don't come and visit yo' sorry ass is to keep you from giving away free heart attacks. I'm supposed to be your friend, Alphonso, an' look how you do me."

"You said you came to help, Danny, so why you tryin' to file a grievance on my ass?"

"Because haulin' this big-ass board up all these flights of stairs is some damn rugged hiking. That's why."

"Look, my main man, once I frame this sucker I stand to make a nice piece of change this time."

"That's what you said the last time, Alphonso."

"We didn't do so bad, Danny. You got to show some of your stuff. You saw some money. What makes you think I'm not gonna hook you up this time?"

When we got to the last landing, I heaved against the board and Danny stepped back up into the hallway, his gym shoes skidding back across the worn carpet as I lifted up. I stepped forward into the corridor, the side of my leg brushing past Daphne's shoulder. She was sitting on the last landing before you got to my studio, her knees held together with a slight shiver. The lavender coat she wore all bunched around her, was mottled with glittering specks of raindrops on the collar and the ends of her hair underneath her scarf.

"Daphne! Where'd you come from, sugar?"

"I've been waiting for you, Alphonso. I was just about ready to leave when I heard you and Danny coming up the stairway. I could never reach you on the phone"

"I've been getting ready for this show I was telling you about. Right, Danny?"

"Mannn, the lady can see what's happening. Evening, my dear, don't get you feathers all ruffled over this snake."

"Daphne, will you do something for me?"

"Yeah, Alphonso?"

"Can you," I nodded to Danny to swing around to the doorknob. "- get my keys out my pocket and open the door for us?"

"Oh! Yeah, where are they?"

"The left hand pocket - the left hand pocket - "

I watched her hair fall into her coat between her collars as she moved her hand like silk through my pocket and grasped my keys. She pulled them free past my belt.

"Tell me which one it is -" she said, fingering her way along my key ring, "this one here?"

"No, the next one -"

"Okay, I think this is it. I'll try it."

She stood there, pulling the strap to her umbrella over her shoulder and trying to jiggle the key in the lock.

"Feels like it's too tight, Alphonso. I can't get it to turn-"

"No, the next one. Try the next one-"

"C'mon man," Danny flashed a grimace, "we can set this down now. We're here. I got to work the blood back into my fingers."

"Ah! I think I got it. Yeah. Okay, Alphonso-"

Daphne looked up at us, her face framed in a half halo from the hallway light overhead. She disappeared inside like a wisp.

"C'mon, Danny," I said, lifting up my end of the board.

"Hold tight, man, hold tight. What's your hurry? Let me get a little breather first. This a dog-gone long way up just for yo' ass to have a skylight!"

"Want me to help, Alphonso?" I heard Daphne call from inside.

"Naw baby," Danny replied, "we got it - we got it."

Danny stood there for a moment glowering at me.

"Man, what you got her up here for?" Danny whispered irritably. "That young heifer come from a good home. She don't need to get all mixed up in this scene you got going on."

"Why you always got to try and convince everybody that somehow I'm in league with the devil? I invited Daphne to come up here and see my work sometime. The way you talk you would think I was Mojo or somebody."

"Yeah, yeah, well, let's get out of this hallway and get this thing inside. C'mon man-"

Danny heaved on his end with me and we staggered my painting inside my studio.

"This is certainly spacious, Alphonso," Daphne remarked as she sauntered into the bars of shadows and emerging afternoon sunshine from the grid of the skylight above. "- are these all your paintings on this wall over here?"

"Yeah. Set it down right here, Danny. All the ones I could hang."

"The particle board paintings we're sliding into the back corner with the rest of the stuff." Danny told her.

Daphne stood a solitary figure before the tan wall that framed those squares and rectangles of varying sizes. She walked up to one painting of a pair of my gloves lain upon a globe of the world. The globe itself was situated on a writing desk next to a personal computer and before the vertical louvered curtains fronting the open window. Daphne gingerly touched the painting with a fingertip.

"What medium did you use for this one, Alphonso?" She asked the painting in the hazy temper of rumination.

"That one is oil, some of the others in acrylic, and there are a bunch of watercolors you'll probably recognize from student exhibits back at the Academy. Here, let me take your coat-"

"These landscapes are quite good, Alphonso," Daphne murmured, looking up at the top of the wall.

"I'll told you man," Danny pointed at me as he headed to the fridge for a beer. "- you ought to concentrate on that for a while and ease on off the nudes and the figurative stuff."

"Aw, go someplace, man. Those are all my drawings along the black wall over there," I pulled the sliding door on the closet and racked her coat. "-and that's all my sculpture over there on the tables against the wall."

Daphne moved with a graceful indolence past the posing platform in the center of the studio. She put a foot on one of the steps that were located at opposite ends of the platform.

"This where you have your models pose for you?"

There was something coy and brazen in Daphne's smile all at the same time.

Yeah, baby," I said, copping an Austin Powers on the woman. "Come on over here."

"What -" She strode over to the black wall with me. "These all your charcoal drawings over here, Alphonso?"

"Some are in charcoal. Some are in pastels-"

"You used cra-pas to render these drawings, didn't you?"

"Oil pastels, yeah. I've been laying down the ground on Arches' watercolor paper for some drawings about you."

I took her by the hand and led her over to the wall behind the platform. I got my nephew to help me grind the various colored pastels in on half a dozen of the papers I was preparing. That left me the charcoal grounds to do on my own. Daphne glanced at me, and then back at the dozen or so brightly hued rectangular sheets that lined the wall. The dark, cloudy, amorphous shapes on the charcoal sheets were interspersed between them.

"Anybody want something to drink?" Danny waved a can of beer around.

"I'll have something-"

"What'll you have?"

"I'll just have some bottled water if you've got it," Daphne called over while she held my fingers. She cocked her head to one side at me. "What makes you think I'll give you permission to do drawings of me?"

"Hey mama, don't you want to end up in an Art Book one day? Opportunities to become immortalized don't just happen every day."

"Alphonso! You are so full of it, Mister High and Mighty-"

"Ain't that something? You know what I hear?" Danny handed me a couple of bottled waters and I handed one to Daphne.

"No, what?" I sighed.

"I hear opposites attract. Probably the reason why there's so much chemistry between y'all and you get along so well is because she's so free of bullshit and, just like the Lady says, you are so full of it." Danny took another swig of beer, then sat in a sofa chair next to the platform and draped a leg over an arm. "Matter a fact, sometimes it be like you're merchandizing your own special brand."

Daphne unlaced her fingers from mine to stifle a giggle.

"Yo-Danny-O, don't you have some place you got to be?"

"Huh?" Danny started to well up with protest, but I just glared at him and turned up the sternness to the max. "Oh. Yeah, I better be getting back to my own studio. I got to finish blocking out the backgrounds to some of those street scenes and urban landscapes I been workin' on."

"Right. Thanks for the help, man."

Danny helped himself to my soul handshake with a crisp snap of the fingers.

"You gotta free pass to my studio anytime, little girl. Just don't let Kid Rap slap the crap on you."

"I'll take your advice to heart, Danny. Besides you've got my back anyway, don't you?"

"Sho' you right. Good night."

Daphne swung away from my attempt to embrace her as we heard Danny's footsteps die down the hallway.

Daphne's high heels clicked on the wooden slats as she paced away. She walked over to a bulletin board on one wall where a papier- mache mask of red and gold glitter hung. The mask was resting against an array of sketches pinned, thumbtacked and paper clipped against the board. Daphne lifted up the mask by its chin and regarded me thoughtfully.

"So this is where you've been making your Art," She nodded again as she surveyed her surroundings. "Why the gym rope, Alphonso?"

"Funny you should mention that. I remembered that photograph I saw in your apartment with you playing Rapunzel and went to a Sporting Goods warehouse and got one."

I watched Daphne's breasts swell as she craned her neck at the ceiling. That was just the hint I needed to spark my imagination. I could easily visualize myself putting her through her poses and making her one of my best models ever. The hunger to turn my passion into something more than a fleeting impulse, to sublimate mere sensation into a constructive realization that would later honor the moment when an experience could be transformed into a pleasurable and perhaps even enlightening product of memory, was fast becoming the mission to be accomplished.

That is the quest that leads the adventurer reluctantly or eagerly to investigate the very real meaning and value of experience itself.

A woman appears in my space being formed by Life as a work of Light, now elected as the primary stimulus of the soul's stirring and craving for transcendence. Why should it be so? What call does matter have to work such a spell upon the mind?

"Just another prop I can use in rendering the body in motion," I toss off casually to this young woman who even now is slowly, subtly capturing my imagination. "Something that I hope will help evoke a scene, enable me to create a lasting pleasure."

Daphne took a folding chair and placed it on the carpeted platform. She took a sip from her bottled water, looking first from the long, horizontal expanse of the black wall filled with drawings and then to the white wall neatly arranged in framed and matted rectangles of oils, acrylics, and watercolors. Finally, she took a long look at me, and her face took on an expression of great and sober solemnity.

"Know what I think, Alphonso?" She took another sip of her bottled water with a sigh of satisfaction. "You want for me to be a muse of some kind to you. I was talking to my father about you the other day and he agreed with me. There's something about real life and the bustle of the world that makes you go into ungovernable ecstasies. At least that's the way my father explained it. I can see his point in a sense. The experience of the sensible world causes in you an emotional response that you can barely master. Now I'm one of those points of perception to you, right? You have to create a way to keep your feelings from overwhelming you and causing some kind of great destruction to yourself and others."

"That's what you think?"

"Yes. I think there is something to that line of thought." There was a merry kind of twinkle in her eye now. "Bring a chair, Alphonso." Daphne patted her thigh. "Come up here and sit by me."

I shrugged and folded up a chair, stepping up onto the platform. I unfolded the chair and sat down, crossing a leg and holding an ankle to my knee. Daphne twirled a long braid of hair with amusement.

"Nice to take a break from mentally undressing me, isn't it?"

"Why? So you can psychobabble me to death?"

"No. I told my parents all about you, Alphonso. They told me they would be very interested in meeting this crazy artist type I've bee seeing lately."

"Oh, so now I'm this crazy artist type, is that it?"

I folded my arms with a narrowed eye. What was this babe driving at now?

"Alphonso?" She looked around in a kind of mock innocence. "Where does that stairway lead to up there?"

"When I get tired, I have to take a break. I have a bed up there and sometimes I crash between projects."

"That right?"

"Uh huh. You want me to take you up there and see?"

"I don't know. Now wouldn't be such a good time." Daphne coolly took another sip of her water. "Did you know I was a virgin, Alphonso?"

She nodded at me with a smile of beatific satisfaction.

Now for all my overwhelmingly intense responses to Life itself, I must admit I was at a loss exactly as to how to respond to this confession. I have always wondered why people placed such a premium on this stage of a development. I have also wondered how it came to be regarded by some as one of the great prizes of Life. Truth be told, there are things I now know about lovemaking and how to satisfy a woman that could never have been taught to me by a virgin. Don't ask me why ignorance and inexperience are so valued in a young woman. A man suffering under these conditions would be condemned for experiencing them one second longer than he has to do so.

Check this out.

What does losing one's virginity mean, anyway? When I first entered that sacred virgin territory with Wilma Durant, I can't recall her breaking down into tears and sobs and wailing that she now was bereft of the very thing that made life worth living. No, it was not like that at all. I remember a look of blissful gratitude on her face that seemed to indicate to me that she felt she was now the proud possessor of a very valuable experience, one that she would be able to cherish and treasure forever. There was nothing lost. Everything was gained as far as I could tell, and you can believe me, that was all good.

Here's the other thing I have often wondered about. What in the world do clergymen mean when they tell young people how great it is to be able to tell your new wife or new husband, that most curious and oft coveted phrase, 'you are the only one I've ever loved.' Think about it. What value can such a phrase possibly have? Besides being obviously untrue; because how could you possibly get through Life without loving, accidentally or otherwise, lots of different people in lots of different ways, who would want to come into young adulthood saying, 'I have never loved anybody until now.'? Am I right? Who would ever marry somebody who has never loved anybody all the way up to the moment they exchanged their vows?

Anyway, I didn't want to freak Daphne out, so I patted my hands together in a light rather than thunderous applause. The way you do when a child first learns how to use a spoon or a fork or even better, how to walk. I held out my arms and Daphne hopped over and curled up in my lap. I stroked her hair and kissed both her cheeks.

"Congratulations, honey, I'm so proud of you."

"I'm saving myself for my husband, Alphonso."

"I know, baby,I know."

"I'm not jumping into the sack with just anyone. I do not plan to be anybody's sexual conquest. I want my love to be just for my husband."

"Doggone, Daphne, I-"

"What is it, Alphonso?"

I was rocking Daphne in my arms like a little girl. Another second and it was certain that she would be sucking her thumb. I kissed her on the neck and caressed her shoulder and patted her back. I hummed a little song in her ear.

"Daphne, I-"

"Yes, Alphonso?"

"I think we better-"

"I know, Alphonso, I know."

"Why don't we-"

"You don't have to say it, sweetie. You want to meet my parents, don't you-"

The folding chair we were rocking in went back too far that last time and we slammed down with a crash that nearly flipped Daphne out of her high heels. We rolled over each other laughing with embarrassment after the initial shock of the event. I should have spoken up a bit sooner that I felt we were rocking back too far in that chair, and that we ought to remove to someplace where we could stretch out a little more. However, rolling on top of her to cushion my fall, I realized that this was the perfect opportunity to end all that psycho-babble . Now that I could feel her breasts crushed against my chest, and could shut her up with big wet kisses on the mouth, I could explore at my leisure this curious concept of being 'the only one she ever loved'.

"Oh, Alphonso, stop it now, stop!" Daphne laughed with squealing zeal, slapping me on the shoulders. "We're nothing but a couple of klutzes! What time is it?"

I was in the middle of cupping one huge teardrop of a breast when she shook me off like a bothersome cur.

"Baby! What?"

"What time is it?"

Time for you to give up that cherry, I'm thinking. Time for you to turn in your virgin license, and get a real library card, babe. Time for you to spread wide, kick high, and let me rock you into Amadeus! Time for me to...

"Come on, Alphonso, what time is it?"

"Why you got to ask me that now?"

"I have to see my parents for dinner tonight." Daphne sat up chuckling and reached for a mirror and a comb in her purse. "You want to come?" I watched her rise to stand on one leg and hop and fiddle back on a lone shoe. "Come on, Alphonso, help me up and help me find my other shoe. I think it fell underneath this platform somewhere. Come on now. Help me find it. Do you see it around anywhere?"

"Hold on, I think I see it under there."

We scurried around looking and finally I got a broom handle. I fished her other shoe out from under the platform where it was wedged beneath a wheel. I slid the platform forward a little as I poked the shoe free...

"Here it is, baby, good as new."

I found a spare chamois lying around from where my nephew had been working and wiped the shoe clean.

"So are you coming, Alphonso?" Daphne asked as she deposited herself demurely into my sofa chair. "My parents would love to have you over for dinner."

"Let me take a rain check on that, Daphne. I really have to get my work ready for this new show. Here's your shoe back-"

"Why don't you put it on me, Alphonso?" Daphne's coy smile settled into an expression of remote arrogance. "I'll have to tell you, one role I never did play in Children's Theater was the part of Cinderella."

"That's because you're too stuck up. Put your shoe on yourself, before I make you sweep out the studio."

I toss her shoe at her and brandish my broom menacingly. Daphne catches it against her blouse and stamps her feet against the floor petulantly.

"Oh, come on, Alphonso! Indulge my fantasy, why don't you? You said yourself you used to be a shoe salesman. What can it hurt to do a little playacting?"

"Sorry, princess, I don't play that."

"You get to be Prince Charm-ming-" Daphne twirled her shoe about her finger.

"Naw. I ain't down for that. Besides, I never wanted to play the lead in somebody else's fairy tale anyway."

"Oh, puh-leeease?"

"Tell you what; you promise to bring your parents to the opening of my show and maybe I'll hook you up. Deal?"

Daphne glared at me with a hesitant flinch.

"Yeah. What better way for your parents to get to know me than through my work?"

"Oh alright," Daphne sighed and lifted forth a dainty foot, "you may shoe me now, your highness."

"That's more like it." I took to one knee playfully, but you better believe I would not be telling any brothers about this anytime soon. "'I have been scouring the countryside for the young lass who fled from my arms at the stroke of midnight. This is all I have left to remember her by. I have come to your abode to see if you might be the owner of this shoe.'"

"'Do tell, my lord. I have often heard it said that should the shoe fit, one should indeed wear it.'"

I brought my hands around her foot in a slow, sensual, heartwarming massage. I worked the shoe carefully into place around and over her reddened heel.

"Alphonso?"

I was in the act of stooping to kiss her instep when the sound of her voice made me catch my breath.

"Alphonso," she began again, looking up at the skylight, "I've been meaning to tell you, I'm taking an audition tape to New York at the end of the month. I'm up for a leading role in a T.V. Soap there. I'm hoping to get the part and if I do, it means I'll probably have to live there for awhile."

I looked up into her face and there was genuine concern registered there.

"Uh-oh. This shoe is not your size, my lady." I cupped my hand to my mouth like a megaphone. "NEXT!"

"Oh, you!"

Daphne picked up her purse and started whacking me across the back with it. I defended myself by running to the closet and getting her coat. I warily gestured towards her and I think she was slightly taken aback that I was dismissing her. She paced over like a penitent little child and I carefully slipped her coat over her shoulders. I gave her a pat on the back and walked away.

"Are you coming tonight, Alphonso?"

"I told you, baby. I got this show to get ready."

Daphne's cheeks reddened as though I had slapped her, and there was a palpable hurt in her expression. She let out a weary, exasperated sigh.

"All right then, Alphonso. At the very least then you can walk me to my car."

After Daphne gave me her family's address, I kissed her goodnight. I gave her a wave as she took off in her green Mercury Cougar. I watched it become a winking red turn signal that soon disappeared under the frosty street lamps.

When I was sure she was safely out of sight, I tore up the slip of paper she had handed to me and went back up to my studio to work.

Victor rubbed my face into last night's torn and wrinkled headlines.

"See this?" He scowled and grunted at me. "This is all your doing!"

The rest of the pages of that edition of the Detroit News went skittering past me out of the alley. The headlines 'HEIRESS AND TEEN STILL MISSING'; skipped and danced between moving cars and into the wind. Victor grabbed my tie and jerked me towards him. I made it up to one knee, but went into a crouch to rush him too late. My head lopped back as he kicked me for a field goal. I felt the toe of his shoe leather against my chin and landed in a heap against the garbage cans just behind.

"What on Earth possessed us?" Victor heaved me up by my lapels. "Why did we ever get mixed up with the likes of you?"

There was no way to convince him now. How I was working on making it all up to him and everybody else. I was being held up on my toes with the blank brick wall behind me. I could barely croak out a word. Now that his forearm was crushed against my windpipe, all I was able to manage was to spit blood in his face while I was fixed to pass out.

REFUGEE FROM THE MORGUE FILE

"**W**hat?" Victor exclaimed with a grimace of consternation. "Are you spitting on me? On ME? Come on over here, boy. Step into my office."

Victor roughly hauled me over and cramped us both inside the grimy alcove of Tony Ghetto's building. He was breathing ragged now and looking around to make sure nobody would see us. I could see the spots of my blood spattered all over the collar of his lavender shirt. I was catching my own breath at this point and deliberating on how I could head butt him and hightail my way out of this alley.

That was when I spotted him again across the street. Clear as day out of the corner of my eye. There he was right in front of me; the slim, muscular dude in the blue turtleneck with the crew cut. Once again he was opening up the trunk to his black Buick Regal. I saw him lift out that same green bag of golf clubs.

Now my thoughts drifted back to Mary Murphy in spite of Victor's hot breath in my face.

Why the 'calculus of encounter' never seemed to add up between me, and Mary Murphy I could not tell you. The beginning of the situation was innocent enough. I would drop by her studio to see how she was doing, but the catch was she would never be there. After I graduated from College we were like that poem with the big black bird in it that Poe wrote. I was starting to get the feeling that we would see each other nevermore, which makes it hard on a dude to say 'thanks for the memories'. I would swing by expecting her to be finishing up a painting and primed for a little break to chat and-whiff! No show and no go past the locked do'.

It would look like strikeout time for the Gentle Man.

But I was cool with it.

Sometimes that is just life in the Big City.

I figured we would run into each other eventually. We grooved too much on the same frequency for that not to happen. There were times when I would come by and just slip the latest sketches and drawings I was working on under her door. I would take a peek through the piece of glass that made a vertical rectangle next to her door to scope on what her latest project might be. I would leave a note to let her know how she just missed me. Little did I know that would be the story of our lives and the future of our history. The routes and the channels were already being engineered by the powers that be.

When we were classmates in college nobody could have told me all this would have shaped up into a first class mystery. I just expected we would get together and talk sometime. There was never any problem when we were taking classes together. We would just run into each other every now and then during school.

Remembering how mellow Mary sounded reciting her own poetry, I often could not help but encourage her to record her own stuff. Go beyond that even and take it to the max. Be some kind of poet laureate for crying out loud. She would smile that sad eyed blonde look, shake her head and wave me off like I was crazy.

"Look," I said, directing her over to the whitewashed bulletin board. "Stand right over there and follow this diagram. Just cop these poses, okay?"

"Sure, Alphonso," She made an impish face at me. "What's this going to be for, anyway?" I held up my trusty Polaroid camera.

"I need your picture so I can put you in the funny papers."

"Why would you want to do that? Wha - are you saying I'm funny looking to you?"

"Yeah, funny lookin' enough to make us both a lot of money!"

"Sure, right. That's what they all say."

"Here, turn like this, okay?" Flash! "Now look up, all right?"

While I was turning Mary's face in profile, I found myself halting for just a split second in the embarrassment of wonder. She was always Mary Murphy to me, the girl who sat across from me in class. Somehow, in the hustle and bustle of preparing for classes I never really took the opportunity to appreciate the uniqueness of her beauty. I was genuinely surprised how easily this aspect of her slid into the matrix of my artistic vision. Pulling her hair back from her neck, I felt as though I were working with the human clay of personality, a material that instantly responded to my touch with the appropriate transformations.

"What's this for again, Alphonso?"

"Didn't I tell you? These pictures are for my Morgue Files. I'll be able to refer back to them when I'm ready to paint your portrait or make you a character in one of my comic strips."

"Morgue File? Ugh! Sounds gruesome! I hope you know what you're doing with me."

I took the last photo and placed it face down on my worktable.

"That'll do it, Mary. Of course I know what I'm doing, honey bun. You're in good hands."

"Yeah, yeah, you don't have to tell me. I'm 'in the hands of the Gentle Man'. I swear Alphonso, sometimes you are so full of it! Is that all you need me for?"

"Yep, this'll do. Your check will be in the mail."

"Right, I wish."

Miss Murphy moved idly about surveying the sketches and charcoal drawings that were mounted on the walls. I was in the middle of framing some of my paintings and applying tissue paper to the cores of my papier-ma'che sculptures. I was gratified that she seemed content to dwell in my studio space for awhile. She cast me a lingering glance that amused me.

"Sorry, I can't pay you anything now. Want a hug for down payment?"

Mary nodded silently and moved swiftly and surely into my open embrace. I held her petite frame in my arms, lifting her off her feet.

The space of the moment was warm and secure, and after several seconds I was startlingly aware of something. She was not pushing back with the palms of her hands for me to let her go. I just knew that I better so that it didn't seem like I was taking advantage of her good will.

"Thanks again," I set her softly down. "You'll be the first to see what kind of Art I make with your pictures."

"I better," she waved as she headed for the door, "don't forget my cut, Alphonso."

"I thought the pleasure of working with the Master was reward enough."

Mary looked at me with a snort and snickered into the palm of her hand.

"Reward enough for you, maybe. You can drop by my studio for additional lessons when I finally have one." She winked and waved at me.

"Season's pass?"

"That's right, bubba. Season's pass. Bye now, Alphonso. Hmn. The pictures came out nice..."

"See ya, Mary."

"See ya."

After that, Mary Murphy just seemed to drop through the center of the Earth. I heard from one of her friends that she found her soul mate, a local rock musician who made her heart go all aflutter. That was as it should be as far as I was concerned. Mary was a sweet girl and I could not wish anything but the best for her. I just wondered why it was so hard to catch her at her studio. The truth was it just wasn't any of my business at that point. Like my dear old mama used to say, you can't make somebody see you when they don't want to. So I just filed Mary Murphy under 'missing in action' and kept on truckin'.

There was not anything really to figure out. I just thought I would casually drop by on her one of these days. We would talk, recharge each other's creative batteries, exchange a hug or two and back to the salt mines we would go.

This is the way I see it - people who try to use their imaginations to make a living deserve all the help they can get and a hero's welcome when they succeed. When they fail ain't nothing to cry about. You just help them dust off their pants and give them a pat on the back for a good try. I always make it my business to encourage and salute artistic vision, even when it isn't my own. I'm just somebody who knows what they're going through because I've been there and am going through it too.

When I finally settled in teaching high school Art and got my own classroom, I decided I could afford my own studio too. I don't know what made me decide to drop by Mary's place for the next round of a half dozen visits. I just couldn't tell you. Somehow, I was feeling geeked about a project I was doing with my students. I was using drawings and illustrations to complement their poetry. I don't know what made me slip their poetry under her studio door. There were still no sightings of Mary on the horizon, but at least she started to answer my notes in poems of her own.

After the big freeze out, it was good to hear from her again. I came to find out she was married to her rock musician and starting to sell her paintings at a local gallery. Hearing how well she was doing made my heart swell with pride, I would have passed out cigars but for the fact that I didn't have any and was standing on the creaking wooden slats of my studio all by myself.

At least we were in touch again. Oh, maybe not so much in touch as within earshot. You never could tell. She might send me a Christmas card every other year or something like that. At any rate, now that I knew she was still on the planet I could call off the search party.

I didn't pay any more attention to Mary after that. I knew where she lived and I knew she was doing all right, and that was that. Now every once in awhile she would send me some poems. I suppose just to let me know that the creative sluice gates were still open and flowing and all that good stuff. As for me, I went back to keeping the faith and defending the faithful.

That was when her notes began to arrive under my studio door.

"Who is the Lady X who keeps slipping you that secret code underneath the door?" Danny uttered injudiciously while I was holding a winning hand. "Seems this is the third time this month she's requested yo' services."

"What's it to you?" I bristled as I threw down three Kings and a Jack. "What's between her and me is my business. Now! Deal with that!"

"You still ain't ready for me, fool." Danny shook his head as he showed his cards. "I'll get you back on the next go 'round."

"You won't be getting nobody dealing a lame hand like that one," I cracked as I slid the coins and dollar bills back home to papa. "Keep your mind on the game and leave my private business private."

"Oh, so she's yo' 'private dancer'," Smiley Thomas leered over his hand, telegraphing to everyone that he was holding a good one. "Well, excuse me-"

"Aww, mannn, stop acting like you know something you don't," I splayed out this new hand between my palms. "You still in the dark about all that."

"Deal." Nathan Eddie passed out the rest of the cards with a lanky assurance. "A man's gota right to his private business."

"I know that's right," I gingerly laid down a seven to test the waters.

"All I know is what's on the bulletin board," Danny laid down a ten just to spite me. "When I see a note up there that starts 'Dear Alphonso' I got to figure you up to yo' old tricks. An' when she signs the thing 'love truly' with a big red kiss in lipstick added for good measure, after writing 'please see me ASAP' I gots to think something's up."

"Right. Now after that, you gon' call yourself my friend? Go ahead - just put all my business out in the street!"

"Ain't nobody tryin' to put yo' business nowhere, man." Smiley sneered at me with a wave of derision. "Don't forget we're your friends, Alphonso. We're just concerned about your fool ass, man."

"Since you all so concerned about me, I'll tell you what you can do." I was stone cold ice when I laid down the Ace, a King, a Queen and a Jack. "Since you all so concerned, you can slap this palm with some mon-nay, ba-bay!"

Nobody bluffs like the Gentle Man can. But what my friends didn't know was that I was hiding a bluff within a bluff this time. I really didn't know what the Murphy girl wanted with me any more than any of them, even though I was just returning from my third visit over to her studio. The little notes Mary was sending could either be cries for help or just her way of saying hello and keeping in touch. The only thing was there was no way to tell until I finally caught up with her.

At first, I wasn't worried because sooner or later the Gentle Man catches up with everybody. That is right. Sooner or later, regardless of the circumstances or the difficulties I find what I am looking for and I get what I want. The Gentle Man is known for this. I just never thought that meeting with a friend for a little chat and a cup of coffee would turn into this kind of mystery. That's why I'm keeping this thing close to the vest for a while. Until everything sorts out I think that's best. I just want to do it before people start jumping to the wrong conclusions and end up turning a simple matter into a ball of confusion. Should that actually occur, you can be sure that many will conclude that the Gentle Man is to blame.

"Deal."

"Um?"

"Gone deal, mah brother," Nathan Eddie crosses his spindly legs and sets back. "What you waiting on, Alphonso? It's either Christmas time in the city and Joy to the World or Judgment Day."

"Yeah," frowned Smiley, flitting a glance at me as he looked up from his cards, "keep yo' mind on the game, Alphonso."

"Hold tight, Smiley, hold tight. You not about to do the Terminator on me with the game you got!"

"We'll see whose got what kind a game in a second," Smiley lays down his cards. "Uh huh, who duh man now? Huh? Huh? Who duh man now?"

Smiley won that round in spite of himself. But knowing him, he would probably lose it all back on the telegraph in the next few rounds. I was filing everything about Mary Murphy away so I could bear down on my game, when Danny comes up with another smart question.

"Alphonso, what does 'MM' mean anyway?"

"Aww mannn, I thought you said you were going to put that down!"

"What you so upset about?"

"Let's play cards, gentleman," Nathan Eddie leans that long cylinder head on his knuckles. "We can talk shop about the ladies later."

"I MEAN-" I shrug with a sigh.

"I think it means Marilyn something-" Smiley mischievously interjects from behind his cards. "Yeah," Danny takes up for Smiley. "Like Marilyn Monroe or Madame Madonna-"

"How 'bout Minnie Mouse or Mabel Moose? Hah! Deal with that!" I exclaimed in victory.

"C'mon- Alphonso man," whines Danny, partly because I won that round and partly because his curiosity is getting the best of him now, "who is this broad who keeps slipping notes under your door?"

"Why won't you let it rest, Danny? She's just some girl I met in school and shared a couple of classes with-"

"Have we seen her? Is it someone we know?"

Sooner or later, our paths would cross again. Something strange was in the hopper that our paths were not aligning naturally in the Seventh House. The only thing was while any man can be cheated in a thousand and one ways, no one ever gets away with cheating destiny in the end. The occurrence that is destined to transpire will make its arrival right on schedule and according to its own timetable. Whoever or whatever is obscured from the purview of the human soul must as a matter of the course of Nature eventually be exposed and brought fully into sight. Somewhere in the nebulous and unforeseen future, the designs of time would fashion a reckoning and a recognition between Mary Murphy and myself.

"No, I would hardly think that would be the case, Danny-O. She was just a fellow creative soul I got caught up with in the flux."

I gave no hint that I was not feeling the hand I was dealing this time.

"So what's the story on the mystery woman, Alphonso?" Smiley stroked his goatee and found himself frowning at his cards. "We see her tracks, but we never spot her in your presence. Where are you two making that secret rendezvous?"

"See? That's just like you, Smiley. That's why I never tell you nothing. Everything with you has to be shady and undercover. There's no hidden intrigue wrapped up in the crux of the matter. The Gentle Man is innocent of all charges in the case at hand. I have this friend I never seem to be able to catch up with. We just keep just missing each other. That's all."

"Sounds kinda freaky, Alphonso," Nathan Eddie took a last drag on a butt before he stubbed it out. "-sounds like something Suckertease would rap about."

"Naw, this ain't as earthshaking as all that," I assured Nathan Eddie, "- ain't no thang. The whole deal is really a casual affair, when you get right down to it. There's some kind of static somehow in the vibes. Something off kilter between yours truly and said young lady. All I know is I just can't put my finger on where this static is coming from at this point."

"Don't let Sammy Turner hear you talk like that," Danny warned me puckishly. "- he'll be able to give you fifty 'leven perfectly rational explanations for what is happening to you."

"Yeah," Smiley put down a pair of Aces on us. "all of them comin' out of some book he read. Boo-yah! Deal with that, y'all."

"The trouble with y'all is that you don't respect the person that reads widely. You act like Samuel Socrates must be under some kind of a curse because he reads so many books. There's a lot to be said for book knowledge."

"Aww, go someplace, Alphonso." Smiley pulled in his pot to his side of the table. "Ain't a person in this room 'ceptin' you don't know Samuel Socrates Turner ain't nothing but an educated fool!"

"Don't be dissing mah man Socrates-"

"You mean 'Suckertease', don't you, Alphonso?" Danny sneered between his cards and his fingers.

"-just because his knowledge comes from books."

"Ain't nobody here got nothing against learnin' and book knowledge," Danny said to me solemnly as he reshuffled the deck. "Don't forget, Alphonso, I got three kids of my own. I'm always bearing down on them to crack open them books. I'm the last one to tell anybody not to seek and get knowledge. The problem with Suckertease is he got more book knowledge than he know what to do with. What he need to do is put some of them books down and give Life a good, square look in the eye."

"I know that's right," Nathan Eddie said, tossing his butt into an ashtray.

"See - Sammy Turner is that further evolution of Tom," Danny continued, and I could tell you almost word for word what was coming up next. "He ain't no Uncle Tom, he's a Doctor Tom, see what I'm saying? The White Man don't use no whips or nooses in the New Millennium. What he uses to keep us Black Folks in line these days is the good ole Information Overkill. He floods our senses with so much useless information, while all the time impressing upon us through increasing repetition the absolute importance of all this trivia we be absorbing, that most of us don't know where we're coming and going on this Information Superhighway-"

"I know that's right," Nathan Eddie said, reshuffling the deck.

"Yeah, but you could say that about just about anybody these days," I countered, "that's nothing that's exclusively true for Black People."

"What are you talkin' bout, mannn," chided Danny, "what part of 'Doctor Tom' don't you understand?"

"The part where you be downin' a brother just because he has a genuine love of learning and wants to better himself by becomin' highly educated. Seems to me if Socrates is your new and improved kind of fool, then you still the ole garden variety."

There's skin and high fives all around when I let that one fly through the bomb bay doors. Danny stews there mortified, but he ought to know better than anyone I don't play that. You want to play smack-down, then step right up. The Gentle Man is not only master of the Kiss, he is also world renowned for the Diss.

"Hey! It don't matter about all this 'emotionalism', baby! I know where of I speak. You're thinkin' somehow Suckertease is sitting on some summit of knowledge. That's right, ain't it - Alphonso? But what you don't know is that all Sammy knows is what the White Man has taught him is important."

"Yeah, tah hear you tell it."

"Straight up. You've seen him around the Playa's Palace. How he be all stiff and carryin' on and so much into himself and his own little world. Hah! He can barely call up the nerve to hit up on a bitch even when it's self evident that she's got her nose all wide for him."

"So? We've all got strengths and weaknesses. Even you. The flip side of every blessing is some earthly kind of curse. There at the root of every gift is some kind of flaw. We each bring a piece to the puzzle, but no one dude has them all. I just respect what the brother brings to the table."

"Naw man, you still in the dark about this thing. I'm telling you the kind of knowledge that Suckertease has is dangerous; not only to himself but to his people. The knowledge and understanding he possesses is just enough to get in good with and be manipulated by white people. It will never go beyond that. The Information Age is an Information Cage for that fool. Why a down brother like you can't see that is what I don't understand."

"Yeah, yeah, keep on talkin-keep on talkin'," Smiley cheered us on as he triumphantly threw down his hand. "Y'all just won me a piss-pot full of money!"

Which he will promptly lose in the next few rounds...

"Check this out. Why we always got to be downin' each other? The way I see it-the more we come together in a loving fellowship with each other, the more we approach and achieve that perfection of being within ourselves."

"Matthew 18:20!" Smiley cried out gleefully as he scooped up the stray coins and dollar bills from the table. "Whoop! There it is!"

"Sho' you rite!" Nathan Eddie clapped his hands together. "Now that I think about it, you and Sammy Turner make quite a pair, Alphonso. Is that where you've been getting all that smart talk from?"

"Naw. I've always depended upon my ladies to school and educate me."

"That's what I been talkin'about," Danny followed up quickly, "everything you know has come out loving relationships with significant others. Everything Suckertease knows comes out of some book, usually written by some white man perpetuating the myth that white folks have all the answers. What you have learned you've learned from people, not from books."

"That sounds like a good point when taken at face value, but I have to tell you it won't wash, mah man. Number one, knowledge is knowledge, and truth can come from the strangest places. Number two, books are written by people too. Lots of people feel like reading a favorite book is like having an intimate conversation with a trusted confidante and friend. Number three, I think it's more generally accepted than ever before that not all important books are written by whites, nor do they have all the answers to everything."

"That sho'is somethin' else," Nathan Eddie stroked his goatee meditatively.

"Whatchu talkin' bout?" I asked, looking over my hand without a flicker of emotion.

"All I gots to do is close my eyes and I hear and see Samuel Socrates," Nathan Eddie said, peering at me with an indolent, discerning curiousity. "Y'all is even starting to sound alike!"

"See what I'm saying?" Danny pointed at Nathan Eddie like that proved his point. "You spending too much time around that fool."

"Not hardly."

Which was true. I spent more time in bed talking about Socrates after a roll in the hay with one of my girlfriends than I did speaking with him personally. The truth was, there were times I barely understood what he was talking about. That's when I would hang a groove with Wilma Durant or Nancy Lawton and after making them kick the air between the ceiling with both feet, I would punch their tickets to board the A-Train. When we returned we would unpack our bags and clean and press our minds together.

Sometimes we even washed out our dirty linen one article at a time.

I have never understood why making love proves to have such a clarifying effect on both my intellectual and creative faculties. I have made cognitive leaps of understanding I would not have dreamed possible plowing between the trembling thighs of my chosen beloved, spilling her rich dark hair across my pillow while I made her softly moan a contented truth. Swirling around and wrapped up in the ecstasy of sex is the mysterious loss of something that cannot be named. The silence and the emptiness envelopes my lover and I, and after dying in each other's arms we await resurrection. The call to new life always comes and we rise, roaring back into the real world like a raging ocean, ending washed up like flotsam on the shores of a new beginning to which we've suddenly returned.

Everything I know that's worth anything comes from my experience of the regenerative power of sexual release. I think it was the Isley Brothers who sang, 'there will be a harvest for the world'. That has been my personal experience and long may she wave. What always rings true, as far as I'm concerned, is true.

The thing is, the name of Samuel Socrates Turner has come up more than once upon the lips of a satisfied lover. Once while I was riding tall in the saddle and roaming the redheaded prairie with Nancy Lawton. I got her climbing the walls with me that time. I was her Amazing Spiderman just before she pulled the ripcord and let all the air out of her balloon. But around about the time she did her final skydive, she bellowed out these sweet nothings in a contralto of deliverance:

"Oooooo! SOC-rah-teeees!"

When she finally floated safely down to the earth, a spinning wisp all spent, I gently probed to find the identity of this mystery man.

"I said WHAT?" Nancy exclaimed, glancing across at me in the middle of kissing the tips of my fingers. "Are you sure I said that, Alphonso?"

"No doubt, mah honey, no doubt. You were testifying it to the highest rafters."

"I DID?"

"Yeah," I said in a half laugh, "why would I lie to you, baby?"

She became absorbed in thought at this.

"Imagine that," she marveled, running a hand along her cheek and wiping strands of sandy red hair from the corner of her mouth. "That is really something!"

"Who is he?"

She looked sideways at me and tittered.

"What? He used to be your boyfriend or something?"

"Nothing so involved as all that. He should be so lucky!"

"Who was he then?"

"Search me. Just some old fart I met on the bus one day. I suppose he liked my looks and when he found out I possessed a degree in mathematics, he did his level best to talk my ear off." Nancy curled up lazily in my arms, "Nothing added up between us. He was extremely well read as I recall, but everything went skew when he tried to come on to me."

"He went down swinging, huh?"

"Oh, I don't know. Maybe had I met him at a party and he was wearing a suit and tie it just might have been different. Face it, Alphonso, what girl rides SEMTA to be propositioned by a total stranger?"

"Yeah, I know what you mean. You gotta watch out for a guy who introduces himself as Socrates."

"No, no, that was his middle name. Just like mine is Maureen. No, his full name was, let me think... Samuel. That's right, Samuel

Socrates Turner. Can you imagine that? A colored guy from the inner city of Detroit has a lot to live up to with a name like that."

"That may be, but seems to me I heard from somebody somewhere that Socrates may well have been black."

"Yeah, yeah, and Jesus may have had 'feet of brass and hair like lamb's wool'. You won't get any argument from me about that. I wasn't there."

I hugged Nancy across her nipples as the receding tapers of light were stealing back into the gathering darkness.

"Evidently he must have made some kind of impression on you. I mean his name found its way out of your mouth while we were free styling in the mellow."

"Yeah, imagine that."

Nancy was wearing that quizzical smile on her face again.

"He was a fascinating fellow in some respects. What I'm saying is to listen to him it was no trick to see he read a lot of books. He even knew about G.H. Hardy and that fellow from India who made those breakthroughs in Prime Number Theory; what's his name- what's his name? I should know this. I did a paper in college on these guys. Ramanujan! That's it, Ramanujan! He admitted he didn't know squat about higher mathematics, but he could name drop about Hardy and Ramanujan. He mentioned two or three other books you don't usually hear talked about a lot except by die-hard mathematicians. That startled me at first, until I questioned him and realized he was just dabbling and looking for someone to help him work through what he couldn't understand."

"I thought you said he was just trying to hit on you."

"Oh, I know that was part of the equation, but there was this other thing going on too. He really did have intellectual ambitions after a fashion, and that's always a point of interest in a man. He made me feel there was something about me, I don't know, that somehow I was arousing in him this desire for higher thought. Now that I think back on it, it was kind of sexy. The only thing was it was totally out of place on a SEMTA bus. I tried to let him down easy. He rode with me all the way to the end of the line and I ended up calling out to some guy I didn't even know to make it appear as if someone were waiting for me. I guess the ruse worked because he didn't follow me off the bus. I kind of pressed my hip against him as I got up. That was to let him know there were no hard feelings. I got off the bus and the rest, as they say, is history."

Nancy turned face to face with me as we held each other close enough to cuddle.

"Who's Ramanujan?"

Nancy shrugged her freckled shoulders.

"Some Indian mathematician I studied about in college. I'll get you some data about him off the Internet later. A little biographical stuff maybe."

"Too bad about old Socrates."

"Yeah, he wasn't that bad looking. He might have hit it off with me under better circumstances. Shame he wasn't as good looking as you, Alphonso-"

"-or able to beat you at chess the way I can."

"Now who's becoming intellectually ambitious?"

"Yeah, but I'm not your Don Quixote, baby. I realize my ambitions."

"That was an anomaly, Alphonso. The opportunity for you to checkmate me never would have arisen but for my having to teach over a dozen kids how to play at the same time! Besides, what do you know about Don Quixote?"

"He was some crackpot old man who jousted against windmills. Am I right?"

"Hmmnn, bet you never read one word Cervantes ever wrote about him."

"No, but my father said he saw him in a cartoon once. Some funny old character who called himself Mister Magoo played him."

"Sounds about right. That's one thing Samuel Socrates got straight. The more media savvy and visually literate we become, the less literate as a society we are."

"Next you going to tell me Socrates has probably read all about Don Quixote."

"I wouldn't be a bit surprised."

"Now tell me this; what good did it do him?"

"What do you mean by that?"

"I've seen that big old book on Don Quixote in the library. That ol' thing is over a thousand pages! Let's say you knew for a fact that Socrates had read that entire thing. What would it be worth to you to know he did that? Would it be worth sitting down and having a cup of coffee with him? Have you ever given any nookey to a man just because he read 'Don Quixote'?"

"Come on, Alphonso, that's not fair. You know it doesn't work like that."

"No, that would be an anomaly."

Nancy spitefully slapped me on the shoulder with a mischievous, smirking grin.

"I said that's not fair, Alphonso. I might put out for Cervantes."

"Oh, yeah? I'll have to see that to believe it, and I've never seen it in my lifetime. See - that's my point. What good did it do Socrates to read all those books? You said yourself the thing that would have made a difference was whether or not he was at a party and wearing a suit and tie. As far as books are concerned - bump that!"

"Socrates didn't have your eyes, Alphonso."

"What about my eyes, woman?"

"He didn't have those eyes that say, 'come to bed with me'."

"You heard what the man said about flattery. We're back to square one, baby girl. Don't tell me you startin' to feel kinda guilty."

"I would like to know about what, my dear."

"You know about what. The lack of value placed on a literate society. I'll tell you what; the next time we groove into the upper stratosphere will you read Cervantes to me when we land?"

"You read it to me and we'll trade up. Deal?"

"Deal! Now give me them lips!"

We went undercover to save the world then, and when we came up for air with the blue dolphins and the humpback whales, there was one other thing Nancy wanted to know.

"Now once we've done Cervantes from cover to cover, we go back to banging each other through higher mathematics, right?"

I could not find a flaw in that argument.

"Alphonso!" Nathan Eddie startled me back into reality as he riffled the deck. "Get yo'self outta Cuntsville, Alabama, brother and get yo' mind back in the game. Gon' be your turn to 'deal a meal' in a hot second."

"Throw down then, guy. Lemme see the U.S.A.!"

The hand I was holding after some seeing and raising was fast becoming an All-Star Cast. I betrayed nothing and let nature take its course. I knew Smiley would sooner or later give himself away with all that emotional Morse Code. The dude couldn't help himself. I decided to just sit around and wait for him to broadcast his hand and then victory would be mine plus his money.

"See, the truth is, you're the flip side of Socrates, Alphonso," Smiley said as though he were reading this off his cards.

"How you figger?" I asked casually as I tossed off a card.

"Break it down to 'em, Smiley," Danny said, putting his two cents in with a Queen of Spades. "School that fool on his A-B-Cs-"

"- and X-Y-Zs-" Smiley grinned malevolently, showing his hand.

"Oh, Knee-grow-please!" I slapped down my cards without cracking a smile. "Show me your DO-RE-MI!"

I started sliding the coins and cash across the table back home.

Smiley's lame attempt to intellectualize me into distraction went into one ear and out the other. The thing is, he won't give up now, because there's always another round to go.

"Ow!" Nathan Eddie howled mirthfully, "He cashed yo' check, mah brother!"

"- an' ran you home cryin' to yo' momma!" Eddie cracked, clapping his hands together in glee.

I stuck a toothpick in my mouth and leaned back, chewing it leisurely.

"You were saying?" I asked him, turning on the sternness.

"Break it down to him 'bout the flip side, Smiley. Come on now-" Nathan Eddie said, choosing now to play the instigator.

"Hey," Smiley shrugged humbly, "I ain't tryin' to signify nothin-"

"Like hell you ain't!" Nathan Eddie snorted, "Gon' finish your play, man. Gon' finish what you got tuh say."

"We got yr' back, Smiley," Eddie said, reaching for his cards. "Break it down to Alphonso about the flip side and the dark side and the raw hide versus the Naugahyde!"

"What's the matter, Smiley? Cat got your cogitate?" Nathan Eddie queried slyly.

"Naw, naw, I'm chill." Smiley looked at his cards and perked up again. "All I wanted to point out was that Samuel Turner loves to learn how to learn and you love to learn how to love."

That's it, Smiley, I'm thinking to myself. Smile that broadcast smile and show me your hole card. The man ought to be president of his own television station; Smiley Broadcast Corporation.

"What's your point, man?" I mutter nonchalantly over my cards.

"Just that you both think you's in the loop when you really just loopin'."

"Uh-oh," Danny nods, and I can tell he is liking his cards too. "Smiley done went deep on the mug!"

"What are you talking about now, Smiley?"

"Just that goin' around in circles is no way to get someplace."

"Oh, so now I'm chasing my tail, is that it?"

"No sir, not exactly. Samuel Turner is chasing his tail. You're just chasin' tail."

"Cop the difference, Alphonso." Danny nodded at me, musing.

"What my man is tryin' to splain to you, Alphonso, is that sometimes the truth you own can end up owning you." Nathan Eddie said, crossing those long legs again and sitting back scopin' real cool.

The skylight overhead cast a grid of shadows out of the clouds over our card table.

"Take Suckertease, for example." Eddie began, returning to his original point. "He thinks there's truth in study and education and all that good stuff you find in books. That's his truth and he's stickin' to it."

"That's nothing new," I replied, still chewing on my toothpick, "everybody got to have some kind of truth they can call their own."

"Sure Alphonso, now you take yourself for another for instance," Smiley tagged up after Nathan Eddie, "you find your truth in pussy and love and getting them fine young things to beg you to take their panties from them."

"Startin' to dawn on you yet, Alphonso?" Nathan Eddie said, gesturing at me with a lighted cigarette.

"Naw man, I got to admit I'm still in the dark."

"You an' Suckertease done each come to the dead end of Truth from opposite ends of the block. Now you both stand facing a wall and wonderin' what comes next."

"Alright, I'll bite. Since you shufflin' the deck, you tell me what comes next."

Nathan Eddie looked over at the dartboard above the storage table where I keep all my brushes and palette knifes. I swear for a moment he seemed like he wanted to throw a butt at the bulls-eye. Looked like he thought the better of it, and after stabbing the thing out in an ashtray, he bridged his fingertips together and lined me up in his sights.

"Everybody got truth, Alphonso. Sometimes you can even run the table with what little you got. But nobody's got enough truth to call the shots all the time."

"So school me, brother. Enlighten me."

"I'm fixin' to my brother. Personal truth ain't gonna get it this time. You can't just go for what you know or fall back on your fade-away pitch. Now you got to go beyond what you know and hit up on a truth that may have been there all the time, but that you never even knew existed."

"Ain't chu deep…"

"Naw-naw, it ain't about all that, my brother. I'm just tryin' to tell you that pussy has no more secrets to reveal to yo' ass, an' there's no use tryin' to read between the lines because the book is about to close on you in a hot minute."

"That book fent tah close on Suckertease too, Alphonso." Eddie nodded as he threw down a card.

"What chu mean by that?"

"Look at it this way, Alphonso. Look at how you keep crossin' paths with Suckertease. Let me call your attention to that time at the Library and then at the DIA when you was givin' your Art Class the grand tour. Now the chump is down at the Playas' Palace every blue moon, takin' notes on us like we some kind of field study and he's some kind of anthropologist!"

"Ask that fool what he be writin' in that little notebook of his and you can barely get a peep out of him." Nathan Eddie sneered as he prepared to reshuffle the cards. "I don't care my damn self, but when you come to a happenin' establishment like the Palace, you should at least come in the proper attire, and you should at least speak."

"I heard he was working on his thesis for his Doctorate." I said, shifting my hand together. I fan out my cards and Pie-yah! This is the hand I was waiting for all along. "Doesn't bother me any, and Socrates isn't bothering anyone. I say let the brother do his business and book. That's all he plans to do anyway, once he takes the next rung up the ladder in white academia. Yeah, once he's got those Doctor papers he'll put us down and leave us to our pigfeet and buga-buga."

"There you go again, Alphonso, there you go again," Smiley threw down his hand, but it is not enough this time. "pickin' the worst possible time to crack wise. Match that, sucker!"

"Aces high, my main man, aces high," I throw down and bring the pot back home, "yeah, ol' Socrates will be hobnobbing it with the Educated Elite while we're still down in the black bottom shakin' our booties."

"Now that's just the kind of crack only one of us can make!" Nathan Eddie snorted.

"Yeah, you need to take that pigfeet - buga-buga mess someplace else, Alphonso." Danny cautioned me as he winced at his cards in spite of himself. "Besides, what could you possibly know about the black bottom? The black bottom ain't no place! The black bottom is a dance, you fool, like what my great grandma used to tell us bout 'fore she would fall asleep quilting."

"Whaddaya know?" Uh-oh, now I got a hand with some teeth in it. "So you don't say, huh? Why don't I do like old Mister Socrates and go make a note of that?"

"You play too much, Alphonso-" Nathan Eddie said, waving me off.

"So far y'all ain't playin' enough. At least not to match my game"

"You play too much, man. I tell you Samuel Turner don't know how to speak, and you go and take his side in the matter."

"-an' he need to keep that superior attitude of his in his pocket!" Danny threw in to help.

"I'm just sick an' tired of you dogging the guy all the time."

"What do you care, Alphonso?" Smiley wouldn't have piped up but he must have a hand he is liking. "You act like the dude is your uncle or something."

"No, don't misunderstand me, Smiley-Miley. I don't care really. I just think it's kinda unfair for four guys to be gangin' up on one guy all the time. Especially when you take into account that he isn't even here to defend himself. I just don't see the sport in it myself."

"So you figger you even things up a little? Make it two against three you reckon?" Danny said with a cagey expression.

"Until my man arrives to set out his side of the story."

"What!" Smiley nearly popped a card when I said that. "Well, that's a fine how-do-you-do!" He cocked his head at me and folded his arms, looking at me like I was growing another ear up between my eyes or something. "You really mean it! You would actually invite that egghead up here to cut a deck of cards with us?"

"Well yeah," I shrugged, "and guess what, Smiley? I think I would even let him use the Rest Room and sit over there at the counter for a sandwich and a beer."

"You play too much, Alphonso." Nathan Eddie reiterated. "I know one thing, that brother better learn how to speak. Because if he don't, I'm gon' have him dusted and parked by the curb with the rest of the trash."

"Now you tell me what that brother ever did to you, Nathan Eddie." I said, really wanting to see Danny's hand and what he's got up his sleeve. "He's just being unobtrusive. He doesn't bother nobody and he don't dip into nobody's business. He sits up in the spiral balcony, sips his wine, watches the action on the dance floor and takes his notes. Face it man, the dude couldn't be more harmless. He's just one of the talented tenth studying up for his Doctoral thesis-"

"He could be the talented titty for all I care!" Smiley declared, as he placed his bet.

"I know that's right," Nathan Eddie followed up, "and I don't care if he's workin' on the Declaration of Independence for Africa! He need to leave that 'too good for you' attitude with those white folks he been dealin' with. Sneakin' around, not talkin' to nobody; people gon' start takin' that as a sign of disrespect. Next time you see the Professor, Alphonso, you tell him that. Tell him he better check himself before he wreck hisself."

"Now! Deal with that, Alphonso." Danny finally showed his cards.

"Alright, big man, will do." I said to Nathan Eddie. "You always been cool with me, and I would never be dumb enough to diss a patron. The Playas' Palace is your joint and you've never known me not to toe the line since you been runnin' the scene. I'll tell Socrates to be more cordial lest his hind be on the line." Now I turned to Danny and gave him the Gentle touch. "Oh, by the way, Danny, my main man, were you looking for this?"

Presto! I held the card aloft like today's headlines hot off the press. Pie-yah! I'm the Ace of Spades, baby!

"Maturity sho'll does become you, young blood," Nathan Eddie nodded sagely with an amused smile. "I'll have to say you growing up at last."

"Help me out, Smiley," I said eagerly as I raked in the coppers, the coins and the lean green to my side of the street. "I need chapter and verse on this; what's that one that goes '-when I was a child I spake as a child-' "

"'-I understood as a child, I thought as a child: but when I became a man, I put away childish things.'" Smiley looked sideways at me out of his ginger ale colored eye and I could see Danny was all drooping jaws too. "That's First Corinthians, Chapter Thirteen, Verse Eleven."

Smiley and Danny looked at each other, then fixed the evil eye on yours truly.

"Sho' you rite! What I tell you? Thanks for the complement, Nathan Eddie, but you see ol' Smiley-Miley just proved my point. There's all kinds of knowledge in the world and there's room for everybody to show what they know. Now you take Smiley there as a test case."

I sat back and chewed on my toothpick.

"Take a phrase-any phrase, and recite a few words of it or a line from the Bible, and I bet you Smiley can give you back Book, Chapter and Verse. He's just got that kind of mind. He's a student of God's word and knows it by heart, or very nearly by heart. Now Danny there is a keen student of Nature. That's human, animal, vegetable or mineral. When he paints his landscapes and street scenes this becomes self-evident. Why he even woke me up out of my post hypnotic state and mesmerization before the female form, lifting my head above the clouds and setting my feet upon the highway of knowledge. Yeah buddy, he saved me from the siren call of tits and ass-"

"Jesus wept, Alphonso," Smiley shook his head in consternation, "you is so full of-"

"Naw, naw, hear me out-hear me out, Smiley. Now you take the honorable Nathan Eddie over there. The mastermind of the Playas' Palace, the finest night spot on the west side of the Motor City.

Started out with nothing but an idea, and then wheeled and dealed it into the reality of a thriving enterprise. Now the Palace is a place where anybody who's anybody has to be seen if they mean to have a rep as a mover and a shaker in the community. I mean-" I pointed to my noggin, "-the man has knowldge and vision! Who commissioned me for my first mural to be painted on the back wall facing the parking lot to his fine establishment? Nathan Eddie MacDaniels; that's who sucker!"

"Now where do you come into all this, Alphonso?" Nathan Eddie crossed his long legs again and turned on the sternness, but I could feel a smile inside of him tickling him to death.

"I come in the spaces in between, like I always do." I said, twirling my toothpick in the corner of my mouth. "The way the Gentle Man should. I heard you was celebrating thanksgiving and I just wanted to be there when you carved up the turkey 'cause I definitely want my piece!"

The buzzer rang in my studio and we all looked up and over to the door. This set off the recorded voice of a female friend in tune with the sounding bells, 'Ooooo-Alphonso! We have some com-pan-eee!"

"Danny, go see who it is, will ya, man?"

Danny grunted and then came back and picked up his cards.

"That was Dougie Dogg. I rang him up."

"Oh? Cool. Cool." I turned my attention back to Nathan Eddie. "See what I'm saying? Right here at this table we got all this knowledge. We're the original society of learned men, but we never recognize each other or give ourselves the proper credit for what we know and what we have done."

"You startin' to sound like your father now, Alphonso." Nathan Eddie almost whispered to me. "That's something he would say."

We heard the buzzer and the recording again and Smiley went to the door this time.

"What up dough, pardners?" Dougie Dogg dropped his duffel bag with a thump and gave soul handshakes all around. "Hey, you got money on this table? Can a brother get in on some of this?"

"Naw fool, get yo' rusty butt back out on the street!" Danny said, tossing in his hand. Dougie Dogg overdid shrugging his shoulders, looking around with his usual deadpan expression.

"Hey, I don't know who you talkin' to. I don't see no hoes up in this mug."

"Pull up a chair and sit yr hind down, man." I told Dougie Dogg.

"What up, Gentle Man? How's the playa?"

"Holdin' his own, my man, holdin' his own."

"Who dat bitch you got tagging me soon as I get out uh Kronk? She keep asking about you, man."

"Bitch?" Danny craned his neck at Dougie. "What bitch?"

"Now was I talkin' to you, Danny? I'm talking to Alphonso here. Matter of fact-" Dougie Dogg bolted out of his seat and went over to the row of windows in the far wall. "I ran into her on the way up here. Yeah, she still down there. Some little white chick-look like Michelle Fieffer, or somebody's daughter. See the one in the green coat hailin' for a cab? That's her. What you do to her man she so afraid to see you? Here. She wanted me to give you some kind of note about something. Hey! Where you going, man -?"

I snatched the scrap of paper out of Dougie Dogg's hand and rushed for the door. Danny followed me and we tumbled down the stairs like a couple of maddened wildebeests. We were barely out of the vestibule when I leapt the stoop calling out her name. I barely got a glimpse of her ankle and the tail end of her coat sweeping into the passenger side of a black and yellow City Cab when I called out her name for the last time. We ran a ways, but we couldn't catch the cab.

"Hey! Wait up! Wait up! Mary?! Is that you? Wait up!"

Danny and I bent over and caught our breaths.

"That your mystery woman, Alphonso?"

"Yeah. I -"

"Hold tight, man, hold tight." Danny took me by the arm as I started to go after her. "We not gon' catch her in this traffic, an' ain't no broad worth gettin' run over."

"What's she playin' at? I -" I copped a glance at the note in my hand, then back up the street and then back at the note.

"C'mon man, let's go back up. Wooo -" Danny pressed his hands against his lower back and spine. "Them stairs is a killer!"

"Why is she doing this, Danny?"

"Who knows what goes on in a bitch's mind? C'mon man, let's head up stairs."

Back upstairs you would have thought we were just coming back from Church's Fried Chicken something. Nathan Eddie was reshuffling the cards again and Smiley and Dougie Dogg were picking up their hands. It was getting drafty in the studio, so I went over again and closed most of the windows. Danny and I sat back down at the card table.

"Gave you the slip, huh, Alphonso man?" Dougie Dogg barely looked up at me from his cards. "White girls will do that to you. Shouldn't be foolin' around with 'em no way."

"Mannn, you don't know nothing 'bout that."

"Don't want uh know about that."

"Yeah, like you and Maxine Baker are living in a paradise on earth."

"At least she ain't got me breakin' my neck, runnin' down stairs trying to catch her." Dougie Dogg put his money down and placed a bet. "You keep foolin' around, she gon' turn you into a trick."

"She ain't my woman, man."

"Could uh fooled me. She sho' was doing the long lost love thang with all them questions she was asking about you. Where you know her from, Alphonso?"

Dougie Dogg stretched out a muscular arm and scratched his back.

"Back at school we were sort of close."

"She the one been slippin' all them notes under Alphonso's door." Smiley told Dougie. "See all them notes on the bulletin board over there? That's her."

"Oh? So she the one. How come all this rippin' and runnin' and duckin' and hidin'? She ashamed to be seen with yo' ass - or something?

"I don't know what going on with her, man."

"Oh. Y'all in some kind uh trouble?"

"Hell if I know. You talked to her. You probably know more about what's up with her than I do."

Dougie Dogg looked at me with that mournful, soulful expression.

"Naw. I don't know nothing. I just hope y'all straighten this out real soon, cause I don't need no white girls waitin' on me to finish up at Kronk."

"Right. You got more than your hands full with Maxine."

"At least she black. An' she gits naked when I tell her to."

"Right. When's the wedding?"

Dougie Dogg looked around at everybody else like I was crazy.

"Say what? What's this fool talkin' 'bout? Ain't nobody said nothing about no wedding!"

"Oh yeah, man, what was I thinking? Don't no bitch put the ring in Dougie Dogg's nose!"

"Hell, naw! Bitches only good for two things; gettin' naked and gettin' down. After that, I got my business to take care of."

You could barely see Nathan Eddie behind a red flaming dot and a halo of cigarette smoke that nearly concealed how he was carefully regarding Dougie Dogg just now. But Dougie was unfazed as we dealt our hands. He did his little gangster pimp frown as he shuffled his cards.

"You know, bitches is people, too," Nathan Eddie pointed out, looking at his cigarette.

"What dat supposed to mean? An' don't you start, Alphonso! Like you an' Miss Pinky Lee is 'goooo-ing to the cha-ap-pel/ and! We're! Gonnn-na git ma-a-a-rried!' "

"Doggone it, Dougie!" Danny exclaimed with alarm. "Please don't sing! Stick to boxing, my brother!"

"That's more like it. Let's everybody stick to what they know best. Dougie Dogg don't know nothing 'bout no marriage. Dougie Dogg don't want to know nothin' 'bout no marriage. Dougie Dogg ain't studdin' no marriage!"

"The Four 'F' Club forever, am I right, Dougie?" Danny was mocking my man from behind his cards.

"That's what I'm talkin' 'bout! Y'all laugh all you want, but you not gettin' my neck in that noose-"

"Somebody lend that fool a Bible," Now I know Smiley must be looking at a real good hand, "and get him to look up First Corinthians, somebody-"

"Look it up yr damn self, Smiley. This ain't no prayer meetin'. Case you haven't noticed, we's dealing in a game of chance at the moment."

Dougie threw down and backed up what he said. That chuckle of his sounded sinister as he drew back the cash.

"What happens when the baby comes?" Nathan Eddie said as he held his cigarette and looked at the ceiling.

"What baby? It ain't mine! I swear the hoe was sleepin' round on me!" Old Dougie cracked nary a smile when he recited the standard line from the manual. "Besides, I make sure Maxine take care of all that before she darkens my doorstep."

"Got all the angles covered, huh, Dougie?" Danny said with a rueful sneer.

"That my job, the way I see it, as the man in the relationship. I'm s'posed to protect this here situation so that nothing goes down that I don't want to go down. Look - there's a time and a place for everything..."

"So I've been told," Smiley says, idly fingering his cards.

"Here I am; barely twenty now and still an amateur boxer yet to turn pro. What am I gonna look like tryin' to raise somebody's baby with no money? I mean, look what marriage did for my man Tyson and he was head up in cash!"

"Uh-oh, here we go again-" Danny groaned.

"Naw, serious business, y'all. Tyson was King of the Hill before he took that little spill with Givens-"

"When you gon' get off that, man?" Smiley whined in exasperation. "Why you always got to make it out like Tyson was Samson and Robin Givens was Deliah? That junk just don't wash, man."

"Just statin' the obvious. You know it too, Smiley. When a chump let pussy go to his head that's when his brains start to ooze away."

Smiley gestured in derision at Dougie, as though he were presenting us with the prize fool for the night.

"Uh-right! According to the Gospel of Saint Dougie Dogg!"

Nobody wanted to laugh, but we couldn't help ourselves.

"I don't know what y'all laughin' at - " Dougie looked around with defiance, but that made it all the funnier, "-that's the problem with us. We don't know how to take nothing serious."

Nathan Eddie tried to hide the mirth in his eyes behind that big ham of a hand, but he was shaking so hard to keep from laughing that finally he just gave up.

"Go 'head up, my man," Nathan Eddie reached out and gave Dougie a big old soul handshake. "Give us book, chapter and verse!"

"I'm about to. What you got to do is abide by the rules of the Four 'F' Club, and when you see a brother back slidin', you offer him moral support. That way you can lead him back into the fold. We got to do with bitches what God intended us to do."

"Cigarette, Dougie?" Nathan Eddie offered him one, before wiping out the corner of his eye. "Woo-"

"Naw, I'm straight."

We sat around and waited patiently for Dougie to finish explaining himself. First time I noticed that the only place that had any carpeting was the place where I posed my models. I made a mental note to take care of that. I also needed to get a heavy black curtain for the times when it would be necessary to block out all the sunlight. I turned around again and with everybody else attempted to give Dougie Dogg my full attention without cracking up. There was a summer breeze coming in through the windows from the street. That helped calm me down. I can't speak for anybody else.

"Come on, Dougie," Danny urged him on, "say what you got to say."

"Bitches got to be handled for what they are." Dougie looked around with a hard scowl. "I don't know what you looking at me like that fo'. Y'all know the rules of the Four 'F' club. You do with bitches what a man's got to do. You find 'em, fool 'em, fuck 'em, and forget 'em. That's the way that go."

"An' after that, son?" Nathan Eddie asked softly.

"After what, after that? After that, you just keep on steppin'"

"'Like a natural man'," Smiley sang out. "Hey y'all, Lou Rawls!"

"Shut your fool mouth, Smiley," Danny said, punching Smiley in the shoulder.

"Naw man, let me write some of this down-"

Nathan Eddie regarded Dougie Dogg thoughtfully before he unfolded his arms. He casually lit up another cigarette and set it in a nearby ashtray.

"Sounds like somebody been schoolin' you on all this, Dougie." Nathan Eddie remarked with a hint of sadness. "How you come upon this new found knowledge you got?"

"Mojo and me was rappin' about it. How come you wanna know?"

"What else Morris teach you?" Nathan Eddie asked, as he reached to reshuffle the deck.

"I dunno. Just things you need to know to get over. We was kickin' around the 'Hammer Philosophy' for awhile."

"The 'Hammer Philosophy'?" Smiley exclaimed as he swiveled his head at us. "Y'all know what this fool is talking about?"

"Don't get him started, Smiley-"

"Wha-you think I can't explain myself?" Dougie was quick to take offense when someone doubted his smarts. "I can explain myself! We was discussin' the 'Hammer Philosophy' as it relates to situations and dynamite."

"Break it down to us, Dougie Dogg." Danny urged him on merrily.

Danny was just messing with Dougie, but he really should have known better.

"Mojo was just tellin' me how to keep my guard up in any situation in Life. He was just sayin' you got to approach Life just like you was the hero in some movie-"

"Oh Lordy, here it comes-" Danny nudged me gleefully.

""He said everybody's got a story, and Life always offers you a script. You can make a quick read of that script if you on your toes. Mojo just told me you don't have to lie down and spread yo' legs like some bitch and accept whatever Life puts down on you." Dougie put up his dukes like he was sparring some invisible opponent. "You can make some demands yourself from Life. In fact, you can hip Life to where it's at. Master Mojo told me the three things a man should let Life know from the get."

"Set us straight, Dougie, set us straight, brother Dogg." Smiley jibed at him.

"You gotta tell Life three things: Number One-You cain't kill me, Number Two- I have to win the fight," Dougie threw a stiff jab at the air, "Number Three-I have to git the girl in the end! He told me that's what the new Black Man needs to tell Life!"

"Oh?" Danny nudged me confidentially again, but I'm wishing he would stop that. "An' what's that got to do with situations and dynamite?"

"I ain't hip on that as much." Dougie's brow furrowed with perplexity. "I'll have to have Mojo break that down to me a little more."

Nathan Eddie leaned back as he took a drag from his cigarette. Now he was regarding me through his tobacco haze with a curious detachment.

"Sound like some of this might be your schoolin', Alphonso." Nathan Eddie remarked.

"Hell, no. I helped teach Dougie how to read, not what to think!"

"I know one thing," Smiley said as he dealt his hand, "your work in that department is not yet finished. Most of that mess that Dougie was puttin' down comes from not reading!"

"You can kiss my black bee-hind, Smiley," Dougie Dogg growled from behind his cards. "I read something new everyday, and for your information, the 'Hammer Philosophy' is the documented thought of a famous celebrity."

"Who?" Danny nudged me again. "'M.C. Hammer'?"

"Naw. Mojo mentioned somebody old school. I forget his name now. He was The Man back in the day before I was born-"

Danny nudged me again, then put his hand over my ear and whispered despite my frown.

"He talking about Fred Williamson; the dude who was in 'BLACK CAESAR' and 'MASH' and 'THE LEGEND OF NIGGER CHARLEY'-"

"Who?"

"C'mon man, the guy your father used to talk about made movies back when they was making the first 'SHAFT' and 'SUPERFLY' and carryin' on. He was a football player before that like Jim Brown. Your father said they used to call Fred Williamson 'The Hammer' before he went and traded in his football helmet."

"So?"

"All that stuff about 'you cain't kill me', 'I have to win the fight' and 'I have to get the girl in the end'; that's his rap. That's what he used to tell movie producers before he would agree to do their scripts."

"Yeah?"

"Yeah, man," Danny finished spitting in my ear, "hold up-hey Dougie! That was Fred Williamson who rapped about the 'Hammer Philosophy' wasn't it?"

"Fred Williamson?" Dougie was liking his hand for the first time during the game. "Yeah, I think so. Somebody like him. I'll have to ask Mojo about that the next time he comes to see me train."

Nathan Eddie came back out of the shadows from the fridge. He was hanging a few cans of beer from the plastic by his fingertips. When he sat down with a plop, he pulled a can free with pop-fizz foam on the top when the tab came off and he guzzle-gulped one down.

"Ahhhh! Anybody want one? Danny? Smiley? What's the deal, Alphonso? I notice you've been kind of mum for awhile."

"I just don't think Dougie should be takin' counsel from no pimp, that's all. The only thing Leonard Morris can teach you, Dougie, is how to fall."

"Let me be the judge of dat, Alphonso. Hah!" Dougie showed his hand and raked in our cash. "Besides, you never would hip me as to how you be gettin' all them bitches to give it up to you the way they do. I cain't help it if I got a professional to share his trade secrets with me."

"How many times I got to tell you there's a world of difference between my game and Mojo's dirty business? I'm creatin' a vision, man. Mojo's a jackal who exploits human weakness and commercializes the human need for love."

Dougie peered at me shrewdly from behind his cards.

"That's your version, Alphonso. Mojo told me all about you. He had me crackin' up about you, man!"

"Mojo don't know nothing about me, guy."

"Oh, he knows a little something about you, Alphonso. The jury's still out on how much he knows, but you let me be the judge of that. I'll bang out for myself whether or not the dude has you dead to rights."

"What he tell you 'bout Alponso, Dougie?" Danny said, nudging me again.

Dougie moved his thumb thoughtfully across the scar on his chin.

"He told me you a real romantic dude, Alphonso, a straight up dreamer. The trouble is you is so idealistic you don't even know you pimpin' all them girls you bring up here to pose for you."

"He told you that, huh?" Danny challenged him back.

"Yeah, buddy,"

"Mojo don't know nothing."

"That's what he said you'd say, Alphonso. You all sensitive about it and carryin' on, but the facts are still facts. He said when you get right down to it, you sellin' sex the same as he's doing. That's why your Art is so popular. You got a sophisticated kind of pimp going on. The thang is you don't even know it. An' he tole me a pimp who don't know he's a pimp is the most dangerous kind of fool going."

Now that did it. The chill of Mojo in the air swirls around the card table and it gets so quiet you can hear the air conditioning in the ceiling and the indoor plumbing go spisssh-knock in behind all the walls. The shadows of early evening clouds come and go over our modest little game through the streaked windows of my studio. Everybody takes a good hard look at yours truly before they will speak again. I curse Mojo under my breath. Nobody ever really sizes him up right. Now I can see how he means for his poison and his filth to reach all the way right up here into my studio, like the fumes of some kind of dangerous urban toxic waste. I curse myself for not taking him more seriously. Now he's fixing to infect one of my friends with his snake logic, and use him as the carrier host for the communicable disease he intends to spread.

Damn that Morris! I should have wasted his ass like I planned to do when I caught him in the act turning Sheba Taylor out. That girl's mother still ain't right about that, what with the plans she had to send her daughter to college. Now Sheba's up and down Woodward after midnight, showing thigh in high heeled shoes to cab drivers, or being hustled off into the passenger side of a Mercedes Benz in broad daylight to some wealthy client in suburbia. I should have shot Morris down like a dog right there in front of the Shakers and the Takers Lounge, the way he so richly deserved. I could have bitch slapped Sheba and thrown her into the car, drove her back to her moms and thrashed the whole thing out, even if it took all night. We could have got Sheba walking a college campus and I had my hand on the trigger, but for Danny stopping me. Look what it's come to now.

Now Morris wants to add Dougie Dogg to his crew.

After all that hard work I put in teaching my friend how to read. Now I gots to be ice.

"I don't care to have any friend of mine associate with Leonard Morris to a high degree of familiarity. How y'all get to be so tight, anyway?"

"What you talkin' 'bout now, Alphonso?" Dougie snatched up his cards. "Mojo came to me! I'm tradin' punches with my sparring partners when he comes down to the gym to check me out." Dougie does that shrugging shoulders thing again. "Said he liked what he saw during my last bout."

"Morris wants to own you, Dougie. I would steer clear of him, if I were you. He's not the kind of company you really want to keep."

"Yeah, but you not me, Alphonso. I hate to keep tellin' you that."

I pulled a folded sheet of looseleaf paper out of my wallet.

"Look, I won't argue with you. Now you should know by now I at least have your best interests at heart. I have been in your corner from day one, Dougie."

"I got lots of people in mah corner, cheerin' me on and carryin' on. What's this you givin' me?"

"That there is a new reading list. I went over it with Samuel Turner and he suggested-"

"What? Now you got that faggot Suckertease involved in my ed-jew-mah-cation? Are you out of your mind, Alphonso? What can that chump possibly teach me, besides how to be a mark the way he is?"

"The fight game is a short career path for a boxer. When you're done in ten, fifteen years at best if you're lucky, you're going to have to take the lessons you've learned in the ring and apply them in a different arena on a higher level." I pointed to the list I had shoved in his face. "I think you should check those books out. One is an autobiography by Muhammad Ali, and there are a couple of other books about boxers on that list. Mister Turner suggested I-"

"Look man, what I got to do to make you see?" Dougie took a brief look at the sheet of paper and then shoved it back at me. "Suckertease cain't teach me nothing! He got more knowledge than he know what tah do with, and more than what's good for him the way I heard Mojo tell it."

"You gon' be the chump you keep listenin' to Morris."

"I'll be the judge of that, Alphonso. I know how y'all feel obliged to do my thinking for me. Mojo kept stressin' how I had to use my mother wit, how I had to think for myself if I was really ever gonna get over; not just adopt the thoughts of a bunch of dead white folks and people who never lived my life or walked in my shoes. That what Suckertease been doin' all his life and where has it got him?"

"The man is studying towards his Doctorate, Dougie-"

"There you go again, man. Because the man got a few degrees that's supposed to make him King of the World! The way Mojo broke it down, Suckertease let his own desire to know get the best of him and ended up involved with some of the shadier elements of society. At one time they had him under lock and key and closed circuit TV. Those dudes picked his brain clean, all without his self even knowing it. After that, they did the bait and switch on him with his one true college sweetheart and shacked him up with a hoe! Now he lives in a room full of books, jackin' off over pictures of white women who would never give him the time of day. Tell me this; why should I read all these books? Reading all these books didn't make Suckertease smart enough to keep from fallin' in the wrong hands. An' it sho' didn't keep him from being turned into a sex addict and the mark for the ultimate mindfuck. You tight with that fool. Ask if he's had a brainstorm about that lately. Degrees! The only degrees Suckertease has are degrees in how to be the White Man's nigger." Dougie giggled away into raucous laughter. "Yeah buddy, he got a degree in the white man's tricknology, 'ceptin' he's the one who's the trick. He got a degree from the Institute of Kiss-My-Ass-ology, 'ceptin' he's the one kissin' ass. Now he's studyin' for his Doctorate in Suck-My-Dick-Technology, and I'm sure he'll graduate from that with honors. Naw, I don't need to know what Suckertease knows, Alphonso. You cain't hold yo' head up high with that kind of knowledge."

"Suit yourself, my main man, suit yourself."

"Straight up, man. Suckertease don't know how to kick no ass and he don't know how to cop no pussy. Those are things a man needs to know to keep going. Since I already know how to do those things and he cain't really school me any further on that, who's got the knowledge?"

"Now I'm hearin' Mojo when I close my eyes," Nathan Eddie said impassively.

"Naw, Alphonso." Dougie Dogg's face took on that soulful, mournful expression again. "I'm for real, man. Who's got the knowledge?"

Now I could have kept on arguing with Dougie Dogg, but that would have just shown I didn't really understand his question. But I really did understand what he was saying. What can you learn from a victim except how to be one? What can you learn from an exploiter and oppressor but how to better exploit and oppress? Which one would you choose if these were the only choices available to you? Yeah, it's a narrow argument, but a legacy of oppression can cause folks to lead narrow lives and to think and see things in narrow terms.

What good is knowledge that does not lift one out of a socially conditioned self-abnegation and self-abasement? What purpose can it serve to anyone, particularly an oppressed people? My friend Socrates knew a lot of thngs, but, as Dougie was asking, did he really have knowledge?

We held our cards and listened to the whirr of the air conditioning.

Most people don't know how easy it is for Black Folks to fall outside the marked socially approved routes and channels and into the street life. I found out personally that as an African American I did not even have to be rebellious or defiant. I only had to be inattentive or careless to find I stepped off too much to the left that time, and now was spinning off the tightrope of social propriety and into the cultural abyss of street life; where you made your own rules in the spaces in between the right and the wrong as you went along.

I knew the mood in the room was Mojo's doing. I was holding a winning hand, but it really did not seem to matter anymore. I found myself remembering how I could have waxed Mojo, but Danny caught my arm and wrestled me back into the alley, where he banged my gun hand against a dumpster before we ended up toppling each other over head first inside. I still have a cut on my back from thrashing around with him inside that dumpster on a broken beer bottle.

I just have to remember there will be another time. I wrote my brothers in Florida and L.A. all about it, and it will be different next time. I'll get Mojo someplace where there's no one around to help him and then we'll settle things about Sheba and maybe even Socrates.

"Alphonso?" Dougie Dogg started, as he threw down his cards, "What it say on that note that white girl wanted you to see?"

"That? Oh, nothing," I remembered how the note began, 'My most precious Alphonso', "it was just about some books she wanted me to read."

That was all I told them that day. Why ruin a perfectly good card game with the rest? How Mary noticed some suspicious dude with binoculars and a green golf bag. He was moving into the apartment across from her. She mentioned how his window fronted mine somehow, but what was that supposed to mean to me?

I clipped Victor a good one with the top of my head just under the jawbone. I twisted and lunged forward to grapple out of the doorway past him. He recoiled in a groan, but somehow latched onto my tie again as though it were a bridle.

"Whoa, little doggie!" Victor snarled as he straddled me like a horse. "Where do you think you're going, my man? Did I give you permission to leave? Back! Back into my office! Our conference isn't finished yet!"

Victor steered me back into the alcove with a choking headlock and a rough knee against my rear end. Between my legs I caught an upside down glimpse of that white dude across the street. I barely managed to see him remove a pair of binoculars from the glove box of his car. This only in the split second Victor slammed my head into the door.

WONDERS OF WILMA

I barely managed to wiggle out of Victor's headlock for a blessed gasp of air. He tackled me again and body slammed me against the concrete stoop, my legs kicking out at nothing. I blocked his hammering punches at my face and head as best I could. That was when some of the stuff I used against Dougie Mack in our sparring sessions flashed back into my mind. I reached up to regain my feet, but Victor kneed me in the chest and I was back on my ass again in the dust.

"Oh? You want to get up now?" Victor sneered at me in a mocking tone. "Here, let me help you up."

Victor grabbed me by the collar and heaved me up against the doorjamb. I felt my back press against a button just barely below my shoulder. We both heard some kind of buzzer go off inside and looked around in guilty apprehension.

When I rang the doorbell to the Wellington establishment and the trumpets sounded, no one could have prepared me for the sumptuous feast that Daphne's parents went to all that trouble to prepare. George Patrick Wellington trapped my hand in his meaty grip with both of his own, the crystal porch light glinting off his green eye. Mrs. Fiona Esther Wellington took one of my hands in her own turn and squeezed it gently. While I studied Mrs. Wellington's handsome, lined face wreathed in graying brunette curls and contrasted it with the prominent forehead and balding pate of the heavyset and squat Mr. Wellington, I spied quickly for a glance of Daphne coming down the marble stairway behind them. I could see she was going to make us await her grand entrance

"We're so pleased to meet you, my young man-" Mr. Wellington nodded soberly.

"Yes, we feel we almost know you. What with all that Daphne has told us -"

"Nothing good I hope -" I quip to them.

"You're right!" Mr. Wellington explodes into a hearty guffaw as some sort of nervous release into hilarity. "However, we understand that everything that they have written about you in the National Enquirer, although true, is to be taken with a grain of salt."

Mr. Wellington throws back his head and his shoulders shake with chuckling glee. Daphne told me all I should do is laugh at her father's jokes if I really wanted to get in good with him. I know one thing. There is no use competing with him in the humor department. The man is clearly his own best audience.

"You got me that time, Mr. Wellington," I pat him on the shoulder.

"Daphne will be down shortly, Alphonso," Mrs. Wellington gathers the folds of her pink silk brocade summer gown. "why don't we all sit down for a moment and chat for awhile to get better acquainted?"

Check this out.

When you've been roped into meeting the parents, you can kiss the old leg wrap and booty hug goodbye. Now you've got to justify your love. Meeting your main squeeze's folks in the parlor gives them a chance to size you up before they waste one morsel of food on you. The mother is usually the one to start sounding you out, so Daphne's mom is acting true to maternal form.

What she doesn't realize is that the Gentle Man has been this way before. I know now I have to set the tone to make sure I'm not eaten alive with what's left over and sent home in a doggie bag.

"Hey," I point to the painting on the wall above a sofa chair, "the gang's all here, huh?"

"That's right," Mr. Wellington browbeats the air with an index finger to remember my name. "Alphonso, that's right, isn't it?"

"Yes sir, you've got it."

"Oh, you don't have to salute me, young man. Just call me George."

"-and you can call me Fiona, Alphonso," Mrs. Wellington said in an attempt to ingratiate herself to me. "Yes sir-ree, that's the old clan all together. Aunt Sarah and George's father Rodney and my father Hiram and Uncle Cyril and my mother Cecilia,"Mrs. Wellington waves off at the painting, "-ohhhh, I'm sure this is all boring stuff to you-everybody's got a family!"

"You're something of a painter yourself, aren't you, Alphonso?" Mr. Wellington turns to me with an amused, curious regard. "How do you suppose we come off in this latest offering by Leon Bournegan?"

I pace around the painting because it's critique time in the Motor City now.

"My man Leon didn't do too bad. He got the 'Wellington Expression' down pat. The guy could have punched up the highlights a little more and put more colors in the shadows, but that's just what I would have done. I respect the way he turned it out. There's a definite family spirit that's going on inside the painting. Hey, that's Daphne over there, isn't it?"

"Yes indeed, Alphonso." Mrs. Wellington said, beaming proudly. "That's my little Daphne sitting next to her Uncle Cyril, and in front of her my other daughter, Theresa Agnes-"

"What's this about the 'Wellington Expression' you were talking about?" Mr. Wellington rested a thigh on the arm of the sofa chair. "What's that all about? How did you come to connote that from the picture?"

"I don't know," I shrugged, "that's just what I see. Something in the way you Wellingtons lift your chins and the steely-eyed way you scowl down at the world now that you've taken possession of it. The expression seems to say 'everybody better kowtow now that we're on the scene'. You know, just one man's way of looking at a picture."

Mr. and Mrs. Wellington seemed to be genuinely taken aback. After thinking about what I said momentarily, they glanced at each other in an attempt to reference the other's feelings. Each gave a nervous chuckle of bewilderment and then looked over at me.

"My Lord!" Mrs. Wellington exclaimed, putting a hand to her throat. "What a remarkable thing to say!"

"Do you really mean to tell us you saw all that in our portrait, son?" Mr. Wellington said in an almost apologetic tone. "'The Wellingtons Cast A Forbidding Gaze Upon The World'?"

"Sounds like a headline for the National Enquirer, doesn't it? Of course, like all truth, it should be taken with a grain of salt. That's right, isn't it, Mr. Wellington?"

"Touche', my young friend, a palpable hit."

Speaking of looking down upon the world, our eyes all turn to the top of the stairs. There she is, a long red scarf draped from her neck around her waist, and fastened just under the bust line of her lavender gown with an orchid broach. There she is, Miss America, giving us a royal wave and the merest taste of the Wellington expression.

"Daphne! Don't tell me you've finally decided to join us, dear." Mrs. Wellington said, pressing her hands together.

"Sorry, Mother. Hello, Daddy. I hope I didn't keep you waiting long, Alphonso," Daphne daintily descended in her ribbed dancing shoes.

"No, we were just getting acquainted a little, that's all." I folded my arms across my chest.

Daphne reminds me of another painting where a female is descending a staircase. I can't remember it offhand, but I am sure it will come to me.

"Mmmmm, something smells like lovin,' " Daphne remarks to the wafting aroma coming out of the dining room.

"We were waiting on you, my dear," Mr. Wellington gently remonstrates her as she plants a kiss on his forehead. "Shall we make our way to the dining room before dinner becomes cold?"

Daphne linked arms with me and we proceeded to grease.

"What are your intentions regarding my daughter, Alphonso?" asked Mr. Wellington as he wiped bits of taboule from the corner of his mouth.

"Regarding Daphne? Thank you, ma'am -" I said to the maid, as she refilled my glass with a nice celery and tomato punch.

"Yesss -" Mr. Wellington nodded as he took a little nip of his white wine.

"I would have to say then that my main intention is to find the image of God within her. When I have come to that, I'll do my level best to transfer and render that image to drawing paper and canvas, and make it a living reality in clay without invoking false idolatry of any kind."

I gave a wink to Estelle, our maid for the evening. She pouted a brief smile before assuming a stiff frown in dignified decorum. She reminded me of something I heard a jazz saxophonist say while I was washing dishes in this nightspot to pay for school. He exclaimed with consternation that brothers were always in the kitchen. I told him where ever the food was at, that would be where you would find me, but he didn't want to joke about it.

Now I could have said sisters are always in the kitchens of white folks, fixing them meals fit for the angels in heaven. However, I did not feel the occasion warranted such a remark. The Gentle Man has no need to play the stereotype for anyone. Let's face it; it really is such a cliché' to always take your cue to play the angry young black man railing against white society. For me to jump at every opportunity to declare my solidarity with the oppressed peoples of the planet seemed absolutely Pavlovian to me, and I was actually interested in salivating about something else for a change.

The dinner table was heaped with generous portions of all this good food. There were chicken breasts with celery root mash after the taboule, baked pumpkin strudel and potato cakes, halibut steak with nettle butter, red snapper with raw spinach salad, rice with cucumber balls, and for dessert a choice between baked papaya with ginger and fresh figs with raspberry cheese. Even the place settings looked good enough to eat. You will forgive me, but when you are surrounded with potato cakes and pumpkin pie, you would be a fool to bite the hand that feeds you. I remember nights I went to bed on mayonnaise sandwiches or stingy portions of black-eyed peas mixed with ketchup. Such events didn't happen often, but it makes you bow your head in prayer whenever you come into the vicinity of all this.

"You're so articulate, Alphonso," Mrs. Wellington exclaims as Daphne blushes over my last remark. "Where do you find such high-sounding phrases?"

"I say it deserves a toast," Mr. Wellington refills his glass with white wine, "eh, Fiona?"

"Let me give it," Daphne touches me on the shoulder as she rises to stand.

"'- to the image of God'," I whisper in her ear before she comes to her full height.

She nods to me with a conspiratorial smile.

"I propose a toast-" She lifts her glass high so that the red evening light can be seen glinting from it, "-to the 'Image of God!'"

"'The Image of God!" Our chorus of four rings out to clinking glasses.

"Here-here!" Mr. Wellington adds savoring the taste of white wine on his palate. "That's going to be a tall order, my boy, don't you think?"

"Sho' you rite. Sounds like a job for the Gentle Man."

"Now I heard you correctly, didn't I? You want to find the image of God within our little Daphne. You wouldn't be saying that just to snow us, would you, Alphonso? Perhaps hoping to lure this young unsuspecting one into becoming just another object of rank titillation? Grist for your artist's mill -"

Mr. Wellington narrowed one eye with a sardonic smile as he sipped more wine.

"George!" Mrs. Wellington playfully slapped her husband's hand on the table. "I believe Alphonso has made a clear enough statement of his intentions for now."

"Oh, I'll grant you it makes a good toast and all, but it sounds too good to be true when you put it through the sifter. Just enough polite chatter to disarm the old folks at home until you complete all your plans to elope with our daughter."

"Daddy!" Daphne glances at me to see where I'm wounded and then at her father. "I for one believe that Alphonso's statements were completely sincere."

"They're the product of a highly original imagination, I'll grant you that." Mr. Wellington pops a cucumber ball into his mouth. "Think for a moment what might have happened had I told your father I was looking for the image of God in you, Fiona. Why he would have run me off with the fireplace poker!"

"Dear! You're not an artist like Alphonso here. Daphne tells us you're preparing a show for exhibit at a gallery soon. We would love to see some of your work, Alphonso."

"I'll get you as many complementary tickets as you need," I assured her as I attacked the celery root mash and shredded a chicken breast with my knife and fork.

Man! I can still taste the olive oil on the chunks of celery and potatoes and the piquant taste of salt and pepper mixed with a little hot milk. My brain is starting to oxygenate with all that good celery and tomato punch. The welcome breeze of fresh air coursing through the gray matter is starting to make me feel a little lightheaded. That could cause the lip to loosen when the sparks begin to fly outside the normally determined routes and channels of the neuron synapse. Uh-oh, I feel a brainstorm coming on! Wait! I know the remedy for that. Let's have another potato cake and more smoked salmon with eggplant sauce on the way! Hold that pumpkin strudel in reserve!

"Tell us, Alphonso, what does the Image of God look like to you?" Mrs. Wellington asks me with that seeking the answer to Life expression. "What does it feel like when you've seen it?"

Forget membership in Dougie Dogg's 'Four F' club. Never set out to hide anything from a woman unless it is absolutely necessary for her safety and welfare. Even then, such deception is best for a temporary or short duration, because eventually any woman will sense you out. It's a womb to tomb thing that the best minds have yet to unravel.

The image of God is everywhere, of course, permeating everything with a shining splendor. However, Mrs. Wellington asked a civil question and deserved a civil answer. Funny, how the image that came to mind first was of Wilma Durant pushing her baby sister higher and higher in a swing and the way the playing field grass looked under her feet. Just one of those things that stick with you over the years like a gem you keep in a hope chest wrapped up inside an old cloth. No one ever sees it but you, but whenever you undo the wraps and rub it off with your elbow it will gleam and shine with its original brilliance.

Some memories are like that. I was riding on the bus down Livernois when I spotted this young girl riding her bike barefooted in shorts. There was something about the clear blue and green day and the sight of her reddened cheeks and thighs and feet on the revolving pedals. The innocent pleasure of it, chaste and pure, was like something out of the Bible. Even now it lives in my mind as a gift from God.

The greatest beauty is unaware of itself. The greatest impressions are without artifice and fly directly into the soul. The spontaneous apprehension of the pleasure of God is at once more than the mind and emotions can tolerably countenance and at the same time the eternal nourishment of the soul. That's all to the good, but unless I mind meld with Daphne and Mr. and Mrs. Wellington for them to see how I felt when Wilma stood in her dark caramel luminescence and all in white teeth and black curly hair pushed her baby sister skyward with big sister joy, and then caught my gaze just long enough to feel my admiration like the welcome sunshine on her skin and all in a split second say, "Hi, Alphonso!" as though she were waking from a dream, they will never really get it.

Therefore, it is time to break it down for them.

"Put it this way, Mrs. Wellington. Just find the time when your husband was more beautiful than you could bear. You don't have to tell me when that was; I know that's personal. I know it already could have been the first time you went out on a date with him, or the first time you knew you were in love with him and it seemed to you his eyes were filled with God. I think you know that whenever you see things with that special faculty and sense that love endows and bestows you with, it will not be long before you behold the image of God in something or someone."

"An interesting analysis, Alphonso." Daphne nibbled at her spinach salad some, took a sip of wine and regarded me thoughtfully. "Do you feel you're seeing the image of God in me now?"

Daphne was as beautiful as that painting by Harry Anderson. That's the one about that broad featured young blonde woman holding the Good Book over her heart and looking skyward to heaven. The shining, uplifted face is a study in the certitude that is rooted in faith and the dignity of spiritual intelligence. How many times have I studied that painting to glean its secrets? Right now, however, I don't want my future model to get too big a head on her. I hold my hand in the air palm down and make like a plane going through turbulence.

"Aaaa, off and on I see glimpses of the magic I might put on canvas, baby." I sip some more of my punch. "I just want to make sure all systems are go in my studio when the Image of God comes in again at twelve o'clock high."

"That is truly remarkable, Alphonso." Mrs. Wellington marveled with a 'what do you know about that' twinkle in her eye. "I do believe I can recall that first time I saw the image of God in my husband!"

"I thought you'd come around." Now it's time for the pumpkin strudel. "You see, Mrs. Strudel, I-what am I talkin' about? I mean Mrs. Wellington -"

"Call me Fiona, dear-"

"Very good, Fiona. You see, Fiona, I don't believe that beauty is necessarily inherent in all things. I think beauty is a spiritual investment in what's goin' on and what's happenin' right now. Just as I believe you intuited so correctly, it's a special way of seeing and feeling about things and others that has to be cultivated by that particular individual. Now let's take Mr. Wellington here as a case in point-"

"George! I'll be hanged if you'll address my wife as 'Fiona' and not call me George!" Mr. Wellington declared with an indignant harrumph. "-and I wouldn't place any bets on you getting my young girl on a bearskin rug in your studio any time soon, young man!"

"Now George, dear," Mrs. Wellington gave her husband's hand a gentle pat, "there is no need to turn the conversation in that direction at this time. After all, we are at the dinner table."

"Momma's right," Daphne assented between chewing her halibut steak, "I already explained to Alphonso that I was taking an audition tape to New York to see if I could land a part in 'Dangerous Loves'. I won't have the time for him to explore the relationship between my inner and outer beauty now."

Daphne points at me with that droll 'gotcha' look and chuckles, sipping her wine with great relish. After that, she nudges me under the table with her foot.

"Now that's a fine 'how-do-you-do'!" Mr. Wellington exclaims with visible relief. "Am I correct in assuming my daughter now plans to be another one of those silly Soap Opera actresses? My Lord, Daphne, when did you decide on all this?"

"I thought you would be happy for me, Daddy," Daphne teases him with a lugubrious pout.

"Momma said it wouldn't take long for you to warm up to the idea. I'll make you very proud of me, Daddy. I promise I will."

"Daphne- my dearest girl! A fellow likes to be consulted about these harebrained schemes of yours every now and then!"

"Daddy! What is so harebrained about my wanting to become a professional actress?"

"Yes, George," Mrs. Wellington takes up her daughter's side, "that's what I would like to know! What is so harebrained about our daughter making a living doing the thing she most loves to do? It's not like it's anything new. She's been performing for us ever since she was in diapers. Now she's going to get paid for it. That's cause for celebration, if you ask me."

Now for the piece de resistance! Smoked salmon in eggplant sauce and for dessert I'll take the fresh figs with raspberry cheese. Mamma too tight! We will grease before we sneeze tonight!

"Don't you think so, Alphonso?" Mrs. Wellington asks, she and Daphne looking my way.

"Uh – run that by me again?"

I am finding it hard to respond with mouthfuls of blessed smoked salmon in my cheeks.

"Oh killer!" Mr. Wellington throws up his hands in despair. "Let's all consult the great oracle of the Blarney Stone, the renowned pontiff of the artsy-fartsy. What say you, my boy? You see how it is with me. Outnumbered three to one by females in my own home. Thank God our Theresa is off to summer camp and not available to gang up on me tonight!"

"Be thankful for what has happened here, Mr.- I mean, George -" I begin, reaching for the fresh figs with the raspberry cheese. "Everyone has to start somewhere -"

"All Hail! The Libertine Hath Spoken!"

Mr. Wellington glares at me with asperity.

"Are you even vaguely aware of the melodramatic balderdash that spews out of those soap operas on a weekly basis? I defy even you to find 'the Image of God' in all that compost heap of emotion."

"Don't bother, Daddy," Daphne remarks dryly as she tests the baked papaya with her fork, "I believe Alphonso has already found God's image in the raspberry cheese-"

"Amen!" I exclaim and dig my fork into more of God's paradise. "All I've got to say is when everybody's happy then everybody's happy!"

The last time I ran into God so unexpectedly was in a steaming hot bowl of chili that went down well with a good gob of egg bread and a cold glass of milk. That chili was so good it moved me to tears.

I was delivered then and there from the dark night of my soul into the realm where epiphany rears it beautiful and awesome visage. That is the true modus operandi of the Great One I have found, the dude will walk right up and shake your hand in the strangest of places, smile up at you from the remotest nook and greater outer limit of the cranny. The most famous place hitter of all time, this slugger will always hit them where they ain't.

"There he goes again, Daddy," Daphne gestured at me with her fork, "Alphonso's doing his thing again."

"Oh?" Mrs. Wellington brought her bifocals to her nose. "Are you going into ungovernable ecstasies now, my dear?"

Check this out. The biggest scam going is that the ecstasy of ecstasies is to be found only in the arms of your lover. Our generation particularly has this propaganda piped in through all the available vents and windows on the world. The atmosphere is saturated with the overwhelming importance of sexual sensation as the officially sanctioned narcotic of the State and the choicest form of social conditioning.

This may sound strange coming from the Gentle Man, and it may well wind up in Ripley's Believe It Or Not, but I think sexual ecstasy is somewhat overrated. Anything that would make people lie, cheat, steal and kill to get it can't be everything it's cracked up to be. Review all of the happiest times in your life and then count how many times sex was actually involved. That will tell you something right there about what makes people feel the most strongly and what human beings truly value. I'm not going to fill in the blank about what you truly value. You are on your own when you get to that, my friend.

I have always wanted to take the feeling I have when I behold a beautiful woman and turn it into something more than Sex. Something more lasting and less evanescent that the whirling, smoking intoxication that intrudes itself and exudes from the hearts and loins of the love struck and sexually challenged. Something less involved with the 'now you see it-now you don't' intense charge of sexual heat. Something you can touch and hold in your hands once you have been all the way through the red surging storm. That self-created thing should be a sort of document, a keepsake and memento of where you've been and where you are now after the rain.

What I cannot understand is why nobody else is down with this.

"All I got to say is my compliments to the Chef," I reply to Mrs. Wellington.

"I daresay Estelle will be pleased to know she has received your highest rating, young man," Mr. Wellington merrily chides me.

"Oh yeah, buddy! She's got that in spades. I'll tell her myself before I leave here."

"You may be right, Daddy," Daphne looks at me curiously while picking at her salad, "it may be that Alphonso is a very self-involved young fellow,"

"Right Daphne, that makes a whole lot of sense," I finish off the raspberry cheese with gusto, "I say go and be a Soap Opera Diva and you go and side with Pops. Help yourself then," I reach for one of those little plastic toothpicks on my napkin, "-stay here and sit your little fanny down."

I sit back and pick my teeth with satisfaction. This has been a night to remember.

"Look-what you love is what you love, Daphne. You don't have to justify it to nobody, or run it up a flag pole to see who salutes it." I sit back a little to relax. I want to prop my feet up but I'm not at home. "That's what it is with some folks. They will have a genuine feeling for something and before long they will have theorized all the life and feeling out of it until they feel downright guilty about ever having the feeling at all. After that, they will go around whining and complaining about how they have no passion for living anymore, when they were the very ones who talked themselves out of it."

"Out of what, Alphonso?" Daphne asked, holding her knife and fork and looking at me out of shrewish eyes.

"Why - out of loving what you love and feeling what you feel. You want to consult with a special somebody? Consult yo'self! Ask yourself if you really love what you think you love; but yes or no answers only, please. Ask yourself how you really feel about it, but trust the feeling that lets you know. An' once you know, then you go."

"It all very simple to you, Alphonso," Daphne glared at me churlishly before bowing her head. She hunched her shoulders, playing with her baked pumpkin strudel. "I bet it's really comforting to be so much in the know."

"Hey, who says everything has to be complicated?" I said, my eyes tracing over those strawberry ice cream shoulders like a pair of hands reaching out of my eye sockets. "My father always told me; the one thing you can trust people to do is what they want to do. People will be sure to do that no matter what anyone says or who's lookin'."

The way those bare shoulders catch the evening sun! The tinge of crimson and the yellow crescent buttered along the edge of her face reminds me of the time I walked in on Wilma while she was taking a bath in the afternoon. The glowing face of high cheek-boned glee beckoned to me as a perfectly arched foot poked a beautiful big toe out beyond clouds of suds.

"Come on Alphonso, git in this wah-tuh with me!"

"You crazy, Wilma! I'm not getting in that water with you!"

"You know you want to -" She said with a coy, teasing expression. "-come on, Alphonso, git in here with me. I want you to wash my back and all over,"

Now Daphne glanced at me all open-mouthed innocence and naivety. Sometimes, I have been told, my expression recedes into a kind of inscrutable abstracted glare when a person's living form becomes the object of my study. Daphne's suddenly aware of being the subject of my artistic scrutiny, and nervously reaches to remove strands of hair from her neck.

Now I remember how it was with Wilma when I wiped and scrubbed the sponge all over her body, squeezed to test the firmness of her breasts, and turned her around and over to see how her well-defined buttocks merged into her sturdy thighs and tawny waist. During moments like these I wished there were a hundred pounds of clay on hand; that I could be both in the tub with Wilma but outside it as well, working a mound of brown dough into the very living image of what I now could see and touch and shape to the heights of my emotion. What a joy to be thoroughly absorbed and yet have the mind and the eyes free, observing from some vantage point on high and bearing a silent and ecstatic witness!

"Why are you looking at me like that?"

That's what they all say. Wilma said it then while I washed and scrubbed her clean, and Daphne says it now while I imagine myself taking her through her poses in my studio. Shannon Wilson woke up out of a drowsy, orgasmic haze when she realized I was studying her breathing patterns and the mask of pain that gripped her face every time she opened up like a flower and gave herself permission to come in my arms. I was getting to the point where I could race her engine, and I think she began to take offense to me working her like a sex machine. I was really getting into the mechanics of how you put an orgasm together, but I can see now as I reflect back how too much concentration on that peak moment depersonalized the whole experience at the very point when Shannon wanted to be most intimate. When you are like me, the things that most rivet your attention are those items, impressions and experiences that most agree with your inner vision of what you believe Life should contain. I walk around primed to encounter those frequencies and energies that will most stimulate me to create. When I fix my sights on a 'Kodak moment', I want to do a freeze frame on Life, clear everyone out of the room and demand charcoals, paints, paper, canvas and clay; whatever it takes to turn this living moment into an enduring work of Art. The aim of my game is to make this moment live in posterity. No need to make any snap judgments right now. Let's revisit in a hundred years and see how it all works out.

"Why are you looking at me like that?"

"Just imagining how I could take what I feel now and put it on canvas. How I could make a painting of this so deep and grand that when others stood in front of it, they would feel what I am feeling right here and now."

Daphne opened her mouth and attempted a frowning disapproval, but the expression on her face sputtered and shattered into a nonplussing groping for the right words. The flicker of a smile broke through like morning sunrise, but retreated behind the horizon again when she realized that her parents were sitting across the table from us.

When I was wrapped up in the sheets with Wilma that first time, there were no questions to ask or to be answered. Once she was asleep, due to our labors of love, and I was aware of dawn light sending its rays through the bedroom windows, I crept carefully out of bed and replaced the covers around her.

Once I was out of bed, I slipped into my boxer shorts and sat on the dresser bureau in front of the mirror. I could see Wilma in front and behind me now. I could also see the way the light came in through the window and glazed her body, those classic breasts and the folds and wrinkles on the white sheets in swirling fingers of red, yellow and blue. This was the moment we were coming toward all along and I couldn't let an opportunity like this slip away.

I started out sketching Wilma on the note her mother gave my mother to cut the grass. I believe Wilma's aunt had died and her mother went down to Georgia to attend the funeral. I saw Mrs. Durant talking to my mother on the porch one afternoon, but didn't know what it was they were talking about at that time. Later, my mother told me how Mrs. Durant had paid her five dollars for me to cut the grass in the front and back and trim the hedges until she came back. Why she didn't pay me I'll never know, as I only saw about two or three dollars of that money

The hard part was the rendering of Wilma's foot, and I placed the covers away from her ankle in several different positions, but still couldn't quite get it right.

That's when I got this great idea. I tiptoed down to the basement and looked around until I found a stepladder. I also found some charcoal briquettes in this barbeque grill that hadn't been used in

I don't know how long. I brought them up later after I was through positioning the stepladder in Wilma's bedroom. I tried several different positions until I got the angle I wanted.

I was hurrying up with the briquettes because I knew the sun would be full out soon and I wanted to take full advantage of the contrast between light and dark while I still could. Back then, I knew nothing about chiaroscuro and couldn't tell you who Caravaggio was from a hole in the wall. All I knew was that Wilma to me asleep and bathed nude in the morning sunlight was ten times as good a subject as that oil painting of The Conversion of Saint Paul.

All the walls in Wilma's bedroom were a kind of beige color. This was a good thing for me because I could use several pieces of the charcoal to do rough thumbnail sketches. I got so into how to get Wilma's hands and feet just right, that before I knew it, the whole wall before Wilma was covered in detail drawings. I sketched not just her hands and feet, but also her head on the pillow from various angles and the way the covers fell away from her breasts and how every sort of shadow was caught in the folds that wrapped around her hips and thighs.

I don't know whatever got into me, but thank the Lord Wilma was such a sound sleeper. That's why I always say you got to love 'em so good you put 'em to sleep. That way the woman won't move when she's in a natural pose you can render in a sketch. I was comparing my number one wall, which was all body parts, with my number two wall, which was all folds and wrinkles in the sheets and covers. I was finishing up my number three wall, which was a series of sketches of the curtains fluttering and the light coming through the bedroom window and the different effects of light and shadow on the pillow, the mattress, the sheets, and the floor. Anyway, that's when I heard Wilma snuffle and I thought she was about to wake up, but without even so much as turning over she closed her mouth and went back to sleep.

Now that the third wall was finished, I could get down to business. My references were all arrayed on the walls around me, and my main subject gently positioned beneath the main light source. I climbed gingerly to the top of the stepladder.

Up above on the ladder, I placed the hard piece of cardboard I found in the basement onto my lap. I fitted the large sheet of paper I had ripped off a calendar onto the cardboard pad with some scotch tape. Now that I was sure up here was the best angle where the light was most evocative, I took a piece of charcoal and started to work.

The more I drew, the more excited I was getting. I was sure this drawing was going to be as fine as anything Charles White had ever done. I was starting to finish up filling in the shadows on the drawing when I heard the doorbell ring.

"Wilma? Willl-maaa! I'm home! I brought Aunt Charlotte with me! Come on down and open up the door, girl! Help us get all our things through the do'!"

I never thought so fast in all my life! I knew the sound of Mrs. Durant's voice. I needed nobody to tell me that if Wilma's mother found me up here in her daughter's bedroom, I would be the shrimp on the Barbie!

"Uhhh-ummm, that you, mama?" Wilma uttered as she roused herself from sleep. She slowly shook her head and rubbing her eyes, sat up in the bed. "Alphonso! What in Jesus' name are you doin' up there, boy?"

She was beautiful from where I was sitting. A full-breasted candy brown woman blossoming into the prime of Life with the morning Sun wrapped around her in stripes of blue shadows. I must have seemed surreal to her, hovering above her like that, with drawing implement and paper poised at the ready. Perhaps she would remember me one day as the dark angel of her beautiful deliverance.

Unfortunately, this was no time for the Gentle Man to admire the view. The gendarmes were on their way, and it was time for me to get out of Dodge. Before Wilma could get out a good scream, I hopped off that stepladder as though it were an ejector seat. I raced over and covered up Wilma's mouth.

"Shhhh, baby, shhhh! I think your moms must have come home early."

"Shoot-I know that, Alphonso! You ain't gotta tell me nothing!" Wilma looked around all wild at the walls. "What is all this stuff you done put all over my bedroom, Alphonso?"

"Look, baby, look-" I was in my pants faster than a quick-change artist. "-help me slide this ladder out the back window so I can run off right quick. Anybody asks, you can just say I was doing some work around the house."

I tossed Wilma her nightgown, but I was keeping the panties as a memento.

"What about all this junk you got all over my walls, Alphonso? What you call yourself doing to me?" Wilma asked as she shimmied herself into her nightgown.

"Bay-bay-" I gave her a good wet kiss on the mouth. "- it's just barbeque charcoal, It'll all come off with a good scrubbing of soap and water-"

"Wilma! Are you up there, girl? Come down here and see about us, Miss Lady!"

"That's my mother-"

"I know, baby, I know-help me get this ladder through the window-"

We shoved on the mug and got the thing down to just under sill level. We looked at each other in terror as we heard footsteps coming up the stairs.

"You got my cellphone number, Alphonso. You call me, hear?"

I crawled out onto the windowsill while I buttoned up my jacket.

"Soon as the coast is clear, sugar," I hung low until my feet touched the top of the stepladder. "Hey, hand me my sketch, will you?"

"That piece of paper? Why you got to draw me naked, Alphonso? Here! I don't want none uh this. Now go!"

"Call you later-" I said, pressing my lips full against hers one last time.

"I love you, Alphonso. Do you love me, sugar daddy?"

"Read the handwriting on the wall, Wilma. You're my Soul Inspiration, girl."

When my feet hit the grassy sidewalk below me, I turn quickly and run all the way home on my toes.

"What are you grinning about now, Alphonso?" Daphne asked me as I felt the sole of her bare foot caress my instep.

"I was just thinkin' about something."

"What?" Daphne starts picking at the laces on my shoe with her stocking toes.

We are sipping wine now and finishing off the last of the desserts.

"Oh, nothing really," I glance over at Daphne's parents and sober up. Judges wearing robes couldn't have looked at me more impassively. Time to 'fess up. "Actually, I was thinking about the time I almost got caught in my lady's bedroom sketching her in the nude. The Sandman couldn't have made a faster getaway."

I chuckled merrily down Memory Lane, but excepting Daphne, the Wellingtons were less amused and I found myself nervously looking for an escape route again.

"Anyway, it was just one of those things. Chalk it up as one of the adventures of a young man. I just remember I left her walls covered with sketches. Like Zorro!"

"Sounds like you rather enjoy the excitement and the danger of discovery. The thrill, such as it is, of almost being caught in the act." Mr. Wellington said, sipping and peering over his wine glass at me with probing eyes. "I hope you're not expecting to play such promiscuous comedies with my daughter, young man."

"No sir, I was barely out of my teens when-"

"The young lady you're speaking about, Alphonso. Do you still see her socially?" Mrs. Wellington asked with pointed emphasis. "Or was she just another notch on your belt? A one-night-stand for a young stud at large?"

"No, it was nothing like that-"

"Watch out, mom, there he goes with the smiles and the teeth again-" Daphne warned her mother.

"What is this, folks? 'Monty Python And The Holy Grail'?"

"Yes indeed. young man-" Mr. Wellington chimed his wine glass with a fork.

All the Wellingtons joined in as one chorus.

"'Nobody escapes the Spanish Inquisition!' "

"Alright, good one. You got me that time."

The Wellingtons seem so pleased to have demonstrated to the Gentle Man that they have a sense of humor. I chime my glass as a sort of salute to Mr. Wellington.

"Touche'! A touch for you that time, sir."

"Hee-hee, I'm surprised you would know anything about 'Monty Python', Alphonso." Mr. Wellington wiped his eyes with his dinner napkin, his cheeks bright as a tomato with newfound merriment. "I'm surprised you would know anything about that, young man. That 'Monty Python' was before your time, wouldn't you say? How would you put it in your vernacular? That was 'back in the day'?"

"That's pretty good. But no, square business - my father was a big fan and he used to have us watch PBS all the time with him. That's how I know about 'Monty Python'."

"What does your father do for a living, Alphonso?" Mrs. Wellington nodded to Estelle to bring us some tea. "Is he a professional man?"

"I suppose you could say so, Fiona. He works downtown in an architect's office for Stoller, Feldstein & Grenwald. He's actually a draftsman, but mostly he just proofreads and revises blueprints before printing them out. He still talks about being a big time City Planner one day."

"A draftsman, you say! That's impressive! That would certainly explain your yen for drawing, Alphonso. Thank you, Estelle,"

Mrs. Wellington takes up her cup of tea.

"Alphonso?"

"Yeah, Daphne," I said, watching Mrs. Wellington's diamond string earrings glint the lights from the chandelier overhead. "-you ready to give a toast or something?"

"Actually, I wanted to ask you who the Sandman was, love-"

"The Sandman?"

"Yeah," Daphne said, her face swaying my way. Methinks the lass a little tipsy with the old bubbly. "Remember? You mentioned he couldn't have made a faster getaway than you did out of your girlfriend's bedroom. Who is the Sandman, Alphonso?"

"My father used to talk about him all the time when we would plead with him and twist his arm to buy us comic books and graphic novels." I paused for a moment to savor the recollection. "We would rave about Cyclops and Storm and the Wolverine and he would tell us they were all chumps and sissies!" I waved off the concerned expressions on their faces. "He was just trying to get a rise out of us. He would wax on and on about the Amazing Spiderman, the Fantastic Four, who were supposed to be the World's Greatest Superheroes, and the old Avengers before Captain America happened onto the scene. 'The Avengers!', he would tell us, 'when you really need to kick some serious booty, accept on substitutes!'."

Daphne hiccupped a little titter and Mr. Wellington let a guffaw get away from him as Mrs. Wellington smiled amiably.

"Yeah, he knew a lot of stories from all over the place. I know he told my mother enough of them."

"He sounds a little like Grandpa Hi, doesn't he, mom?" Daphne said, looking to her mother as though remembering something.

"That man!" Mr. Wellington shuddered at the memory.

"Oh, don't get your father started, Daphne-" Mrs. Wellington admonished.

"A perfect scoundrel that man was! It's a miracle your mother and I ever got married with that buttinski around!"

"Oh, don't you start that now, George. Think about our guest, for heaven's sake.."

"I still want to know who the Sandman is, Alphonso." Daphne plied me again.

"The Sandman was a famous nemesis of the Amazing Spiderman. He could change his body into sand anytime he wanted to do so. The cops would chase him and try to grab onto him, but he would slither and fly out of their hands on the wind. Once he was successful in eluding their grasp, he would reform all his particles again and run off. He could also make his body rock solid and pulverize his foes with pile-driver blows. The Amazing Spiderman finally had to resort to using a vacuum cleaner to capture him!"

"I hope it was a Kirby vacuum cleaner!" Mr. Wellington quipped.

"Might have been-might have been. It was definitely some kind of heavy duty brand."

"So! That's how you perceive yourself, is it, Alphonso? As a sort of slithery confidence man who goes around stealing woman's hearts and their virtue? A sort of evildoer whose very insubstantiality makes him a virtual Invisible Man, existing just beyond the grasp of reason and the bounds of the Law?"

"If you say so, sir." I thank Estelle for my tea and take a sip. "Actually I always saw myself as a young man postulating artistic projects in order to increase his self awareness and self knowledge. Mine are the adventures of the Soul, not cops and robbers."

"Consider this, young man," Mr. Wellington glares at me with resolute determination. "The situation may be that my daughter may not want to be just another of your artistic projects. Have you ever considered that?"

"As a matter of fact, I have been considering it," I said, taking another sip of tea, "that's why I related that little incident about one of my main squeezes when I was younger. This, by the way, bears some relationship on the major turning point that Daphne wants to make in her life. You remember earlier I was saying that everybody has to start from some place. I started out drawing the pretty girls in my class on the fly leaves of my textbooks. I was always groping for away to make sense of the wonderful feelings that beautiful women inspired in me. How could I take this nearly unbearable bliss I felt when interfacing with the warp and woof and the stuff of living creation and turn it into a tangible construction of reality? Whereby another could behold such a construction and finally see what I see, feel what I feel, and encompass my most ardent thoughts with understanding? Everyone starts from someplace and comes from somewhere. This one starts from his high school sweetheart's bedroom and after sketching the living grandeur of her nude body as it is sculpted and formed in the gathering light, realizes sex is not enough. It's too much like looking at infinite bliss through the aperture of a pinhole camera. But he starts from here, mentally undressing the most beautiful women he can find in an effort to gain greater understanding of the handiwork that is God all about us. That one, perhaps, starts from in front of the camera of a Soap Opera television show." I gestured towards Daphne and she opened her mouth in assent, but no utterance came forth. "Perhaps, here she can at least begin to explore the meaning of emotion and what priority the value of performing for others has in her life. Maybe it begins and ends as an actress for 'Dangerous Loves'. Perhaps 'Dangerous Loves' is only a door that leads to someplace else further afield. That's not for me to say, because in the end it has to be Daphne's thing. What is for me to say is, 'here I am!' This is how I define myself without guilt or pretension. Reference that as you need to in finding your own way."

"You're full of grand and lofty sentiments this evening." Mr. Wellington scowled over his raspberry cheese. "Aren't you, my man?"

"That's the first time I have been accused of that! Most of my friends would say I'm full of something else."

The women tittered and hid their smiles with their napkins while Mr. Wellington chuckled to himself with a sneer.

"You're a member of the 'ME' generation, as is my daughter, unfortunately." Mr. Wellington patted his lips with his napkin and pushed back from the table. "I pray she isn't suffering from a terminal case of the disease. Between her plans to be an aspiring actress and your plans to be a great painter, what plans have either of you made for raising a family?"

"I swear to God, Daddy-" Daphne exclaimed testily, "-why do you have to make it seem like it's the height of selfishness-"

"Now don't take the Lord's name in vain at the dinner table, dear," Mrs. Wellington said raising a finger to her lips for Daphne to shush.

"Heaven knows she's vain enough as it is!" Mr. Wellington patted perspiration from his balding pate and took another sip of tea.

"- when there's something I really want to do with my life?" Daphne paused to regain her composure, cradling her cup of tea in her hands. "I thought the two of you would be happy that I wanted to leave the nest and become self sufficient."

"I just think right now you want to have your pie in the sky and eat it too," Mr. Wellington crossed his arms over his burly chest. "I think I'm warranted in wanting to know what place will family have in al this 'Search for Tomorrow'? "

Whoa! Mr. Wellington was throwing out the zingers tonight!

"What about you, Alphonso?" Mr. Wellington bristled when I joined in on the laughter.

"Uh-sir?"

"I would be interested in knowing what plans you have for rearing a family, once you and your ilk have ushered in this New Renaissance you're masterminding?"

"Family, sir?"

"Come on, my man! Certainly that subject is not too outre' for a sophisticated young chap such as yourself. Well! I'll be a son of a Saint Bernard! I do believe I'm the one introducing a new and novel concept at the table now!"

"No, not at all, sir. I believe in Family-"

"George, you don't have to be so-" Mrs. Wellington began to caution her husband.

"No-no, really, Fiona." Mr. Wellington waved her away. "I've been listening to this Grand Vision you've been painting for us-"

"Daddy, pleeease-" Daphne pleaded just above a whisper, cupping her head with her hand.

"-and I must admit, as far as I can see, the whole thing revolves around you. It's all about you! Where do all the rest of us fit into all this? I have yet to hear you say 'I want my son to live in a world where-', or 'I want my daughter to live in a world where-' and then you itemize all the particulars. What's the matter, my man? Don't you like kids? Where do they fit into the visionary scope of your creative prowess? Come on, Alphonso! When are you going to have some kids you can foist all these opinions on, my young friend? Or are you going to cop a plea with your generation and the generation before you? How does it go? 'I wouldn't want to bring children into a world like this where-', and I dare say you know the rest. How about it, Alphonso? Are the youth of today still whining that old song? I'll admit I may be a little out of touch with the times, having to run a business and raise a family and all. Thank you, Estelle-"

Mr. Wellington stirred the spot of cream that Estelle dropped into his tea and regarded me with a smug expression.

"Let me ask you this-" Mr. Wellington began again as he was beginning to feel frisky now.

"Oh George, really-" Mrs. Wellington cast a sympathetic eye my way.

"Really, Fiona! We're just making polite conversation. Tell me, Alphonso, you've been dating Daphne for awhile now," Mr. Wellington kept stirring his tea meditatively, "do any of your plans for my daughter include the prospect of marriage, young man?"

"Really Daddy!" Daphne tossed her napkin into her lap. "Alphonso and I have just been getting to know each other."

"Nevertheless," Mr. Wellington peered over his cup at me as he sipped his tea, "I would love to know Alphonso's 'opinion' on this one. Have you considered the subject of marriage with my daughter, young man?"

"Naw suh, I'm too young to die," Daphne kicks me under the table when I admit to this. "I'm just looking for real live sources of inspiration that stimulate me to create."

Daphne flinches at this, but there is method in this Gentle madness.

"So! You're just roving the landscape in search of a creative fix. Is that it, Alphonso?"

"I would hardly put it that way, sir."

"Oh?" Mr. Wellington thinks he's on a roll now. "How would you put it, my friend?" He glances at Mrs. Wellington, whose head is bowed in chagrin, his eyes twinkling with the notion of a new joke. "Perhaps you be Count Gentle, a mysterious prince in search of new life to suckle for blood. No necking with Alphonso, Daphne! He vants to drink your blood! He must have new prey to renew his creative essence!"

Mr. Wellington's eyes widen in wild-eyed relish, as he raises his hands and clenches his fingers as though they were fangs.

Now even I have to laugh at this whack mess Mr. Wellington is putting down. I clap my hands and lift my cup of tea in a toast.

"Whoop! Dere it is! Bingo, Mr. Wellington, you got me dead to rights!"

Daphne and Mrs. Wellington look askance at me with lifted spirits as I have lightened the mood somehow in their eyes.

"You don't say?" Mr. Wellington raises his teacup with evident satisfaction. "I'll drink to that! A toast to all your fallen comrades before you; and to all the sex crazed, bloodsucking beaus of Daphne's to come!"

This is one whack rap that Mr. Wellington is free styling, but I have to admit in that weird white bread way of his, he's somehow keeping it real. Mrs. Wellington reluctantly raises her cup, and Daphne sneers at me like I have 'phoney' written all over my forehead. But hold tight, it be the Gentle Man's turn at bat directly.

We click our teacups together.

"Here, here, y'all!" I exclaim with gusto.

"- and a word to the wise, Alphonso. Daphne is already engaged to a very dear friend of the family"

Daphne flashes an expression to me that it's all news to her.

"Victor Basehart, Alphonso," Mrs. Wellington confides to me, "he has also become a key executive and a top producer in George's company."

"So thank you very much, Alphonso, but you have as much chance of getting into my dear young daughter's pants as King Kong has of going through the eye of a needle!"

"Daddy!" Daphne quickly gives me the once over to see where I'm wounded. "Alphonso is my friend, you apologize-"

"No-no, baby," I take Daphne gently by the wrist, thereby nipping in the bud her big scene of running away in tears. "- your father has a right to say what's on his mind."

"I don't care to agree with you, Alphonso." Mrs. Wellington's eyes seemed to glint with the fire of the final red and yellow rays of the Sun flaring in the window. "No matter how charitable a point of view you wish to take in the matter."

"Ladies, ladies!" I hold my hands up in a conciliatory gesture. "A man has a right to speak his mind in his own house."

"You're wrong to treat this young man that way, George. You know it!" The blood was rising into Mrs. Wellington's forehead and temples as she spoke. "I can tell you one thing, were you talking to Grandpa Hi like that, you would be dusting off the seat of your pants."

"No, no, ladies," I gesture soothingly for them not to leave the table, "it's all good. If you can't tell people what you truly think in your own home, where can you tell them?" Now I believe Mr. Wellington was just about to say this, but as you can see, I beat him to it. "Besides, I've been blazed worse than that playing cards with the dudes I grew up with in the neighborhood, and them guys are my friends! No," I loosen my tie and pour myself more tea, 'please sit down, ladies. That is the one thing we always says about white folks; they can be so afraid to offend and feel so guilty when they do and become so polite and sweetness and light that they never again dare tell you what they truly think or really feel. The one thing that's respected among Black Folks is a person who's real and genuine. Don't get me wrong, that can be a hard thing to be, but we really treasure realness and genuineness when we can get it. I don't agree with everything George just put down, heckie-naw, but I gots to respect him for keeping it real."

Mr. Wellington sits there regarding me with arms folded against his massive chest. Now his breathing seems labored and that immense fury nearly spent. He begins to grumble to himself as he rocks softly in his chair.

"I imagine it must be your very presence, Alphonso. Somehow you've inspired me to new heights of creative honesty." Mr. Wellington said snidely, hoping this one last dig would get a rise out of me. When that fails, he lets out an irritated sigh. "Perhaps I have overstepped the bounds of propriety as a host. Don't mind this old man, I get that way sometimes. I get Estelle's good cooking into me belly and start to act like the king of the castle. I hope you can see past all that."

Check this out.

Mr. Wellington and I both know he's already hit me with his best shot and has even emptied both barrels on top of that. But it's mate in three for the Gentle Man and he is going to have to suffer through it. See, the thing of it is, I really can see his point of view. Maybe it comes from all those portraits that my friend Danny encouraged me to do. I not only see inside of him the way he was demonstrating to his wife what he could do to me, I can also sit inside behind his eyes and look out and see what he sees. But let's quickly review the facts as we know them.

The hubris of the White Race or Western Man or whatever, is its pride in having all the answers and knowing how to get the straight dope. Of course, for those of us who are members of recently oppressed peoples, the dope isn't always straight. It's just dope, and highly addictive to boot. The point is, oftentimes its not enough for a member of the White Race to beat you, given the history of such encounters. No, he has to beat you so bad that you'll have this overwhelming fear rise up and smother you if you even think of opposing him again. Now of course, when he puts that kind of whopping on you, well, that's how Slavery Time was born.

No, it's like my father used to tell me when my brothers and I used to go down to Bakers Keyboard Lounge and bring him home to sober him up. There are times when a white man does not just want to beat you; he wants to wire everything he did to beat you step by step on a circuit board so that it 'works every time'. He will systematize and computerize the whole thing so that whopping yo' sorry behind is standard procedure and business as usual. He'll have all the routes and channels on his circuit board mapped out so well he knows where you've got to go before you do because he designed the Golf Course. Pop used to argue that we black people have been scurrying around like mice along the highways and the byways of the White Man's imagination for so long, many of us would self-destruct if through sheer will power or by mere accident we hopped permanently out of the routes and channels designed and 'wired' for us to travel. Dad used to call it 'popping a groove'. That's why he loves jazz musicians so much. He told us somebody like a jazz musician knows how to 'pop a groove' without self-destructing and then is free to create in the spaces in between the routes and channels of the White Man's society and the orbits of his world. I can't say exactly what he would have said about Billie Holiday or Charlie Parker, but sometimes you have to see how a man is right before you take a look at how he's wrong.

Dad said all the true heroes of freedom possessed this quality in common, the ability to 'pop a groove' and go where the road doesn't lead or beyond where the proscribed boundaries of humanly regulated space would dictate they should go. He told my brothers and yours truly we could be sure we were creating our own space anytime we chose not to follow the markers along the road that somebody else mapped out.

Oh yeah, it can get real deep.

Anyway, what I did with Mr. Wellington was 'pop a groove'. I didn't go where he expected me to go, and therefore ended up steering him where I needed him to arrive. The first mistake he made was outright opposing his daughter's plans for the future without leaving her a dignified and honorable way out. Naturally, when I sided with her as honestly as I could, this only served to strengthen my position. The second mistake was announcing to me that Daphne was already engaged to another. Whether true or not, there was no need to give a near total stranger this information. After all, their daughter's engagement was, strictly speaking, a family matter. However, when Mr. Wellington did announce Daphne's engagement, her true feelings about making such a commitment undeniably surfaced in her startled expression. Young adults in America have a awful phobia about their parents acting as matchmakers and 'fixing them up'. Making this announcement could only further fuel Daphne's desire to look to me for a way out. The third mistake was making personal attacks upon my character thereby hoping I would do the same. When I did not respond in kind, this demonstrated that I was not some kind of hotheaded loudmouth who could not control his temper. The mothers of daughters love this by the way, because it signals that their little baby is not involved with someone who might be the cause of domestic violence.

When Mr. Wellington's personal attacks against the Gentle Man culminated in him declaring that I would never get into the pants of his little girl, it was then mate in three. The emotion used and the manner in which he made this statement made it inevitable that the exact opposite would be the case. There is something mathematical about this inverted truth, but you would have to see it for yourself and even then you would probably not believe it.

Hold tight. You'll see it for yourself soon enough.

A quick note of interest here for later reference. The unenlightened might assume that I made a mistake in not declaring any interest in marrying Daphne, but as events unfold, you will see wisdom not madness, in the method of the Gentle Man. Just remember that you never confide to a honey that you have the desire and intention to marry. Quite frankly, that's not your job. Your job is to get out on your own and establish your place in the Sun. Once you've made your rite of passage and have proven you can take care of yourself, the honeys will drop by to see how well you do this. Now it doesn't take much deduction to realize that if you take care of yourself well, there are honeys out there who will be happy have you take care of them too.

The average woman is suspicious of the man who is too eager to marry. The dude who needs a 'good woman' to help him get it together need not apply. A good woman is looking for someone who can make it on his own. Ladies usually avoid dudes who are seeking to marry. This often suggests to them someone who is looking for a woman to take care of them, as did their mothers. The strange truth is that a man who appears to be strenuously avoiding the matrimonial noose has a better chance of getting hitched than the one who avidly seeks it. Women find the man disinterested in marriage more attractive and interesting than those who pine for it. The ladies will scream to high heaven protesting this, but a true playa makes his own observations. You don't have to take my word for it. Conduct your own experiments and draw your own conclusions.

This is just one of those inverted truths that Christ liked to rap about so much. What you want you usually have to cross the burning sands to achieve. What you don't want often shows up uninvited at your doorstep.

When I declared I have no intention of marrying Daphne, I immediately increased my own attractiveness and interest in Daphne's eyes. When her father began to question and examine the validity of my intentions I became the underdog, and let's face it, playas, honeys love to champion the underdog. Most especially when, in this case, they have just been made one too by their own father. Now that I have determined that I am no threat to the peace and security of the Wellington Clan, and am not somebody who flies off the handle at any provocation, I'm sitting in the catbird's seat.

Check it out.

Just like I said, mate in three.

Anyway, let's return to 'Days of Our Jive'.

"That's all right, I ain't mad at ya. These eats have been like a Christmas dinner to me. For a feast like this, you can call me King Kong-Ding Dong or Mah-Jongg! Just please, baby, please gimme some more of that raspberry cheese!" I reach out to Estelle and dig in for second helpings. "Funny thing about Christmas-" I continue between mouthfuls.

"What's funny about it?" Mr. Wellington asks with an air of resignation.

I wish Smiley were here. I can hear him in my mind's ear quoting Proverbs Chapter 26, verses 26 and 27. That last verse, according to Pop, made famous by the Lone Ranger!

Hi-ho, Silver! Awaaayyy!

Daphne and Mrs. Wellington give me weak, affectionate smiles of sympathy. I suppose it is their way of showing moral support for me. Probably the ladies have it figured I'm just laughing to keep from crying and to cover up how much my feelings are hurt. Everybody's entitled to think like they want to think, I just want more of this raspberry cheese.

"The thing that's funny about Christmas is how it's supposed to be Christ's birthday." I resume my discourse with Mr. Wellington. "Right?"

"That's the general idea, bub."

"Okay then, how come it is nobody gives Jesus anything for his birthday on Christmas?"

"What a novel way to look at it, Alphonso," Mrs. Wellington looks at me with a baffled expression, the way women do when they've heard what you've said, but are not quite sure they've caught the emotional drift of what you've uttered. "Don't you think so, dear?"

Mr. Wellington sighed with exasperation and eyed me with a grim look, the chartreuse curtains behind him fluttering in the evening breeze.

"What kind of sophistry are you brewing up now, young man?"

"Naw, I'm just trying to be real, Mr. Wellington. Now your birthday's probably come and gone, but I'm sure your wife and Daphne got you something. What did you give Jesus for his birthday last time around?"

"I'm not quite sure I follow you. What did you get him, young man?"

"A pair of socks and a box of cuff links!"

Daphne lets slip a yelp of a laugh before covering her mouth and playfully kicks me under the table.

"Al-phon-so," Daphne slaps me a nick on the shoulder.

"Alphonso's right, dear. What did we get for Jesus last Christmas?" Mrs. Wellington pipes in and glances slyly at me because she wants in on the fun now. "I don't believe I got our Lord anything special, you know."

"I think the matter might be slightly different with the King of Kings, Alphonso." Mr. Wellington said as he snapped a bread stick in half. "After all, Jesus is the son of God. Let the Holy Father arrange a birthday party for him in heaven."

"Yeah, but Square business, don't you see how whack that is? Everybody gets something on their birthday, and on Christmas everybody gives everybody gifts. But on Christ's birthday he gets nothing, not even a card or a letter. Ain't that a trip? See sir, you were talking about Daphne and I being members of the 'ME' generation awhile back, but how do you think Christ feels when nobody's thought enough of him to get him a Christmas present in two thousand years?!"

"Talk about your 'ME' generations, Daddy!" Daphne mugged at her father triumphantly.

"Yes, well," Mr. Wellington scoops more baked papaya into his plate, "I'm sure that's an oversight, however regrettable, that your generation will remedy someday-"

"That's just it, sir. The way I see it, we gots to. Think about it; two thousand years of all of us just rippin' and runnin', grippin' and grabbin' at everything we can lay our hands on and what do we give to Christ?"

"I'm still not sure I completely grasp what you're driving at, Alphonso," Mrs. Wellington glances uncertainly at her husband as she pours him more tea. "I think you may have side-stepped some important theological considerations that should be noted before we proceed any further."

"That may well be, Fiona, but I humbly submit this idea for your inspection; what would you think of people who hold a party for a guest of honor whom they never give any presents? On top that now, they go even further and go through the ritual of being cannibals who devour his body and drink his blood! They even do this regularly on Sunday! What would you think of such strange customs were you a visiting alien tourist from another planet?"

"That's shocking, Alphonso!" Mrs. Wellington exclaimed incredulously. "Clever conversation is one thing, but there are matters in the world that you should not speak so lightly of, my dear young man."

"That's my sentiment exactly, Fiona. A few moments ago, George compared me to a drug addict roving the artistic landscape for a creative fix, or a mysterious prince sucking the life blood out of the culture for sustenance. Yet many of us dine regularly for Sunday dinner on the body and the blood of Christ, and drop to our knees for the Almighty to mainline us a spiritual fix. Are those of us who do this; always taking from Christ and God and never giving them anything back, any less the addicts and bloodsuckers?"

Daphne gazes upon me with rapt attention. Now she's got that thing going on, at turns she looks like that girl in the Harry Anderson painting holding her Bible, and at others like the girls in paintings by Botticelli and Ruebens. Every once in awhile, with the Sun still simmering just a bit through the flaring chartreuse curtains, she takes on the aspect of one of the women in the Bible. Now as I related to you before, it would be a trip to transfer all that beauty and glory from the throb of real life to the posterity of the canvas. That way, everyone would get to see her in her best light and she would become more than just another piece of puff-n-stuff.

"No, I think I get what Alphonso is talking about." Daphne looks to her parents and then to me and then down at the table to collect her new thoughts. "Alphonso isn't saying you're wrong or right, Daddy. That has nothing to do with it. I also don't believe he is condemning Christianity as a strange rite indulged in by a bunch of self-serving primitives, attempting to sublimate their desires for cannibalism. What I believe he is saying is that certain activities viewed from different cultural perspectives can take on new and startling connotations, and thus be interpreted in ways that would seem strange to the persons involved in such activities according to their cultural training. I think it's something like that."

Daphne turned to me with a diffident, hesitant expression.

"I didn't mean to put words in your mouth, Alphonso. That's something like what you were getting at, isn't it?"

Bingo! Let's give a little hand to the Gentle Man! I serve up my best German accent, as I give my favorite impression of Einstein and applaud Daphne.

"The idea you haf, my child. Wunderbar!" I exclaimed as Daphne made a face at me.

"The point is," Daphne turns back to her parents, "we can condemn Alphonso for wanting to draw, paint and sculpt women who appear beautiful to him. Just like you said, Daddy, it does on the face of it seem shallow and superficial to us to go into ungovernable ecstasies over the shape of a woman's face, or her physique and whether or not her legs and feet are good-looking. That's because our values and our belief system causes us to focus on and highlight those things in our environment that reflect our values and beliefs. I got it!" Daphne darts a look at me with a glitter of an idea and then reaches a hand to her parents with an expansive gesture. "Suppose everyone at this table was a painter or artist of some kind in the pictorial arts. Why, I bet you then Alphonso's behavior and interests and 'ungovernable ecstasies' would then be in perfect keeping with the values and beliefs of the people with whom he broke bread."

"Now Daphne-" Mr. Wellington began to interject.

"No, George, let Daphy have her say-" Mrs. Wellington gestured a finger at her husband as though it were a baton. "I think we might be coming to something here."

"That's nearly about it, mother. You can see how were everyone at this table involved in the acting profession, my intention to become an actress on a leading Soap Opera would probably receive unanimous approval."

"Just as in the opposite vein," I reached over and patted Daphne's hand, "were we all parents raising families and Daphne appeared to be suggesting that she was willing to abandon her responsibility to her children in order to pursue a career as an actress, she would probably be met with unanimous disapproval."

"The point being?" Mr. Wellington's arms were folded across his chest again.

Daphne looked over to me to pick up again the main thread of the argument.

"The point being that we all seem a little strange to each other, arriving here from different paths and points of view by dint of the values and beliefs we cling to and hold dear. Since no two persons will value all things equally or rank their beliefs identically, what we value and what we believe will shape for each of us differently how we perceive and see the world."

Daphne sighed with relief and I patted her hand once again.

"There's plenty for us to make each other feel guilty about and to censor and condemn. At the same time there is really nothing to censor and condemn. All of us have worked hard and undoubtedly earned the right to be where we are right now." I took another sip of tea. "There's no doubt that the value of family has been underappreciated by myself and my generation. I can't exactly say why, but that's one of the challenges I will have to confront with the rest of my friends and contemporaries. I can't say I've grown to embrace the concept as successfully as you have, Mr. Wellington. My truth is a limited truth; perhaps it's even a shallow and superficial truth, as I've heard you have said. The fact still remains, it is my truth, and I came by it honestly, you dig? I just hope as the years pass, I'll be lucky enough to add to it a little more and a little more. I just know I won't add anything to it by lying and pretending to be something I'm not, just for the sake of obtaining some temporary advantage. So I want to thank you again for communicating your true feelings and for keepin' it real."

I also wanted to say I was still curious. How would you get King Kong through the eye of a needle? I was having this feeling I was close to finding out, then I could run and tell Bill Gates. Of course, he might have already found a way through Cyberspace. You never could tell.

"You really are remarkably articulate, Alphonso," Mrs. Wellington reiterated as her husband nodded in assent.

"Whatever else you are or are not, I'll have to give you that, young man."

"Thank you. The both of you seem very well read as well."

"We would be interested in knowing how you came to be able to express yourself as you do," Mrs. Wellington sipped her tea, "what kind of books would you say helped you develop your language skills?"

Should I tell them the curious tale of Stella Yamamoto? How I met this Japanese coed who was majoring in the Graphic Arts? Sweet Stella was an oriental version of Andie MacDowell with the figure of Bettie Page. Before I met her in college, I could never have explained to you how I came to understand the true meaning of a literate society. I drummed my fingers thoughtfully on the dinner table. How could I put this as delicately as possible?

"I've always been a reader, mostly of Art books, I suppose. But I met this young lady in college who could read anybody under the table! I believe when she woke up in the morning, she would reach for a book. I would pass her running up the stairwell to class, and there she would be, sitting on the top step of the landing, her head bowed over a thick paperback book. I found myself carting a lot of books around just to get her interested enough to date me!"

The truth was even more interesting. Stella was always making reference to things she read in her books, but these comments usually fell on deaf ears. That's because nobody knew anything about the books she read. Most of the fellows who attempted to hit on her could hardly care about that, we were all so thunderstruck with her 'light up the street' beauty. But one day, after I attempted to win her company and failed once again to get to first base with her, I went to visit Hideki in his studio and to report that I was stumped

"What do I have to do to get next to her?" I complained with irritation, casting about wild glances at the abstract expressionist art Hideki was working on to find some sort of clue.

Hideki pushed back his black-rimmed glasses onto the bridge of his nose. He gave me his most ingratiating smile and asked me humbly to pass the palette knife. He was also working on a figurine of a Siamese cat in clay.

"Weed hew books, Alphonso," Hideki said as he added and scraped away clay from his cat.

"I've tried that," I replied bitterly, "I talk about books with her-"

"No, no, Weed huh books. Have huh weed huh books to you, Alphonso. Help her learn the language bettuh. She will be most gwateful. Bye now."

Hideki told me to hit the road with such appreciative enthusiasm I was out in the hallway before I knew what happened.

Hideki was right, as usual. The next time I met Stella in the cafeteria, instead of making brief comments about what she was reading, I asked her to read me a few pages of her 'Grapes of Wrath'. You would have thought Edison was lighting up Times Square, the way all of Stella's lights went on when I said that. She eagerly began to read to me and to ask me whether or not her pronunciation was correct. She would stop at the end of certain passages and ask me that. Suddenly I found myself entering a whole new realm of communication with the Lotus Lady. I found myself checking 'The

Grapes of Wrath' out of the library, just so I could talk to Stella about the tribulations of the Joads in California. We would sit in the cafeteria for long hours thumbing our way through identical copies of 'Les Miserables' and 'Crime and Punishment', with nothing but the chiming bells of the pinball machines along the wall rhyming with our chatter.

Soon came a time before long when I realized I simply couldn't keep up with Stella. The fact is she was just a voracious reader, who could just as easily pick up Fuller's 'Synergetics' and digest it as she could a romance novel by Danielle Steel or a techno-thriller by Tom Clancy. Just about the time when my own literary interests were beginning to wane, Stella, to my profound and grateful astonishment, started ladling in greater and greater doses of sexual sensation to serve as a mental stimulus to our Olympian endeavors.

Now the Gentle Man was on jam!

We went at it, armed with dictionaries and thesauruses and the site of battle changed many times. Stella and I were bivouac in the cafeteria in the beginning, reading volleys of passages at each other over lunchroom tables, scouting far afield for the meaning of theme or atmosphere. No strangers to paradox and inverted meaning, there were times when we clasped hands and dived together into foxholes of mutual confusion, when we simply didn't know what the mellow yellow the author was talking about! Once the smoke cleared, we would raise our heads above level ground again and make a safe retreat to a more secure position. Stella would await my signal to lay siege once more, and like that bare-breasted Lady Liberty in Delacroix's painting proudly carry forth our guidon onto the quaking grounds of new understanding. During our campaign against the enemy, I became the most highly decorated soldier in Stella Yamamoto's army.

After the battle of 'The Grapes of Wrath', I was awarded an honorary kiss on the cheek. During the skirmish of 'Tristram Shandy' I was near mortally wounded, and received The French Kiss of Honor for courage under fire above and beyond the call of duty. While under a withering bombardment during the campaign into 'Ulysses', I found it necessary to conduct a raid on the panties and we eventually established a beachhead in Stella's bedroom.

Now from there we fanned out in all directions and liberated all occupied territories. The minions of Dickens fell before our onslaught, and we were able to send a message for reinforcements in code once we made it up 'To The Light House' where Virginia Woolf was being held hostage by terrorists. Stella and I then dug a tunnel under our POW camp just beyond the barbed wire fence where the searchlight rotates and the Machine Gun Towers stood. I was half dragging and half carrying Stella across the river into our greatest escape when we both collapsed from exhaustion and rolling down the sloping hill wound up inside 'The Tale of Genji'.

"What's it called once more?" I squinted at Stella .

Stella adjusted herself again in a half lotus and holding the book in her lap, began to spread her notes out on the blanket. She flicked and tossed her shiny, straight black hair over her back and about her shoulders and fixed me with the most beautiful expression of earnestness.

"'The Tale of Genji'. A vehy impotant novel in my country. Lady Murasaki very famous Japanese writer." Stella glanced quickly at the locket watch that was draped between her glorious breasts. "Please. You read and then I weed like before. We will discuss all the major ideas we may find just like before. Okay?"

Stella Yamamoto was herself a major idea whose time had come and gone. She was the very opposite of the sex starved dowager princess of the Orient. Stella was starving for the society of learned men and women. There must have been many of them at the universities she attended in Japan and Hawaii. She was yearning to be the center of attention in some European cafe where students while away the hours discussing Schopenhauer and Hegel, Camus and Lao Tzu. Stella's greatest desire, more than anything else, was to have intercourse with great ideas. That was why, before we began our literary workshop, every time I reached for her in a carnal way, I felt like I presumed too much; was guilty of suggesting that I, of all people, should be permitted to take liberties with the royal personage of Stella Yamamoto. She would shrink away from my touch as if to say, '-how dare you!?'

How dare I indeed! What did I know of real passion or desire beyond the encircling lust that I exuded to suffocate her? Could I ever really understand what she truly thirsted for, what she truly hungered for, beyond what broke the limb's strength? Could I really recite the secret password that gave access to the abode of her greatest ecstasy and learn to dwell there with her?

Often it seemed to me that a book to Stella was like a passport from some nether region not unlike hell to a place of more temperate condition. She could book the flight or the voyage at any time; what she lacked was companionship, a person willing and able to travel on these expeditions with her. She was carefully testing and exercising my intellectual fitness preparatory to some future journey whose hardships even she could only dimly contemplate.

"Dante! He writes about the Inferno, but what does Dante truly know about hell?"

"You askin' me, Stella?"

"No. I tell you this time, Ahponso. No one who has not been to Hiroshima and Nagasaki can ever truly know Hell."

"Yeah, I guess you right about that. Of course, I can't think of anyone who ever mapped the place so well. I think maybe everybody has to look deep within themselves to find out what Hell is really all about. Seems to me human beings create new brands of Hell everyday."

"You almost sound like Buddhist, Ahphonso."

"I do?" I remarked as I flounced a couple of pillows against the headboard. I straddled myself around Stella's hips and bare back and reached through strands of straight black hair to tickle a swelling nipple with my fingertip. "Do you think that's good or bad?"

"Hmmmnn, you want to do the Tantra with me, Ahponso?" Stella mused as she swayed in my arms, both her nipples now erect like ripe berries. "You want to do the Tantra with me, eh? Honey Chile?"

"I just want to groove you, baby," I nibbled and licked at her ear before sticking my tongue inside. "do I have your permission to groove you, sugar?"

"Swow down, Alphonso, not so fast." Stella said, twisting her head and halting me with a raise of her index finger. "Emperor say you must help Miss Yamamoto with her paper first. Please be so kind as to give Miss Yamamoto your version of Hell, please."

Stella closed her eyes and heaved a deep breath before slapping my hand away from her breast. After that, she dutifully picked up her notepad and pencil.

"We humbly wequest your version of Hell, please."

Stella's face settled into a beautiful repose of seriousness. The expression she assumed was the spark that fueled my impulse to create and, as you may have realized at this point, the impulse to create is something the Gentle Man always chooses to obey. I found an open notebook and a spare pencil also resting upon the mattress and propped myself up.

"I'll tell you what, Stella, let me sketch you just the way you are now and I'll give you the straight dope, okay?"

"Okay. I will listen and you talk. Now go."

I blocked in the lines of Stella's eyes and high cheek bones .The pert nose and the prim and intelligent studiousness of those sweet lips set above a small, strong chin were the new focus of my creative thought. Now what could I say that was deep enough to keep her from changing the very wonderful dignity of her current expression?

"My version of Hell would be a cage with many trap doors whose hallways all led back to the main room of the cage. It doesn't matter by what door you leave the cage. No matter what corridor you walk, the next door you open leads right back into it. That would be the bare bones mechanics of my version of Hell. However, the overriding philosophy that governed the conduct of its inhabitants would be an entirely different matter."

I paused to erase part of my sketch, where I had given Stella too much chin.

"The inhabitants of my version of Hell would be forced to associate with individuals who don't see things their way, don't value what they value and don't believe as they do. As well, at the very same time, overwhelming force would be brought to bear on them to adopt the mindset of their new abode. That is, to see things as the people who run the place see them, value what the minions of Hell value, and believe what the hired help believe. Or---"

I paused to work in the areas around the mouth, nose, and eyes. I didn't mean to, because at this point Stella turned her head towards me.

"Ahponso? Please go on. You were saying 'or'-"

"Don't move your head now, Stella. I just about have you down now."

I started putting in the highlights in the hair and smearing the graphite to create tones and shadows. She set her head back where it was and I continued.

"Well?" Stella shrugged, showing me the palms of her hands.

"Right, baby, right. Well, you know how it is, you believe what Master tells you is right to believe or get tortured eternally beyond the last inch of your life. Now that's my version of hell. It's your turn, Stella. How about you? Don't smile -"

Stella resumed her serious demeanor.

"I 'member a movie I see once with Andie MacDowell and Bill Murway. The name of it I think was 'Groundhog Day'. You see it?"

"I might have--" I said, more interested now in getting this sketch right than anything else. "You tell me about it, but keeping looking that way."

"Simple story. Selfish man lives the same day over and over again forevuh. Nothing he can do to live tomorrow the next day. I read in a magazine once, idea put simply."

"Oh?"

"Yes, Ahponso. I find old magazine in library. I quote; 'Hell is the enforced repetition of times past' unquote. This is my version of Hell, Alphonso. You live the same experience over and over again eternally. You never grow or develop to ever experience anything new. "Groundhog Day' is all you know forevuh."

Sounds like the Chinese Water Torture, but Stella's Japanese. I wonder whether mentioning this would appeal to her sensibilities?

"'Enforced repetition of times past' huh, Stella? Never heard of that one before. I think I get it though. Sort of like paying for the roller coaster ride at Cedar Point, only you're never able to get off. You just go on and on and on---"

"Exactly! 'Groundhog Day'!"

"So, how do you get out of 'Groundhog Day' and live to see another day?"

"You rent me movie and we find out togethuh."

Stella's face settled into that Oriental inscrutability and that was just the expression I was able to capture in my sketch.

"I was dating this Japanese coed in college and she wouldn't even talk to me unless I read to her everyday." I told Mrs. Wellington, coming out of my reverie. "She would ask me lots of questions about what certain words and phrases meant. We used the dictionary all the time. She knew the English language well when she came in as a freshman, but by the time we graduated, she knew even the fine points that a grammarian would quibble about."

"You must have been quite fond of her, Alphonso." Mrs. Wellington adjusted an earring with a twinkle in her eye.

"Put it this way, Fiona. I just remember how the prettiest teachers were always the meanest usually. But when they were nice to you, it was like you were released from Hell and given a ticket to Seventh Heaven. Now I'm seeing this Japanese honey who is as pretty as any teacher I ever dreamed about, and she's not only seeking me out to study with her, she rewards me for the favor by going out with me. What could be a more rewarding study experience?"

Daphne regards me now, glowing with a newfound respect. I don't know why, really. I'll study the whole Encyclopedia Britannica when you give me sex, and the more I studied and widely read with

Stella, the more she let me reach into the honey pot at the end of the rainbow. What more motivation and incentive does a young man need to pursue higher education?

We even thoroughly studied the subject of Human Sexuality. We read what everybody had to say about it, including Chinese and Japanese authors, and you know what? There is nothing more stimulating than being able to intellectualize about sexuality and sexual technique in ways most people are too shy to discuss. Since we were going out with each other, we could of course be more hands on than students in other classes.

Now I will tell you something else. When you devote yourself to studying what the experts think, there is always the chance you might wind up an expert too.

That is why I take my hat off to Samuel Socrates Turner. We would be cracking up when we saw the mug carting away books from the Main Library. There were no honeys helping him get a leg up on the road to higher learning. We would chide him because it was evident that he loved books and study more than pussy. That's why I was so surprised when I was wringing Stella out to dry from our sweaty embrace, that the last three syllables that escaped from the throaty throes of her final orgasm were this:

"O - Soc-uh-teasssssse!"

"Alphonso?" Daphne playfully tugged at my sleeve with a quizzical expression. "What's on your mind? Are you thinking about that Japanese girl?"

I looked up and the Wellingtons are studying me intently.

"Huh? Yeah, well, as a matter of fact, I was on the verge of crying like a baby when I drove her to the airport."

I have to stop here. I've already said too much. Generally it is bad policy to let on to a woman that you are almost ready to beg her not to leave. I'm giving this to you on the down-low, after wringing Stella out she was the one who hung me up to dry. Oh, she thanked me profusely for a valuable once-in-a-lifetime learning experience, and how she would share everything she learned with her countrymen back home. The thing of it is, there was never any doubt that she was booked for her flight and ready to go. I was her American adventure, already indexed and filed for easy reference.

I knew this would come up next in the conversation. I just wasn't sure which one of the Wellingtons would broach the subject.

'Did you love her, Alphonso?" asked Daphne as she twisted a strand of hair around her finger.

"She was one of the ten best things that ever happened to me."

Mr. Wellington, who by now was thoughtfully nosing an El Producto, peered at me over his cigar with shrewd regard.

"We want to hear whether or not you loved her, young man." Mr. Wellington said, finally breaking his silence.

Now this is definitely against playa policy. This is bait you don't want to bite unless you have to do so. A skillful playa will always find a way to dance around this subject. Here's a way to handle this you might find useful.

"Absolutely!" Notice the one-word affirmation that substitutes for those dreaded three little words. Again. "Absolutely! We were good to each other and good for each other. There were times when we absolutely brought out the best in each other. You asked me how I came to be so articulate, well, Stella is one of the reasons that I am here."

I feel Daphne's foot again, rubbing against my own.

"Do you miss her, Alphonso?"

What can I say about Stella? I mean, how many times in your life do you run into a woman who will put out for great literature? Such a one would be a rare Oriental jewel.

"Sometimes. But Stella and I gave everything we could to being happy while we were with each other. I doubt that either of us would report any regrets."

Regret.

You may think I don't know the meaning of regret, but you would be mistaken. There are lots of folks who wish they could go back in time and relive some important turning point in their lives. When the relationship you've experienced with someone is particularly satisfying, there is no desire to go back and relive anything. There may be only a handful of people one can say that about in anyone's life. Stella Yamamoto will always be one of those individuals for me.

"What is it, Alphonso?" Daphne asked me, intrigued. "You seem to be pondering some important matter. Do you mind sharing with us what it is?"

"Nothing earthshaking really-"

"Probably just catching his breath, Daphne, after blowing all the air out of his windbag!" Mr Wellington quipped as he searched his pockets for a lighter.

"Oh, don't light those dreadful things up at the table, dear." Mrs. Wellington waved her hand at imaginary smoke as Mr. Wellington continued to finger his cigar.

"I was just thinking about this dude who keeps coming up in the conversations I have with the girls I date. He's a high school teacher by the name of Samuel Socrates Turner."

"Who's he?" Daphne asks to further probe the mystery.

"Oh, the ladies keep telling me tales about him. I first ran into him teaching History at old Northwestern High on the Boulevard."

"Socrates!" Mrs. Wellington repeats with airy marvel. "That's an impressive middle name. He probably received a lot of ribbing in school, being named for a Greek philosopher and all."

"Yeah, a name like that could end up making you a walking insult. I'm afraid the truth is that already in some parts of the neighborhood he's known as 'Suckertease' rather than being identified with venerable old Socrates."

"Oh dear!" Mrs. Wellington exclaimed, "That really is unfortunate, Alphonso. Why in heaven's name would anyone want to call him that?"

The Wellingtons look to me in naive bewilderment, much to my delight. The expression on their collective faces is much like that of suburbanites stranded at night in a tough section of the city due to a flat tire. I break it down to them as best I know how.

"See-there are those among us who value street knowledge over book knowledge. I have no particular preference myself. Knowledge is knowledge as far as I'm concerned. But some call Sam Turner 'Suckertease' because for all his book knowledge, he can be easily played out here in these mean streets and he's too nice and kind for his own good. Some think he's barricaded himself behind walls of books to insulate himself from the way life really is out here."

"What do you think, Alphonso?" Daphne asks me with deadpan seriousness.

I look up and realize that all the Wellingtons are taking me seriously now. Somehow, I must have turned on the sternness without knowing it. Anyway, I decided I would make the most of the opportunity to be more than just the jester for the night.

"This is the way I look at it. I think sometimes you can use knowledge to hide from knowing yourself. Samuel Turner may be guilty of this in certain departments, and to this extent, he is no Socrates. He walks around with his pockets full of puzzle pieces, more than anybody else maybe, but I don't think even he can put the whole thing together yet into a total picture. I have just now lately come to recognize and respect the potential that he represents for us. I sometimes think Socrates could take us to the threshold a of new knowledge. What he's got to somehow do is adopt a fresh perspective on what he already knows and, well, the jury's still out on whether he's smart enough to do that."

Estelle darts in and out to remove our plates and silverware and asks us every now and then whether or not we want more tea. I shake my head and put my hand over my cup. I feel I better press on while I have still got the Wellingtons' full attention.

"Stella told me 'fore she booked for Japan that a man like Socrates in her country would be highly honored and respected for his attainments of knowledge. She scoffed at the notion that we would ridicule any man of advanced learning. I guess it's just not done in the Eastern world. As she put it, even a fool who attempts to make himself wise should be applauded."

"I'll drink to that!" Mr. Wellington said, as he poured himself more wine.

"She said our attitude towards learning and knowledge exposes the truth of our history. The Western Man is still in many respects a hairy barbarian, stumbling out of the Roman Coliseum searching for the next orgy and sporting event where the combatants fight to the death."

"Hmph!" Mrs. Wellington gave me her frowning disapproval. "I'm not at all sure I like the sound of that!"

"Yeah, well I'll have to admit she gave me a new way to look at school. According to her, that's why American teenagers place more importance on being partygoers and excelling at Sports activities than they do on achieving important skills through the acquisition of greater knowledge. Stella believed that even though the bodies of Western men were far removed from the Circus Maximus, their minds were still up in the stands cheering on the gladiators and thrilling to the Christians being devoured by the lions!"

"Why, that's the most preposterous thing I ever heard in my life!" Mr. Wellington blanched as he coughed out his objection. Mrs. Wellington thumped him on the back as there was something stuck up his throat. "There's nothing in Life to validate such simplistic drivel!"

"There, George, there now," Mrs. Wellington wiped the drool from the corner of his mouth as he reached for a glass of water. "-don't upset yourself so-"

"Do you believe what she said, Alphonso?" Daphne asked me gently, the translucence of her blue eyes seemed especially probing and piercing at this time. "Is that the way you see us?"

There was a palpable silence as the night breeze went floating through the curtains.

"Naw, not after you done fed me and everything!"

The Wellington sternness creaked a crack as Mrs. Wellington emitted a tiny giggle.

"I mean-don't get me wrong. I can see her part of the argument. That would explain why the highlights of our entertainment focus on so much sex and violence. Many of us have not yet outgrown the tastes we cultivated lusting for blood in the coliseum!"

"Please, young man, please." Mr. Wellington's coughing fit was now subsiding. "Spare me these erudite snap analyses of the Western Historical tradition. I have a feeling things may be a bit more involved than all the explanations that the savants of the East might give."

"I agree with you, Daddy," Daphne said with a slow hesitancy, "-but then I don't agree as well-"

"What could be plainer?" Mr. Wellington sneered at Daphne, as he patted his mouth with his napkin. "'East is East and West is West', and all the rest of that rot-"

"All I'm saying is something must be wrong when a man like Samuel Socrates Turner can be studying for his doctorate and can't get no respect, while a big time pimp like Leonard Morris, also known as Master Mojo, becomes the role model of choice for our African American youth. I have a nephew fixin' to turn eighteen and I'm not sure which path he'll choose to tread. The path that leads to street knowledge and the Leonard Morris' of the world, or the path that leads to book knowledge and the Samuel Turners of this world-"

"Perhaps," Daphne looks up, and barely raises her voice to the level of a whisper. "Perhaps your nephew will blaze his own path, Alphonso. Maybe you should pray he walks the path that leads towards self knowledge, regardless whether that takes him into books or the streets."

"I like the way you put that, Daphne," Mrs. Wellington remarked with a nod, "-yes, I think that was wisely put."

Daphne is starting to sound like Stella now.

"Yeah, well, I'm his Uncle and I going to have a hand to play in this somehow, too. I just don't want him to miss the bus when it's time for him to get on board for the major turning point of his life."

"Oh, I think you're probably serving him as a good role model already, Alphonso." Daphne said to the surprise of her mother and father. "You're a college graduate and all. You don't seem all wrapped up into the street scene and its mythology, and I think that's a good thing. You have definite plans and goals for your life and that's got to be appealing to anyone. Don't you think so, Daddy?"

Mr. Wellington shrugs and makes a little grimace of a smile. He's getting antsy to find someplace where he can smoke that El Producto. Mrs. Wellington admonishes him with a stifling glare.

"Oh, it sounds all right for a bill of sale," He idly taps the shaft of his cigar, "but sooner or later you've got to go over the fine print and examine the goods for what they are. I hardly expect that a young fellow like yourself would know anything about that, Alphonso-"

"I don't know. I examine the goods plenty when I'm working on a drawing or a painting. Plus I have my secretaries go over the contracts I have my models sign in minute detail. I think I have some limited understanding of what you're talking about despite my youth."

"Going into business for ourselves, are we, young man?"

"Gonna build me an Empire one way or another, sir."

"I just hope you've got the stomach for the tough choices that have to be made to keep an enterprise thriving. I've been in the Greeting Card business for over twenty-five years now and I don't mind telling you, I've had to cut the fat from the bone many a time."

"I gotcha. I'm just the opposite. Sometimes it seems it is all I can do to nail down agreements to keep things from running away from me. There's this young poet named Mary Murphy doin' the 'now you see me-now you don't' game, and I-"

The air is ripped across with this bloodcurdling, heart-piercing scream coming from the kitchen! Estelle dashes out, her washcloth pressed against her face, now a ripening red shade of mahogany.

"Get it away!" She exclaims in terror, wildly flitting glances at all of us. "There's a snake in the sink! Get it away! Mr. Wellington! Y'all do somethin'-"

The Wellingtons move as one mass of bodies into the kitchen before Daphne comes bolting out on the hoof, followed by Mrs. Wellington.

"Aaaaa! Alphonso!" Daphne puts her hand to her mouth and makes a retching sound. "You get that snake! What are you still doing out here?"

When you talk to my running buddies, they'll swear up and down I know everything there is to know about women. Putting the hype to the side for a moment, however, I'll have to admit there are several things about the opposite sex that mystify me.

A couple of these in particular are worthy of mention.

Once I saw a photograph of screaming females at an airport, being held at bay by security guards because this sixties rock group, I think they were called the Beatles, were coming off their plane. I'll never forget the look of wild frenzy in the eyes of these ladies. You would have thought they were being sent to Buchenwald or something. It is strange to me how the most intense of pleasures can seem to resemble the most profound pains.

So I am asking you now. What on earth is all this carrying on these women do all about? I just want you to know I see the 'how', but when it comes to the 'why' I don't have a clue.

I mean, what is this?

The other thing is why do women go into apoplexy when they see a centipede or maybe a caterpillar or a worm crawling over ears of corn or squash or lettuce? I say just flick the creepy crawler off and rinse as needed. Why make a big production out of it, and do 'The Creature From The Black Lagoon' on the mug?

Anyway, Daphne's pulling and jerking on me to get up and help her father handle that snake in the kitchen. I stumble through the entrance and I feel like Sherlock Holmes in 'The Speckled Band'. I see Mr. Wellington resolutely holding a Teflon skillet in a meaty fist. I immediately snatch up a broom, and advance with the business end towards the green and grayish-brown thing coiled about the faucet.

"Looks like a garter snake, Mr. Wellington," I said, stepping slowly forward.

"Pssst! Young man!" Mr. Wellington bid me over with a jerk of his head. "This way! Drive the little devil over here and I'll flatten the filthy thing."

"Yeah, that sounds like a plan, sir. Let's send this sucker to the Happy Hunting Grounds!" "We're of one mind on that account."

I take another determined step forward and stab at the striped snake with the broom to somehow catch it up in the bristles.

"Good, m'boy, good. Have at it again!"

"Right, sir. Here goes---" I said, as I prepared to make another stab.

That was when the lights went out and I heard another scream come from the dining room!

We heard a shriek pierce the air. Victor caught me with a hard uppercut to the stomach that left my head swimming. I held him by both his shoulders the way a drowning man clutches a life preserver. I squeezed my hand around the back of his neck. Just as he was about to push me into the door, I elbowed him in the face as hard as I could. I felt bone and something soft like his eye or his mouth give; I don't remember which.

Victor shrank back in stunned surprise.

The shriek dissolved into a bunch of well-dressed girls ambling by in business attire. We glanced at them chattering away a good distance from us. They giggled past the alleyway oblivious to any of our struggles. Victor felt around his face with a handkerchief to see whether or not there was any blood. He gave me another grim, steely glare.

"All right. Are you ready to talk?"

"Talk about what?" I wheezed and protested lamely. "I already told you I don't know nothing."

"Wrong answer, Mister." Victor told me as he wrapped his handkerchief around his right hand. "I'm going to find out what you have done to Daphne even if I have to beat you to a pulp to do it."

There was nowhere to run and nowhere to hide.

I put up my hands again and clenched my fists...

MIND OVER MANHOOD

I stepped away from the alcove. I was on my last breath. My ribs hurt and my head ached. I felt like I was going to throw up breakfast and lunch. But none of that made no never mind. I could tell by the way Victor stood on his feet with that unsteady sway that he was close to hanging it up too. I slowly raised my hands to defend myself. I attempted to mentally review everything Dougie and I went over while we sparred before his big bout.

Victor went down in a crouch with his fists held high.

"Very well, Mister Gentle," Victor said with a malicious chuckle, "I must say I've been looking forward to this. I..."

"Where did you hear all that?" I asked Dougie as I shuffled the cards.

"What you talkin' 'bout, man? Everybody's in the know on this one."

Back at the studio, Dougie Mack was all poker face and there were ugly gray storm clouds gathering up beyond the skylight. Nathan Eddie flicked cigarette ash off the crease of his pants leg and Danny, Smiley and Baldy were looking at the backs of the cards I was dealing them. I shrugged and kept on passing out the cards, hoping to elicit from somebody a favorable reaction.

"Hey Alphonso, how come you got these honeys on the backs of these cards?" Danny asked with an indignant expression. "You think lookin' at yo' women while you play cards with us gonna give you some kind of edge?"

"Naw man, it ain't about all that. It's a new wrinkle of an idea I've been workin' on for my enterprises. How do you like it?"

"The women is fine, Alphonso, but they ain't showin' much skin." Dougie Dogg muttered as he sucked on the tooth pick in the corner of his mouth.

"What's the big idea, Alphonso? Who are these heifers?" Smiley asked as he surveyed his suit. "Sort of look like movie stars, but no one I can remember ever seeing at the Star."

"They're the best lookin' girls I could photograph when I was going to college. I was thinking of coming up with my own brand of playing cards. You know, something like 'The Playas' Playing Cards'. What you think?"

"You should of made them bitches show mo' skin, Alphonso. Straight up." Dougie Dogg threw down a card. "For all we know, these could be the 'Lost Women of the Bible' or some such carryin' on. Hey now! I know this little bitch, man. That's yo' little bitch, Alphonso. She's the one who came up to the Gym askin' 'bout yo' sorry ass. Ain't that right? What the hell you got her ass on the back of these playing cards for?"

"You ack like she the only one on these cards, Dougie Mack, my man." Baldy said, as the lights glinted off his glasses. "Old Alphonso's got the whole stable kickin' up on these things."

James 'Baldy' Badewell and I go way back. He came back from Desert Storm and became a foreman on a construction crew. But I remember him when he was just Baldy and the best hoopster in the neighborhood. We were sure he was going to the NBA before he went over to Irag and got busy.

Now he's got a wife and two kids. Those basketball days when he was a hero are just recollections to past the time while we play poker. He still cuts all his hair down real close to the skin the way his father used to when he wanted to save money. He throws down three-of-a-kind like he's got the lowdown on all of us.

"Square business, Alphonso." Baldy winces when Danny sets out four-of-a-kind. "Why you got your women on the back of these cards?"

"Just lookin' for another way to make some money. That's all, Baldy. I thought I would try this idea out on my friends first, you know what I'm sayin'?"

"See - Master Mojo got you dead to rights, Alphonso. He said it wouldn't be long before you would start workin' some angle to make money off them bitches of yours." Dougie scowled at his hand because all he had was two pairs. "You got the instincts of a pimp, nigger, whether you admit it to yo'self or not!"

"Watch your mouth, youngblood," Nathan Eddie cautioned as he took another drag of hiscigarette, "we can do without that kind of talk around here."

The cards have not been kind to the Gentle Man this evening, that's why I brought out my own brand and started shuffling. Unfortunately, events have come to such a head I need to pump Dougie for the latest out on the street. I sidestep all that Mojo mess and put it to him straight.

"You trippin' Dogg. The only one gettin' an angle worked on 'em is you! You need to find a john and heave that unenlightenment Morris is feeding yo' silly be-hind down the toilet. Just because Morris gets his high holding the power of Life and Death over some bitch, don't mean I have to see female flesh in terms of dollars and cents. This is the twentyfirst century, Jack! Morris got you thinkin' that holdin' the reins on some babe who is strung out on you is the highest virtue of Manhood. That stuff is real whack, Dogg. I mean, where's the beauty in that?"

Dougie lets out a breath and trains me in his sights like he's fixing to take a poke at me.

"Straight up, man," Dougie says as he nods at me, "you pretty stupid , Alphonso, for a guy who supposed to be so smart with the ladies. There is nothing more beautiful than standin' over some fool whose ass you've whopped! Bitches be the first one to drop to their knees and worship a nigger they know can kick ass. You kick a nigger's ass and suddenly you be lookin' real good to these bitches. Mess around with you, Alphonso, and you'll have us all down at the Library with Suckertease; reading books and getting dissed day in and day out."

"That's Socrates, fool. What you got against Samuel Turner, anyway?"

"Now look who's trippin'! Turner done sold his soul to the Devil, man. Why can't you see that? Sure, he's got all the knowledge in the world, but he signed away his manhood to get it.

Just like whitey sold away his humanity to run his little tricknology game on the world. You know what you need to do? You need to stop callin' him - you need to stop callin' him - whatchamacall it? So-so-social disease-something?"

"That's Socrates, fool."

Dougie held his nose and snickered like he smelt something bad.

"Yeah Socrates-"

"I bet you don't even know who or what he was-"

"Don't need to know that whitey mess! I bet you strip the both of us down he couldn't kick my ass-wham! You snooze you lose, Smiley!"

Dougie threw down a full house and slid the cash his way.

"Why everything got to be a fight to you, Dougie?" Nathan Eddie threw down his hand with a sigh of resignation. "I'm out, gents. Anybody want a beer from the fridge?"

We all shook our heads. Nathan Eddie got up to stretch his long legs and then ambled over to the windows. He lit another cigarette and looked out on the green wide lawns of the boulevard.

"Because that's what Life is all about, Mister Eddie Man. It's Trial by Combat from the womb to the tomb. Faggots need not apply. Just get out the Vaseline and bend over cause it's coming. The rest of us know Life ain't about to hand you nothing on no silver platter, and that goes double if'n you black. You have to be prepared to compete for what you want, and let's face it; to the victor go the spoils, just like in any game. That's just common sense."

"I heard that." Baldy pulls out his hand with a flourish. "Read my flush and weep, brothers. Ol' Baldy come to break the bank! Hey, Dougie-"

"What?"

"I bet I know something you don't know,"

"What's that?"

"That Socrates was a faggot his own self. You ever heard uh that?"

"I have," Smiley nods to us as I reshuffle the cards. "I heard he was sweet on the young boys he was-"

"What I tell you - what I tell you, huh?" Dougie looked around with a triumphant scowl. "Now what in the world do I want to learn from some fruit? What can he teach me except how to let somebody else's horses in through the barn door? Nothing! You tell me, Alphonso, where the wisdom is in all that?"

"That is your problem, Dougie." I said, grunting in disgust. "Can't nobody tell you nothing, bro. Common sense should tell you that you can learn from anybody. Even when their cultural experience doesn't square with yours and you don't necessarily see eye to eye with them."

"All I know is that you should stop callin' Sam Turner Socrates, man." Dougie threw down a card. "People will start to get the idea he's some kind of wise man. That faggot ain't no ways a wise old philosopher. He's just a bad imitation of some dead ole white man."

"Right. That sounds just like something yo' ignorant ole ass would say." Baldy snorts as he places down his bet . "Sammy's black, an' there's no way on God's green earth that any black man could ever be as wise as any white man-"

"Oh, so now you gonna take Alphonso's side in this, eh-Baldy?"

"Hell yeah!" Baldy checked his hand and then went mum.

"I should have known -" muttered Dougie.

"That's because you is coming from an ignorant ass position!" Danny threw down his hand with gusto. "Straight flush right back at you! Ain't seen that one in awhile have you, friends?"

"See-" I begin as I reshuffle the cards again, "-we admire white folks so much in all those movies and books about their doctored-up version as to what went down back in the days as it's immortalized in storybook and song, we tend to forget in our sincerest flattery of imitating them we're actually imitating ourselves."

"Damn Alphonso!" Dougie exclaimed, because he's holding a bad hand. "Cain't you say nothing plain? Ain't no white folks around for you to impress now. Break it down for a brother so he can understand."

"I'm just saying that a lot of what they have is actually ours, and a lot of what they've done is actually modeled after our deeds, and a lot of what they are is a synthesis of what they've observed as they've sailed the seven seas. You would be surprised how much of what they are actually comes from watching us and peoples like us."

"I bet you didn't put it like that when you was havin' dinner over that white girl's house." Dougie said, as he chewed on his toothpick as though its taste was bitter. "You never did finish tellin' us what you did with that snake when the lights went out."

I shrugged as I finished passing out the cards.

"I just did what a man's got to do. I took care of business and protected the ladies."

"Yeah, I bet you did, Alphonso." Danny clapped his hands together with amusement. "I can see you scurryin' around that dining room now. Anything to get your head up under that white girl's skirt!"

There a supressed feeling of something around the table that breaks out into an uproar of laughter.

"Now y'all," Smiley motions for everybody to calm down, "you leave Alphonso and his white women alone."

"That's the one thing I ain't never liked about you, Alphonso. You is a down brother in every other department. You got your own business goin' on, your own Art Studio and you ain't got to answer to no one-"

"Least of all you, Dougie Dogg-" I point out as I check my jacket for a cigarette.

"-but I hates the way you is with them white chicks! You gon' be black, you gotta be black all the way; an' you know the sisters don't appreciate that monkey business."

That was when Nathan Eddie broke in again. He was still standing by the windows, cool as you please. He was looking through the pale blue of the panes like he was at the aquarium at Belle Isle. Nathan Eddie did not even turn to look at us, he just spoke through the window out at the boulevard.

"Ain't you about nothing, Dougie. We spend three - four hundred years tryin' to get our rightful freedom just so you can tell Alphonso what he ought to do."

That was Nathan Eddie for you. When he really laid it down, you could hear the judge's gavel drop.

"Rightful freedom? What's so righteous about having the freedom to beat the White Man across the finish line so's you can put his woman on a pedestal?" Dougie took one more card to add to his suit. "Now that we've freed our bodies, we gots to free our minds."

"-then 'yo ass will follow'!" Baldy quipped as he laid down his bet. "You all check out the Funkadelics when you searchin' for truth."

"That's what I'm talkin' about!" Dougie gave a nod to Baldy and some skin. "There ain't nothing to be found in the White Race that you can't find in the Black Race. We got our very own version of Sharon Stone, Julia Roberts, and Catherine Zeta-Jones. You can find Sophia Loren and Rita Hayworth, Marilyn Monroe and Ingrid Bergman right here in yo' own backyard. The White Man found that out when he kidnapped us and brought us over on the boats. Else why he gotta mix his blood so much with all of that Brown Sugar? Huh? Tell me that! He know the Truth. He know the darker the berry-"

"THE SWEETER THE JUICE!" Everyone at the table joins in the chorus with Dougie.

"Sho' you rite!" Smiley throws down a royal flush. "Dougie's got a point there, Alphonso. Thank you, gentlemen," Smiley rakes in his cash. "-ain't no need to quote scripture about that! That right there that Dougie just signified is a-what-they-call-it? Self-evident truth. Thank you, my friends, thank you again for your kind donation."

"I don't think you have to tell Alphonso all that, Dougie," Danny turns one of my cards around and squints at the picture on the back, "from what I can see he might understand that part better than any of us. Hey man," Danny glances at me, "this Sheba Taylor you got on the back of this here card?"

"Yeah man, I was all set to do a painting of her. I got her mother's permission and all that good stuff when Mojo moved into the cut."

"I feel you, my brother. That there mess was a damn shame. Sheba was the last young lady I would have figured to get turned out by a snake like Mojo."

I do not have to turn on the sternness now. I am feeling deepest, darkest Africa all inside me now where not one ray of light will enter. I look up at the skylight overhead, because it is a suffocating feeling, but all I see in the open space in the ceiling is the grayness. I feel like I am underwater and all I can hear is my heart pounding, and my head is fixing to explode in a red roar.

"You shouldn't have grabbed my arm like that, man -" I seriously tell the table.

"Don't go there, Alphonso man, don't go there," Danny starts to wave me off.

"You shouldn't have held me back, man-"

"Naw? Held you back, huh?" Danny looks around at everybody like he cannot believe what he is hearing. "How many times I got to tell you, fool? What I did was stop yo' stupid ass from gettin' smoked that night. Got dog-it-"

Danny starts to get up out of his seat and walk away, but Smiley and Baldy herd him over into a corner of the Studio by the cream leather couch. They are over just a few feet from the window where Nathan Eddie is standing with his smoke. I feel like their hushed whispers are coming from inside my head and it is all I can do to keep my fingers from balling up into fists.

When I look up, Dougie Dogg is regarding me thoughtfully, that toothpick still planted in the corner of his mouth.

"Ain't no thang, Alphonso, ain't no thang," Smiley grinned tentatively as he and Baldy escort Danny back to the table. "We came to play cards, let's play some cards."

Danny lands back in his seat, but now the wiry little guy is doing his own smoldering. He scowls at me and then hides his mouth with his hand as he looks away and starts to mutter. Now he jerks a piercing look at me.

"I told yo' ass to focus on landscapes instead uh them nudes. I told you to leave them white girls alone, but naw, I was puttin' a damn crimp in your 'artistic freedom'. The problem with you Alphonso is you think with yo' dick, and that dick of yours is going to lead you straight into hell. Got Dog-it! I thought once you calmed down, you would have seen the sucker play Mojo was maneuvering yo' ass into, but you still in the dark!" Danny turned in his seat and gave me the shoulder. "When have you ever seen Mojo at the Shakers and the Takers, man? Never! Oh, but you go there all the time. So ain't it a real coincidence that just as you fixin' to go into the place you spot Mojo and Sheba Taylor in the parking lot, big as Life and dressed to the nines."

I open my mouth to say something, but nothing comes out. Suddenly I feel the gazes of everyone at the table on me, and they are wearing these tight little smiles. Danny's dark scowl is blazing at me, Smiley is imperceptibly nodding at me the way you do when you are teaching a little child how to read, and Dougie Dogg with that toothpick in his mouth is the very image of inscrutable Ghetto Soul.

I can hear the clock on the wall and the refrigerator whirring. There is an airplane overhead that passes a droning shadow over us through the skylight.

"Startin' to get the picture, Alphonso?" Nathan softly asks the window with eyes uplifted.

"First Corinthians, Alphonso," Smiley mumbled as he nodded gently, "Chapter Thirteen, Verse Eleven."

"That don't do it," Nathan Eddie resumes his conversation with the window, "check out that Ecclesiastes, Chapter Ten, Verse Eight, brother."

"Mojo put the most beautiful bait he could get on his hook to get you to come where he wanted you to go, Alphonso," Danny's brows nearly met in an angry 'V' between his eyes. "He knew all he had to do was show Sheba Taylor off anywhere and there you would be, led by your all-knowing dick! But just to make sure, he decided to show up someplace where everybody knew you hung out all the time. So he set up the play, because he knew all you would see was Sheba and how much you wanted to get her back to her moms. What he didn't count on was that one of your friends might see how he was triangulating you between himself and two young guns on opposite street corners. You didn't even see the frame, Alphonso, and you just catchin' on to it now! That's cuz you still cain't stop thinking with your dick when the real deal goes down."

"Yeah buddy," Dougie Dogg flicked on his toothpick, "that's just about the way Mojo sized it to me."

"See what I'm sayin'?" Danny gestured towards Dougie Mack. "There you go."

"Yeah buddy," Dougie Dogg nods to himself, "Mojo schooled me that you didn't have what it takes for situations and dynamite-"

"That situational dynamics, fool!" Danny snapped at Dougie.

"I know what it mean," Dougie glared at Danny. "Mojo was fent to pull the old 'bait-and-switch' on you, Alphonso, but he couldn't run the number 'cause you got friends. Danny pulled on yo' coat last time and he figgers it most likely be somebody else the next. So he's chill for the minute. But Suckertease is another matter. He such a lone wolf, he don't bring his friends, if'n he got any. Mojo ran it down to me how Suckertease bought whole cloth that crazy ole White Folks idea about 'rugged individualism' without reading the fine print. Anyway, he was explaining to me how he worked the 'bait-and-switch' on Suckertease before with success, and now he's got it down to a science. The word out on the street is the 'bait-and-switch' is on for Suckertease because Mojo need to pick his brain about something. He just ain't found the right bait, but that's what he's got his soldiers scoutin' for now."

Dougie's face takes on that mournful, soulful expression again as he looks straight at me.

I wanted to ask what all this has to do with me, just as a thought flashed into my mind before I could open my mouth and stopped me cold! Something added up for me in that moment as unyielding as any modular equation and I suddenly saw how the whole thing was being tooled to run down.

"Yeah buddy, the way Mojo put it - this here Motor City ain't big enough for the both of y'all." Dougie sucked on his toothpick and looked at me through his cards. "The way Mojo see it, you be givin' people the wrong ideas about where the action is in this community. He been takin' note of how you been pullin' all the best lookin' bitches in the city into your studio."

"That's might be how Morris looks at it, Dougie," Danny interjects, "but the women are only a small percentage of Alphonso's workload. Especially lately, he's been doin' a lot of portraits of people in the neighborhood and the 'rainy night in Georgia' type of street scenes that are his trademark."

That's one thing I have to give to Danny. Nobody ever boosted me the way he can.

"Street scenes may be his trademark," Baldy began, as he rubbed back the skin on his head, "-but it damn sho' ain't his specialty!"

"That's what I'm talkin' 'bout!" Dougie fiddled with his cards before throwing one down. "Mojo been scopin' the style uh hoe you be turning out up in this mug. The kind uh bitch you be dealin' with is a different kind of merchandise from what Mojo puts out on his shelves. Mojo's hoes is more the professional business woman escort service type. That is, the ones that can pull in a 'C' note a night, or a grand or two for a businessmen's weekend."

"You got me all wrong, Dougie." I told him as my face set into the cold sternness that was welling up inside me. "There's a whole world of difference between what I do and what Morris perpetrates. For one thing, my business is legit and on the up and up. My ladies go on to bigger and better things even when they don't continue their careers as models. But what it comes down to is I am not peddling flesh and that's the sum total of Mojo's action. Now gon' run tell that!"

Dougie is chill and shrugs like I have ruffled his feathers. Smiley, Danny and Baldy all nod with agreeable smiles. Nathan Eddie could be on another planet, ready to phone home for all that distant focus in his eyes. I reshuffle the cards and start to divvy up again.

"What you signifyin', Alphonso?" Dougie whispers in a sinister tone. "You tryin' to say I'm Mojo's messenger boy?"

"You tryin' to say you not? This the second time you come in here, crashin' our card game spoutin' words of wisdom from Mojo. Like I give a damn what he got to say! You keep spendin' so much time around him, you gon' start seein' things with the same snake vision that he do."

"I ain't nobody's messenger boy, Alphonso." Dougie nearly tears a card in two, he's holding it so hard. "Mojo and I was havin' a conversation, and I'm just givin' you the blow by blow because whether you dig it or not, you was all in the mess he was puttin' down. That is just the way it is. While he was runnin' to me how he wanted to promote my career once I turn Pro, he kept askin' me all sorts of questions about them bitches you call yourself paintin'. The way he tell it, they're the wholesome, college girl-next-door kind he has a hard time gettin' his hands on to sign up with him."

"That's a no-brainer!" Smiley snorts as he admires his hand. "What good Christian girl gon'

get herself mixed up in Mojo's slimey smut?"

Dougie shrugs as he lays down a winning hand.

"Don't know nothin' 'bout all that," Dougie hitches up his pants and twirls the toothpick in his teeth. "A bitch is a bitch as far as I'm concerned. All I know is that Mojo kept tellin' me over and over again how he would like to get a percentage of some of that young spring chicken pussy you been warehousing over here, Alphonso. He kept tellin' that to me like I was hard of hearing. I been in enough scraps to know when a body is fent to call you out. Right now, Mojo just wants to know what he got to do to get some uh this you got established for yourself, Alphonso. No doubt in my mind he means have him a slice, by hook or by crook."

The room seems to darken even though there is nothing wrong with the lights. I can hear Nathan Eddie's labored breathing blend with the sounds of the street and children playing outside. We descend into a space so quiet that the gathering shadows of the evening seem to whisper a warning in our ears. While Nathan Eddie is a statue at the window, all we players at the card table dip our minds into the well of some deep ancestral emotion and sigh as one soul with resignation. I half expect Smiley to quote us something from the Bible, but I don't hear a peep out of him now.

Yeah, that must be why we call it the blues...

"My-oh-my, apple pie," Danny breaks the silence with a sardonic chuckle, "yeah, the whole thing all checks out now. That's why Mojo showed with Sheba at the Shakers and the Takers, my man. He wants in on your business as a silent partner, Alphonso. Probably figgers he can get you to front for him and help him launder his money. Anyway you look at it, he wants you to sign on the dotted line with him or else."

"Or else what?" I croak as I reach inside my jacket again for a cigarette.

Damn! My throat is so dry I have to take a drag off something. I've been quits for months, but now I've got an urge for some of the leaf.

"Hey somebody," I say as I reach into my jacket pockets and come up empty, "somebody let me bum a coffin nail."

Danny reaches over with a Newport Gold and lights me up.

"Or else," Danny resumes as he snaps his lighter closed, "you end up outlined in chalk, all laid out on the floor of your studio, Alphonso. Ready for the cops to sweep you out and put a tag on yo' toe."

"Mojo is serious business, Alphonso." Dougie idly sniffs at his cards.

"Morris' muscle don't mean nothing to me."

"Morris ain't about muscle, Alphonso." Nathan Eddie's voice haunts us from the window. "He will talk that sweet jive to test you; to see whether you're in or out. When you decide you're out, he'll have you lookin' down the barrel of a piece." Nathan Eddie turns to us, a silhouette in the last flaming glow of the Sun. "Morris ain't about muscle. He means that to be Dougie's department. Morris is all about the guns."

"Shoot-I ain't never said I was gon' do no work for Mojo." Dougie scoffed as he threw down a bad hand. "My man came down to the Gym and gave me the rundown. I was just polite enough to listen to his rap." Dougie's eyes narrowed as he pondered darkly, chewing on his toothpick. "I'm gon' let this thing between you and Mojo set. When y'all finally come on with the come on, I figure Trial By Combat will set everything straight. Time gon' come when the both of you lock horns and then we shall see what we shall see. Somebody's gettin' his ass kicked and somebody's going home with all the chips. Ain't no way around that. There was one thing that Mojo said been kinda botherin' me though-"

"Oh yeah? Enlighten us, my brother-" Smiley chided now that his hand was looking good again. "Lighten the load of your troubles with us."

"Yeah, you real funny, Smiley. Don't you go and quote me no Bible, neither" Dougie kept probing with his toothpick. "Mojo couldn't stop braggin' what a boss hoe Sheba was turnin' out to be and how he knew she used to be tight with you, Alphonso. That's when he said somethin' about you and her that didn't quite register with me. What does it mean when a dude calls a bitch some fool's 'Helen of Troy'?"

"Helen of Troy?" I asked with a puzzled frown. "What's that got to do with anything?"

Dougie glanced at me with indignation.

"That's what I'm asking you, Alphonso! Mojo said that Sheba was your 'Helen of Troy'. Now what that mess supposed to mean? He said you would know and that I ought to read up on it to better understand the History of Bitches. So do yo know what he was talkin' 'bout or not?"

Danny grabs me by the elbow and Smiley slaps my shoulder so hard, the cards I'm holding nearly fly out of my hands.

"Come on now, Alphonso," Baldy gives a relieved chuckle, "the young man desires some mo' schoolin'. Come on now - break it down to him."

"Helen of Troy? Mojo compared Sheba Taylor to Helen of Troy, did he?" I remarked to Dougie as I inhaled on my cigarette in reflection. "That's a Greek Mythology riff. You sure you want to hear it all?"

"That depends on how well you can set out the story." Dougie refolded his arms as the toothpick jerked in his mouth. "You ain't got to read the Encyclopedia to me, just give me a general picture of how it all went down."

Helen of Troy.

There may be a tale in African Mythology or African American Folk Tales that compares to this story. Still, I haven't found one yet, truth be told. This story of a Grecian white woman, so beautiful her husband was willing to wage a war for ten bloody years to get her back, stands out to me as emblematic of the Western mind-set. The first thing a brother would say is what woman could possibly be so fine as to be worth going to all that trouble? Even yours truly has been forced to meditate on what kind of beauty is that which inspires so much death and great destruction. But white folks love to put photographs of movie stars like Rita Hayworth inside atomic bombs before they nuke somebody, or send the Air Force or the Ku Klux Klan out to rescue Fay Wray or Helen Hayes. I bet some of them would even say that preserving the honor of white women and restoring them to their rightful place upon the pedestal of mankind is vital to the birth of nations. At least that idea was good enough to give D.W. Griffith the idea for the title of one movie. That Helen of Troy is one outstanding example of how the desire for heavenly sex can lead one into the hell of armed conflict and deadly violence.

Now to break it down so that Dougie can deal with it.

"The best way to put it, I guess, is that Helen of Troy was a babe who got snatched from her hubby and he went to war for her to get her back. The report was that the war lasted ten long years and thousands upon thousands of people died."

Dougie mulled this over while he chewed on his toothpick.

"Did he get the bitch back?"

"Yeah. He fought an army and destroyed a city to do it, but he got her back."

"Damn!" Dougie marveled, as he looked around at Smiley and the others. "All that for one bitch! When did all this go down, Alphonso?"

"Back in the day before Roman times. I think it was during the Golden Age of Greece or something like that. I'll get you a book. You can check it out for yourself."

"Ummm, who was the joker who copped that bitch?"

"Some dude named Paris."

"Paris? That's the name of a city in France, ain't it, Alphonso?"

"Yeah Dougie, but this Paris was a man, not a city."

"All right. What they call the dude who got her back?"

"Helen's husband was Menelaus. I think he was King of Sparta back then."

"I know he bitch slapped that hoe when he got her back home! Whoa! Ten years fightin' head up like that. That hoe's pussy must have been lined with gold!"

Danny and Smiley cracked up and Baldy nudged me again with a playful elbow while I just reshuffled the cards again.

"Go on, Alphonso," Smiley cackled with delight, "you started this. Now go head on and you finish it."

"I'll get the book for you, Dougie." I said, rubbing the sweat off the back of my neck. "I think there's a little bit more to it than just how good her pussy was to him."

"There oughta be. Straight up, Alphonso, that's some high hell to be paid for one heifer." Doug set out his hand on the card table. "So. That's how you feel about Sheba Taylor, huh? You ready to go to war for her, man?"

Dougie's eyes and the eyes of all the others focused on me. I looked over at Nathan Eddie for moral support. He was still rooted by the window, coolly eyeing me with curious regard. There is this heavy feeling in the room that I am about to make something jump off with respect to Mojo and the Lady Sheba. That may or may not be true, but for now I am holding my cards close to the vest.

Now I know this is supposed to be the part where I tell Dougie Dogg that I agree with his little analogy about Helen of Troy and Sheba of Detroit. The problem is the idea came from Mojo and is therefore laced and backed with a diabolical intent. The truth is, we live in a society that is dedicated to the image as a substitute for the substance of things to come. Where it seems everybody is striving for his fifteen minutes of fame and the photo opportunity of a lifetime. This being the case, it becomes harder and harder to resist the seduction of face values and break through the skin of the apple to its very core where the seeds of renewal await.

That being said, what am I really putting down? Just this; that black folks are always being urged to see things from the paradigms of the historical experience of white folks. We are all supposed to swallow whole cloth the glorious significance of the Greco-Roman tradition whether or not there is a one to one correspondence to the situational dynamics of our own lives.

Mojo has Dougie tell me that he thinks Sheba is my 'Helen of Troy'. Now I'm supposed to get all swept up in the Grandeur that was Greece and, likening myself to King Menelaus, start seeing Sheba as Queen Helen and Leonard Morris as Paris.

A sucker's play if ever I heard of one.

You don't have to take my word for it. Read up on the mug and then draw your own conclusions. Rest assured I have already drawn my own. The door to the bottomless pit of degradation swings wide when black folks start imitating the affairs of white folks.

Think about it for a moment and you will see how the whole notion is whack. The idea of a woman so beautiful she is worth the wholesale destruction of men, women and children; not to mention an entire city. That's right, just turn the whole world into a butcher's slaughterhouse for the honor and glory of restoring a kidnapped Queen to her rightful place back home. Oh yeah, let's put Helen back on her throne so the whole world can once again be her footstool.

Now scope it all from the point of view of the African American male. The first thing I'm going to think is that it must have taken more than a face to justify the launching of a thousand ships against an enemy host. Knowing just a little bit about my history, I am forced to reflect on the millions of lives lost as kidnapped slaves were brought through the Middle Passage to their places of residence in this New World. There are those who would contend that all the black souls dumped into the oceans of the world for garbage disposal, and the product control and effective maintenance of merchandise while in route on ships as cargo, far outnumber the casualties of the Jewish Holocaust. I would not know about that, and after the first few millions who keeps count anyway, other than the ones who survive their lost ones?

The point is, you could easily ask yourself why a thousand ships weren't launched to reclaim the lost liberty and physical well being of the millions of African men, women and children who were forced along with their subsequent generations to work here in the Americas for the next three or four centuries without drawing a paycheck. That line of questioning opens up a whole new can of worms, of course, and delves into the sense of guilt the African American male can feel with regard to his ability to protect the African American female. Beyond that, it shows just how absurd the situational dynamics can be between peoples. One white man kidnaps one white woman and a whole war erupts and is waged for ten long years to get her back. Millions of blacks are kidnapped from the continent of Africa and nobody there ever even considers launching a canoe to get those hostages back.

Now don't you find that somewhat strange? Seems to me an invasion force rescuing and restoring kidnapped blacks to freedom would have made a better story than a bunch of whiteys fighting for a decade over pussy. I know it makes me wonder. Is sexual desire and the need for female companionship really a stronger motivation for war than human freedom? The argument may seem specious, but you have to admit that's the way it looks at face value.

Check this out.

I take my nephew down to bookstores all the time to look at the new Figure Study Art books that have come out. I'll tell you what, you try this as an experiment. Look through all the Art books there are that treat the subject of Anatomy and report back to me how many have black models in them.

There was a time when the answer would have been none instead of next to none. Be that as it may, I want you to take a look for yourself. When you've made a thorough examination of the Art Anatomy books on display, I have a question to pose to you.

Why do you think that is so? Why do you think it is that there are no Anatomy books that feature black men and women as the primary models, instead of as instruments of tokenism?

Don't answer that yet. Look up the word tokenism first in a good dictionary.

Why is it that black men and women don't represent themselves in the Anatomy Books of the world as it pertains to Art Instruction? Better yet, why is it that no one even considers or talks about the idea? After all, it is just an idea, isn't it?

That brings us back to 'Helen of Troy'.

Morris tells Dougie that Sheba Taylor is my 'Helen of Troy'. That's supposed to be my cue to go for my guns and to do drive-by and whatever else it takes by any means necessary, no matter how many innocent bystanders end up being collateral damage. No, Jung to the contrary, the archetypes of this particular mythical construct do not apply to my present situation. Time to do the unthinkable, the forbidden and 'pop a groove'. I don't think I will ask myself this time what Holmes would do, or attempt to assess my scene through the eyes of white folks. I think I will examine my experience with my own eyes, and, as Danny would say, 'make my own footsteps and follow those'.

"No Dougie, there will be no war for the Queen of Sheba. I told her moms I would get her back home some kind uh way, and I aim to do it without bringing the whole world to the edge of Doomsday the way some outraged whitey would invent to do. I may not give war a chance, but I am willing to be the Orkin man and do pest control. At the present moment, Sheba is in the wrong place at the wrong time. This condition is endemic to African Americans and has its roots in historical precedent. When I'm through, Sheba Taylor will be in the right place at the right time and hard at work cramming for classes in her freshman year at college. I pledged to her moms that would be how it would go down, and I aim to keep that pledge."

When I sat down in her mother's parlor lined with those turkish rugs, Sheba Taylor was in the right place at the right time. I handed Mrs. Taylor my pen so she could put her signature just beneath her daughter's on the dotted line. That rainy afternoon, she was just about to sign her consent for her daughter to begin as my model, when Sheba sashayed her way over with our hot chocolate.

"Do you like yours creamy or thick and rich?" Sheba asked with an inviting smile.

"Hush child, give the man his hot chocolate, girl," Mrs. Taylor scoffed as she scribbled in her autograph on my contract with Sheba. "Pour us some of that stuff and sit yourself down."

Sheba was a darker than milk chocolate African American version of the voluptuous and comely Rubenesque. She was a full-featured, full-figured sprawling work of classical proportions stepping out of the marble of Michaelangelo or seemingly floating free of the Sistine Chapel. Even Charles White could not have fashioned a more marvelous John Henry woman out of a hundred pounds of clay or graphite and drawing paper. Lord! The most insignificant gesture she made seemed to move heaven and earth. She would touch the sheen in her black hair and cast a wary glance in my direction with eyes that would crinkle into a knowing smile that spread wide in the broad cheekbones of her regal face. I do not mind telling you I was salivating and chomping at the bit to get her back to my studio so that I could touch greatness. Every artist needs to encounter one great model to really step up to the plate and bat for posterity. Sheba Taylor was going to be my one for the ages; that boundless treasure for the roving eye, designed to nourish the future generations of humanity with food for the soul.

"How's that hot chocolate working for you?" Sheba asked, as she pursed her lips and blew into her own cup.

"No complaints, Sheba. This is just like at home, Mrs. Taylor."

"Don't get too comfortable, Alphonso," Mrs. Taylor cautioned me with a wagging finger. "Explain yourself, baby. What are you going to have my little girl doing in that great big studio of yours?"

"I was hoping we could get to that, Mrs. Taylor," I said, as I reached into my jacket pocket for the slides I brought with me. "Here -this should give you some idea of what I've done so far-"

While Mrs. Taylor held my slides up to the lamplight in the parlor, I made eyes at Sheba over my cup of hot chocolate. Perhaps it is a sin to worship at the altar of the female body, and I must admit that those who accuse me of such idolatry would often find me guilty as charged. The robust bloom that youth gives to the human form is only a prelude to the story Life will write upon the subject as character and destiny interact to etch and chisel out a true likeness of the spirit. I can only admit that I travel the topology and the smooth contours of the human flesh with a great marvel and a rapture, such as might be experienced by those in the throes of religious ecstasy and the consecration of devotion. These hands wish to scan, to pluck and to probe the richness in the ripeness of the human weave and design. Before time leaves its own marks and impressions on the living sculpture of God which is every man and woman, let's note the first unfolding of the leaf and the flourishing of human efflorescence with a lasting tribute of eternal gratitude. Thank you, Lord, for the honeydew melons in the hug-a-mug and the juicy roast rump in the hump-a-bump! Thank you, dear God, for the glide in the thighs with the supersize and the real deal with the fine ankles and heels and the meal on wheels when Sheba shows her toes. Let's get some paper and some canvas on this award winning Mother of the Universe!

Sheba and I first met when we were security guards for Social Services at Seven Mile and Gratiot. The alarm system went on the fritz due to a computer glitch and I volunteered to do an all-nighter until the system was gotten back online. Sheba went off shift around four thirty in the afternoon and left with her book bag slung over one shoulder, looking as always as though she were poured into her uniform.

"Don't let the boguh man get you, Alphonso-" Sheba said, with a saucy toss of that fleecy ebony mane floating like cotton candy drift about her shoulders and the small of her back. "I'm headin' down to Shifty Twisty's to pardy hardy tonight, Alphonso. I'll bring you back a nightcap after hours maybe, huh?"

"I'll be here, baby," I said, running my nightstick over my shoulder.

"Oh, I knows you will," She said with a light lilting laugh, "an' you can stop grabbin' my behind with yo' eyes!"

"What? You ain't showin' me nothin' I ain't seen before."

"Never can tell about that, honey. You be good and take care of the house while sweet mama's gone and you just might get to see all this and heaven too."

"I'll be here, Sheba. I'm not goin' no place."

Sheba blew me a kiss as she teased those heartbreaking proportions through the glass doors and with a sensuous, earthy stride lit up the parking lot.

Now that she was gone, I had all two floors of the Social Services office to myself. I paced across the rust gold wall to wall carpeting, swiping my nightstick through the air. I went over to the elevator next to the lectern, where everybody signed when they first came into the building. I pressed the button in the panel next to elevator and took it to the second floor. Just as I thought, the lights were still on upstairs.

While I surveyed the tables and the chairs and the office cubicles ranked along both walls to my left and right, along with the file cabinets and the Xerox machines, I couldn't help thinking that this was how I wanted my studio to be one day. All this mother loving space to bend to the hand of the Gentle Man!

I came up here to get my mind off the way Sheba filled it with her voluptuous form. I even brought a book with me to show myself approved of the Lord. But I couldn't study about Degas and Da Vinci in a joint like this. My imagination got the best of me. All I could see was where I would set up my stands and my easels. Where I would rack my paints and stretch my canvases for the master works to come. Store the moist, wet clay over there by the water cooler where I 'll put a clay table for making busts and figurines. Love that lowered ceiling and the indirect lighting from the florescent bulbs. I'll put the posing platform for the models in the center and get some spotlights for partial and full silhouettes. The models can use that room to disrobe before we get down to business.

That was just the beginning of my vision as I calculated which walls I would use to post my sketches and drawings. Yeah man, it was only a matter of time before all that I eagerly imagined passed through the veil from hazy dream to living reality! I started to read, but I was just too excited for that. I took a poster off the wall and began to sketch how the room would look all decked out with everything I would need to begin Gentle Enterprises.

Every hour on the hour I would patrol the building after checking the clock on the wall. I did eventually get in some reading for a class, thoughts of Sheba floating in between passages about Whistler and Rodin. Around two in the morning, I thought I heard somebody thumping on the glass doors out front and went down to see.

There was Sheba with all her physical charms and comely glory stuffed into a maroon party dress. She gestured for me to unlock the door, and spilled in all wagging wiggles and giggling plump pulchritude, holding a thermos and gesturing with her hands like she was raising the roof. I knew she was glad to see me when she wrapped arms around me in a big-hearted high.

"You miss me, honey?" Sheba grinned as she ran her finger around my ear.

"Couldn't get my mind off you, Sheba,"

"I missed you too, Alphonso. I brought you back some punch."

"What happened, Sheba? I would have thought dudes would have been breakin' legs and necks to take you home."

"That was about the size of it." Sheba sauntered around me so that I could drink her in with my eyes. "Them triflin' brothers ain't about nothing far as I'm concerned. Those fools made me feel like a lump of honey in a nest of flies, the way they hit on me all night to dance with them. Besides, I promised you a nightcap, sugar."

Sheba leaned a hip against one of the conference tables. She eyed me playfully while she shook and swished the contents of her thermos.

"Let's go upstairs, baby," I said with genuine affection as I placed my arm around those gorgeous, burnished, strapless shoulders, "I'll get us some cups for that punch and we'll have us a toast to Social Security."

I shepherded Sheba carefully over to the elevator and pressed the button.

"You need to quit, Alphonso, always makin' with the funny-"

Sheba glanced at me over her shoulder while she cradled her thermos against those gold medal breasts. She kicked and scuffed at the carpet in her open-toed shoes and caught me looking at her well turned calf as plump and fine as the fat end of a baseball bat. She made a little chuckle to herself with bowed head.

"We could have this in one of those stalls over there." Sheba declared with a toss of a head full of long, tapering braids. "Whatchu takin' me upstairs fo' anyway, Alphonso?"

"I just want to show you something, baby -square business. I drew up this sketch and-"

"That sound just like you, boy," Sheba slapped me on the shoulder, "always tryin' to draw up a plan about something!"

We didn't have that long to wait before the elevator went ding and the doors slid back.

"After you, my dark and lovely," I bowed and with a sweep of my arm ushered Sheba into the cage of the elevator, "I welcome you to my studio-"

"Yeah, right, nigguh-you wish-"

We stood together in the cage as it lifted us up, and Sheba licked her lips and shook her punch in the thermos. She gave me a nervous, quick look up into my eyes like she was expecting something. That was when I knew it was time to lay one on her. I took the thermos out of her hands and turned her around as I pressed my lips firm against her own without any tongue. I cupped a huge tear drop of a breast in the palm of my hand and squeezed until the nipple swelled and popped erect. We surged and plunged into a deep breath together and when I felt her buckle at the knees, I swept her up into my arms and swung her out of the elevator just as the doors slid open and we came up for air.

"Uhnh! That was juicy, Daddy. Can I have some more?" Sheba breathed into my chest as she tugged at the collar on my uniform.

"Oh yeah, baby, all you want. There's a whole lot more where that came from too!"

"Oooo-that's what I want to hear-" Sheba fluttered her legs in the air while I held her in my arms and then languorously kicked off her shoes. "Send me, baby, send me! Ship me off air mail or special express, any way you can-but send me, please-please, send me!"

"Hush up, woman, so you can git yo' whoppin'!" I threw Sheba over my shoulder and gave her a smart slap on the rump. "I'll send you, moma, I'll send you alright-" I grabbed her by the thighs and made like I was about to toss her, When she yelped, I set her gently back upon her stocking feet. "Yeah, I'll send you. Every which way but loose!"

"Oooo-Daddy!" Sheba squeezed my hands until I felt the thrill go through her fingers into mine. "Ooo-baby-ooooo, you know what I like!"

"Hush up, woman! You heard me! Let me get a good look at you before I pop that coochie into Kingdom Come!"

Sheba jumped into my arms and kissed me deeply. That was when the warm, wet, heart pounding and red rising haze came out of my stomach and climbed into my heart before pooling in my throat. We baptized each other in plenty of tongue galore this time; enough to make a blind man weep in the Motor City. While she hugged me about the waist with her thighs, I made the room revolve around her like a spinning top. When I was sure her head was swimming, I turned up the thermostat on the sternness and thrust her back away from me. Never would I pass this way again and I knew I would have to make the most of every moment.

"Wha-" Sheba said in surprise, catching her breath as those tremendous melons shuddered in earthshaking tremors. "What you want me to do, baby?"

Sheba reached for me again, but I held her at arms length, softly kissing her fingertips. She was all expectation and I knew now was the time to set up the ground rules and lay down the law. While Sheba licked her lips in anticipation, I slowly paced her about by her fingertips. I studied the way the light hit her at every angle. I made a mental note on how the spidery fingers of bold shadows caressed the geometric forms of that divine body in motion.

"Oooo, come on, Alphonso!" Sheba murmured, rubbing my fingers against the full set of those sumptuous lips. "Do me, baby, do me!"

"You gon' do everything I say and not talk back?"

"Everything, honey, anything! Just let me show you-"

Sheba went down on her knees and embraced me around the legs. I could feel her tears wet against the crease in my pants.

The passion in that simple gesture should have told me something. I think looking down into the beauty of Sheba's cherubic upraised face must have shorted my antenna on all frequencies at the time. I should have got down on my knees and rocked her with tender loving in my arms. I just didn't fully comprehend the way she was setting out all her cards. Sometimes when the moment erupts into its blossoming, you cannot possibly capture all the petals that spill out from the flower.

"These are my conditions, baby-"

"Yes, Alphonso, oh yes, baby-"

"Listen up now! I give you all the signals and call all the plays. Nothin' open to negotiation. You got it?"

"Oh baby, you got it," Sheba's teary eyes glint up at me with loving adoration.

"Now get up off yo' knees and gimme me those lips!"

Sheba hopped back onto her feet and stood up on my toes. While we laced fingers and then slowly nibbled our return into slow, wet, deep kisses, I felt Sheba's lips flutter against mine as her dress rode up her hips.

"Hold tight, baby," I took Sheba by the hand and over to one of the luncheon tables where I snatched a huge table cloth into the air and twirled Sheba inside of it until she was a living sculpture inside masses of diaper folds, spiral folds, zigzag folds, pipe folds, half-lock folds, inert and drop folds.

"Come over here, woman," I marched Sheba over to a full-length mirror against one wall and then stepped back to size her up. "Now. I want you to get buck naked for me, Sheba."

Sheba was careful to hold the generous folds of the giant sheet she was wrapped inside of always at her neck. She shimmied out of her party dress and tossed it into the air where it chased its own shadow until it floated to rest on the cream carpet. Next came her stockings, which she sling-shotted my way one by one. Finally, those huge cotton domes of her bra seemed to sail away in super slow motion and landed at my feet. I solemnly placed these sacred objects upon a nearby conference table and deftly caught her panties, spinning towards me like a freshly snapped green dandelion.

"What you want me to do now, Alphonso?" Sheba asked me with demure amusement.

"Stand by, baby, stand by, I gotta make sure I set this up right!" I told her, as I quickly slid two desk tables on either side of the mirror and aimed their lamplights before clicking them on. "Now! That's better!"

I took a corner of Sheba's body turban in my hand and paced away slowly. I observed with scrupulous note how as I unraveled and unwrapped this ebony assemblage of spheres, cubes and cylinders she was just as rapidly rewrapped in the spiral arms of light and shadow exuding from the lamp lights and bouncing upon the full-length mirror behind her to frame her head in a flaring halo. Sheba emerged from her shroud in a slow, sensuous spin, a Nubian Queen recently released and set free from the royal cocoon of silky afterlife. She lightly skipped and capered in such an airy manner, her toes barely touching the cloth wreathed about her feet in so profuse a collection of inert waves and slashes of white folds, that for a moment, she rose and soared above the pranking shadow that loomed against the opposite wall and until now, seemed larger than her life. Sheba paced herself beyond the idea of the Mandingo woman on the auction block. and the concept of nudity as a badge of slavery for conquered peoples. She was the royal blood of Mother Africa, the sacred dust of the earth scooped up by the hand of God and formed together with the rib of the first man.

"Just a moment," I quickly tore my uniform off and tossed it away, "-stay there until I get over to you, Sheba-"

When I was completely undressed, I went over to one of the lights and adjusted it to make even larger shadows. After that, I went over to Sheba and reached for her hand. I passed my own hands over all her body, measuring and examining and testing the tenderness and the tautness of sinew and muscle tone, dipping her head and wonderfully formed limbs deep into the inky black shadows I had made and back out again. I revolved us into a slow eclipse and just as slowly out again as gradually as the phases of the moon.

"Alphonso," Sheba glanced at me and our shadow clad figures in the full-length mirror. "I don't mean for you to worship me. Just groove with me, honey, groove me,"

The lady was right on the button this time. I told you before that some times real life looks so good you wish you could put it into a painting or a sculpture that would live forever, or at least a glossy full-color magazine. Just as sometimes you will see something in a glossy full-color magazine or a painting and wonder to yourself whether or not you have ever seen such in real life. Now I was seeing through Sheba the 'you can't touch this' of real life and at the same time the shimmering splendors of the sights that inspire the hand of the master artist.

"Alphonso!" Sheba caught her breath and shrank from me, reaching down to scoop away the gathered cloth at her feet before quickly stepping back to be swallowed up into the darkness. "Did you hear that? Do you hear that now -that thumping downstairs? Somebody's tryin' to get in here!"

"You stay here, baby, I'll go see -" I said, as I grabbed at my uniform heaped on the carpet.

"Hurry Alphonso," I heard Sheba's whisper reach out of the darkness at me, "can't you hear it? There! I think it's getting louder!"

"Oooo-Alphonso! This here girl ain't got no clothes on!" Mrs. Taylor exclaimed as she held one of my slides up to the light. "I hope you not thinking Sheba is going to have any part in something like this!"

I nearly spilt my hot chocolate in my lap when Mrs. Taylor said that.

"Uh-naw, not really, Mrs. Taylor," I moved out of my sofa chair and peered over her shoulder. "Oh! That's something else all together. Naw, I was thinking really of doing something a little Lichtenstein with Sheba, or maybe a portrait or a landscape-"

"What did you just say, boy?" Mrs. Taylor craned her neck away from my slide, "You say you wanna do a 'little lickin'' with Sheba? Did I just hear you right, boy?"

"No, Mrs. Taylor, no, that's Roy Lichtenstein! I was saying I wanted to do something sort of a little in his style. He was a famous Pop Art painter. This big comic strip I drew in pastels is something like he would do." I reach for another slide off the lamp table and hold it up for her to see, "See what I'm sayin'? Don't you think Sheba would make a great super heroine?"

Mrs. Taylor drew back like she smelt my breath or something.

"That there is some stuff, Alphonso," Mrs. Taylor narrowed an eye at me, "I'm talkin' bout this slide right here. Did you really have some woman posin' for you butt naked holding," She held the slide up to closer scrutiny, "-what is this? This a bow and arrow she's holdin' up here?"

"Yeah, Mrs. Taylor, but that was just a study-"

"Lord-a-mercy! Ump-ump-ump! Just what on earth was you studying, Alphonso?"

"You know, Mrs. Taylor-"

"No, I don't know! I want you to tell me, Alphonso,"

Sheba just sips her hot chocolate and seems to enjoy watching me squirm in front of her mother.

"It's like this, Mrs. Taylor, you have to understand the human body in order to draw and to paint it. This was just a study in Anatomy, that's all-"

"Oh, so you drew this out of some kind of textbook, did you?"

"Nooo, I can't really say that, Mrs. Taylor,"

"What can you say about this, Alphonso? This is some real live person you got down on one knee with a bow and arrow in her hands?" Mrs. Taylor looks over at Sheba with an incredulous expression, but Sheba is mum for now, stirring up her hot chocolate. "Who is this little girl you got with her legs all open and carryin' on like that?"

That's pretty much what Smiley said when he finally threw down that straight flush he was broadcasting all over Times Square he was holding.

"Pie-yah! Time for 'the last to be first', my good gentlemen. Y'all be cool, 'cause your brother Smiley gon' pass the hat now,"

"Hey, what verse is that, Smiley, my man?" Baldy asked as he wiped all the sweat from the sides of his face. "Ain't you gonna give us book, chapter and verse?"

"You can look it up," Smiley raked the coins in with an indignant expression, "ain't nothing keepin' any of you from diggin' a little gold out of the Good Book. Hey Alphonso-"

"I hear you, Smiley-" I said, reaching out to reshuffle the cards.

"Who is this little heifer you got on this card here," Smiley holds up the back of one of the cards between his fingers. "lookin' all ferocious and stuff? She look a little like that young babe that played 'Xena: The Warrior Princess'. You know who I'm talkin' bout?"

"Yeah, Lucy Lawless." I said as I riffle the cards for the next hand.

"Yeah, that's the one!" Smiley snaps his fingers with a flash of recollection.

"So?" Danny shrugged, as he glanced at his watch and took his hand. "What about her?"

"Nothin'." Smiley starts to mull over his hand. "'Cept don't you think this girl kinda favor her some?"

"How you run into her, Alphonso?" Dougie asked, fanning out his cards and strumming his toothpick in his mouth. "Who she be? I don't ever remember seeing her around Playa's Palace any askin' for you."

"We were in a class together in college. She would model for me from time to time."

Baldy took a look at the back of one of his cards and then squinted. He looked up at the far wall and pointed a finger.

"That's her up there in that drawing you got on the wall! Ain't it, Alphonso?" Baldy did a double take between the back of the playing card and the wall drawing. "Sho' is! The naked bitch lookin' all proud with the bow and arrow in her hands."

Rebecca Colleen Brooks. Smiley was right. The defiant glare that often seemed fixed upon her face, even in repose, did make her seem like some kind of Warrior Princess. I can still see how she was blushing when I first told her so.

"Xena? Oh, I don't know about that-"

We were studying the Life and Times of Frank Lloyd Wright in a room full of twenty-five to thirty students. When I laid eyes upon her casually one day and Zeus' thunderbolt struck, I knew I would never rest until she brought her heroic stature into my studio. I hid my sketchpad in my textbook and made quick gesture drawings of her in between my notes on 'Fallingwater' and the Guggenheim Museum. When I finally worked up the nerve to approach her, she was more than willing to model for me.

"I could be dying of thirst in Death Valley, Alphonso," Rebecca began, "my next breath dependent upon whether or not you would give me so much as a thimble full of water from your canteen, and I will guarantee you could not get so much as a head cock or a change of expression from me as a model-"

"That's cool, Rebecca, but hey, take a look at these and tell me what you think."

"- and don't get any ideas that you can sweet talk me into taking my clothes off for you in any way or for any reason. The world could be coming to an end and you would still be out of luck in that department. So don't bring it up, because it's not going to happen."

Rebecca and I walked across the dusty lawn between buildings. The Sun broke through the gray clouds massing overhead and we surveyed our surroundings. Rebecca held my sketchpad against herself, tossing her waist-length hair from her frowning face across her square, broad shoulders. "Jimminy! Where is everybody?" Rebecca asked, as she held her hand up to shield her face from the Sun.

Months earlier, the paved walkways between buildings were clogged, straining and some times even bottlenecked with students scurrying to classes. Spaces designated for entertainment would be jammed to overflowing for young people and young adults such as ourselves, when the musicians came to croon and groove to crowds swaying with the Wave. Now, even those with the tattoos and pierced noses and eyebrows were getting scarce. The absence of bodies in the hot mix of the hustle and the bustle made the blue and green scenery yawn open with the scratchy lament of the simmer in the wind. There were now so few to note that only the pigeons seemed willing to attend to the heat vapors passing between spring and summer.

"Whatchu think happened to everybody?" I scoffed at Rebecca. "It's winnowing down to the hard core, baby. The grind of the Academy is separating the wheat from the chaff, sister."

Rebecca looked askance, down her nose at me from head to toe with mock distaste.

"I guess that means you'll be blowing in the wind soon, huh, bro?"

"Come here, you-"

I grabbed Rebecca by the shoulder and threw my arms around her. I cannot tell you what a joy it is to wrap a rear bear hug around a big-boned, big-breasted woman. My pleasure was short-lived however, as Rebecca shrugged me off her shoulders with a hearty chuckle. She playfully put her head down in some kind of practiced maneuver and gently stomped my instep while digging her elbow into my ribs. She stepped back into a wide-legged karate stance, her fists held low in a guard position. Rebecca looked like something out of a textbook, and I could tell by the way her cheeks glowed with a rising pink turning red, that this position was something rehearsed by her at least a thousand times.

"Wha-you want a piece of me, Alphonso?" Rebecca demanded, her blue-gray eyes narrowing into a steely glare. "Whataya think, Mister Gentle? Do I look like I'm finally ready to earn my Black Belt?"

Rebecca was always going for her Black Belt. At least it seemed that way to the rest of us. She was really crestfallen the last three times she tested and didn't make the grade. Earning the coveted Black Belt was something of a point of honor with her, as one of her brothers was a 1st-dan expert in Tae Kwon Do and the other a 3rd-dan in Shotokan karate. Besides that, she had an uncle who was a Defensive Tactics Instructor for the Police department and her grandfather on her mother's side taught Tai Chi Chuan at a community college in Rochester. Needless to say, this young lady was well connected when it came to the Martial Arts.

The hardest thing in the world was to get her to talk about her training, or to get her to the point where she would show some of her moves. Rebecca normally played it nondescript when it came to hanging out with her girlfriends, and except for that intense Brooke Shields scowl that she fronted when being hit upon by eager overachievers, was just like any of the other pretty coeds on campus. The only difference being she rarely smiled until you mentioned Chuck Norris and Michelle Yeoh. The first time I spotted her she was sitting in the campus library, thumbing through a martial arts magazine that featured Bruce Lee's daughter on the cover. Unlike many of the young ladies whose eye the Gentle Man has caught, the first time Rebecca and I locked gazes I got the distinct impression she wanted to know who I thought I was to be looking at her like that.

There was a recognizable quality about Rebecca that made you recall and meditate about the cave women of Frank Frazetta's art, and the warrior women of Boris Vallejo's book covers. I remember when I used to rummage around for exciting and adventuresome nudes to look at while browsing the book shelves of Paperback Unlimited. Sooner or later, I would inevitably find myself gravitating over to the Fantasy calendars, where I would busily flip to familiar images of the female nude barbarian.

Whether in repose on an animal skin after a glorious battle, her trusty broadsword hung faithfully inside its scabbard from a spike embedded in the cave wall behind her, or found by slavers to be frolicking in the high grass with jaguars and peacocks, or yet again languidly reclining on the sloping verdant bank of a stream shimmering with sunlight, the female barbarian, hair spilling about her shoulders and down her back, as naked to the sacred world as Eve herself, was a favorite subject of mine. The mysterious world of sword and sorcery, where robust women with tremendous physiques became the sport and object of Emperors and Kings vying in fierce combat for trophy wives, was a constant source of seductive wonder to me. Here was a grim world that seemed to be crafted by bloody conquest, where the only thing worth having was whatever could be gained by the victory of arms. The waxing of passions found their release in the struggle for force and then still greater force. The sword in this world was more to be revered for battering down doors than any imagined master key to the universe. Whatever survived in this world owed its continued existence to its own pugnacity, hence the dot ray of pride glinting in the eye of the female barbarian. There were those in the land who were prepared to spill blood to possess her. She was finally the fairest object of love to be coveted in the clash of cultures and the war of worlds. The value she held in men's eyes was never in question or doubt. The royals themselves were willing to kill or be killed to win her comely and ravishing presence.

That brings us back to Rebecca Brooks and the drawings she dutifully thumbed through in the library when she sat down with my sketchpad. She would stop every now and then when one of my drawings seemed to particularly capture her essence. There was a hint of fascination at one point when she came to a sketch of her seated and studying one of Frank Lloyd Wright's earliest blueprints. She gave herself away with a glance of furtive admiration before adopting her usual warrior princess scowl.

"When did you do this one, Alphonso?" Rebecca said softly, even though her arms were folded across her chest. "I think this one's maybe the best. I-I mean, it's all right. I could see it as a painting one day."

"That's what I'm talkin' about. I would love to have you pose with some of your martial arts equipment and maybe a bow and arrow one of these days."

"Bow and arrow? Oh, I don't know about all that, Alphonso. What's that stuff all about, anyway? Where did that come from?"

"Greek Mythology, baby. Don't you remember Artemis, Goddess of the Hunt? She always went around with a bow and a quiver of arrows."

"I don't see what that has to do with me."

"We in a library, mama! Let's look it up and enlighten ourselves."

I got up quickly and went over and plucked an 'A' volume of the encyclopedia out of the reference section. I came back to our table and handed it to Rebecca.

"Here. It's A-R-T-E-M-I-S. Look it up."

"Hmnnn, 'the goddess of childbirth, hunting and the moon'," Rebecca puckered her brow and frowned, "Oh! She was a virgin goddess, too. I think I better write that down."

"Here's a pen for you, baby-"

"Ho! This hunter, Ach-Ach-Ach-I can't pronouce his name-"

"Let me see," I take the book from her hands, "-yeah, that's Actaeon. Say, 'Ak-Tee-uhn' for me-"

"Ak-Tee-uhn. Ak-Teeeee-uhn. Ac-tae-on. Actaeon. Is that right, Alphonso?"

"There you go. That's perfect, baby." I hand her back the book.

"Thanks Alphonso. Yeah, this hunter Ac-tae-on was a worshiper of Artemis evidently. At least that's what it says here. Says he accidentally caught her bathing naked one day and she turned him into a stag. Way to go, girl! Aw, poor guy. After that, he ended up devoured by his own dogs. Bummer!"

Rebecca leaned closer to the book to glean every word for content.

"Let that be a lesson to you, Mister Alphonso Gentle, and a word to the wise to boot for you." Rebecca glanced my way and let out a sigh of exasperation. "Alphonso! Are you sketching me again?" She reached out and caught my pencil hand. "That's enough. Stop. Alphonsooo-"

We playfully pulled at each other's hand and I slapped hers away.

"Ow!" She gave me a punch in the shoulder. "There! That'll teach you." We were starting to get a little loud and settled down when the library aide looked our way. "What I cannot begin to understand,"

Rebecca whispered to me, "is why you would want to turn me into an object of worship. What purpose would it serve for you to deify me?"

"You can celebrate the beauty of a person, place or thing without it being deification, my little honey mama," I swept her dark brunette hair carefully back over her shoulders, "I'm just as proud of what God gave you as you are."

"I bet you are." Rebecca said with a snort. "I think it's still pretty superficial to be in love with the way a person looks. There's something base and shallow about that kind of love."

"That's because you don't see you the way I see you." I tapped her fingertips with my own. "How does it hurt you, my Ladyhawke, to have me bring out your best qualities and frame it all in an artistic presentation?"

"You wouldn't feel that way were I sporting a wart on my chin; and fifty pounds under or overweight."

"When you model for me, Rebecca, I'll make a believer out of you. You come to visit me in my studio and I'll make you see that what really turns me on is the force of your character and the uniqueness of your personality."

Rebecca snatched her hand away from me with a snarl.

"Oh, give it a rest, Alphonso! We've already established that's not going to happen. My girlfriends told me to watch out for all the malarkey you would be dishing out to get into my pants!"

I patted Rebecca on the back with a soothing chuckle.

"How have I not been straight with you, Rebecca? I have freely admitted that I find your beauty fascinates me and stimulates in me something more than the glimmer of sexual arousal."

"Oh really?" Rebecca replies with frosty wariness.

"Really. I admit I have a weakness for good-looking women. That's why I am always looking for women who can take me beyond the erotic and into the aesthetic. I am always grateful to the women who can take me one step beyond my admiration for them and stimulate in me a valid creative impulse that improves me as I honor them."

"You sound like you want to be saved from your own lust, Alphonso," Rebecca scoffed as her voice lowered into a whisper.

"Why shouldn't I worship the one who delivers me from that and empowers me to transform my passion into tangible, valid works of Art?"

Rebecca thoughtfully regarded me for a moment, and for an instant there flashed in those gray-blue eyes the fugitive escape of a spark of hope and belief as her flushed lips parted. She was searching my expression and scanning my face the way women do when they are checking to see whether or not you are for real. She started to say something, because women are great believers and inspirers of belief, as you are probably aware from your own experiences and observations. There are those like Rebecca with thick walls of resistance. You have to keep whacking at them until the walls come tumbling down, but once they do, the deluge of wholehearted belief can be simply overwhelming. That is the delight and reward of dealing with women who possess great personal reserves of composure and a strong natural passion such as Rebecca.

"You hit all the right notes, Alphonso." Rebecca lowered her head and shook it as though she were snapping out of a posthypnotic suggestion. "But I'm not buying it. You tell me that you are interested in my character and personality, but I really think all you are interested in is how my atoms and molecules are arranged at this moment in my youth."

Rebecca gave me that warrior's scowl again and then there goes that look! My warrior princess gives herself away with that needy, hopeful expression that you play around with at your peril. I have seen this expression on the face of a homeless person when they finally come to spy someone through a restaurant window, mightily enjoying a feast with a circle of friends and the laughter rings and rolls and resounds again and again around the dinner table. However, when a women reveals such a feeling, it is a revelation of almost confidential intimacy. She unwraps herself and opens up that which is meant to be hidden. The unwise can trifle with this keepsake kept safe and find themselves swilling ground glass or turning over onto their sides to find a shiv up in their Adam's apple.

This is serious business.

"I was taking this philosophy class once, you know," Rebecca glances at me diffidently and then looks down into her thoughts again, "-and our teacher was discussing with us the spiritual principles of animism and the use of fetishes in primitive religions-"

"Oh, so now I'm being primitive," I place the fingers of my hand inside the collar of my warrior princess' neck and I feel her purr like a kitten even though she makes no audible sound. "Is that it, Rebecca?"

Rebecca casts wildly around to see who's looking at us and then quietly takes my hand in her own, She can tell that nobody in the library cares much what we do, and she lowers those hooded eyelids with the thick lashes and slowly rubs her fingertip over the nail of my index finger.

"You-you sound that way sometimes, Alphonso," She quickly glances at me to see whether or not I have taken offense, "- you know? The way you talk about putting my soul into clay and capturing my spirit in paint on canvas for the whole world to salute and take notice. I don't want to be revered like that, Alphonso. I don't want to be treated like that."

"Like what, baby?" I asked softly, as Rebecca placed her feet gently on top of mine.

"You know what I mean. I don't want you to make me into something that I'm not. I don't want to become some kind of object for the world to worship. There's no need for anyone to worship me and my body. Least of all you, and you should know better."

"I think you're taking this way too seriously, Rebecca-"

When Rebecca closed my mouth with her own, I found I couldn't finish my sentence. The taste of mint on her tongue send a feverish thrill through the both of us and Rebecca grasped my hand just as I reached to clutch her breast. She set my hand with care back on the table and put her own in my lap, smiling with the satisfaction of a triumphant siren.

The moment lingered, and then just as suddenly vanished into Rebecca's stony scowl and was closed up in her hope chest as a keepsake. She dutifully closed the encyclopedia volume we had been perusing and with a visible effort of will stood up.

"I'll tell you what, Alphonso," Rebecca declared, towering over me with that tough expression intermittently interrupted with that look of hope and need. "I get my Black Belt and we'll discuss it some more, okay?"

"I'll help you all I can, Rebecca."

"We'll see." Rebecca turned and headed for the bookshelf. "I'll put this back for you."

Smiley slammed down a full house and brought me out of my reverie. He collected high fives all around and raked in his pot again.

"Pie-yay! Proverbs, Chapter Sixteen Verse Thirty-two." Smiley nodded to himself smugly. "Read that and try and understand it, Dougie. You'll know what I think of all yo' trash talk when you go check that out in the Good Book."

"You is trippin', Smiley." Dougie surveyed his cards with exasperation. "I been to church enough to know God ain't studdin' yo' ass while you playing games of chance. Why would he bless you to have a full house anymore than he would bless me to have a straight flush? Naw, God ain't no ways in this little card game of ours and you can stop quoting the Bible now."

"Amen." Nathan Eddie said, inhaling on his cigarette by the window.

"Straight up, Alphonso," Dougie continues, "you gotta come down to Kronk and spar with me sometime. I could use another man with a long reach to practice counterpunchin' and work on my combinations for this bout I got comin' with the Marine."

"That Marine gon' kick yo' ass, Dougie," Smiley leers at him to catch his goat.

"I heard tell he broke a dude's jaw in one of his fights-" Danny idly comments to his cards.

"Yeah, an' y'all figger like niggers. I got somethin' for Mister Marine right here." Dougie raised up a clenched fist. "I got the goods on 'em." I just got to fine tune my strategy a little bit more to make sure I serve up his whoppin' right."

"I wouldn't do you no good, Dougie. Boxing really isn't my thing. Besides, Boxing is a dirty business far as I'm concerned." I said, as I looked over my cards.

"Just glorified cockfightin' for white folks is what it all boils down to in the end." Danny throws in his two cents, taking up my side.

"Aww, so y'all gon be a couple of pussies about this, huh? That's what I get for thinkin' y'all would have the balls to help a brother out."

"Oh yeah, that white boy got you spooked, don't he, Dougie?" Smiley said with a nod and a confidential smile.

"Ain't no thang," Dougie said evenly, "you a big enough fool to bet against me, that's gon be yo' problem."

There is a look in Dougie's eye that tells me that this time he might figure to need a little help before it is all over. Something about the way he hesitates before he throws down his card suggests this latest exercise in the art of pugilism is a long way from adding up to be a walk in the park. The shadows fold long across our card table, and there is an expression on Dougie's face I have not seen since we used to meet in the Library, and he would look up from his book for me to help him piece the syllables into words.

"What times are you up at Kronk now?" I shrug my shoulders as I stack my cards. "I may as well drop by and see you in action."

"Afternoons from two to six and on Saturdays from ten to four," Dougie blurted out as he tried to mask his eagerness, "just spar with me man; I need to practice with an opponent who has a long reach."

Danny looked at Dougie and then over to the window where Nathan Eddie was standing.

"Somebody give this fool a news flash." Danny sighed in exasperation. "Don't you know that the white man will fight to the death to defend your inalienable right to entertain him? We live in a system of things where the program to nullify us by the numbers has already been published and activated with success. It was called 'slavery' and variations upon the theme of good business practices. Tell me, man, what do you plan to do once your fight career is over and done with?"

"I don't know. I ain't thought that far ahead."

"Yeah, that sounds just like us, don't it?" Danny said, as he nudged Baldy with an elbow.

The way Dougie looked at Danny, you would have thought somebody had asked him to read the tax code out loud to us.

"What you signifyin'?"

"Whatchu think I'm signifyin'?" Danny bristled at Dougie. "You got to think beyond the White Man's game and make a game plan for yo'self."

"Oh, so now the White Man is just runnin' a number on me, that what you call yourself tryin' to tell me?" Dougie started to clench and unclench his fists.

"Look at the hand you been dealt with, my brother. When you see us on the six o'clock news it's either for a felony, a melody or an athletic specialty. When we contribute to World History, it ends up being HIS-story, we play society's game but it's always his game. You try an' break the rules and you end up a felonious fool, tossed to the sidelines onto the trash heap of our wonderful modern tricknological life."

"What you 'spect me to do about it without some ends, man?"

Dougie looked daggers at Danny and I could see it was time to chill the scene down.

"Look Dougie, Danny ain't tryin' to put you down or nothing-" Baldy wiped the sweat from his jowls and threw in his hand. "He was just givin' you the Front Page on what's been typical in the Black Experience. Danny just don't want you to become the White Man's rerun is all. He don't want to see you end up with a recall barcode stamped on yo' sorry ass is what he's talkin' 'bout."

"Amen." Danny threw down his hole card.

There is something I have a hard time getting my mind around. I remember duirng my days as a security guard how I passed this elderly Caucasian couple fishing with a coat hanger to unlock the door to their car. I came over to the curb to see whether or not I could be of any assistance. Somehow I was able to help ma and pa solve their little problem. They wanted to pay me something for helping them, but I refused. That's when the lady in the party said something to me that I will never forget.

"I'll tell you what. Where do you live? We'll come and visit you."

Back then I was doing everything I could to get out of the nest, and on my own away from my parents. I started and flinched at the idea that I might be called upon to cultivate a friendship with two more persons of the parental experience. At that time I just wasn't up to it. I was doing everything I could to make my great escape, so that I could paint beautiful naked babes until my last breath took me to the happy hunting grounds.

I remember how the old man looked down and took his wife by the arm as he walked her over to the passenger side of their car.

"Come on, dear," he said, as he gave me a parting glance of chagrin.

Every once and awhile I think of that old man and his wife. When I do, I always have this vague, intangible feeling of having failed in my responsibility to them as a fellow human being. I know that probably sounds odd just setting it out like that. The thing that stands out in my mind when I think of them is this palpable sense of having rejected them somehow. Can you get to that? Here were two old white people, a man and a woman, feeling rejected by a young black man! The strange thing is I don't think they felt rejected because they were white particularly. What came across to me was that they were feeling rejected by me because they were old! That's right. Those two were feeling lonely and old and useless. They didn't really need someone to open their car door for them. What they really needed was someone they could visit and who would visit them now that their sons and daughters, if they had any, were all grown up and out on their own.

Every now and then I will think upon that moment. How I could have been big enough to go beyond the troubles and the problems of my own little world, and how in the end I did not make the grade. I failed to make the grade, some might say, not because I wasn't black enough but because I wasn't human enough. I could not bring myself to enlarge my compassion to include two people who might have been feeling as lonely and isolated as I did at that moment in time.

I don't know what exactly made me think about that while I was playing cards with the rest of my crew.

All of the above may seem like the last gasp of humanism rearing its hoary head. I will admit I do agree with some of the tenets of the Humane Society, but I refuse to be accused of being a humanist. No, as far as I am concerned, we excuse too many of the horrors of Life on the grounds that we are only human. The humanly challenged have to rise above their disability and embrace an even higher truth.

"I'll tell you what, Dougie. I'll come and visit you." I heard my voice say from far away.

"Straight up, Alphonso. You mean tuh say you up to tradin' blows with the Dogg man in a good cause?"

That old couple should see me now. Let us say I ran into them this day. I'm all set up in my own crib and got my studio and everything. What would I say now to the old lady's request to come and visit me? Why, I do believe I would flash her my business card, and tell her she and her husband can stop by my studio anytime and have a tea with me.

Yes, that is exactly what I would say.

The trouble is, you have to fertilize the seed when there is real need. There are some things that cannot be done just at your own convenience. Cultivating a real friendship is one of them. I suppose I will never know how it would go in this day and age. That is, unless I run into Ma and Pa Kettle again.

"Hey Alphonso," Baldy snatches some thought off the upper shelf of his mind, "what you ever do about that snake once the lights went out in yo' honey's crib?"

I could not help but snicker. Daphne and her moms ran around and did the Charleston in the dark. Estelle raced around after them like she was trying to retrieve their bouncing heads. I did what I could to usher them out through the sliding doors that led to the cedar-boarded deck. The semicircular deck was fronting the spacious, sloping lawns which they called their backyard. I will have to admit the air was invigorating in the deep blue moonlight.

Daphne seemed rooted to the wall, gesturing to her trembling mouth with her hands. I went over and grasped her by the wrist. I was literally wrestling her through the glass doors.

"Come on, baby, come on-" I said as soothingly as I could, but I really needed a crowbar to pry her off the wall and out of the dining room.

"Where's Daddy, Alphonso?" Daphne cast distracted looks all about her in the darkness. "I want to be with Daddy-"

Mr. Wellington was making his way down to the fuse box and left me in charge of the women. I started to tell Daphne that her father was heading down to the basement when I heard a fresh scream come out of the night air from the deck. Mrs. Wellington and Estelle high-tailed it back through the sliding glass doors just as the lights came back on again.

"I saw some eyes glowin' in the dark out there by the barbeque grill!" Estelle panted as she put her hand to her breast bone. "Do somethin', young man, do somethin'-"

Daphne's shrill scream was accompanied instantly with an identical reaction from Mrs. Wellington as both women pointed to the ceiling.

"Aww-shit-" Estelle bolted for the kitchen again, quickly followed by Mrs. Wellington while Daphne grabbed at a poker from the fireplace on the way. "- let me get out of here-"

"Aaaaaa! Look! You see it, Alphonso? Do you see it?" Daphne pointed at the chandelier clasping at the golden poker. "There! There!"

I looked up and was startled for a moment. I will have to admit my heart lurched when I saw that the garter snake was placidly coiled about the branches of light in the chandelier. I am not easy to scare, but I must confess I was in a state of awe this time. I was half expecting our little visitor to malevolently leap out from his perch on the chandelier and fang us. Almost out of reflex, I closed my hand over Daphne's and led her around towards the kitchen. I reached again for the broom handle I was wielding, shaking the bristle end at the interloper who was hovering over our dinner table.

That was when the lights went out again to a chorus of renewed screaming.

Daphne darted behind me, brandishing her poker like a golden sliver of light in the pitch black. The lights in the dining room flickered weakly on again and I could feel Daphne's fingers tugging my sleeve at the elbow.

"There it is, Alphonso! Ugh! Get it away!"

"Shhhh, baby, shhhh-" I patted her hand on my elbow, "you get back in THE KITCHEN-"

I stabbed forcefully at the garter snake with the broom to knock it off the chandelier. The living necklace of grimy green and yellow bands sailed away and flattened against the far wall as it ricocheted onto the waxed floor and slithered under the clothed dinner table. That was when the lights went full on again, and Mr. Wellington came huffing and puffing up from the basement.

"Fiona? Daphne?" Mr. Wellington whirled around with an expectant expression. You would have thought he wanted to know how the Tigers were doing in the bottom of the ninth. "What happened? Is everybody all right? Estelle? Alphonso?"

"Yo! Sir! We're over here," I gestured Daphne around me with a nod, "Daphne! Go into the kitchen and see if you can't get me a garbage bag, okay?"

"But Alphonso-" Daphne objected as I flipped a corner of the table cloth up onto the top. "Aaa! Alphonso!" Daphne stamped her feet. "Don't do that! What are you doing?"

"Shhh, baby, go 'head on now. Get me a garbage bag out of the kitchen. Go on now," Daphne reluctantly moved off towards the kitchen as I waved her away.

"What have we got here, Alphonso?" Mr. Wellington said, as he came over with his own poker to hand. "Our little friend still on the premises?"

"Yes sir, I think he's underneath this table somewhere," I grabbed another corner of the table cloth and snatched it up. "-there he is! Around that table leg-"

"Here, Alphonso, here!" Daphne came back to our side, rattling and snapping the black garbage bag open. "Get it! Get it! Please!"

Mr. Wellington barreled stoutly over, the lights from the chandelier bouncing highlights off his pink balding head. He took a stab at the snake as it jiggled and darted away from the table leg and back under the table. He cursed softly to himself and looked up at me to join him in taking up the hunt.

"Come on, young man, we've got to surround him," Mr. Wellington waddled over to the far end of the dining room table. "I'll chase him your way and you snare him in that garbage bag."

"Sounds like a plan. Daphne-see if you can't get your mother and Estelle out here to help."

"Alright, Alphonso. Daddy, are you going to be all right?"

"Yes, dear," Mr. Wellington bent down and peered, squinting beneath the table. "Go see about mother and Estelle- I think I see him over that way, young man-"

"Yeah, that's him! Drive him over by me-" I flapped open the garbage bag fluttering a big gaping black hole in the night breeze. "Yeah, that's it! Stab at him a little more, sir-"

The garter snake seemed slow and stolid until we tried to nab him, and then he would skitter and skip out of our clutches with the nimblest instinct for survival. We were nearly on our knees, crawling about on all fours when the business end of a poker struck just inches from my dodging fingers. The golden metal point of the poker nicked through the coarse skin of the snake, and scraped quickly over the floor in front of wiggling toes strapped into dancing shoes. I looked up the heels and around the contours of Daphne's shapely legs and into her towering reddened face, flaming with loathsome outrage.

"Uhn! I got him!" Daphne exclaimed with some relief. "Catch him, Alphonso! Don't let him get away!"

I caught the little monster in a net of black wrapping and snatched him up in the hood of the garbage bag. I danced away with it in jubilation and nearly waved our captured prize in little old Daphne's face, but thought the better of that. I pointed to the kitchen.

"Well done, Alphonso!" Mr. Wellington said, wiping the bare crown of his head with a handkerchief. "We got him, we did!" He rose from the floor with his hand against his side.

"I saw a big jar in the kitchen, Daphne. It's on the counter." I said, as I gestured her to go in that direction. "Go get it for me, please. Quick now -quick!"

"Okay, Alphonso. You don't have to yell," Daphne was back in an instant with the jar and Mrs. Wellington and Estelle in tow. "What are you going to do with it now?"

"Screw the lid off. That's it-" I said, as Mrs. Wellington and Estelle paced warily around me holding the swaying bag in one hand. "I'm gonna put him in this jar and take him with me."

"Ugh. Why would you want to do that, Alphonso?" Daphne held up her nose and turned down the corners of her mouth. "Just toss that ugly thing in the dumpster, I say."

"Naw, this is better." I poured our little slithery friend out of the black garbage bag and into his new home in the jar. "I'll put him in the back," I quickly took the lid from Daphne's hand and screwed it back on, "in the trunk of my car. That way I can sketch studies of him and you don't have to worry about him escaping out of the dumpster to get revenge or something like that."

"Man!" Estelle held her hands to her face as I held up the snake in the jar. "Lord hav' mercy! What you gon' do with that thang now? You better kill that snake, boy!"

"I'll be back," I chuckled as I cradled the jar under my arm, "let me take this to the car and you won't have any more trouble with this little guy. You wouldn't have a screwdriver handy by any chance, would you, Mr. Wellington?"

"Uhh!" Mrs. Wellington gave a sigh of relief. "I'm so glad you captured that nasty little monster, dear. Do we have any screwdrivers in the house, George?"

"Yeh, somewhere down in the basement, I suppose," Mr. Wellington irritably gestured in that direction, "but I'm not going back down there. I'll have Estelle turn on the light for you this time. You should find one on my tool bench, Alphonso."

Mr. Wellington wearily parked and landed his squat frame back at the dining table with heavy emphasis. Estelle patted her bushy gray Afro and started to collect our dishes. I followed Estelle back into the kitchen carrying a stack of dishes. When we deposited them in the sink, she turned on the light that led down into the basement.

"You be careful now," She warned me with a hint of suspicion in her face, 'what you need with a filthy ole snake is more than I can tell."

I found a good hammer and a slotted screwdriver and punched holes in the lid out on the deck. I was just about all finished up, when Mr. Wellington waddled out onto the deck with this something under his arm. He came over with his face in half silhouette under the backlight and held out a box to me, flipping the lid open.

"Cigars, young man," Mr. Wellington winked at me confidentially. "I believe this calls for a celebration. Now that the women are safely sequestered indoors, let us men enjoy a smoke out in the lively night air. What d'ya say, my good fellow?"

I proudly placed the jar like a trophy on the wooden two-by-four railing, and reached for me a stogie. Mr. Wellington clicked out his monogrammed lighter and we lit up, our ears keening to the sound of the crickets in the grass. We both regarded these nice, long, Cuban babies with a polite, satisfied admiration. After a few casual puffs, we lazily surveyed the deck, our eyes at last coming to rest on the barbeque grill next to the potted plants and deck chairs. We were aware as well of eyes next to the grill, glowing red and green in the darkness.

"What do you think it could be, Alphonso?" Mr. Wellington asked, jetting puffs of smoke out into the night air. "There are all manner of the wild out here, you know."

"Hard to say, Mr. Wellington," I said, inhaling on my cigar, "doggone! This here is one mighty fine cigar!"

"George, m'boy, George, please. We're past all the formalities at this point."

"Yeah, I guess you got a point there, Mister-George." I took another long drag on my cigar and considered for a moment. "Might be a rabbit over there, or maybe an opossum scrounging around for scraps of meat from the last cookout."

"Doubtful it would be an opossum, Alphonso." Mr. Wellington gazed off dreamily into the night sky, flicking ash from his cigar at the Big Dipper. "No, hear that thrashing around in the tree over there by the millstone fountain?"

I followed Mr. Wellington's cigar as he pointed beyond the hedges. Sure enough, I could see the leaves swaying towards the ground in a way that could not be accounted for by the wind. "That's an opossum, young man." Mr. Wellington nodded with certainty as he drew in on his cigar again. "I can't say who's looking out at us from behind the barbeque grill."

"Why don't we just enjoy our smoke and maybe he'll come out and say hello?"

"That sounds reasonable enough."

The silence of the nocturne filled the deck as we stopped talking.

Finally, after listening to and making note of all the intangible sounds that fill in the void between what you can and cannot see, Mr. Wellington cleared his throat and turned to regard me with narrowed eyes of discernment. He pointed at me with his cigar.

"The truth now, Alphonso. What are your intentions with regards to my daughter?"

Now I looked at Mr. Wellington's cigar in sober reflection and cleared my own throat.

"Man to man, huh?"

"That's right."

"Might as well face it, George, you have raised a beautiful daughter. I'm sure she can have her pick of any man she wants. I know I wouldn't mind crossing the color line for her." Mr. Wellington stiffened at this and the air around us became tense. "But I don't believe she's for me. Now don't get me wrong, there's many in the club who fantasize about getting into her pants, and I would be less than honest to say I am not a card carrying member." I chuckled and watched my last puff drift off into the moonlit night. "The truth is, I've spent too many hours drawing nudes out of art books and wandering around art museums seeking out the images of beautiful women painted on bare walls and hanging in gilded frames. I'm so much into that I tend to reduce nearly everything down to that common denominator. The trouble is, of course, that in the end nobody in their right mind wants to be equated with a painting on a bare wall or one that is hanging in a gilded frame. No, I understand where you're coming from, sir. You and your wife are making plans for some young man to become a member of your family and, Lord willing, help extend your family into the next generation by making you grandchildren. I know you don't see me as a prospective son-in-law and for once we're in complete agreement there." I breathe in deeply the invigorating aroma of this wonderful cigar and chuckle quietly to myself. "Besides all this is purely academic. The deal is already closed, isn't it, sir?"

Mr. Wellington looks at me as though there's a word written across my face that he can't quite understand, but he nods to himself that at least he understands the general idea in context. I see him nodding once again that that's good enough for him. The way a person does when they're trying to convince themselves of something they don't have all the facts for yet.

The only thing is sometimes the devil is in the details, as you will behold later.

When Mr. Wellington finally speaks again, his voice starts to come out in a hoarse whisper. He puts a hand to my shoulder before patting me on the back.

"Don't be so hard on yourself, Alphonso. Even while it's not in the cards for you to be a member of our family, we would be more than happy and honored to have you as a member of the wedding."

"That'll work. When do I get a wedding invitation?"

"Just leave your address with us, young man, we'll be sure to send you one."

Mr. Wellington slaps me on the back with a hearty laugh. I point out something interesting scurrying in front of us from behind the barbeque grill.

"What do you know, sir. A raccoon! That's what the ladies saw out here!"

"Now what do you make of that?" Mr. Wellington exclaimed with wonder.

"Yeah, can you get to that? Who was that masked man?"

We lean against the railing watching our raccoon friend make his way into the bushes and then up a nearby tree.

"Tell you what, Alphonso, why don't we go back inside and see how the girls are holding up after their traumatic experience, eh?"

"I can deal with that. I think I'll go help Estelle with the dishes if that's all right with you, sir." I said, as I carefully remove my garter-snake-in-a-jar off the railing.

"Certainly, young man, certainly. I'm just sorry I didn't bring my hunting rifle out here. I could have bagged you a coonskin cap." Mr. Wellington quips as he takes me by the arm and opens up the sliding door.

The women are inside washing and drying and stacking the dishes and want no parts of me when they see me bringing my jar into the kitchen.

"Alphonso, my dear!" Mrs. Wellington nearly leaps out of her skin. "Please don't bring that creature in here. I thought you were taking that dreadful thing out to your car."

"Mr. Wellington and me thought maybe we could get you to cook us up some French-fried snake meat!" I said with a cackle as I held the jar and its wiggling contents over my head. "What do you say to that, Estelle?"

"I say you bed not bring that nasty ole thing into my kitchen!"

"Yeah," Daphne glanced warily in my direction, "you know where you can go for your French-fired snake meat!"

Mr. Wellington shrugs and exchanges expressions of innocence with me as we hold our cigars at the ready.

"My Lord! What's gotten into them, Alphonso?" Mr. Wellington asks in all sweetness and light. "You would think some monster had been after them."

We looked at each other again and burst out in raucous laughter as we exited from the entrance of the kitchen.

"You've got to promise me you'll come back again sometime, Alphonso," Mr. Wellington placed a brawny arm about my shoulders as he ushered me out through the living room. "Next time I want you to tell me more about your family; your father and your mother and any siblings you may have."

"That can be arranged, sir," I said, as I spy Estelle replacing us at the entrance to the kitchen. "My brothers should be coming to see me soon and I know they appreciate good eats such as what you set out tonight."

I cradle our dinner guest in the jar against my stomach. Estelle starts to approach us since there's thumping at the front door we both can hear.

"Now who could that be this time uh night?" Estelle passes by us wiping out a coffee cup with a dish rag.

The thumping at the front door takes me back to the time I was hustling myself back into my guard uniform. I pressed the lighted red button on the elevator to go down and see who might be breaking into Social Services at this hour.

"Be careful, baby," I heard Sheba call after me in the darkness as I rode the elevator down. I paced quickly to the glass doors, gripping and twisting my baton in my hands. My mouth dropped open when I saw Danny banging and slamming at the shaking doors. The fury in his face made me think he was going off his nut.

"Danny!" I exclaimed mystified, as I reached for the keys he left me in my pocket. "What the holy hell are you doing bangin' on the door like that?"

"Man, unlock this door, fool! Who you got up in here wit you?"

"Why! Who wants to know?" I fumble over the keys until I get to the one that fits.

"Don't play with me, man. One of my boys said he saw you let a woman in here!"

"So what? Like you never have friends over when you pull all night guard duty-"

"What is wrong with you, nigger? Don't you know they got cameras in here? You 'bout to lose yo' job over some tail, fool!"

Danny shouldered his way through the door in gruff indignation. He looked around with an anxious distraction . You would have thought he was expecting a full floorshow of strippers to come traipsing out of the stalls for the caseworkers.

"Alright, where she at, Alphonso?"

"What you all up in my business for anyway, Danny?"

"Look man," Danny grabbed me by my collar, "I'm not here to play with yo' ass. You bedder tell me what I want to know and you bedder tell me right now!"

"Dog, man," I angrily snatch Danny's hand away from my collar. "Why don't you gon' with that stuff? Who you tryin' to be? Elliot Ness or somebody?"

"You got anybody down here with you?"

"Naw-"

"What about upstairs?"

"Well, that's a different story. I got a little lady in the penthouse I'm discussin' my plans with. What's business is it of yours?"

Danny gave an almost imperceptible sigh of relief. He turned and looked at me with dead level earnestness.

"You got that babe Sheba upstairs with you. Huh, man? That's right, ain't it?"

"Yeah, there might be something to that. What's it to you?"

Danny shakes his head like he's about to cuss me out.

"It's live down here, fool! All the cameras is on down on the first floor. The staff call they self savin' money, but the cameras upstairs come on around six in the morning."

"Shoot man, there's three or four hours to go before that."

"Man, you get Miss Comely up out uh this joint! Don't you know they can put yo' ass in jail for this? You supposed to be in here by yo'self!"

"Why you illin', man? She just stop by to bring me something and to talk."

"Come on, man, give that bitch her walkin' papers, before the Social Services folk find out how you up to no good."

"Who done told you so? Far as you know, Miss Taylor and I have been study partners for the evening."

Danny looks at me as though I just lied on a stack of Bibles.

"Study partners, huh? Okay, you be that way. I'm gon' let you stew in yo' own mess this time."

Danny turned to head for the door and I reached out to grab his arm.

"Naw, naw, loose me, now. Loose me!" Danny snarled, twisting out of my grasp.

"Danny, man," I started in cajoling him, "we gon' keep everything undercover -"

"Oh yeah, I want to see how you explain to the Social Services folks how you and your little partner in crime weren't trying to case the joint to rob it." Danny was holding on to the door and halfway out before he said, "- this time I'm gonna let yo' dick end you up where you was always headed anyway."

Before I could get in a word in self-defense, Danny was through the door and walking towards the alley that cut through the parking lot.

"Who was that, baby?" Sheba asked when I came out of the elevator.

"That was Danny," I said, my head bowed.

"Oh?" Sheba asked, as she looked over the sheet of paper that was in her hand. "What he want?"

"Nothing really," I shrugged as I looked up at her, "just watchin' my back like he always does."

"I thought you and him was tight." Sheba was sitting up on a long conference table, the white table cloth coiled around her nude ebony frame.

There was something about her statuesque figure, and her glowing complexion shining under the strategically placed desk lamps I positioned around her that dispelled all doubts for me. I was ready to gamble with the risks just to have an opportunity to capture such African beauty in at least a few sketches. I scurried over to the broom closet and pulled out a long roll of wrapping paper. I feverishly pulled a drawer out of a desk to grab me a fistful of markers and Sharpies.

"Alphonso, what you got this paper all marked up lookin' like the inside walls of some kind of box for, anyway?"

When Sheba looked up at me holding that sheet of paper in one hand and the table cloth just under that huge dark caramel buttermilk gum drop of a breast in the other, I did not need anymore advice from anybody about what I ought to be doing. Thank you very much for stopping by and please come again soon. The lighting was just right and the time was nigh to now tape my sheets of wrapping paper against the walls just as I rendered the scene in that sketch that Sheba was holding with such a naturally regal air. Now was the time to turn the second floor of Social Services into my studio of the future and as its resident artist of renown get busy!

"Alphonso-"

"Don't move, baby-" I eagerly tore huge sheets of wrapping paper from the roll I pinned to the carpet with my knees.

"Alphonso!"

"What I say! Keep yo' head cocked the way you had it, woman!"

"Alphonso! Why we always got to go through this, anyway?" Sheba pouted in a sulk, but an admonishing glance from me stifled all that. "Why you always gots to be drawin' me and all carryin' on like you tryin' to put me in some Art book or something? Why can't you just let your nature rise and let us groove in the sweet meat?"

"You just hold that body still while I cop that pose, lady."

"Alright, man," Sheba let out a sigh of exasperation. "Guess who I ran into at the party?"

"Who baby?"

I was only half-listening while I taped the final sheets of paper against the wall and started to uncap the Sharpies.

"Leonard Morris, that's who!" Sheba giggled and raised up her shoulders. "He was tryin' to get me drunk so he could talk that sweet mess to me. I knew the nigger was talkin' mess just so he could call room service for me, but my-oh-my, he was talkin' that mess sweet!"

"You moved, Sheba. I told you keep still. Go on, put your foot back like you had it."

"Yeah-yeah, man, I moved. So doggone what? I am flesh and blood, Alphonso! I'm not studyin' to be no statue like them other heifers you be toyin' with. Why you all the time got to turn me into a bunch of pictures before you can get down and graze yo' lady in the grass like respectable folk do?"

"All good things, baby, all good things-"

Estelle turned from the Wellington's doorway with a suspicious look on her face. She looked me up and down and made a clicking sound with her mouth.

"Somebody at the door say he wanna see Alphonso Gentle. That's you, right?"

"Yeah," I said, nodding at Mr. Wellington as I approached the open door.

"Well, why don't you see who it is, man," Estelle remarked with some impatience, "I got to go back and put those dishes up before it gets too late."

"Okay then," I motioned to Estelle and Mr. Wellington that I would be right back. "Lemme see who this is-" I set my snake jar on the nightstand by the door.

The short little guy in the dread locks kept motioning for me to step outside onto the concrete landing, so I slipped through the screen door and gave a little finger soul to Temperance Wilson, poet laureate of the Diamond Hut.

The Diamond Hut was a little club over there by Belle Isle where Elmo Washington ate catfish sandwiches and gave Poetry Slams to make his joint out to be high class. The Black Illuminati of Detroit would collect there during the wee times of the witching hour and pontificate and hold forth on all subjects animal, vegetable and mineral. The Temp Man was the newly elected High Priest of the Holy Order of Riffdom, and it was vested to him to track down all up and comers who would deign to take up the open mike.

"What it gon' be like, Alphonso?" Temperance put it to me with a deadpan demeanor. "I know you don't want me to get all in yo' jibs about the Slam tonight. You comin' through the set or what now?"

"Yeah man, you got my thumbprint on the dotted line, don't you? Just let me wrap up having dinner over my lady's house and I'll be down in the cut before you know it." There was heat and the expectation of something about to jump off in the summer night. "Hey, you wanna come inside for a minute and have a little dessert with us?"

Temperance gave me thumbs down on that idea.

"Naw, I'll get me a little love later. Right now, I gotta take care of this business." The hand flew out from Temperance and I knew he was gone. "Bring your little friend down to the Hut if she's got a rap in her, and bag that dessert for me, jack. Don't leave me hangin' Alphonso, and make it look like I hyped you for nothing."

"Solid."

"Peace out."

We wrapped our fingers around our palms and Temperance skipped and zigzagged his way down the Wellington's front porch. He made his way around the curb and to the other side of the lemon yellow Chevrolet Corvette Convertible with its black top. He was parked in front of my sky blue Eagle Vision. I saw a fine head crowned in Afro-curls and rimmed in lip gloss wave dayglo nails at me from the passenger seat. Temperance gunned up and was gone before I could spy who his little somethin'- somethin' might be.

"Who was that, Alphonso?" Daphne asked from over my shoulder.

"Huh?"

Daphne wrapped her arms about my shoulders as I sunk my hands deep into my pockets. Something in the tone of Daphne's voice made me think back to that time with Sheba. How I slid and refitted those panties up and around those Rodin thighs and buttocks in the wee hours of the morning. The glowing satisfaction that highlighted that grateful smile framed in that wide face with its proud, high cheekbones made the birds sing the night into the morning breeze. I hitched up those rich, creamy, molasses dark chocolate mulberry nipple wine vessels of mother's milk back behind the bulwarks of the bra that stored them with the loving touch of the supplicant.

We took turns redressing each other, and the love in Sheba's sparkling eyes told me that the good fight waged was now won. She was at this moment a newly christened soul in the Holy Church of God in Gentle. Sheba cast quick glances around the walls as she hastily shimmied her way back into her stockings and her gown.

"Jesus wept, Alphonso!" Sheba marveled like a child coming down the steps for the first time to see all the presents under the tree. "You drew all this about me? Where did you find time to do all this in the middle of the night?"

"We was makin' time, baby, we was makin' time."

"Damn, Alphonso," Sheba went up to one of the more than dozen drawings and touched it with her finger tips. "-this is some freaky stuff! I give you pussy and the next thing I know I'm in some kind of Art Gallery! This the freaky-deaky for sure! Doggone, even favor me some-"

"More than a little bit-"

"What you gon' do with all these pictures, Alphonso?" Sheba paced along the walls in a dazed wonder as she pulled her open-toed shoes back onto her feet. "This end up on the Internet, it's yo' ass, niggah!"

"Naw, Sheba, naw. These are just studies-"

"Studies for what, Alphonso? What you call yourself studyin'?"

"Studies for when I immortalize you on canvas, my lady. What you think?"

"Oh yeah? When that s'posed to happen?" Sheba reached for her thermos to pour us a little drink.

Now all I can think about is what Kazantzakis riffed about back in the day. Sheba leans against my drawings and I realize I still want more of her. She moves about this space on the second floor and continues by the grace of her very presence to turn it into my studio. How would that old wily Greek have put it? I captured Sheba's image in the hope of filling my soul with her flesh and my flesh with her soul. We have consumed each other and still some inner need of mine waxes yet towards some truer, more ultimate spiritual satiation. Every time she moves, even in the most casual way, she seems to sow the seeds of new urges and yearnings that the imagination seeks to reconcile in a shower of ever new images. Every time I answer the call of the wild I am left to ponder deeply one particular question anew. When will there ever come a time when the images will be enough?

"You got me trippin', baby," Sheba says as I sit next to her on the edge of a conference table. "There are times when I can't tell whether we're deep in Love or going off the deep end into Lust." Sheba thoughtfully sips the wine from her thermos. "Want some?"

"Yeah, I'll have me some more uh that-" I said, taking a sip and considering what she just said. "Why can't it be both, Sheba?"

"I don't know, baby, I don't know," Sheba gives me a searching look. "I just know that sometimes when you groove me, I feel like I'm the only woman in the world for you. Then I see all this and I don't know. I feel like Pinnochio or somebody."

"Pinnochio?"

"You know what I mean, Alphonso." Sheba slaps my knee. "There come times when I feel like you lovin' me to get to something else," She gestures around at all the drawings on the walls, "and this is it! Sometimes I feel like for you to love me is not enough. There's gotta be this or no dice."

"You is trippin', Sheba-"

"That what I told you, lover man. Whether it's Love or Lust between us, I don't know. I don't even know whether you can call this Art or some kind of porno trip you into just to make the sex so good you can't stand it. I don't know-"

"At least you thinkin' about it."

"That's what I'm tryin' to tell you, Alphonso. Sometimes the way you love me makes me think more than I feel. Shoot -man, might as well come right out and say it. You always making me think when we make love, Alphonso. Sometimes more than I want to, when you get right down to it. Sometimes more than either of us need to, I believe. All I'm sayin' is that I don't always want to make love just to reach a new thought about somethin'. Sometimes when I make love I don't want to think about nothing. I just want to feel, Alphonso." Sheba gives me that searching look again. "Do that make sense?"

"Yeah, I suppose so,"

"See? I don't go off like this with nobody else but you, Alphonso."

"What? You want me to tell you whether that's good or bad, Sheba?"

"Yeah, tell me somethin', lover man. Now that you done turned my pussy into an open book."

"I read you loud and clear, baby, but that don't necessarily mean I read between the lines this time." I neatly pin Sheba's flower back onto her dress. "Look woman, we better cover our tracks." I shift around for some things Sheba can take with her when she leaves here. "Dawn will be comin' in soon close on the heels of the night we just loved away. Help me take these sketches down and roll them up. I'll find some school books or something you can take with you."

"Schoolbooks?" Sheba looked around in disbelief , as she stood on a chair and up on her tiptoes to pull one of my largest sketches free from the wall. "What I need with schoolbooks?"

"Danny told me the cameras on the second floor turn on at seven a.m., Sheba," I head into one of the janitor's closets where a makeshift 'Lost and Found' has been setup for this floor. "You leave here with schoolbooks under your arms, people will think we been in here studyin' all night." I snatch up mathematics and social studies books and toss them onto the conference table.

"Here, take these with you, baby -"

"Ain't you somethin', Alphonso," Sheba steps down from the chair rolling wrapping paper up in her arms, "so you gon' make like we was study partners or something pullin' an all-nighter, huh?"

"Somethin' like that. What time you got now?"

"Just a little after six, yeah -" Sheba glances at her wrist and flashes the digital display, "so what you gonna do with all these drawings, Alphonso?"

"Here-" I dump the science and literature books into her arms with the rest. "- think you can take my sketches home with you and I can come over and get them later?"

I kiss Sheba full on the lips for added incentive.

"Man! I can't take this mess home with me! Here-" She thrusts the drawings into my hands and I place them carefully onto the table. "How am I supposed to explain to my moms all these drawings you done did of me buck naked?"

There was nothing I could really say to that. After all, working with live nude models in a sexually repressive society desperately attempting to broadcast to all the world its achievement of sexual liberation is hard enough these days. When you add to this the cultural legacy of the African American female, well, you could find yourself diving into a foggy bog of carnivorous octopi.

There are a number of very plausible reasons why any black woman might object to celebrating the Body Beautiful.

While white women can have painters liken them to Greek statuary of alabaster hue and Roman sculpture of chalky and marble tinged sheen, fit for the Acropolis and the Parthenon, the situation is not so adulatory for the African American woman. The sight of her naked form is more likely to harken one back to the photographs and anthropological studies of the National Geographic magazine to put it gently. While to put it more bluntly, nudity for a member of a conquered race is a badge of slavery, rather than an emblem of approbation for high-minded and clean living citizens of the Republic. The sight of a nude white woman, myself included, makes me think of the murals and the paintings in the great museums of the world. Whereas putting on public view and display the nude form of the black woman, myself excluded, causes many to flash back to the Slave Trader's Auction Block and the need of many white men to take a trip down to the slave quarters for belly warmers and a little of that old time miscegenation. Nowadays in our enlightened times the sight of a black lass au naturel rarely inspires a poet, a writer or a painter to adopt her as his muse and that's too bad , I suppose. More often she comes to the cattle call to play the role of black-hearted Sapphire, indomitable matriarch or madame of the night. She is enlisted with zeal as the woman of lusty humor and easy virtue, trafficking in easy favors for easy money, her comely form exuding the faint scent of prostitution at the behest of her pimp.

How it all came to this, I could not even tell you. All I know is it's a long way down from the Black Woman as the image of Mother of the Universe.

Now that I've laid this on you, there will be those among you who will rush to offer forth examples of how this is not actually true. How my observations are partisan and chauvinistic. Let them spill their beans and you will see for yourself. Just remember it's the exception that proves the rule in every case.

That brings me back to the mystery of the Queen of Sheba. I kiss her again full on the lips and hustle her over to the elevator so she can press the down button.

"You gon' walk me to my car?" Sheba asks with a glance of suspicion.

"Yeah baby, I'm a member of your Imperial Guard."

"Hmph. You can save that sweet talk for the next time you 'bout to get inside my drawers, Alphonso."

"All right then, m'lady. 'Flame Off ' until I see you again."

"Alphonso?" Sheba nuzzles the edges of the books she is clutching carefully with her chin as we descend in the elevator. "When I was kickin' it around with Leonard Morris, he mentioned somebody he said I ought to talk to whenever I got the chance. He said you would know who he was talkin' about."

"Who's that, baby?"

"Somebody go by the name of Soccer-tease. Who that? You know him?"

"Yeah, I know him. Samuel Socrates Turner." The elevator comes to rest on the first floor. "We'll talk about him later. But I don't want you mixing with Morris anymore. He's not the kind of company for a young lady such as yourself to be keeping."

I take Sheba by the elbow to escort her to the door, but she twists away at the last second.

"Nig-gah? Who you supposed to be? You ain't my daddy! Next thing, you'll be sending me to bed without any supper-"

"You would like that, wouldn't you-"

"I ain't no child, Alphonso-"

"Did I say you was?"

"I can handle myself, Alphonso. I talk to who I want to."

There are some who would have hauled off and bitch slapped some sense into her right then and there. Perhaps the Gentle Man was remiss in his duties at this particular time, but I really did not see the need to ruin a wonderful and productive evening with a dispute. I sealed our time together with one last kiss.

"O-kay. You be that way."

We said our goodbyes and I unlocked the door. I watched Sheba walk to her car loaded down with the books I gave her.

Smiley threw down his hand with childish glee. I finished rapping to Baldy about that snake I helped snatch up out of the Wellington's dining room.

"Pie-yay! Four-of-a-kind, my brothers, four-of-a-kind!" Smiley reached for a mint in the center of the table as he raked in his cash. "Let me see now, let me see-"

"Man!" Dougie sucked venom out of his toothpick with a resentful frown. "Shut up that mess! You ain't gotta quote no more scripture while we gamblin', Smiley."

"When the Good Book ever do you any harm, youngblood?" Smiley winced around with a pained expression. "You ask me, you could use all the scripture you can get-"

"Yeah? Well, I ain't askin' yo' sorry ass." Dougie gets that gunslinger's look on his face. "Play cards, Smiley, but stop tryin' to turn this game into a Sunday Service."

The buzzer to my studio blared out while Dougie was trying to get Smiley to punch his woof ticket.

"Somebody's comin' up." Nathan Eddie said matter-of-factly, but I saw his hand go inside his jacket just the same. "You wanna take a look, Alphonso?"

There was something in Nathan Eddie's voice that made it more like an order than a request. I got up with alert quickness and looked over Nathan Eddie's shoulder out the window.

"I don't see nobody."

"That's cause they just came inside."

"Who was it?"

"Two dudes. They was kinda on the large side, you know?"

Baldy twisted around from the table and tried to wave me back.

"Hey Alphonso! You holdin' all the cards and we waitin' for you to shuffle. Come on back over here!" Baldy wiped the sweat off his jowls with a handkerchief. "Besides, I want to know what you did with that snake you caught."

"Hold tight, Baldy, hold tight," I wave him off from the window, "We want to see who's on their way up here. I got that snake around here some place. I'll show him to you."

"YOU WHAT?" Danny threw down his hand in consternation. "Ain't that about a bitch?" Danny twists around again, looking at everyone around the table. "Somebody tell me I didn't just hear what I think I heard!"

Danny makes me smile inside, because I know what he's going to say next before he even opens his mouth. That's the way it is between best friends. Yeah, brother, I am thinking to myself. I got him in here and he's still alive, too. I even got a she-snake for the little sucker to see if I can mate me a few more. I'll show you where I'm keeping them in just a second.

Standing at the window with Nathan Eddie, I go back to that night I carried my little prize snake-in-the-jar out to my car. We all got together and threw in to help Estelle finish the dishes. I helped to stack them so she wouldn't be up all night. After that, I took my little friend out to the trunk of my car and stowed him. I could still hear the clack of Daphne's sandals as she came down the lighted walkway to where I was closing the lid of my trunk.

"Are you leaving now, Alphonso?" Daphne asked, as she caressed her bare shoulders in the summer evening breeze, her face framed in the yellowish-blue tinge of the moonlight.

"Yeah, I gotta give Temperance my riff at the Slam tonight."

"You should kill that snake, Alphonso." Daphne looked down at the ground and stamped her feet. "I poked him good in his side. Finish him off and put him out of his misery."

"I don't know. The way I see it, he was just in the wrong place at the wrong time. I know how that feels. I might just take him down to the vet and get him all healed up before I return him to the wild."

Even now, I can see clearly in my mind's eye the way Daphne's lips were parted and the way the strands of her hair were blown back in the night air, a mixture of moonbeam halo. She stopped herself as though she suddenly thought the better about what she was going to say to me. She chuckled, mocking at herself while she crossed her arms and looked down at her feet.

"So you're going to be in harmony with nature and 'talk to the animals', eh? Doctor Dolittle? Better that than follow the advice of some bloodthirsty paleface, eh?"

"You said it, girl, not me."

There was another uncomfortable silence as the wind whipped through my pants legs and Daphne's green gown.

"What did you and my father talk about, Alphonso?"

"Just things. We both agreed I was too much into physical beauty to be a serious contender for your affections."

"Is that right?"

"Yeah, that's about the size of it."

There was another uncomfortable silence, but I was ready to call it a night.

"Look, I'll call you tomorrow, okay?" I walk around to the drivers side of my car and open the door. "I'll let you know how the Poetry Slam went when I see you again."

"I've never attended a Poetry Slam before."

"Yeah?" I said, shrugging it away. "There's nothing to it, really. I'll try and bring you a tape tomorrow, okay?"

"Okay."

"Bye."

"Bye."

I got into the blue Eagle Vision and started up the car. Before a moment passed, I heard tapping against the passenger window. I looked up and there was Daphne, gesturing and pulling at the handle to the car door. I pressed back the button for the automatic lock and Daphne opened the door and swept herself in beside me.

"You forgot to kiss me good night, Alphonso."

There was such an earnest look on her face that I grabbed a hank of hair at the back of her neck and pulled her towards me. Daphne surged forward and mashed her lips against mine until the furnace heat in our hearts raged on full and a sparking flame spat between us. Daphne's hands pressed back against my chest and we both sat back against the cushioned upholstery.

"That's better, Alphonso," Daphne put her hand to her breast to catch her breath, "I sure would like to see what a Poetry Slam is all about."

I slipped the gear into 'D', and grabbed Daphne by the hand. We veered away from the curb and arrowed off into the sweltering night.

Danny came back from the door and I saw my brothers Willie and Earl behind him looming large. I turned from the window and nudged Nathan Eddie.

"Hey. Were those the two guys you saw comin' across the street?"

"Yeah," Nathan Eddie nodded with relief as he stubbed out his cigarette, "That's them."

"What's up, Alphonso?" Earl scratched a scraggly beard above his police windbreaker. "You got a little action goin' on up here, man?"

"Always, always," I traded soul handshakes with them, "'bout time you suckers showed up in the cut."

Willie looked around with a dour expression and nodded with grudging approval.

"Looks like you comin' up in the world, little brother."

"I don't know about that," I looked around as I gave Willie a hug, "all I know is at least I ain't sleepin' in no garage sufferin' for my Art the way Bobbie is doing."

"Hey, don't be dissin' Bobbie," Willie warned with a wagging finger, "he may not have much sense, but the boy is all heart."

"No doubt, no doubt. Let me introduce you to the fellas. Hey y'all, these is my brothers!" Earl took my hand away from his shoulder just as I got my mouth opened good. The next thing I knew he was giving me a lecture in front of all my friends! I should have known he would try and pull rank just because he was a couple years ahead of me.

"Let's dispense with the formalities, Alphonso. I know you E-Mailed Willie and I got your letter from my wife." Earl was simmering with annoyance. "Look, I don't know what kind of bad blood there is between you and Mojo, but the answer is 'no'!"

"Damn straight." Willie muttered.

"I just wanted to tell you to your face so that there's no mistake about where we stand on this matter."

"You done come up with some whack ideas in yo' time, Alphonso," Willie said, his face impassive behind his shades, "but you ain't never come up with one that could get somebody killed before!"

"Look, it's a damn shame that Mojo turned Sheba Taylor out; a damn shame. But that don't give you or nobody else the right to plot to gun him down. We're not vigilantes, Alphonso." Earl's bloodshot eyes bulged at me. "You hear what I'm sayin', little brother?"

"What you 'spect me to do?" I protested, and rightfully so, I might add. "He was fixin' to ice me! You tell me what I'm supposed to do? Just wait for him to get the drop on me again? Why on earth should I do that when I can nip this thing in the bud right now?"

"Man," Willie flipped his hand at me in derision, "you is trippin'. Who gon' help you, huh?

That's what I want to know. Who gon' help you? Earl's a police officer and I got some military training and a few medals for gettin' shot at; but guess what? Neither one of us is gon' help yo' crazy fool ass! So who gon' help you? These gentlemen here gon' step right up and be yo' posse when the real deal go down?"

"You been watchin' too much television, Alphonso." Earl said, with a edge of resolve in his voice. "This is a police matter. File a report with them and let it go, Alphonso."

"Now." Willie said, as though that were the final word on the matter. "You got some beer up in this joint, Alphonso?"

There was silence then as everybody at the table looked down at their cards. Even Smiley did not seem to have a quote to cover the situation. I could hear the whirr of the air conditioning again and the pock-knock of the water pipes in the walls. We were a room full of statues, except for Baldy wiping the sweat from his chin. It wasn't until Dougie Dogg sucked on his toothpick that everyone seemed to break from their trance and come back to life.

"Yeah buddy," Dougie grabbed a beer as we passed them around for Willie and Earl, "Helen of Troy - Helen of Troy -"

Victor stepped back when I stung him with my jab. I knew with my longer reach I might be able to keep him back with stiff jabs to the head. I could not let him close in on me because that would be courting trouble. Victor sported the build of an Olympic athlete and already knew he could throw me around like a rag doll.

The main thing was to keep to my height and reach advantage. I figured I would keep him back with my jab every time he came at me. He was already slowed down some from wiping up the alley with me. I discovered with some relief all that tussling before was making it easier for me to tag him at will. I found I was still lighter on my feet and dodged and flicked my jab as best I could until I saw a hickey begin to form on Victor's cheek. I coughed a little blood onto the alley flagstones and went back to working Victor with that jab. I staggered and danced like Ali as much as I could. Just working that jab – working that jab – work, work, working that jab! I jabbed at Victor until my knuckles went numb and I could feel a dull pain in the palm of my hand.

The tide seemed to be turning despite the fact that I ached all over. Victor wheezed with every step he took towards me. Finally he sighed and with one last desperate lunge tackled me to the ground.

SUCKERTEASE AND TRIXIE

"W hat?" Victor demanded as he hammered me with angry blows that carried less and less force. "Do you think I'm toying with you? Is that what you think? This is not a game!"

Somehow I shook him off of me. I struggled back to my feet. I staggered over to the wall and reached vainly time and again for the fire escape. I coughed and wheezed and looked over at Victor. He was down on his knees, quivering and moaning for Daphne now.

"This is not a game," he kept declaring at me, "this is not a game."

He said it so often I was forced to respond somehow hoping that would shut him up. That took a huge amount of doing as I was very nearly out on my feet. I wheezed and coughed and regarded Victor with a fading resentment despite all the pain.

"I know that, man. I know that." I mumbled through swollen lips.

"How could you know anything? Daphne! Daphne! I'm going to find you. I swear before God I'll have you home safe again."

Victor continued to call out Daphne's name and I let him.

Meanwhile, I would have to get out of here now. I could not afford to let rumbling with Victor throw all my plans into a tailspin. I reached for the fire escape again, but just did not have the strength any more to pull it down.

The black door at the top of the landing loomed above us as a mute mocking witness.

Rap Robinson went back through the black door in the red building with me. We crossed over the concrete floor between the red Volkswagen Beetle and the gunmetal grey Mazda RX-7 Turbo

II suspended and hovering above us on hydraulic lifts. Lucky the back garage door was all the way open. The fumes from the oil and gas leaks were enough to make me breathe fire. I could just spot the white Cadillac Eldorado, seated without wheels on concrete blocks and in the middle of the process of being cannibalized. Rap and I stood fronting the grassy apron to the big open lot that was filled with chopped down weeds, sand and rut marks.

We were standing there between the open hoods of a green Ford Contour Sport and a lavender Ford Thunderbird with a green/tan interior. Rap was wiping the grime off his hands with a nasty, shredded rag. The engines to both cars were all hooked up in a web of chains and bars and pulleys. Naturally I wanted to know how come. Old man Rasmussen was sitting on an old red cylinder of a gas can in the shade and chuckled to himself. He didn't say anything; just spit a long trail of tobacco into the grass.

Taxi drivers! You ask them something about these steel chariots they have such a jones about, and they'll look at you like it's the first day of school and you ought to be sent back to kindergarten instead of to the first grade. Now Rasmussen and Robinson gave me more than a glance as Rap checked the chains on the Sport. Old man Rasmussen stood up stiffly and dusted off behind him with the Detroit Free Press. While he sat back down and opened up the paper to do some light reading, I squinted through the tall chain link fence at the silver and black taxicabs.

The headlights of about nine cabs gleamed in the Sun as they fronted the fence. All things considered, I ought to be home copping some Z's, but times are tight now and I need to collect on a favor from the King of Woodward. Old man Rasmussen ruffling the Free Press in his lap makes me catch the morning headlines in bold black letters. I nervously turn back to Rap as he takes a screwdriver and a mallet to separate the leads from the battery inside the Sport. Now that he can see good, I watch as he starts to remove the air cleaner from the engine. He grunts for me to hand him tools, but I can see those letters off the headlines still flashing like that old useless neon curled up in the dust around the dumpster out back. 'WELLINGTON HEIRESS MISSING ALONG WITH TEENAGER!'

"What you do with that little girl, Alphonso?" Old man Rasmussen asked his newspaper, his lips curling into an amused expression in spite of himself. "Tole you to leave them white girls alone..."

"Naw, that wrench right there!" Robinson snarls at me as he points beneath his tool chest. "Yeah, there you go-"

I hand him the wrench as Old Man Rasmussen rattles his Free Press self-righteously.

I resentfully grunt at Old man Rasmussen as I turn my face away and tighten my folded arms across my chest. What does he know anyway? Forget that old fool! The one time I do right and everything turns out all wrong.

That big hunk of bull steer Andre Johnson held off on the shower of sparks he was making welding a new muffler in place.

"Betcha he got her in the trunk in a plastic bag!" Andre said helpfully, flipping up the welder's shield so we could all get a good look at his Leadbelly face.

"Gentlemen! Gentlemen!" Old man Rasmussen clapped his hands together with suppressed glee, his feet literally dancing over the concrete floor. "We's all presumed innocent until proven guilty."

"There ain't nothing funny in that," Robinson uttered solemnly as he twirled the wing nut off the air cleaner and removed the lid pan, "for all we know, Mojo has struck again! What you think about that, Alphonso? Could be Mojo copped that high class cream and your nephew too! The way I see it, he's probably turning her out as we speak, the way he worked that miracle on Sheba Taylor. Probably got your nephew Antonio runnin' errands for a piece of the cream. C'mon man, run it down to me how you see it."

"Look inside the punk's trunk," I hear Andre's voice boom from under a new shower of sparks, "that'll answer all yo' questions. Stop playin' with his bitch ass and make him produce the body."

I clench my fists and start to move over to where Andre is welding.

"Hold tight, Alphonso." Robinson gestures towards his toolbox again. "Gimme that bar over there and that crowbar too-"

I rummage around and hand him what he needs for leverage.

"Besides, that's not the half of it now that Antonio's about to get his picture pasted on milk cartons and telephone poles. Here, pull up on this-" We started to pull the engine up out of the frame. "-unnhhh! You got your sister Alicia to answer to now."

"Aww shit!" I hear Andre's big mouth boom out again. "Ain't no use in goin' home! Bet yo' nephew killed the bitch an' gone!"

"Boy," Old Man Rasmussen starts leafing through the Sports section, "you better thank yo' lucky stars this didn't happen down South about fifty years ago. Them white boys would have your nuts in a pickle jar by now."

Andre Johnson has finished welding on the muffler to the red Volkswagen. He lumbers over with his welding mask under his arm. I feel like grabbing another crowbar and using his skull as a scatter drum.

"Come on, nig-gah," Andre racked his welding mask, "fess up now. Did you 'Bigger' that bitch? I bet you tried to get Antonio to help you, but he ran off! Or did he 'Bigger' that lily white paddy and when you caught him red-handed flew the coop? Yeah, I bet it's something like that. I know it's got to be one of those two scenarios."

"Unnnhuh! Since you got me dead to rights, Sherlock Homey, why don't you get the fuzz down here and have 'em cuff me? Hey Rap, my man, tell me again what we supposed to be doin' here-" Robinson worked the chains and the pulleys and after nodding with satisfaction, flashed me an incredulous expression.

"We switchin' engines on these mugs, Alphonso. Don't you remember when I broke it down to you? We're gonna need an engine with a little more kick to it to run the little number you got in mind."

"I just hope you didn't forget about the distributor and the coil," Old man Rasmussen said as he ruffled his Free Press again, "you oughta thought about detachin' that air cleaner fore you start settin' up to switch them engines."

"I thought about it, Old Man," Robinson readjusts the chains and rachets up the pulleys. "That's cool, Alphonso, that's cool. Who's doin' this anyway, me or you?"

Old man Rasmussen shakes his head mournfully while the hot breath of summer blows a dry breeze through the drafty old garage. He riffles his paper with fastidious gentility.

"Umph, umph, umph. We'll know soon enough who did what once you switch the ignition on this shell game you and Alphonso got goin'." Old man Rasmussen launches another wad of spit at a pigeon scavenging inside the afternoon shadow next to a rusty hubcap. "I know I ain't puttin' my name on the order form to none of that mess. I gotta reputation to consider."

"Don't you worry bout a thing, Old Man. This gonna be all our doin'; Alphonso and me. Black Lightning Taxi not gon' be liable for nothin'."

Andre looks up from behind the hood of that tan Ford Mustang he's fixing the points on with the chrome wheels and tinted windows. He fixes me with a stony glare that's at once soulful and serious as Old Man river. He gestures at me with a wrench in his fist and a prickly feeling goes up and down my spine. The way he looks at me, it's like he's trying to take a mental snapshot of the way I was the last time he saw me alive. Robinson is mum, sprinkling sand and grit over all the grease spots staining the concrete floor while Andre runs his mouth some more.

"I just wanna know what you did with the body, Alphonso, and where you got yo' nephew holed up at. You among friends here. Come on, nigger, you might as well come clean and tell us what you didn't tell the poh-lice."

Robinson sat down on the concrete abutment between the green Sport and the lavender Thunderbird. He poured the can of orange juice he got out of the vending machine into the fizzing plastic cup that held his Sprite. He frowned and shrugged at Andre like he was static coming out of a boom box and he was fixing to change the channel.

"Aw, go suck on a football, ya goober-headed blubber ball! You don't know nothing!" Rap stirred the orange juice into his sprite and held up his cup. "Want some, Alphonso?"

"Naw man, I'm straight."

Robinson shrugged and started to sip his beverage.

"How come you shaved off your mustache, Alphonso?" Robinson asked his cup as his eyes narrowed and he looked off into space. "Ahhhh! You sure don't wanna hit some of this, man?"

"Naw, knock yourself out."

Andre keeps peeking his head out from behind the hood of that Mustang, but I'm not saying nothing for him to go run and tell. He already has got his own ideas as to why I shaved my mustache. I decide to just let him run his mouth and jump to his own conclusions. The shade fades across the garage with the late noon Sun, as the cabs come up the asphalt driveway and through the wire fence to crunch and skid gravel for the next shift. You can see the motley crew of college boys and old timers bopping and stumbling into the office with their clipboards and trip sheets.

Andre tries to convince Robinson and Old man Rasmussen that I shaved my mustache so nobody will recognize me when I go to dump the bodies. He is close in that assumption, but no cigar yet. Old man Rasmussen grunts when he hears this idea, but doesn't look up. He just keeps on reading his paper and scratching his forked beard.

Now he's going on about the Band-Aid I'm sporting on my forehead. He keeps barking while he gets ready to back the Mustang out for a test drive that somebody should make me roll up my sleeves; that I probably got scratches on my arms and other signs of struggle on my body. All I know is Andre won't be that somebody. He knows better than to put his hands on me lest he draw back a nub.

There is not much I want to say to anybody right this moment. The truth is, it has been a long night, what with police officers grilling me all evening long doing their Mutt and Jeff routine. The way my sister, Alicia Marie, went ballistic smashing vases and carrying on when she found out Antonio was missing, well, I don't even want to think about that. I'm just glad I escaped her crib with nothing more than a gash on my forehead.

The main thing is to put all this back right before my name is mud in this town.

Sometimes, you go over and over a thing in your mind and examine every little thing just to spot that one little action you could have done differently. The thing that gnaws at me is how it all went wrong once I thought everything through and decided to do right.

Now I was all set to take my leave of Daphne and the rest of the Wellingtons when she decided to hop into my car. I should have made that mama say goodbye from the curb rather than agree to have her ride shotgun with me. I will admit I was rather tickled to be able to draw one more French kiss out of the deal, but I didn't expect to be paying so dearly for the privilege of Miss Wellington's company.

We were making that good fast time down Jefferson, the street life lighting up on both sides of the street with peoples sharp and down all around us scurrying to and fro to get to the clubs. Daphne's hair was streaming and flowing in wisps and strands of corn silk in the summer night's breeze. She turned from the lit up ghetto dark, squirming on the passenger side to regard me through hooded lids and slightly parted lips that made it seem as though she were purring or singing or maybe a little bit of both. Daphne would always make me flash on the electric babes who flickered via satellite across the television sets and poured out capering in the seemingly never-ending stream of lights and shadows from movie-never land. Every nuance of gesture and movement she made seemed to be another letter newly transcribed on the Rosetta stone of visual literacy. She was, without even knowing it, some living, breathing, three-dimensional collage and compendium in dreamy slow motion of every button-pushing advertising and merchandising glitz that ever stapled its navel or wore the wings of Victoria's secret in the slick paper night air. Now that I was riding with her in my chariot, I was the man of the hour, holding my ticket from the Publisher's Clearing House to my very own fifteen minutes of fame.

When we came up on the lighted spiral sidewalk amid the rolling lawns that fronted the low, squat cylinder of the translucent multicolored glass building, Daphne's upturned eyes melted into a marvelous gaze.

"Gee, Alphonso," Daphne exclaimed, clutching her rhinestone purse to her as I opened the passenger door and took her by the hand, "this is really living large!"

"Nothin' but the best for the Ice Princess." I whispered in her ear as I prepared to shepherd her up the curving walkway. "I'll show you the ropes, then we'll see whether or not you have what it takes to be an Ambassador of Good Will."

"Slow down, Alphonso," Daphne took a couple steps back, the night breeze ruffling her aquamarine gown in shivering, coiled and draping folds that lifted and gathered again around her waist and stocking sheathed thighs, "not so fast. Gee-"

Daphne took in the whole scene like a sightseeing tourist traveling through France on a bicycle. We could already hear the rhythmic clapping and shouting going on inside as we watched the shimmering globe atop the Diamond Hut spill winks of glittering light against apartment buildings across the street. Daphne stood there so long she was turning into the statuesque voluptuary of the joint; her flowing, streaming, spilling hair and fluttering gown streaked and tinged blue in the diaphanous moonlight. The whole thing was getting sort of spooky. The more we stood out there in the night, with the club goers coming across the street and over the curbs, the more that Daphne seemed to be cloaked in a kind of impervious white privilege. What tripped me out was how she didn't even seem to be aware of it. I gently put my arm around her to see if I could kind of get her started towards going inside with me.

"Don't you want to see the inside yet, baby?"

I was just about ready to make her walk a straight line she was so drunk with awe.

Now I know I never would have noticed Leonard Morris standing across the street at the cross light, but for the clanging, warbling shrill Doppler of the EMS truck roaring its way down Jefferson. He stood there with his eyes fixed on Daphne, and didn't move even when the walking sign flashed green. Morris remained at the curb, a calm eye in a colorful, swirling sea of passerby and pulled out a cigar without his gaze ever leaving Daphne. Sheba Taylor was standing by his side with a red fur stole around her shoulders. He linked arms with her, admiring the stars in the night sky while Sheba pulled a gleaming silver lighter from her purse and lit him up. Morris held her hands while he puffed and the tip of his cigar began to glow red. I caught him snatching yet another peek at Daphne through Sheba's fingers and cursed him silently to myself.

"Who's that you're looking at over there, Alphonso?" Daphne asked.

"Nobody. What do you say we head inside now?"

"Wha-"

I gently but firmly urged her forward, my hands pressed against her bare shoulder and back.

"Alphonso! Who is that comical looking fellow with the huge red feather sticking out of his hat band.?"

"You don't wanna know. C'mon, let's go, woman."

"Why -"

Daphne moved forward to the entrance with me stride for stride. I glanced at her studying to decipher my sullen expression with a mixture of surprise and intrigue in her smile. The volume of the rocking beat and the rhythmic clapping din of hands rose to a swelling bass crescendo. The raging, tumultuous ocean of sound fairly threatened to engulf us as we moved up past the lights in the curved sidewalk. There was Temperance Wilson standing in the lighted doorway with his head wreathed in braids and his eyes shielded behind shades. The towering form of Big D the bouncer loomed intimidatingly over us. Temperance and I exchanged soul handshakes while Big D, of course, checked everybody out. While I introduced Daphne to Temperance, he gave her the once over and with nodding approval stamped a Black Eagle with an ink blotter into the palms of both our hands.

"Damn!" I overheard Temperance exclaim out of one ear to Big D as I ushered Daphne down the ramp and into the Diamond Hut. "The deal don't never fail! Alphonso be clocking these high-class super model bitches into the joint on the q.t. all the time." I could hear hands slapping behind me. "The brother gon' be the Mayor of Playas if'n this keeps up."

The Mayor of Playas getting down with the Ice Princess. Mercy –mercy -me! How the Soul Folk sure can talk. What can I tell you? Even the gentle man has a reputation to maintain. Daphne and I swoop down into the iridescent swirl of the mirrored pit in the center of the dance floor. We make our way past the swaying and waving bodies of young and ghetto America hanging over the guardrails of the upper balconies and grooving and moving to the sweet tunes of the Rap Room. We find our way to a table not far from the edge of the stage and the open mike. I pull back Daphne's chair from the table and she spots Leonard Morris and Sheba making the scene just as I scoot in her sweet cheeks.

"There's that man again, Alphonso-" Daphne points out as I seat myself.

"Forget about him, Daphne, and that's the last time I'm going to say it. Just take my word for it; you don't want to know no parts of him over there. He's a bad nightmare that will go away when you wake up and realize I'm the only man who deserves your full and undivided attention at this moment in time."

I take Daphne by the hand and look deep into those twin pools of blue, turning on in full all the sternness at my command. I watch her blush and swell with the lightness rising from her heart. She sighs deeply with the love light glowing in her eyes.

"Alphonso," She utters in a soft, confidential tone.

"That's what I'm talkin' bout," I rise with Daphne in hand and we make our way through the crush and press of undulating bodies and the sweet raw scent of passionate sweat, "c'mon baby, time to shake that groove thang."

We were a tight squeeze in a slow dance and it was no problem guiding Daphne's hips with my hands in synch with the music. She playfully slid my hands up to her waist and scolded me with a wagging finger. Soon after that, her arms were about my neck and I could feel her fingertips running through the hair at the back of my head.

"How'm I doin', Alphonso?"

"You'll be all right, once you learn the ropes the Gentle Way."

"What makes you think you'll be the one to teach me?"

Daphne discreetly places my hand once more against her spine just above the beautiful, romantic, muscular curve of that classical virgin ass.

We became one with the swaying, pulsating vibration of bodies on the dance floor. Daphne and I slow danced until we were enclosed within the booming bubble of the stereophonic mood of the Diamond Hut. We were alone among the many couples, finding secret shelter within the bare space of our most intimate sighs, gliding inside a melody insulated from words or even the sound of voices.

When we rose to the surface from our underwater trance, we could hear someone calling from the shores of the rhythm island.

"Daphne! Is that you, hon? Daphne! What a surprise to see you here!"

Daphne turned her face in a dreamy expression in the direction of the voice, and her eyes widened in startled disbelief.

"Victor? What are you doing here?" Daphne asked, as she reflexively put a step of distance between our partnered bodies. "I thought you were on a business trip in Chicago? How-how did you come to find me here?"

"Chalk it up to serendipity, I suppose," said the Chosen One of Daphne's parents, sticking his chiseled, cleft chin between us. "I actually came to see Vanilla Thunder perform tonight and lo! What do I find? My beloved in the arms of another man!"

Victor Baseheart chuckled, throwing back his square shoulders and putting out a hand to me in all good humor.

"How you doin' there, I'm Vic Baseheart."

"Oh!" Daphne slapped me on the shoulder as though she were absentminded. "I cannot believe you two have never met. This is Alphonso, Vic. You remember my telling you about him?"

"Ohhh, that's right, the artist friend of yours. Daphne keeps going on about how talented you are, Alphonso."

Victor thrust out his hand and gave me a hearty lumberjack's handshake.

"Vic right?" I place my piano fingertips tapping in the hollow of Daphne's back. "We were discussing your engagement to Daphne tonight during dinner."

"Really?" Baseheart clownishly contorted his features into a lugubrious scowl. "Darn it! I wanted so much to make it a proper surprise for you, Daphne," Baseheart touched her hand with a searching look, "I was really looking forward to just the right moment when I could,"

Baseheart looked nervously over at me with that 'three's company' expression on his face. "Excuse me, Alphonso, could I cut in here?" He slapped me on the shoulder with a conspiratorial little wink. "I wasn't expecting Old man Wellington to blab my intentions to strangers just before I was ready to announce my engagement."

"Naw, ya'll gone on ahead. Nice-"

Before I could finish telling Baseheart what a treat it was to meet him, he swooped Daphne around and twirled off with her in a space between jam-packed bodies. Now that I was dissed and dismissed, I thought I would make my way through the chorus line and blaze a trail to the bar where I could get me a brew. I would watch the happy couple cut a rug somewhere beyond the vicinity of the dance floor, and as a 'stranger' make disinterested observations for further field study and research.

But the thing of it was, I never made it through to the sidelines. The colors and swirls of light kaleidoscope across the mirrored dance floor and bounce off the walls as I move on up out of the pit. I was fumbling with the inside pocket of my jacket for a smoke, when I got turned around by the vivacious smile of Wilma Durant. My girl was flouncing her Afro curls about her bare shoulders and ready to do some serious damage to any male hearts around. Temperance Wilson played peek-a-boo behind her with his hands on either side of her hips.

"What up, mah niggah," Temperance moved his head like a snake on either side of Wilma's glowing face, "you ready to get - down wit duh get - down?"

"For real, you know you need to quit, Temp," Wilma moved the hands of Temperance to cover her belly button and gave me the once over. "Ooomm, how you like me now, Alphonso?"

Wilma swayed in Temperance's arms to the soulful sounds wafting from the dance floor.

"Actually, I was on my way for some refreshments when you lit up the joint, Wilma. Why don't we retire to the bar, where I can recover from your blinding fineness?"

"Man, you know you talking that stuff!" Wilma giggled as Temperance blew in her ear. The red flowers that were pinned to her shiny, brown shoulders jiggled with her mirth.

"But it's the stuff that dreams are made of, baby," I assured her.

Wilma and Temperance nodded to each other smugly.

"Like I said, don't nobody stir as much sweetness in they mess as you do, Alphonso." That was when Wilma held out her hand for me to take. "I think I am going to accept your invitation, guy."

"Yeah, I kinda figured you would."

I took Wilma by the hand and we glided past a table where Leonard Morris and Sheba Taylor were commencing deep into the conversation. We came up to the bar and I ordered some kind of spiked passion drinks for the both of us. Wilma nonchalantly stirred her swizzle stick and sort of too casually looked over to the dance floor with a sly smile.

"I saw you out there with Miss Gold Medal flour," Wilma took the cherry from her toothpick and sucked on it before she popped it in her mouth. "What it gon' be like, Alphonso? You fixin' to knead all that white dough with your rolling pin?"

"Naw, it ain't hardly about that, Wilma. We're just good friends, that's all."

"Y'all was dancing mighty close to be such good friends."

"Yeah, well, she's engaged anyway."

"Who's she engaged to, honey?"

"You're lookin' at him."

We peered down onto the dance floor as the final strains of the chorus began to echo and fade away. Our very vision seemed to part bodies and reveal Victor and Daphne wrapping up all their country high stepping with a flourish. Wilma and I watched them make their way over in our general direction.

"That him, Alphonso? The Kirk Douglas look-alike?"

"Yeh," I said, spying Temperance over by the stage and nodding that the show must go on.

"Hmm, they make a beautiful couple, don't you think?"

"That's what the front page used to be about us."

"Yeah, but you was too fast for me, Alphonso."

"That's what they all say, sugar pie-honey bunch,"

"Don't you 'honey bunch' me, Mister Gentle! For all I know, you plannin' to frame her panties right next to mine the first chance you get in that 'studio' you call yourself runnin'."

"There you go again, mama, jumpin' to conclusions."

"Oh, my bad! You haven't gotten around to sketching all that out yet, have you?"

"Shhhh! Why you gotta be so loud? I thought you would have gotten over that by now, but I can see you still upset. What I gotta do to make you forgive me?"

"Hmmm,"

The screech of the mike as Temperance Wilson adjusted it on stage made everyone turn their heads. A growing knot of club goers gathered in front of the apron, some with drinks in hand and already high, others simply stepping forward to join in and clap on time with the beat. Daphne and her beau came up to us with hands clasped, their faces flushed with expectation.

"That was really something, Alphonso!" Daphne exclaimed excitedly, "What's about to happen now?"

"Hey fella," Baseheart reached out and shook my hand again, "Daphne and I really tripped the light fantastic out there. You have great atmosphere in this place." Baseheart nodded with an amiable delight at Wilma. "Hello there-"

Victor Baseheart took Daphne by the hand and we all traded introductions.

"Hooooooo! Everybody in the house!" Temperance took the mike off the stand and began to wave his hands before a bopping crowd echoing his exclamations. "Hooooooo!"

"Hoooooooooo!" The gathering clustered around the lighted stage with an answering chorus amid giddy squeals and peals of laughter. "Hoooooooooo!"

"Callin' all Rappers-callin' all Rappers! Doin' the 911 on all Rappers in the house!"

Wilma and Daphne and Baseheart and I looked around and exchanged glances with each other. I gently urged Wilma forward, pushing against her bare back. She swatted at my hands with mock irritation.

"What you lookin' at me for, Alphonso? Loose me, man, loose me!"

"I thought you was down for some 'Poetic Justice' woman,"

"What's your hurry, Alphonso?" Wilma snatched away from me. "Somebody would think you just dyin' to get slammed!"

"What? You tellin' me you got what it takes to get the job done? That the case, step right up, little girl."

I signify Wilma some soul gesticulations before I give her both thumbs down.

"You step right up, brother man. I always allow losers they last request."

There is nothing more to be said. I proceed for the stage and Daphne catches me by the forearm.

"Alphonso! Alphonso!" Daphne exclaims breathlessly. "What's about to happen?"

I look around and down into the exploding stage lights flashing in Daphne's eyes.

"We Rappers and Poets are about to fight/ for our right/ to par-tay!"

Baseheart snuggles up to Daphne and slides an arm around her waist.

"Let's get a ringside seat, hon. We'll be sitting at that table over there, Alphonso. Please come join us when the dust settles and the Slam is done."

"There you go, dude. This gon' be a contest to decide who is the best in the East and in the West!"

"Wow, Alphonso! You sound just like a Rapper-" Daphne sighs with fascination.

Daphne freezes as she catches the eye of Leonard Morris quietly appraising her with his feet propped up on the cocktail table. Sheba solicitously pours him another glass of what looks like champagne. Morris indolently flicks the ash from the stub of his cigar.

I feel Wilma tugging at my sleeve as my eyes narrow and my hands start to clench again.

"Hey guy," Wilma said, snapping me out of it, "- come up on this stage and get you another whopping!"

Temperance Wilson is waving us to get up on the stage when a cocky skinhead white boy in baggy jeans and a Day-Glo black T-shirt flashes past us. He swaggers towards the stage in buster brown brogans, sporting a nose ring and covered in tattoos. The young rapper responds to the roar at his arrival by jumping to the stage and reaching for the mike that Temperance hands him. He paces the stage like a tiger and twirls the mike by its cord like a whip.

"You've got your hands full now," Victor Baseheart warns me as he ushers Daphne to a table. "That's Vanilla Thunder and I've heard he's quite a wonder. I hear he gives no quarter and takes no prisoners. Daphne and I will be over there to offer you moral support."

"Ciao, Alphonso-" Daphne waves at me playfully.

The time has come to take on all comers. Wilma follows me down the aisle on the side and through the purple curtain backstage. We come up the little steps and stand with about a dozen other people in the wings. Vanilla Thunder is all revved now and coming to the end of his rap and the verve of his words are punctuated from end to end with clapping in time.

> "'-I was swingin' with Jane
> When the bullet creased my brain
> Got caught in a trap
> 'An couldn't beat the rap
> Now I'm stuck in a cage
> Filled with nothin' but rage
> Ain't studdin' bein' no Sage
> (Audience joins in now)
> Man-oh-man-Tarzan!' "

Vanilla Thunder holds his peace signs high to uproarious approval and waves them around. He trots into the wings so full of himself, if you stuck a pin in him he would explode. He looks at all of us to see who would dare challenge him.

"Alright, brothers and sisters, show me what you got!"

"Show you what I got?" I look around and wave my arms expansively at the rest of the Rappers. "Show you what I got?" I fold my arms and give the kid the once-over. "I'll show you what I got! I got 'NOWHERE TO GO'! Hooooooo! Hooooooooooo-"

I take my war cry out onto the stage and proceed to snatch up the mike. I do a little Mack strut and pound my palms over my head. The audience is already chanting 'GENTLE MAN!' and keeping the beat with their hands and their feet. Even though it is hard to see who is out there in the darkness beyond the bright lights, I stiffen my backbone with pride and pull the rip cord on my Rap. Now is the time for yours truly to dive for the sky, sprout wings and swing to the aid of all good men in the party!

"What up, y'all, what up? Glad you could show up, Detroit, cause
this is 'NOWHERE TO GO'-

Nowhere to go
    yes, I suppose so
    guess you got it on the down-low
    else how would you know?

Been so long that I have run this show
    gon' be hard to believe there will
        be nowhere to go
Better take it slow
just move on with the flow
the lunches, the punches, the
footsteps crunched in the snow
the hummers, the summers, the
hot winds that blow
the movement of students,
impudent to improvement-but
then, all that you know
the studious seemers, the
leaners and the screamers,
the beaming dreamers all
lost in a fog
and here I am, with nowhere to go
    like a bump on a log

There is no fire to retire
    for I've gone wire to wire
    more time won't take me no higher
    all the time I've spent

with all my friends here,
    I really ought to crow
    jus' this feeling keeps nagging at me
    'cause there's no place to go

Down Woodward to Euclid
    I think of everything that I did
    with all my friends we sure got paid
    we made the streets pay off in spades
    I wonder now for all the rest
    I have been tested
    and passed every test
    Lord knows
    I gave the babes my best

Down East State Fair to Eight Mile
    Just let me recollect awhile
    now all my memories just make me smile

The challenge of the years
The conquest of my fears
that outpaced all my tears
when I think of the careers
that could have brought me cheers
there's no fantasy or dream that nears
the feeling that I get
knowing just how well I fit this bit
when I took up my place on the field
this was the real deal

Now I'll make space for you a taste
    all this Gentle know-how and experience
      can't let it go to waste
    Stop cryin' little honey, now-go and dry yo' face!
    You know where I stay - buzz me any time-any
    day-any place
    Don't be supposin' that you'll be imposin'
    Since you always know, that for you, baby, I've got
    nowhere to go!' "

I replaced the mike with a flourish and Temperance Wilson rushed out of the wings to give me a high five. I pointed a finger stage left at Vanilla Thunder and left him to wonder. I gave a wave to Wilma, shook hands with a couple of folks hanging over the edge of the stage and then headed back into the wings to mill around with all the rest of the rappers awaiting their turn. Wilma was ready to tee off now and gave me a hug as Temperance Wilson introduced her and she stepped out into the glare of the lights.

There were soul handshakes all around amongst the little knot of late night soothsayers and wordsmith riff playas that collected around me. Vanilla Thunder a.k.a. Vincent Duncan Trudeau, shook hands with me and grabbed my arm, sticking his face so close to mine I could see the acne scars on his jaw and the twitch of the nose ring he sported. I inhaled the smell of the beer he must have downed just before he made his way on stage.

"Word -that sho' was righteous, my brother," Thunder patted me on the shoulder, that gold front tooth flashing in his mouth, "we gotta do a whole set one of these times. Just you and me, if you down with what I'm sayin'-"

Yeah, right. Canuck comes through the Windsor Tunnel across the Detroit River to show everybody down on Jefferson just how black he was in a past life. He even has the tatoos and the scarification down in case he runs into an African tribesman one of these days. I know my moms would break his face about wearing the wrapper without living the history or even knowing it full up. I can hear Rap Robinson going on with his riff right now -

"See -it's just a fad with them, a phase they goin' through, Alphonso. Dudes like Vanilla Thunder do their tour of duty with the homies and then go on to run their father's hardware store. Or sit in on the board at General Motors." Robinson took another sip of orange Sprite from his plastic cup. "We're just another excellent adventure as far as they're concerned."

"- just another footnote in history to the conquerin' hordes," Old man Rasmussen mumbles refolding his Free Press and turning to the

Comics Section. "Them paddies only want to know enough to kick yo' ass and keep on steppin'."

"See-they love the style as long as they don't have to walk the mile to get to it." Robinson continues after nodding to Old Man Rasmussen and taking another sip. "We look good to them as long as we can turn them a profit -end of story. They don't need to know about our history and our Timeline except where they come in and scoop up the gold. Long as we can hoop, sing, rap and do the fiddle-de-dee on the trumpet and the saxophone, we uh damn asset to humanity! Huh, Rasmussen? What you got to say to that?"

"I know that's right!" Old man Rasmussen crackles his paper with an indignant scowl.

"We're the greatest natural resource known to Man! Forget that Saudi oil! The real black gold comes out of the blood, sweat, tears, muscle and brains of colored folk from all over the world. I bet ya the real reason Vanilla Thunder is hobnobbing with us now, gettin' his rap thang goin' on and fine tunin' it, is because he sniffs big bucks in between the assemby lines and he is gonna work the system till he gets his percentage."

"That's cold, man," I tell Robinson as we watch Andre hulk his way over to the wooden stand where my man Rap has got his latest go-machine under a tarp. "you act like you can't just get to know people without being out for something. Face facts, white folks are people, too."

"Ain't this a blip?" Robinson looks at me with a glare of disbelief. "Tell them that, my man, you oughta know. The next time you get yo' weldin' torch ass deep in that white hot pussy you tell the bitch that tole you that we black folks is people, too." Robinson glanced warily over to where Andre was pulling at the tarp on his go-machine. "Hey-hey-HEY! Andre! What you call yourself doin' over there, man?"

"What it look like I'm doin'?" Andre peeked under the tarp, a wrench in his right hand. "I just wanna know how come it's taking you so long to get all the parts for that Classic Blue you done had under wraps goin' on like forever."

"What's it to you? Get away from there, Dickhead!" Robinson walked between the chained suspended engines, hovering next to the raised hoods of the green Ford Sport and the lavender Ford Thunderbird, and out next to the wooden stand. "Gone now! The bike ain't done yet. That's all you need to know."

"Why don't you chill, man?" Andre grimaced at Robinson with a sullen expression. "I just want to see what parts you got missin'. I might can pick you up something next time I'm out at the junkyard."

"What made you decide to be so good to me?"

"Skip yo' bitchass, Robinson." Andre Johnson said, raising up to his full height and towering intimidatingly over the both of us. "You been tinkering with that bike the whole year and ain't been going no place. What good it gonna do to have a Harley you always workin' on, but nobody ever gets to ride?

Robinson looks over at me, but no sympathy here. There is not a soul in this garage who does not know how selfish Robinson can be with his machines. As far as he is concerned, the bikes and automobiles he hauls in here might as well be three-dimensional jigsaw puzzles. He never has enough of his endless tests and once he has built something from the ground up and got it working, he would be perfectly content to dismantle it piece by piece and start all over again.

Robinson grabbed a shoulder and shrugged without remorse.

"For all you know, this is just a spare parts bike. Something I can use to just get the feel of the make. I can get me another one just like it later, and customize it just the way I like it."

"Nig-gah! What's the matter fo' you? Huh?" Andre sat down on the edge of the wooden stand. "You act like Classic Blue Harley Davidsons grow on trees!" Andre started banging his wrench against the side of the stand. "You were lucky to get yo' hands on this one!"

Old man Rasmussen rolled his paper up in his lap and let out a weary sigh.

"Christ Amighty, Robinson, show the man what you got. That's just what the White Man wants, and that's just what we do."

Rasmussen gets up stiffly and turns for the john. "We always at each other throats like crabs in a basket, pulling each other back down before we even got a leg up good. Take off that damn tarp so Johnson can see what you got. Y'all put both your hands on it, you might end up puttin' together a pretty good machine. Go on, Robinson, before you get on my last nerve and I dock you a day's pay." Rasmussen started to head for the Rest Room and he was muttering to himself. "- had no business bringin' that raggety-ass motor-sickle in here no way, takin' up all that space-"

Robinson looked down with folded arms and rubbed the steel toe of his boot in the grit and sand on the concrete floor. He looked at us with a surly, almost petulant expression. He took a step onto the wooden stand and pulled away the tarp.

The bike was an incomplete thing of beauty. The strange thing was how its incompleteness, how its cutaway textbook look seemed to add to its beauty. We got up on the stand, pacing all around with Robinson as he surveyed the frame. That is, the front forks or steering, the engine cradle and the swinging arm or rear suspension. Andre looked over the mufflers while Robinson thumped all around with his fist to check the brackets, guards, fenders and shields. The guards and the shields were a shining, brilliant deep royal blue. Andre continued to check the chains and the wheels and Robinson went over the brakes and the cables. Around and around they went; I could see them mentally ticking off what Robinson had done and what remained to be done. Every once and awhile Robinson would touch the handlebars and Andre would squint at the instruments. After the examination, Robinson and Andre stepped off the stand one after the other and took one more step back in nodding admiration of Robinson's handiwork.

"You got it, baby," Andre confirmed solemnly, running his thumb over the crescent wrench in his hand, "she is looking sweet."

"Yeah, I painted the fenders and the shields myself," Robinson said, grinning with everything but his eyes, "all she needs now is a heart of fire."

"Got any idea where to get the engine?"

"I'll scrounge around to see what I can find."

"I got your back on this one."

"I'll second that emotion. That said, should be small potatoes for the King of Woodward."

I cannot tell you what took me so long to realize that the main parts of the engine were missing. Once I discovered that you couldn't ride this baby down the street, I was ready to step off that stand. I am not too keen on standing around anything that has missing parts.

"Naw Alphonso, where you goin', man?" Robinson waved me back next to the bike.

"Ain't no happenings, Rap." I said, showing him my hands. "What you gonna do with a bike that's got no engine?"

"Hold tight, Alphonso, hold tight for a minute." Robinson looked down and studied the floor for a moment, and then he looked up as though an idea had suddenly occurred to him. "I'll tell you what; get up on the bike."

"Do what?"

"Get up on the bike, man. The engine's out so you won't be in any danger."

Robinson got back on the stand and slowly paced around again. While I swung onto the seat and grabbed the handlebars, I could hear the toilet flushing in the Rest Room as Robinson checked the shock absorbers once again.

"I heard your moms got Willie and Earl to cop her grandmother's peacemaker off you."

"Yeah," I said, careful not to show how surprised I was Rap already had this information. "- she decided to donate it to the African American Museum where she works."

"Damn shame," Rap kept pacing around the bike, "does the seat feel loose, Alphonso? You can tell me the truth. I want your honest opinion."

"Yeah, it's cool. I mean it feels snug to me."

Andre appears to be grunting resentfully out the corner of my eye. He starts drifting back to that tan Ford Mustang he was fixing the points on. The next thing I know he is aiming that crescent wrench at me while he swaggers away.

"Uh huh, enjoy it while you can, Hell Rider! I'm just waitin' to see where they park yo' ass when they finally find that bitch's body next to your nephew's. Uh huh, you ain't gettin' way with this one, you little trick."

Andre moves back to the Tan Mustang and puts his head back under the hood. I spot a crowbar racked against one of the walls and hop off the Harley in its direction. I'm overdosing on Andre's bullshit and I figure it is time to supply the cure. Robinson reads me right in the eyes and makes me halt with his hands against my chest.

"Whoa, tiger, whoa! Check yourself before you wreck yourself-"

"Naw! Naw! He ain't got no right to diss me like that!" I can hear my heart pounding and my mouth is getting dry again. "Come on over here and say all that again. This time say it to my face! You a mighty big man in this joint long as you walking away-"

Andre pokes his head out from under the hood again, while Robinson pushes me back to where Rasmussen was seated on the red gas can. Andre leans again the Mustang with a smug look on his face while he wipes his hands with a grease-smeared rag. Old man Rasmussen comes out of the Rest Room dragging ass with a haggard look on his face.

"What?" Andre exclaims, trying to act all cool. "You gon' do somethin'? Huh? You gon do somethin'?"

Old man Rasmussen whirls slowly around to check out the scene.

"What y'all frontin' bout? I can't leave for two minutes to take a dump even and y'all fools is at each other throats!"

Andre's eyes glitter with anger as Robinson continues to push me back. I'm breathing hard and thinking all I need is something to chop that big dumb country nigger down to size, and he'll never mouth off at me ever again. I twist with pained annoyance away from Robinson's grip.

"Stop pushing me, man! You ought to be holding him back; that's what you ought to be doin'."

'Naw, you ack like you bout to start something. Step right up, nigger! Now you actin' like you want some uh this." Andre steps away from the Mustang and slaps his chest with both hands. "What? You gon' do somethin'? Ain't no honeys round here now to take yo' bitchass side. What you gon' do now? Ain't no honeys round here to impress. What you gon' do now?" Andre slaps his chest again. "Wanna go for the World title? Come on with it, I'm ready to go -"

"That's enough out of you, Johnson-" Old Man Rasmussen snaps at him.

"Naw, the nigger keep actin' like he gon' do so much! I wanna see it. I'm ready to go. I just wanna see what he gon' do."

"Fightin' ain't allowed in here, you fool-" Robinson barks irritably as he gestures at me with a warning expression in his eyes.

"That's right!" Old man Rasmussen snarls as he juts his forked beard at Johnson. "You so ready to go, why don't you hurry up and finish the job on that Mustang? You a day late and a dollar short on that one, ain't ya?"

That statement momentarily halts Andre in his tracks and suddenly he can't find Old man Rasmussen's eyes.

"He the one actin' like he gon' do so much," Andre starts to make his way back over to the Mustang. "Give me a damn break. Nigger ain't gon' do shit. One thing to be neck deep in them hot white thighs stoppin' to smell the roses; but it's a whole new world in here, punk. An' you figurin' on givin' to me what you gave that bitch, then think again, trick. Yo' sister Alicia done already kicked yo' bitch ass over how you lost her little boy. If you was on the up and up, you'd be figurin' on how to produce her son for the rematch. You the Black Man's Curse, Alphonso. If anybody ever asks, you heard it from me first."

Now I'm clenching my fists so hard my knuckles hurt.

"We can always take this outside -" I hiss through my teeth.

Old man Rasmussen turns his muscular face at me and he's filled with rage.

"Now Alphonso," Rasmussen picks up his Free Press and slaps it against his thigh, "you want to go outside, go right ahead. It's a beautiful day and the fresh air might do you some good. Be that as it may, that young gentleman over there," Old man Rasmussen turns and points with his finger and his forked beard, "is stayin' right here. He's gon' fix that car and finish my job order. Now," Rasmussen takes a wobbly step forward and fixes me with a narrow-eyed glare, "have I made myself clear?"

"Yeah, Old man Rasmussen," I mumble out the corner of my mouth.

"What? I don't think I heard you good -"

"Yes sir, Mister Rasmussen,"

"That's what I thought you said. Now do you have any other business with us today?"

"Well, I -" I scowl when I see that big sucker head ugly bear Andre smirking from behind the hood of that Mustang. "I suppose -"

"Let me and Alphonso finish up our business 'fore he goes, Mister Rasmussen," I hear Robinson piping from behind me.

Robinson is dragging that aluminum colored tarp to pull back over that Harley machine.

"Hey Alphonso, help me with this, okay man?" Robinson asks while he slips the tarp over the back wheel of the bike like a hood.

I turn back to Old man Rasmussen for the okay.

"Say hello to your mother for me, Alphonso." Old man Rasmussen slaps me against the shoulder with his newspaper and heads back to seat himself on his red gas can. "Where's that cushion I had over here some place? I swear - you can't have nothin' around here -"

I help Robinson pull the rest of the tarp snugly over the Harley and we head out through the open garage door into the sun-filled lot. We kick at the ruts left by the tires in the sand. Rap moves over to the silver grey Dodge Intrepid on blocks in the lot, almost totally cannibalized now. The vehicle is barely more than a collection of fenders on a chassis; even the brake pads and shock absorbers are gone. Rap shakes his head as he surveys the door-less, scavenged mass of metal.

"T'was a sweet ride back in the day," Rap says as he squints into the sunshine, "t'will be again when I get the parts."

"This thing don't look like a ride no more, Rap," I told him as I leaned against the pole holding up the wire fence, "looks more like a piece of Installation Art to me."

"Instant what?" Robinson squinted at me. "This ain't no 'Instant Art'! We put in a lot of man hours strippin' this sucker down. Hey Alphonso, let me ask you a question man; what you do with all them hub caps I let you have?"

"I added them to my collection," I folded my arms and then pressed my back against the wire fence, "then I sketched me out a design and welded and drilled those bad boys into a frame until I had me a decent piece of Installation Art."

"'Installation' Art? Did you say 'Installation' Art?"

"Yeah, man, you come to my show and I'll show you what I'm talking about. It's sort of like when you take a space and redesign it with spare parts from your own imagination."

"Yeah? What you wanna do that for?"

"What you think? To see how it would look in the real world."

Rap mulled this over for a while and then shook his head again.

"Sound like an awful lot of trouble to go to just to see how somethin' gonna look."

"Not really, when you think about it. I seen you go to an awful lot of trouble just to see how to make something move."

"Lookin' and movin' is two different things."

"Tell me about it."

Robinson traced a pattern in a sandy rut with the toe of his boot. He looked about him with furtive caution to make sure no one was about who could hear us. He dug his hands deep into the pockets of his overalls and looked sideways at me with stern resolve.

"You leavin' the Focus with me for awhile?"

"That's about the size of it."

"I'll have yo' ride ready day after tomorrow."

"Music to my ears."

Robinson pulled the key fob out of his pocket and popped open the trunk on the Intrepid. He took another quick look around before he went over and rummaged around for the jumper cables and the lug nut wrench. He motioned for me to come over with a jerk of his head and pulled out a grimy old cigar box secured with rubber bands. The kind cab drivers keep for their Trip Sheet and fare money. Robinson shoved it into my ribs with a grunt.

"Here. I'll have you outfitted for the night as soon as your Focus is done. I just thought you might need a little sumpin'-sumpin also for now until then, Alphonso."

"Solid, Rap. Sure you ain't got a tire iron in there so's I can crack that nigger Andre in his skull?"

Robinson dryly shook his head and chuckled as I helped him close the trunk.

"Black Folks! All we be is clubbin'! I give you a box of cigars to light up with and still that is not enough."

We leaned against the back of the Intrepid and folded our arms.

"It ain't about all that. Just want to cover all the bases."

"This ain't no time to be thinkin' outside the box," Robinson tapped the lid on the cigar box as we watched the Sun set in the leaves of the trees, "-you can leave coverin' all the bases to yours truly. That's what the King of Woodward is all about."

"Hmph. Thinkin' outside the box is what the Gentle Man is all about. Whadduh the drums say on Socrates?"

Robinson looked down and rubbed a weed loose with his foot. He looked up again at me and then scratched his jaw, like he was too cool for school.

"Mojo found the bitch he needed. Sammy boy is a marked man from here on out. Mojo got him bugged with the best bitch bait goin', and it's all wholesome and sophisticated and wired to be deadly as sin. Tapped into the nigger's dreams and found the nut he's dyin' to bust, but can't crack. Don't look good for your wise man, Alphonso. I know you respect him for all that book knowledge he got, but I'm afraid Mojo's holdin' the owner's manual on Socrates this go round."

"That how you got it sized up?"

"No doubt."

We didn't say anything for awhile as Robinson carefully felt the three-day growth on his chin. I glance over at Robinson, but all I see in his face is end-of-story. The words of Old man Rasmussen come back to haunt me. I can recall how we signified on Socrates while we knocked back cans of Mountain Dew. We were cackling cracking up about that Samuel Turner so bad.

"Silly sucker!" Old man Rasmussen clapped his hands with glee. "He read about what the White Man do, he read about what the White Man say, he read about what the White Man think, he read about what the White Man feel. Now," Old man Rasmussen claps his hands again on this point, "what he gotta show for all that study and research? They ain't one damn thing he got to show for it! Still don't know what he gonna do 'less the White Man tell him, still don't know what he gonna say unless he done read it some place in one of the White Man's books. What he gonna think unless it's a Xerox copy of what some white man thought back in the day when they was workin' out how to rob and murder people and snatch up they land? What can he feel unless it's simpatico with what the White Man need to feel to be right with the Lord for the rape and plunder of countless folk to gain and get gold? All that readin' and gettin' knowledge, and when he punches out at the end of the day he's still the same as any of the rest of us. Just another nigger with no idea of what he can do, what he ought to say, what his true thoughts and feelings really really are. Because his whole life and everything is all submerged under a mountain of lies, and covered under the cold white snow job of the White Man's history."

"Preach it, Old man, Preach it!" Robinson is spurring Rasmussen on.

"Nowadays Sam the Man will tell you he got it all worked out to the lowest common de- nominator. All you really got to know is 'People is People'-"

"Right," Robinson gurgles another swig of Coke, "just put that on a bumper sticker and you're good to go!"

"Silly sucker! Don't you know good and well tricks is for kids? You can't just go reducin' Life to just any ole one thing! Sound just like those fools who try to reduce Life down to the one Master Law of Nature, or boil it down to the one Master Equation of Mathematics or the Master Code of Science or the one true Cosmic Vibration of Jazz or-"

"How 'bout this one?" Robinson wipes his mouth with the back of his hand. "'Politics is Everything'?"

"There you go! Life ain't bout to be reduced to nothin'. You go about tryin' to reduce Life to its lowest common denominator and you going to end up being that lowest common denominator. You dig? Life is bigger than your biggest understanding, young Gentle, so always be ready to add a little mo' to what you already know."

"Hey Alphonso," Robinson tossed his empty pop can at the wastebasket and missed. "Uh-Uh. Whoa. There goes my shot at the NBA. Hey Alphonso," Robinson gets up to retrieve his can, "-what you got to say about all that, huh?"

I look around at all the giddy faces and shrug to myself.

"Hellifino. Rap, my man, throw me another can of Dew."

The Sun is low in the trees and taking all the green in the leaves with it. Rap and I just stand with our asses pressed against the trunk of the Intrepid, our arms folded and our heads bowed. Our faces are closed books, not open to inquiry or even scrutiny as we consider all the angles in the setup.

"I used to watch them white boys cruise by in their fancy cars and on their souped-up bikes just like in the commercials on T.V." Rap clears his throat, "- sometimes when you look around, it can seem like White folks got the best of everything and Black Folks just here to make sure they get it and to cheer them on. Yeah, this one racist bitch monkey-"

Rap nodded to himself and then looked over to me like I just materialized out of thin air or something.

"You think I'm jivin', don't you? You watch the Discovery Channel and all you learn is how White Folks invented everything and we never did shit. What Black Man got enough smarts to invent new technology? Did you see that show on PBS about how Richard Spikes invented the automatic gear shift?"

"No, I think I missed that one-"

"How about the show they did on Joseph Gammel, the dude who invented the supercharge system for internal combustion engines?"

"That must have been on BET. When you see that, Rap?"

Rap hid his chuckles behind a grease stained hand.

"There ain't no shows like that, fool! Them brothers was Black. Everybody knows Black Folks can't invent and develop 'superior' technology. Where you from, country? You got to get your mind right!"

"Why you gotta play me, Rap?"

Rap is still snickering and stifling his chuckles as his shoulders shake with silly delight.

"I dunno man, just sumpin' to do, I guess." Rap wipes a trickling tear of laughter from the side of his nose he is so tickled. "Old man Rasmussen said he never thought the Iron Curtain was gonna fall in his lifetime, and now they's sellin' Big Macs over in Moscow like a Big dog. So I guess they's hope. You never know; the day may come when I turn on the television set and see a science program that can break down for a layman like me the thought process of a Alice Parker, the black woman who invented the heating furnace, or maybe even a John Standard, the man who I understand invented the refrigerator. Who knows? Maybe another movie'll get made about that Thomas Edison, only this time they'll show how Lewis Latimer helped invent the filament that goes inside the light bulb. What you think, Alphonso? Do you think we'll ever live long enough to see on T.V. how we been busy inventin' white folks happiness ever since we were brought over here?"

"You is whack, Rap. Like I'm gonna turn out all the lights and curse the darkness until America admits that's Lewis Latimer's stuff inside Edison's light bulb! We don't need nobody to tell our story no more; an' a good thing, too. You wanna preach the Gospel of Black

Invention, go right ahead! Just make sure you get paid for all your time and trouble, that's all I got to say."

Robinson went back to digging weeds out of the ground with his big toe as the bars of shadow get long across the ground and the back of the Intrepid we were leaning against. He looked over at me again with reserved amusement.

"I'm just keepin' it real, Alphonso. I was hangin' with this honey one time and when we went back to her crib it was wall-to-wall Science Fiction! Books galore and movie posters and all sorts of autographed glossies of Harrison Ford and the Matrix Man-you know who I'm talkin' about-who is that guy?"

"Keanu Reeves-"

"Yeah! Keeno Reeves and that baldheaded sucker. Who is that?"

"Lawrence Fishburne-"

"Yeah, that's the one! Anyway, we're layin' up beneath the sheets after I done raced her engine some, and she starts bringin' up whether I'm into Science Fiction or not and have I ever read any I liked. I tell that bitch hell naw! I'm living Science Fiction! What I need to read it for? White Folks everywhere tryin' to conquer the world and the stars with their got-damn machines. Why I gots to read about their dreams for the future in a universe without colored people? What good it gon' do me to read about their heroic exploits, battlin' back aliens from other planets like they was roaches? Anyway, I told her just lay back again. I'll send you to every planet in the Solar System in a minute!"

"That's an ignorant-ass position to take, Rap, when you got a babe in bed. How you expect her to serve up the cream of wheat when you tellin' her to her face you don't respect her mind?"

"I didn't say that; and you shouldn't be readin' stuff into it that ain't there. I was just about keepin' it real. Science Fiction ain't nothin' but a White Boys' Club no way, like the Presidency or Hockey Night in Canada. Niggers need not apply. Straight up. White folks dream of a future they can custom design and fine tune to their most intimate desires, a future where they can make the Great Escape beyond the

Stars and leave all their troubles and crimes behind. Black Folks just dream of gettin' White Folks foot out they ass!"

"Oh -so now you an authority on the Dreams of Black folk and what they think. Is that it?"

"Naw, don't put words in mah mouth! I'm an authority on what the King of Woodward think, brother!"

"Yeah, well, you shouldn't go dissin' somebody just because they read Science Fiction-"

Robinson shrugged and scooped up a rock to throw at a squirrel perched on the dumpster and eating out of a fast food wrapper from some restaurant.

"What I care whether a bitch like Flash Gordon or Buck Rogers? Free country. That don't mean I got to like it, too. Why I got to read some book to walk around in some white man's imagination? Niggers done enough uh that already, and still can't find the road home."

"That's about the most ignorant thing I ever heard, Rap!"

"See, you a college Joe, I wouldn't expect you to understand." Robinson goes back to rubbing the rooted weeds out of the sand with his foot. "I like to read about stuff where Black People is in charge, not where White People is in charge and we're just helpin' out. Let White Folks walk around in our imagination for once. Let them step up on the auction block in one of our fantasies they wanna feel our pain so bad."

"'Mandingo Was A Slave Master', huh?"

"Naw. 'Mandingo IS The Master of the Universe'." Robinson spots another squirrel at the dumpster and hurls another rock. "Git outta there! Gotta discourage that kind uh thing, Alphonso. Next thing you know, it'll be rats."

"No doubt. But even squirrels got to have a place in the Sun, you know."

"That sound like something you would say. Dougie tole me about that snake you put in a jar at yo' bitch's house. You a trip, Alphonso!"

"Yeah? Well, that's your opinion. Which is not shared by many, I want you to know."

"Ain't no skin off my nose. Like I was tellin' you about my lady; she was within her rights to have a jones about Science Fiction and I was within my rights to want no parts of it. When you read them books its all about white people. Just like when you turn on the tube it's all about them sellin' you something. Naw, I'll pass on that dose of brainwashin'. Straight up, though, when somebody writes a book about Black Folks from another planet invadin' Earth to herd White Folks into ships to take them somewheres they can be sold on the open market like horses and sheep, you better believe I'll be at the book signin' for an autographed copy. Straight up."

"I imagine you will. You've got an insight into engines and cars, Rap, but you too hung upon Race. It doesn't take long to see you can't blame White folks for everything. Part of the bill is for us to pay. Besides, you know if your battery went dead and you were standing on the corner of Six Mile and Woodward with jumper cables in your hands, you wouldn't give a damn about the color of the person who gave you a boost!"

"That where you wrong, homie. First of all, you wouldn't catch the King of Woodward ina fix like that. I would call Triple A for one thing. Second of all, I'm not lookin' for some white angel to come out of nowhere at the last minute to solve all my problems and rescue me. See-you need to change the mind-set on that little number, cuz. I solve the problems in my life and I have whiteys come to me to fix their problems for them."

"That's a refreshing viewpoint, Doctor Robinson."

"Yeah, and my very own invention, Money."

Now that I have heard Robinson's standard riff on the Race Question, we can get down to the business at hand. I hold the cigar box close in my folded arms and look around to catch the last of the cabs coming in at the end of shift. Beyond the wire fence, Black Lightning has its own gas pump and a place where you can check the antifreeze and change oil. We cast glances over our shoulders as we note the black and silver cabs queuing up for servicing.

"You got the pictures, man?" I ask Robinson with tension in my voice.

"Right here, my man," Robinson pats the pocket over the chest of his overalls, "I drove my boy from Kennedy Photographic around with a telephoto lens and we caught all Mojo's bitches in they natural habitat."

"Let me see what they baitin' Turner with, man."

Robinson produces the picture and I nod in recognition.

"Theresa Loretta Cartwright is what she's known by now," Robinson continues, "she goes by TLC to some, but among most of her colleagues she's known as Trixie. Strictly high class; the usual escort of businessmen and politicians, so Samuel Turner must have really stumbled onto some classified dope to be movin' up in the world like that. She put herself through college on her back and earned a bachelor's and a master's degree in the Social Sciences. Mojo flexed his connections and got her planted in the same high school where Turner teaches. Don't look now, my brother, but you can bet she's pickin' his brain even as we speak. After that, it's bait and switch by the numbers true to form and 'This has been a Master Mojo production'. Here-"

Robinson hands me the photograph. I can see it is the same woman I noted as I made my way past the congratulations and all the way down the steps at the side of the stage through the purple curtain. I have a good memory for faces and movie stars and I remember watching Ms. Cartwright waxing philosophical with Mister Turner, and thinking to myself how much she looked like a cross between that old school actress Sandy Dennis in 'UP THE DOWN STAIRCASE' and the other one; that creepy broad in that movie our father took us to see. What was that called? Oh yeah, 'CARRIE'!

Anyway, I remember how the dance floor was grooving and rocking and how the sound of the music seemed to spiral endlessly up from the pit as I moved between tables to get back to little ole Daphne and her dearly beloved Victor. Some people love the sound of voices and the rich flow of fifty dollars words and big ideas.

Every once in a very great while I have run into a babe where just my voice was enough to fill her with a thrill that made her wet inside and shot her all the way to the stars. Watching the open, glowing expression of beatific contentment that exuded from Ms. Cartwright's face, you would have thought Samuel Socrates Turner was down in the coal mine with a diamond tipped drill and striking enough sparks to build himself a Stairway To Heaven! That look of transfiguring joy that babes usually kept wrapped up in a hope chest deep inside their heart of hearts was smeared all over Ms. Cartwright's face like dandelion butter. What was so deep was how platonic the whole thing seemed. The innocent bystander would scope the scene and conclude the fortunate couple were somehow making love with their minds, and dining with gluttonous delight upon the spiritual ambrosia of their own conversation. Have you ever seen two people in deep conversation rapping the night away until something seems to rise up out of the very air between them like a smoke ring from a cigarette? Some kind of energy frisbee spins out from between them in slow motion and ever expanding rises up to be engulfed in the very atmosphere. Watching Socrates and Trixie go at it with nothing but words and ideas made me flashback to the way I would feel when listening to some of John Coltrane's super-extended improvisations on the saxophone. Man! What could he be telling that broad that made her seem so elated and eager and ever loving open to the touch of his voice? That bespectacled, bow tied, pedagogue was rousing this top shelf beauty to such sweetest ecstasy, you would have thought he had her spread-eagled over the table with her ankles against her ears as he ran a wet red and white candy cane in and out of her until her juices boiled and flowed free, spilling and oozing all the way down into the river of whee. How could I deduce all this in a matter of moments? Besides my own observations, this was not the first time I was a witness to the handiwork of Socrates. There were the rare times when the Spirit moved him, when he was really on top of his game teaching and his students, that especially includes the ladies, would leave his classroom almost walking on air. These encounters usually produced their most powerful effects one on one. When I would come to Turner's high school as a visiting artist, I was privileged to be in the presence of a few of Turner's brainstorming sessions with a pretty Science teacher and an attractive librarian. He would make even me look down from the scaffolding where I was painting my mural to marvel at the super intellectual riff he could wax on a woman.

Now that I look back on it, that might have been the first time I began to recognize that I was starting to see things in a new kind of light. Miss Ford, the head librarian could easily have passed for that woman in that T.V. movie. The one who played Rosa Parks; you know who I'm talking about. I think her name is--the one who played Michael Jackson's mother--Angela Bassett. Yeah, that's the one! Anyway, it was a trip to me the way Miss Ford and Mister Turner were all lovey and grooving on each other's thoughts and feelings in the library, now that after school time was here and the students were gone.

There was nothing in their behavior to look down upon. What could be more innocent than to have a conversation with a colleague at a circular table across a pile of books? I was up there in the lights and like any other fly on the wall was privileged to a ringside seat that permitted me a grand view of the evening's festivities. Each was working on their little task for the school, but it was obvious that they were quite unexpectedly stoking the flames of intellectual ecstasy in each other. That was when it began to dawn on me that there might be more paths to bliss than the usual route that led between a woman's legs. This was a fugitive thought, and it seemed to me to run counter to the prevailing wisdom of the times. Who was there to deny that the most wonderful thing in Life and in the world was the revolutionary emancipation of the orgasm? What kind of pleasure could compare to the after glow radiating out of your woman's face after you've rocked her world through her womb? The answer would have been obvious to my homies. There were no happenings to equal the pleasures of pussy. Still, what did they know? Most of them, I am afraid to admit, couldn't see farther than down the block. Even in their daydreams they were hard put to imagine what lay for them beyond the horizon. Most of them didn't want to know and couldn't be bothered to care. The pleasures of pussy were immediate and real. No, pussy couldn't get you into college or a high-rise apartment or a Mercedes-Benz, but it sure was the greatest consolation prize ever invented for the exploited and oppressed.

The only thing was, no man could stand in the shadows of Love forever. Sooner or later, a guy was bound to cop the attitude of the ancient Hindus and ask Santa what else he's got in that bag on his back. The truth is Stella and I used to kick this one around a lot, and she used to contend that the Lord would not have been so hard hearted as to furnish Man with only one route to bliss; and such a narrow one at that. When my head wasn't swirling in the intoxicating sweetness of her sex, I would make an earnest effort to see what she was concluding on the matter. This wouldn't last long, as she was so heartbreakingly beautiful to look at I could barely concentrate on what she was saying to me. I would pick up bits and scraps of her line of reasoning before I finally managed to successfully part her from her panties. I would then change the subject to a demonstration of nonverbal communication, where at least I could say I had done my homework.

That's the strange thing about understanding. Sometimes you don't grasp a thing all at once, bolt-of-lightning style. There are times when snips and shreds of ideas just percolate inside you until they are ripe enough to begin to emerge from the fertile ground of your thought. I think intellectually I was always prepared to accept, like Old man Rasmussen would probably say, that there was more to Life than pussy, that you couldn't observe or examine the subject of ecstasy by only putting your eye to the keyhole of sex. But it wasn't until I saw Miss Ford and Mister Turner together enjoying the rapture of conversation as though it were a peak experience that I could emotionally accept what Stella was attempting to ring my chimes about.

Ecstasy was an entrance through an aperture to a path that led to an ever-expanding whole new world.

When you have never known what it is like to own a car, finally walking around with your wife to pick out your favorite ride might really make your spirits swim in the nectar water. The day when you can finally have a catch with your son might be the milestone that makes for the eternal buzz. Coaching the little league team or the high school basketball team to a winning season and perhaps a Championship may bring you a happiness that can never be found in sex.

Check it out.

This may sound like a paradox, but what is more filled with paradoxes than that ball of confusion known as human behavior? Anyway, I believe people make love and have sex in order to know a happiness that can never be found in sex. That sounds like a trip, doesn't it? But that what I think people really want. They want that happiness that can never be found in sex, but they are chained to bodies whose greatest joy is sex. Therein lies the paradox, between what the spirit wants and what the body wants.

Some people like my grandmother simply needed a cool breeze and a good walk around the block in the Sun to restore the roar and flow with the glow. Just scoping at Miss Ford and Mister Turner out the corner of my eye from my perch on the scaffold, where I was mixing gesso and paint, I began to sense and perceive that there are probably as many ways to reach ecstasy as there are people to know them; and even though I was serving up no complaints at this particular time, I could see how in the long run, the physical means of achieving ecstasy might eventually leave something to be desired and have its limitations in the end.

There were ecstasies probably to be found in the love of the community for the community that might never be found between the sheets of lovers; but once again, this is merely speculation on the part of the Gentle Man. Unfortunately, as I continue my rampage through a vigorous and passionate youth, I will have to admit I am not yet falling all over myself to find out. I simply say to each his own freaky-deaky.

I know not what others might rap, but as for yours truly, give me pussy or give me death!

The Gentle Man has spoken.

Be that as it may, as Socrates and Miss Trixie did their Orgasmic Mind thing, I whipped panned over to Daphne and Victor motioning me over to their table. While I approached them, I found myself envisioning their togetherness in a way I never thought to imagine it. I could see myself being invited over for Thanksgiving dinner with all the trimmings and dodging and doing end runs around their grandchildren and congratulating their sons and daughters for making such fine parents and raising such fine children. We were all old and grey now, and as we collected around the table piled over with juicy browned turkey and dressing and cakes, cookies and pies, the Basehearts asked me whether or not they could prevail upon an old friend such as myself to say grace. The vision was so vivid with all that steaming hot food, it made my mouth water.

I know before you even say it, what a Tom thing to get all worked up over. Just like Old Man Rasmussen used to say, don't take more than the blink of an eyelid to get all wrapped up like a sucker in some white man's dream. The next thing you know, you're the best supporting factor in the movie of his story and you don't even get a percentage of the gross!

But even now, I will have to admit that the vision at the time seemed to appeal to the angels of my better nature. I could see Daphne and Victor holding hands at the head of the dinner table and it was all good. Faithful, old reliable Alphonso felt the pangs of compassion break like winged eagles from his breast as the Baseheart clan raised their glasses in anticipation of yours truly giving the toast. You could see the family terrier through the picture window, and hear him barking in hot pursuit of a rabbit on the rolling lawns outside. Everything seemed as though it were meant to be. The Baseheart family clinked their glasses, downed their sherry, and then gave a little hand to the wooly, cotton-headed Gentle Man. One of the Baseheart daughters pulled back my chair and made me feel like an honored guest. What more could an old man want with a free meal? I creaked my rear end into the cushioned seat and prepared to dig into the Thanksgiving feast.

What could I possibly offer Daphne to compare with this high class version of wedded and domestic bliss? Endless sketches and figure studies of her after making love with me, draped in the folds of our bedsheets? Perhaps a half dozen really boss paintings, and a motley collection of finely burnished pieces of sculpture? That was not a lot to build a long-term relationship upon. I was forced to concede to myself that compared to the Baseheart vision of Daphne wallowing in the lap of luxury, all I could offer were polished wooden slat floors where she could stand next to my easel while I was painting. I could see her in a nightgown, barefoot and pregnant and holding our latest bundle of joy in her arms while she shrewishly asked me when I was going to take my turn and burp the baby.

There's no use pretending to anyone now. I used to have nightmares that my poor wife and children would have to take to begging in the streets, as destitute and homeless as any of the characters of Dostoevski or Dickens. I could picture my wife with a pleading look of concern on her face for the children, wearing cotton winter gloves without any fingers to them, attempting to sell my charcoal sketches to passerby on the streets for a little meat to put on the table just before the eve of Christmas and in the dead of winter. The more well meaning among those who stopped to survey her wares would ask whatever become of her husband. She would turn her face away and reluctantly explain in the shivering cold how I ran off because the pressure finally got to me.

The one thing I did not want was to be like my brother Bobbie. Sleeping in abandoned garages and taking showers at the YMCA when he could get them, in hock to everybody and his momma and calling himself doing a Van Gogh for the sake of his Art. No, I wasn't down with that kind of scenario. I vowed to myself long ago I was never going out like that.

Sooner or later, everybody has to face up to what he or she really wants. The truth was, I was too involved with making a successful career out of my Art to be contemplating wedded bliss and the ecstasies of parenthood. As I approached Daphne and Victor Baseheart, it seemed to me a new kind of understanding was dawning on me.

This was my big chance! You know how it is when you come to some major turning point in Life and the choice you make at that moment is like the switching point in a switchyard? How the track of your life will be set for many years henceforth depends on how you play the setup that lies before you. I watched Daphne and Victor pave their little bubble of intimacy around them and somehow saw what I ought to do.

The time was finally upon the Gentle Man to put the greater good before the coochie.

All I needed to do was play my cards right, and I could get myself promoted out of the rank of artistic cock hound and into the rank of serious artist of note. Even though I knew Daphne was having the hots for me, I made up my mind to let this hand pass. I would give Baseheart a wide berth and let him have his dream with the maidenhead intact. I would do just like my moms always wanted me to do. What was that poem she woke me up with one morning, reciting to me at the top of her lungs? Something she read about being 'a friend to Man'. Yeah, I got it now! Something about sitting at 'a house by the side of the road and be a friend to Man.' That's what I made up my mind to do. I would let Daphne and Victor weave a dream that their parents could applaud and friends like me could celebrate. This would be my first step in creating community goodwill, and later on the Basehearts would come to me to have their portraits painted and those of their children and it would be all good. After all, just looking around the Diamond Hut I could see a thousand and one subjects worthy of my brush and my palette knife. I would take the high road and become a painter of the people. I would grow old and end my days rendering glorious sunsets and sunrises. I was easily envisioning the shingle above my front door. It read, 'ALPHONSO GENTLE: A FRIEND TO MAN!'.

That was when I ran into Dougie Dogg and the main squeeze he was sporting on his arm, Maxine. She was all curves and mammary melons tightly packed into a low-cut pleated burgundy dress. Dougie Mack was styling a pinstripe suit with a red kerchief in the lapel pocket. You would have thought he was returning from a weigh-in or something. When we brushed shoulders and I recognized him, he smacked me on the chest with the back of his hand.

"What up, dough, Alphonso?" Dougie introduced me to Maxine and she nodded at me with a smile. Dougie looked over at Daphne and Victor and shrugged. "Polly want a cracker, huh, my man?"

"Looks that way."

"- just -"

"Just what?"

Dougie gave me a steely-eyed scowl while he playfully fingered the tear drop earring dangling from Maxine's left earlobe. She giggled and whacked him playfully on the shoulder.

"Gone now, Dougie! You need to quit!"

"Hush up now, baby, hush up." Dougie admonished her as he shrugged at me again. "Just I thought you was the dude she came in with, my man."

I opened my mouth to reply when the crowd's response to Wilma's rap distracted me.

"NAW NIGGA-OH NIGGA! NAW NIGGA-OH NIGGA! NAW NIGGA-OH NIGGA!"

The chanting chorus of the crowd gave me that underwater feeling, but when the sea of waving hands parted, I had to admit that Wilma was looking good as Alice Walker with that mike in her hand. She was bopping to the beat of the clapping as she bounced her spiel off the walls.

"'Naw nigga-it ain't yo' deal
    why don't you come on now
        please be real

Naw-nigga-now
      don't be nasty
    just roll them dice
      an' when I hit
    don't ask me to be nice-
    'cause I'm bout tuh pull a fasty!

Naw-nigga-no!
    you got tuh go
I'm 'bout tuh get mah damn coat

    cause you 'bout to rock the boat
you ain't gotta choke now
cause you can't match mah stroke-POW!!

Oh-nigga-oh!
That really was neat
You done called mah hand
Ooooo-you so sweet!

Go-nigga-go!
    Don't be so slow!
There's more where that came from
    If you really want to know
Show me what you got
and I'll tell you -I'll tell you -I'll sho tell you
when you've hit the jackpot!

Now-nigga-now!
    Don't be so mean
you got me payin' off, baby
    like a slot machine

Down-nigga-down!
> You done gone the mile,
> I started down on a frown
> Now you done made me all smiles!'"

Wilma went on until the crowd took up its chanting chorus again: "NAW NIGGA-OH NIGGA! NAW NIGGA-OH NIGGA! NAW NIGGA-OH NIGGA!"

Dougie Dogg was clapping his hands in a rhythmic beat with Maxine. He looked over at me with a look of indignation and shook his head.

"What you oughta be thinkin' about is how you can get back up in that rye meat Wilma is ready and waitin' to set out for yo' sorry ass," Dougie said, sucking his teeth at me, "-a little of that AFRODISIAC might fix what been ailin' you, Alphonso."

"I'm cool on that score, Dougie," I look over at Daphne and she's still waving for me to come over. "Hey man, why don't you come over for a second and meet Daphne and her fiancee?"

"Them yo' friends, Alphonso. I'm tryin' to reduce!"

Maxine looks over from her clapping. She gives Dougie a quizzical look

"What you talkin' bout now, baby?"

"Alphonso wants us to go over and meet his friends."

"What's wrong with that?"

"I don't need no mo' honkies in my life! I'm tryin' to tell him I'm tryin' to reduce the number of whiteys I got to deal with now."

"Aw man," Maxine flaps her hand in Dougie's face. "-don't mind him, Alphonso, he kinda mental like that-"

"Watch your mouth, woman. Naw I ain't! Whiteys is just dead weight. You deal with em fo' a minute and you keep on walkin'. Now Alphonso, I know how much you love you some white folks, but that don't mean I got to get all wrapped up in they lifestyle with you-"

Maxine hears this and halts in mid-clap. She turns and looks at Dougie in disbelief, folding her arms under the burgundy folds of that wonderfully proportioned bosum. She makes a little tap with her shoe.

"Take a chill pill, Dougie. Damn! Alphonso just wants us to socialize with some of his high-class friends, I don't see nothin' wrong in that. All you gotta do is thank Alphonso for being nice enough to ask, that's all."

Dougie looks up at the ceiling. You would think he was counting to ten, the way he starts mumbling to himself. He tells the ceiling what he wants Maxine to hear.

"Why you dissin' me, Maxine?"

"Why you dissin' Alphonso, Dougie?" Maxine fires back with a counterpunch. "I thought y'all was tight. I don't do my friends like that. An' how am I s'posed to be dissin' you, anyway? I just said I thought you ought to thank your friend Alphonso for being nice enough to ask us to meet his friends. That's all I was signifyin', honey-"

"I oughta whop yo' ass fer that-"

"Unh-uh. You ain't about to put a dent in all this good stuff I got for you, man."

Dougie turned to me as he herded Maxine to his side with a hand on her shoulder.

"Thank you, Alphonso. Bring yo' friends to ringside. I'll be happy to give them my autograph when they come through. Come on, woman-"

Maxine blew through her lips, fanning them into a pout.

"Now ain't you high and mighty, Dougie! You act like Alphonso tryin' to get you to sign a contract with the Devil, when you got Mojo Morris for that-"

Dougie drifts off with Maxine nattering under her breath. I sort of wish she would cool it in a way, because I know Dougie, and he's not above slapping a woman around to put her back in her place and keep her in line. A true playa should be above that business, but I don't mind telling you that true playas are rare and a breed apart.

I make my way finally over to Daphne's table and sit down. Victor Baseheart half rises out of his seat and offers me his hand.

Daphne's face seems suffused in a kind of love-light. She eyes me, carefully sipping from her champagne glass.

"I'm impressed, Alphonso. You should have told me you were a rappa!" Victor gives me a hearty, grinning handshake and turns eagerly to Daphne. "That was outta sight, wasn't it, honey?"

"Uh huh. I think Mister Alphonso has been full of surprises tonight."

"Just a little sumpin'-sumpin' I picked up from the hood, that's all."

Baseheart goes on and on about the entertainment and the atmosphere at the Diamond Hut. While we're kicking it around about how he's being groomed to take over all the Greeting Card subsidiaries that the Wellingtons own, I slowly come to realize that Victor Baseheart is a veteran long distance bourbon drinker. He keeps telling the waitress, all decked out in her sparkling, twenty four carat diamond uniform, to bring us another round. He explains expansively how he would like for me to submit some paintings, preferably landscapes, to his Art Department. I keep telling him I'll take him up on that. I also suggest to him that he ought to take advantage of Daphne's ability as a performer and custom design some commercials for her to do. He does nothing more than grunt at this, and by the time I've brought it up for the third or fourth time, I start to realize he's slowly, deliriously sliding down into the bottle he's drinking.

"I think you've had enough now, dear," Daphne says as she attempts to push the bottle away, "why don't we go home now?"

"Nonsense, nonsense-" Victor pulls the bottle free from Daphne's fingers. "-I want our ole Alphonso here to be fully aware of the tremendous business opportunity I'm placing before him-"

He goes on about how productivity has increased since he got on board at the Greeting Card concern, but it's getting harder and harder to understand him as he keeps refilling his shot glass. Finally, Daphne let out a sigh of exasperation and looks up at me with a shamefaced blush.

"He's normally not like this," Daphne begins by way of an apology, "-this drinking of his is really the only thing I can find fault with him about-"

"You don't have to explain unless you want to," I tell her, "we Gentles have some first class drinkers in our family. My father could really tie one on after a late Friday night at the Blue-print Office."

Daphne attempts to give me a grim little chuckle.

"Victor? Why don't I take the keys now? You've had enough and we need to get home."

Daphne dutifully reaches for the key chain on Victor's belt, but he brushes her hand away.

"Nonsense, darling! Just because I've had a few doesn't mean I still can't handle myself. I ask you, Alphonso, do I look like a man who can't handle himself?"

There's such an earnest expression on his face, I'm laughing in spite of myself.

"I think you're having such a good time, you ought to let Daphne drive you home so you can concentrate on that. Why –why –why -why don't you; hey, belay that brew, brother-"

"Nonsense, nonsense!" Baseheart keeps repeating himself, but his words are starting to slur now as he rises to his feet unsteadily. "Why I'll go out right now and get the car and we'll-"

Baseheart slips and slides, spilling onto the floor in a heap as Daphne gives a little yelp of surprise. There's a wounded look of consternation on Baseheart's face as he sits up on the carpet. I motion to Daphne to get him up under the arms.

"Come on, Daphne," I tell her, "let's get him into a chair again,"

"-my mother keeps telling me it's his Irish and Welsh heritage-" Daphne begins as we heave Baseheart back into a chair.

"For real? So my father did all that boozing because of his Irish and Welsh heritage! I'll be sure to let him know."

"This really isn't funny, Alphonso."

We sit down across from Baseheart and listen to him mutter and hold forth on various and sundry subjects. I look across the table at Daphne and realize that Baseheart's dream and vision for them both has a decided dark side. No one can truly forecast the future, but even I can see the occasional thunder storm on the horizon for them should they marry. Before we know it, our dear Baseheart has begun snoring and now Daphne lets out a sigh of relief.

"Let's call a cab for Victor, Alphonso," Daphne says, slapping her thighs with resolve, "my poor baby will feel better in the morning once he's slept this one off" Daphne pulls out her cell phone and makes the call. "There. Do you think you can take me home, Alphonso?"

"Sure. You think that will be all right with Victor?"

"I don't believe he will mind. We've had to do this now and again since we've been dating. We'll deposit him into cab and I'll call one of his friends who stays in the same apartment building to look out for him."

All the while that we're figuring out what to do with Victor Baseheart, I can spot Leonard Morris out the corner of my eye, silently observing Daphne and me. We seem to be his entertainment for the evening, and with Sheba serving him food and beverage does not appear to be going anywhere anytime soon. Daphne catches me looking his way, and the question I refuse to answer appears on her face once more.

"Alphonso?"

"I hear you, Daphne,"

"Why does that man keep looking at me?"

"Face it, Daphne. You're a beautiful woman. You've got him spellbound, that's all."

"You're doling out the blarney now, Alphonso. What is it about that man you don't want me to know?"

There was a tense silence between us as I searched for the right words to say.

"All I can say is that it's personal. Right now, he's not a part of your world and there's no reason why he should be. Later, I'll tell you all about him, but for right now, I don't believe it's a good idea."

"Alright, Alphonso."

Daphne glances Morris' way once more before the festive mood congeals into another kind of murky silence. Daphne takes one more sip of white wine and reaches for her cell phone again. I can see the yellow checker cab parking outside, and I know that's my cue to start getting Victor Baseheart on his feet.

"Hold on, Alphonso, I'll help you as soon as I let Phil know that Vic is coming home-"

"Alright, baby-"

Daphne slaps her thighs again and then slings her purse across her shoulder, as she stands up and takes our snoozing Victor by one arm while I grab the other.

"Dog -Daphne! Feels like I'm cartin' one of my sculptures to the elevator," I exclaim as we half-walk and half-haul Baseheart to the front entrance, "-this guy's all muscle!"

"He ought to be-" Daphne clucks her tongue, "-this is a Lifetime Membership to FIRST FITNESS we're sending first class in seersucker-"

"I feel ya, girl, I feel ya,"

We deposit our Baseheart into the taxi as Daphne plants him a kiss for postage. We return his oozy-boozy wave as the cab makes its way around the spiral driveway and off down Jefferson. We're back inside the Diamond Hut in no time, and leaning over one of those winding balconies high up with a bird's-eye view on everything. We're scoping it all and sipping on that sherry wine so fine. The dance pit, the stage, the bar and the dining area are all laid out down below us in some kind of swirling regal fast life glow of hip-hop Life and Soul. There's Socrates Turner and Theresa Cartwright waxing philosophical about the price of swishy fish or something over at the edge of all the whirling bodies in the dance pit, and Leonard Mojo Morris giving out free soul handshakes to all his associates as they stop by his table to pay their respects gangsta-lene style while poor Sheba makes sure to keep his cigar freshly lit, and of course Dougie Mack and Maxine Green down in the pit going blow for blow, mixing it up and mincing steps and sweating hog wild into their groove thing, while the dining room swells with more and more paying customers bopping to the boss beat of the Rasta Man Band AFRODISIAC!

I point out Elmo Washington and Temperance Wilson to Daphne. We chuckle to ourselves, watching them nod smugly with proprietary interest at all the goings-on in Late Night Soulville.

"Who are those guys on stage playing that weird spacey music, Alphonso? They've really got it going on!"

"Where you been all this time, gorgeous? Ain't you never heard of AFRODISIAC?"

"That what they're calling themselves these days?" Daphne sips her sherry with reserved satisfaction. "Quite a band by anyone's standards, I must say."

"If it please your majesty-"

"Yes, my Lord Gentle?"

"Shall we retire to dine or continue with our leaning?"

"Oh, by all means let us lean, my dear Alphonso, let us lean -I say!"

"As you wish, your highness, as you wish,"

So we continued leaning against the rail of the winding balcony, duly noting the events of the evening as Daphne played footsy with me on the sly.

"I hope you won't hold it against us that Victor got bombed out of his mind tonight."

"Ain't no thang, little momma, ain't no thang. Everybody's got a hole in his soul somewhere. The real man rises above the flaws in his personality."

"You know, Alphonso, there are times you almost make me believe you really know what you're talking about. What makes you so wise, anyway?"

"I'll make a believer out of you sooner or later, Daphne Duck. There's some little thing gone wrong with everyone and that's just the way of the world. For Victor it's the lush embrace of the bottle; for me it is –"

"- the lush embrace of a beautiful woman. I know, Alphonso, I read you loud and clear."

"Check it out. There hasn't been a perfect man or woman since God gave Adam and Eve their eviction notice. So why are folks so greatly surprised when those closest to them prove this true in every case?"

"What about me, my liege?"

I look down my nose at Daphne from head to toe, sizing her up.

"What about you, sister?"

"Oh, you know, Alphonso. What did you call it?" Daphne snaps her fingers. "What's the hole in my soul! Right. That."

"Oh, so it's all about you now, huh? That right, Snow Queen?"

Daphne slaps me on the shoulder and we both look down into our thoughts and chuckle again.

"Are you trying to tell me in your inimitably indelicate way that I'm too self centered for my own good?"

Daphne kicks the back of my calf with her toe.

"Hey, I don't know. Should the shoes fit, see whether or not you can get them on discount, Cinderella."

"That's awfully cryptic, Alphonso. What in heaven's name is that supposed to mean?"

Daphne knocks shoulders with me, but I say nothing and chuckle alone this time. We share one more amused silence before Daphne casts her gaze in the direction of Leonard Morris. Now her brow wrinkles, and her face tightens with apprehension and concern.

"I think you ought to tell me now, Alphonso."

"Tell you what, baby?"

Daphne points down into Morris' direction and nods at me with a discerning frown.

"We're way up here and that guy is still checking us out. What's his deal, anyway?"

There are some things worse than opening Pandora's box, and I have that strange feeling this might be one of them. I reluctantly shake my head and examine the lint on the cuffs of my suit coat. I hold on to the sternness for Daphne's sake.

"Come on, Alphonso, tell me," Daphne implores with a hint of genuine alarm in her eyes, "-please? What is that bozo's problem?"

We watch as Morris motions over to where Dougie and Maxine are beginning to exit the dance pit with the other couples. Dougie takes Maxine by the hand and stops to palaver awhile at Morris' table. The two of them trade soul handshakes and Dougie accepts Morris' invitation to sit down and stretch his legs. Maxine looks off like she's sighting for the nearest escape and then with a resigned sigh scoots up to the table with Dougie.

I rap my knuckles against the rail of the balcony. Seeing Dougie with Morris is tripping some alarms in my own mind. Morris looks up at us again with a wide Cheshire grin and pulls a fresh cigar out of his breast pocket. I can feel Dapne's head against my shoulder as she squeezes my arm. We watched as Sheba is again Johnny on the spot with the silver lighter for Mojo.

"He's still looking this way, Alphonso," Daphne tells me as I feel her cheek shuddering against my arm, "what does he want, anyway?"

"He's looking at you, Daphne."

"Why? Don't leave me in the dark like this, Alphonso. He's been like that all night. What is his problem? Does he have some kind of fetish for white women or something?"

The old adage goes that Knowledge is Power, but in this case, I would have done a whole sight better by keeping my mouth shut. The only thing was, it did seem unfair to Daphne to pull rank on her like that. Besides, I thought it might go easier with her once she understood the whole scene as it was laid out before us.

"He just wants to market what God gave you, Daphne."

"Wha - what do you mean?"

"It's nothing personal with him, really, just business. Leonard Morris peddles flesh and right about now you look like an excellent business opportunity to him. He's studying you now to see what the markup might be and what kind of clientele you might best appeal to in today's open market."

My mouth is going dry again and I'm feeling tempted to have a cigarette, but calling myself trying to quit, I forgot to bring me some. Daphne takes a step back as though someone dropped a scoop of ice cream in her lap and is all aghast as I knew she would be. I stop searching in my suit pocket for a smoke as Daphne tries to make light of my remark with a nervous laugh, but nobody in all these centuries has found being inspected for the auction block a subject of amusement yet.

"What did you say?" Daphne tilts her head as though she's hard of hearing

"I didn't want to get into all this, but you insisted. You asked me; I told you. That fellow down there has been figurin' and calculating all night what he would have to do and what it might take to turn you out."

Daphne takes another step backward, furiously blushing.

"Are you serious?" Daphne's nervously touches the Adam's apple of her pale white throat, and you would have thought she was in the middle of coughing or choking. "Please tell me you did not say what I thought you just said."

"There's nothing wrong with your hearing."

Damn! I knew I should have kept this to myself. Now Daphne is casting about glances to see whether or not anyone else is passing us by on the balcony within hearing range. I watch her eyes narrow as she drums her fingers on the balcony railing.

"That's the most incredible thing I have ever heard! What on earth would make him think I would ever agree to such a preposterous proposition?" Daphne began to fume as she fingered her rhinestone purse with uneasy agitation. "Why! I've half a mind to go down there and slap his face for that!"

Daphne half turns to descend in a huff down from the balcony, but I catch her by the elbow.

"Whoa, mama, whoa! You don't want to mess with that critter unless you've got disinfectant and plastic gloves. Besides, there's no law against havin' private thoughts."

Daphne whirls around to confront me, her face turning beet red.

"Are you defending him, Alphonso?"

"No, that's the last thing I would ever do. But that there mug is so well connected with the sewer system here in this city, it's hard to be in the same room with him without soiling yourself."

"He's not the only one who's well connected. My father has golfing buddies in the various police departments of this state. What's his name, anyway?"

Now I'm kicking myself in the ass for having gotten Daphne involved in all this. Whatever made her decide to go cruising with me on tonight of all nights, anyway? None of this slumming she was so keen on doing was my idea.

"He's Leonard Morris," I mumble with a forlorn sigh, "he services with the Gentlemen's Escort Business and deals in Showgirls. Down in the hood, dudes know him simply as 'Master Mojo'-Daphne! Put that down-"

"'Master Mojo', that's rich-" Daphne scoffs imperiously as she scribbles something down on a sticky pad with the eyeliner pencil she took from her purse. "I'll have my father-"

"Daphne, put that down!" I grab at the pencil between her fingers, but she snatches away from me. "Don't let him see you writin' nothing! He might get it in his head you're some kind of Narc or an undercover agent!"

"There!" Daphne puts the sticky pad and the eyeliner pencil back inside her purse. "I'll get this to my father and have him alert the proper authorities. I wish I were a law enforcement officer here. Looks like you need one! Some people should know better than to let their imagination runaway with them in the future."

When I glanced back down across Daphne's shoulder that was when I knew, and a chill ran through me colder than the almighty Hawk ever sent through Cadillac Square on a windy winter's night. The Cheshire grin Morris was sporting disappeared and now he became the Great Stone Face in a twinkling of an eye. I saw him lean over and whisper something into Sheba's ear, and he made a gesture straight at us.

Do you know that Daphne was in the act of waving back at that buzzard?! The next thing you know he would have sent Sheba over to invite us to his table and it would all start all over again. Leonard Morris trying to collect another piece of my life to grind between the gears of his Mojo Machine. No, I couldn't let the endgame go down like that!

I laced my fingers between Daphne's and turning her around away from Morris, bent her half way back over and laid one on her. After that, I raised her up slowly making sure my back was blocking Mojo's view of her. Daphne's indignation shattered into a startled smile, as her fingertips brushed my cheek.

"Alphonso? Why-"

"Dumb bitch!" I whispered softly into her ear.

"Wha-?!"

I grabbed Daphne and tossed her over my shoulder. There was no time for a discussion. I figured to get her down from the balcony and out of the Diamond Hut before we were swirled any further into the Mojo mix. I literally danced my way down the winding marble step, dodging people going up and folks going down.

"Uncle Alphonso! Hey, Uncle Alphonso!" I heard a youthful voice dimly within earshot. Daphne attempted to wiggle down from my shoulder, but I slapped her on the rump so as to reduce her struggle and protest as we made good our escape.

"Ow! Alphonso, what in heaven's-"

The ashy hand of Temperance Wilson stabbed out at me.

"Dynamite rap, Alphonso!" Temperance exclaimed as we managed a soul handshake, but now I had to put Daphne down on her feet. "You came through true to form and did us proud as always, my brother."

"A privilege and a pleasure as you very well know, my main man," I said, as I took Daphne by the hand and spied behind me for any sight of Mojo. "I was just telling Daphne what a treat it would be to bring more of her friends here sometime."

"Yes, I'll be sure to tell my -" Daphne begins swaying unsteadily beside me.

"Look, I gotta book, Temp-" I pull Daphne in the direction of the exit, "-say good night, Daph-"

"Whoa!" Temperance holds out his hand like a traffic cop. "Slow down, playa, slow down! I got someone here I would like for you to meet-"

"Ain't got time now, Temp, my man-" I curse under my breath at Daphne for getting us interfaced into Mojo's shit. "-we got another party to catch-"

"Hey, Uncle Alphonso!" Now I recognize that voice! "Uncle Alphonso! Don't do me like that! I know you hear me callin' you!"

I follow Daphne's gaze until it comes to rest upon my nephew, Antonio Gentle, according to his mother's maiden name, and his little teenybopper hip-hop girl friend, Gelisa Dukes. At least he's not embarrassing me. He's dressed to the nines in that casual, but immaculate Gentle style, and his squeeze don't look too bad either, except those piercings in her nose and eyebrow do nothing for her. Antonio is a nice looking version of his mother and my sister, Alicia Marie. He favors Tiger Woods sort of, except he's taller and slimmer. Gelisa, the girl of about an hour, has that Brandy thing going on with the corn rows and braids. I gave Antonio a summer job to shut my sister up, and he's been running errands for me back and forth from my Studio after school. I see him raise his hand for the soul handshake, but this is no time to socialize.

"What are you doing here, Tony?" I asked through my stern face.

"Aw, don't do me like that, Uncle Alphonso. Just cuz you tryin' to sneak outta here with that white girl don't mean you should leave kin hangin'. Gelisa, my Uncle Alphonso."

"That your nephew, Alphonso?" Daphne tugs on the sleeve of my suit coat.

"Yeah, that his nephew, girl -" Temperance pulls Antonio over next to me like before and after pictures in some kind of magazine. "- don't you see the family resemblance?"

"I see the resemblance. How come your nephew's cuter than you are, Alphonso?" Daphne teases me.

"Look - you should be home, Tony." I said, pointing an accusing finger at him. "Look, I wish Daphne and I could stay for awhile and socialize, but we really have to be going -"

"That's just like you, Uncle Alphonso. Grandma always said you stay in the streets too much." Antonio hands are sky high over his head so he can signify. "Why don't you give yo' lady an answer to her question before you go? Explain to her please how come I blaze you in the looks department!"

"That's to make up for the brains you ain't got! Come on, Daphne-"

"Alphonso! That's no way to talk to family-" Daphne chastises me as I tug her along.

Little Gelisa whispers something into Antonio's ear and they giggle together.

"Uncle Alphonso! You can't do me like this! You can't just hit and run on kin. Don't let that 'Jungle Fever' do you in like that. Hey, Uncle Alphonso! You need a prescription, you know where to come," Antonio puts his arms around Gelisa's shiny, dark carmel shoulders, "report back to the Love Doctor as needed."

'Jungle Fever', huh? Report back to the Love Doctor for a prescription, right? Right. Take four white girls and call me in the morning.

"Hey, Uncle Alphonso!" Antonio cups his hands around his mouth and stands on his toes. "Mister Turner wants to know when he can come over and play a little poker with your buddies. What should I tell him?"

"Tell him to give me a call, Tony!" I said, waving my way through the glass doors of the Diamond Hut.

"Nice meeting all of you-" Daphne signals with her flashing rhinestone purse in farewell.

Great! I can just see Wilma, Dougie and Maxine clustering around Temperance and my nephew wondering what has gotten into me. They all step aside though, when Leonard Morris bulls his way through, snapping his fingers and pointing to his feet to get Sheba to his side.

"What's your hurry, boy?" I hear Morris' deep baritone rumble out in the night air. "That honey not gon' fly away! What's the matter, you can't speak, boy?"

Morris takes out yet another cigar from his vest pocket but this time waves Sheba away.

"I ain't got nothing to say to you, man." I hurriedly tip the valet and open the passenger side of the Focus for Daphne to sweep herself inside. Daphne and I look up the curving walkway at the rotund silhouette of Morris in front of the Diamond Hut. "We don't have no business to do that I know about."

"What's the matter. Alphonso? Yo' daddy never teach you no respect? We might have a little business to do just on account uh-"

I did not catch the rest of it because I was too busy gunning the engine to get us out of there. We swept our way back down Jefferson to the Lodge. There was an uneasy, disquieting silence between Daphne and me as we took the fast lane on the freeway.

"I'll take you back to your parent's place, Daphne."

"How come? I don't think I want to go back there tonight, Alphonso. Why don't you take me back to my apartment?" Daphne gives me a nervous glance and then looks off into space. "I'll fix you a cup of coffee, and then you can explain to me what this thing is between you and this Leonard Morris/Master Mojo fellow or whatever he calls himself."

"Leonard Morris is a pimp, Daphne."

"I gathered as much. I just don't follow how you're involved. I also don't understand why you're so afraid of him."

"The girl that was seated at the table with him? Remember her?"

"Yes, Alphonso, I remember her."

"She used to be my girlfriend. She was going to college and everything. Mojo got a hold of her sweet-talked her into the Life, sunk his claws into her and turned her out."

"You mean… she's one of his prostitutes now?"

"You're catchin' on-"

Daphne started with a nervous laugh, and then squinted at my forehead as though there were characters of foreign script she was attempting to read between the lines of my furrowed brow. She attempted another laugh, and then turned to look out the window at the rushing scenery; a finger between her teeth. She looks at me again with that question in her eye.

There was just the air rushing through the window to fill the silence now.

"I must say, Alphonso, I never thought you could see me in that light."

"What light?"

"What made you think I could ever agree to that kind of a Life? Why I would rather be dead than endure that kind of degradation! That's not to even mention what my father and my mother would do were they to find out I was involved in that lifestyle. Why my father would kill me, and my mother would disown me and have me written out of the will! There's not enough money in the world to make me sign up for that kind of grief!"

Daphne glances at me again through the glare of a street lamp.

"Why on earth would I ever do something like that? I have everything I could ever want or need now. There is nothing that could possibly induce me to consider such a thing!"

Now I really wish I had a cigarette. After I take a deep breath, I let out a long, weary sigh.

"That's Mojo's game, darlin'. Don't you think he's asking himself the very same set of questions you just put to me? The only thing with him is he's not ruling anything out. He sees the whole thing more in terms of a sporting challenge. Like I said, there's nothing personal in this for him. Especially since he doesn't even know you. As far as he's concerned, you're just an interesting problem with special characteristics. He was pondering about you the way a physicist would ponder about a problem in quantum mechanics, or a mathematician would ponder about an equation involving irrational numbers. Just the sight of you started the wheels of exploitation turning in his head. Now he's figurin' and calculatin' and searchin' through his mental files for special cases. He wants to see whether or not there are precedents already established involving high class women and the kind of trade he sponsors and advocates. He would still just be kicking it around in the workshop of his mind, but for the fact that he saw you takin' notes on him. Now, no tellin' what he might do."

All the time I am breaking it down for Daphne, the streetlights and shadows lick across the most incredulous expression on her face.

"Alphonso!" Daphne shakes her head and looks out the passenger window flustered. "I –I –I -forget it! There's no way; it's not going to happen! There's no telling what my father might do when I tell him we ran into that sort of character. When my father finds out what you've just been telling me, this Mister Mojo will be lucky if Daddy doesn't put out a contract on his life!"

There is another uncomfortable silence and for the first time a cultural chasm seems to open up and yawn between us.

How do you explain to a lady the propensities of the male mind? Women tend to focus, in my experience, on the whys of emotional motivations, whereas fellows tend to focus on the hows of stress and leverage. The first kind of intellectual exploration is great for counseling abused children and battered wives in a halfway house I suppose, and the second type of method is good for construction sites and building bridges. The problem comes about when you attempt to take these modes of thinking out of the domains of thought and fields of activities for which they were intended. Combining stress and leverage with the subject of social and human relationships tends to conjure up for me unwholesome connotations I don't even want to think about. Whereas the subject of human motivation, as fascinating and inexhaustible for insight as it may be, must take a backseat to an understanding of mechanical advantage in a machine shop or a lumber mill.

"Alphonso?"

"Huh, baby?"

"What did you mean when you said this Mister Mojo character turned your girlfriend out?"

"Just that," I regard her evenly, "whatchu think I meant?"

"Alphonso! That isn't telling me anything!" Daphne scrunches around in her leather seat. "I mean you said, 'he turned Sheba out'. What does that mean exactly?"

"Let me break it down to you this way; it's like you take a glove and turn it inside out. That way what was on the inside is on the outside, and what was on the outside is now on the inside, safely tucked away or ready for the trash bin."

Daphne sat back and nodded thoughtfully.

"So when you turn someone out, it's like you reveal to the outside world their true nature. Is that what you mean, Alphonso?"

"Now you're catchin' on, Daphne. The thing is, it all depends on what you're looking for and what you intend to do with what you find. The prevailing wisdom is you can draw anything out of anybody once you really know it is already there. At least that's how guys like Mojo think. The question to a dude like him is simply a matter of how much stress and leverage would he have to apply to bring out the side that he can make money on. Once he's sure he has successfully calculated that, all he has to do is press the right buttons and put out the job order for a brand new spankin' clean hoe to come hot off the assembly line!"

"That's an awfully cold-blooded way to view the world."

"Yeah, tell me about it." I quickly shift out of the fast lane and look for the exit. "See -"

I quickly glance at Daphne with uncertainty, and then back at the road.

"Alphonso?"

"Huh?"

"You were saying?"

"I don't know if I should be tellin' you all this-"

"You started this. You might as well tell me everything now."

I started this! Like I was writing up Mojo for the Feds or something. Still, I might as well read the fine print to her, just in case the deal goes down we really are in contract with the devil.

"Come on, Alphonso," Daphne nudges me, "give me all the dope about Mojo."

I look at her again and sigh, because we are treading on shaky ground about now.

"When you view your whole life through a prism of pain, the way you look at things can get twisted a hundred and eighty degrees without you even knowing it. I think that must have been what happened to Mojo because of some kind of mess in his life. Anyway, Mojo figures that beneath the soft, sweet, innocent, loving and compassionate breast of every woman beats the heart of a skank, bitch-ass hoe ready and willing to seduce a john to his knees and spin a trick out of all his ready, available cash. He's been tellin'us homeboys for years that it's a bitch's true nature to spread her legs for the rewards of Life. That whorin' is as natural to a woman as her menstrual cycle, and all he does is liberate a woman to be her natural self. The point is, Mojo looks for any and every opportunity to prove that his brand of pander logic is as scientifically valid and correct as any of the laws of Gregor Mendel or Isaac Newton. He's an absolute fanatic about the idea that inside every woman is a whore waitin' to be primed to pay off like a cash register. So nowadays he looks for the women whom men would declare least likely, or put out of bounds with the 'never in a million years' designation, and he trains his sights on them to prove his universal Law of Life."

The freeway wind streams through the deep, probing silence that settles upon us once again. Daphne carefully mulls over what I have said.

"That's my exit, Alphonso! You just missed it-"

"No I haven't. I'm taking you home to your parents."

Daphne looks behind her at the receding sign posted against the overpass.

"But - what is this, Alphonso? Do you think you're rescuing me or something? I'm not in fear of some lowlife just because you say he has unmentionable designs on me."

"See - that's why I got you out of there. You walk into someplace and you don't know where you are. The best thing to do is to keep a low profile until you see how things go down."

"I don't recall my ever flaunting myself, Alphonso."

"That's not the point, Daphne." I look over into Daphne's imploring indignation and deep down I know that it is my bad for taking her down there. "When you're someplace you've never been before, you have to chill, because any little thing you say or do might be taken the wrong way and get your ass in a sling."

"Alphonso! What are you talking about? I've been to nightclubs before. I know how to comport myself. Why don't you just come right out and say what you mean, for God's sake!"

I heave another sigh of disconsolation and look Daphne straight in the eye.

"Why do you think Morris followed us out of the joint, anyway?"

Daphne narrows her eyes slowly, not comprehending at first, and then just as slowly her eyes widen as a thought slowly dawns upon her and she convulsively grips her rhinestone purse.

"Nooooo-" She exclaims with a hushed whisper.

"Oh, yeahhhh-"

"-but-but I was just writing on a stickypad with my eyeliner!"

"Funny thing how that caught his attention, huh?"

Now the gravity of the situation finally sinks in as Daphne senses how she inadvertently is swirled up in the Mojo mix. She huffs with a little scoffing laugh, and then looks at me for moral support, but I'm looking straight ahead and I'm not smiling. Daphne presses her back against the seat and folds her arms testily.

"Take me back to my apartment, Alphonso. I don't care to be driven back to my parents home tonight."

"No can do, sister. You need to be someplace safe. This is your big chance to tell your pops all about the shady character who was eyeballin' you all night at the Diamond Hut."

"I can do that anytime," Daphne waves airly, "I'll probably call Victor tonight and see what he thinks I should do, but right now, you can take me back to my place."

Now I am beginning to feel a mounting frustration rising inside me. What do I have to say, what must I do to get through to this poor little rich girl? I grip the steering wheel until all my knuckles hurt.

"Naw Daphne, you don't seem to understand. Leonard Morris is a card carrying member of the Shady Characters of America Club. All he has to do is flex his connections and someone dies. He's thick as thieves and under the table with the Greeks, the Italians and Chicanos; and I cannot gurantee that the black Mercury Cougar that' been in my rear-view mirror the last few minutes isn't his idea of a tail!"

Daphne takes a quick, apprehensive look over her shoulder and then catches herself in a little self-conscious laugh. She slaps me on the shoulder with a feigned air of playfulness.

"Alphonso, now you've got me doing it! You can stop with all the melodrama. I refuse to be infected with your paranoia. What you've given me is a personal account of your relationship with that Mister Mojo fellow and the woman he came in with-what's her name-?"

"Sheba Taylor-"

"That's right. It seems to me that your whole assessment of tonight's events is highly colored by your emotional experience with them. After all, you say that this Sheba Taylor was your girl friend and that she was going with you, isn't that right?"

"Yeah. What's that got to do with anything?"

Daphne slaps her thighs and folds her arms again.

"There! There you are! It seems to me that it might be pertinent to ask what you did to that poor little Sheba, 'playa', to estrange her to the point that she would seek refuge in the slimy embrace of a wolf like our Mister Mojo."

"What? Where did you get that idea? I didn't have anything to do with Mojo turnin' Sheba out."

No time to lodge an official protest. All other questions I planned to answer with 'no comment' or simply plead the fifth.

"That simply doesn't wash, Alphonso. She was your girl and she was going to college, or so you explained it to me. What would make a lovely girl like that suddenly desert a 'dreamboat' like you and the prospect of a dignified and respectable life, all so she could throw in with a criminal and pursue a career in prostitution? I've been wondering about that ever since you hustled me into this car."

I will have to admit I did not expect Daphne to take me to court on this.

"Now is not the time to get into all that, Daphne."

"Hmph. That's what I thought you would say. You see now, Alphonso? I'm not such a dumb bitch, after all."

I can tell Daphne is fishing for a compliment to smooth over hurt feelings, but times are tight right now, and she will just have to check back tomorrow during store hours.

"Don't you see, Alphonso?" Daphne clutches at her purse again petulantly. "Where I think you made your mistake is in too closely identifying me with Sheba Taylor. Perhaps I should be the last one to point this out, but Sheba, I'm gathering from what you've told me, probably comes from a single parent home without a strong male role model, has struggled with poverty all her life and the cultural disadvantages of being an African American woman. I was fortunate enough to be raised in a loving two parent family that's well off and, rightly or wrongly, still enjoy all the advantages granted to a white woman of Irish and Welsh descent. I think it's best for you to bear that in mind-"

Daphne goes on and on with her never ending story. I suppose partly to show me she can relate, and partly to show her solidarity with the oppressed peoples of the world, whose pain keeps her awake at night under those plush covers. Women and children! It's just like Rap and me used to observe when we were pulling stickers and labels off those videotapes coming down the conveyor belt at Technicolor. Women and children! You can't be nice to them. Daphne goes running off at the mouth about how she wishes Sheba and her could have gotten the opportunity to know each other better and on and on and on and when she shuts her mouth nobody knows! Now comes the kicker at the end of all this.

"I was really surprised, Alphonso, when you kissed me and then in the next breath called me a dumb bitch. Anyone else, and I would have left my handprint tattooed across their face. The thing of it is, that was the first time I felt a spontaneous connection of honesty between us. Something of the real you finally came through that facade of charm you strut around behind all the time. Right now in your own alarmist way you're actually trying to protect me, and I have to admit it's refreshing. Especially when I consider how you've spent all this time playing me to get into my pants."

"Now you are trippin', girl! I'm droppin' you off at your parents before you land us both in a world of hurt."

"I just want you to know I am not a dumb bitch. I'm not in the least afraid of that Mister Mojo slime ball. Also, I don't care to be taken back to my parents place. I thought I made myself clear on that point." Daphne's face sets in a sullen scowl. "I'll have Victor meet me at my apartment seeing as how you're so concerned about my welfare."

"Look Daphne, this is not about what you want anymore!" I said as I see the exit to her parents crib coming up. "You may think you're down with the setup, but let me tell you, sister, you're in the wrong place to be real right about now."

"That some more of your ghetto wisdom? I said don't take this exit, Alphonso! Look, I'm calling up Victor on my cell phone right now-"

We are coming up the ramp for the straight shot to her parents crib when we behold a curious sight. There are two people scuffling nearly in the middle of the street when I see a flash of metal reflected in our head lights. Daphne and I watch as the bodies thump and roll in a wild embrace, and finally collide against the curb where the posted sign for the bus stop vibrates in the night air. I bring the Focus to a sharp, screeching stop at the edge of the service drive. Now I can see it's a man and a woman thumping head up with each other, almost teenagers really, and the woman somehow knocks the flashing metal out of the man's hand as he straddles her body to slash away.

"Alphonso, look -" Daphne tugs at my sleeve and points through the windshield.

We watch the knife fly end over end in the air until it lands with a clatter on the asphalt. It slides and slithers to a stop just shy of falling through the drainage grate next to my front tire on the driver's side. Daphne seizes for the door to the car.

"For heaven's sake, Alphonso, he's trying to kill her! Don't you see that?"

I quickly grab Daphne by the arm and pull her back, thrusting her into her seat.

"Naw, baby, naw, this is not for you," I say as I open the door to the driver's side, "- just stay in the car and let me see-"

The look of protest on Daphne's face is hard to shake loose as I hustle and lunge for the knife before my man can retrieve it. My fingers snatch for it and nearly knock it down into the grate before I have a hold of it. Our midnight assailant stops just short of me as I feint at him and slice menacingly at the air. He cracks a desperate smile now that I've got the drop on him.

He looks to me like a short, muscular medium complexioned man in the headlights.

"Aaaaa - what's the matter? You want some? Come on, man-" I lunge at him again.

Now that I've got the weapon in my hand, Mister Big Stuff chooses this moment to turn tail and run. I rush off after him until he disappears, well into the darkness of the trees in the park. I hear the car door on the passenger side slam behind me. I turn to see that Daphne has done just the opposite of what I told her to do. She is out of the vehicle and rushing over to the weeping young woman at the side of the curb.

Daphne is helping the distraught young lady to her feet. She takes her hand and begins to dust off the woman's burgundy pants suit around the legs and the behind. Daphne pulls blades of grass out of her fleecy hair and generally aids in straightening up her disheveled appearance. I come back across the street, wheezing under the street lamp to my car and get the surprise of my life.

"Are you alright - who was that -!!" I stop and Daphne glances at me with a tense questioning expression as I bend over to get closer. "Miss Ford? Is that YOU?!"

Sure enough, I realize this is no teenager before us. I am peering into the face of the head librarian at Mister Turner's high school. I help Daphne guide Miss Ford over to my car with a consoling hand on her shoulder.

"Miss Ford –what –how -why are you out here this time of night?" I splutter out as Daphne gives me a stifling look and hands Miss Ford a Kleenex from her purse. "Daphne, open the door so we can get Miss Ford somewhere safe."

"Lord have mercy!" Miss Ford exclaimed between sobs, close to breaking down. "Lord have mercy! I was coming from a party, walking back to my car across the park. That's when this -I don't know who that was-came out from behind a tree or something and attacked me! I kept screaming and running to get away from him, but nobody came out to help or anything. I don't know what would have happened if you all hadn't stopped to help me!"

"Alphonso?" Daphne looks at me again, as she opens her passenger door. "Do you know her?"

"Hell yeah, I do. Excuse me, Miss Ford-" I said, and then swore softly to myself when I saw that black Mercury Cougar cruising around the park from us. "I was the one who painted that mural on the wall of your high school library. Remember me?"

Miss Ford dabs her eyes with Daphne's Kleenex, gives me a look of irritated discernment before she recalls where she saw me last and the light goes on in her eyes.

"That's right!" She points at me like I'm her attacker. "You're Genner, aren't you? The one Principal Landry hired to do the artwork for our school. How are you, Genner?"

"Gentle, Miss Ford. Alphonso Gentle. I'm fine, I - get in the back , Daphne, will you? I-"

"Look Genner, I didn't want to ruin the evening for you and your lady friend," Miss Ford is close to breaking down into tears again, "I just wasn't expecting-"

"We understand, Miss Ford, we understand,"

"Did you get a good look at him?" Daphne asked meekly as she crawled into the back of my car. "That'll help with the police and things-"

"Who?"

"The one who attacked you, Miss Ford -"

"Oh!" She waved at us in disgust as she dabbed her eyes again. "He came out of nowhere so fast I hardly got a chance to see anything. The most I remember was he wore some kind of black stocking cap or something. I nearly pulled it half off when he grabbed me and I started hitting him with my purse. My purse!" Miss Ford twisted around looking anxiously. "You didn't find my purse anywhere, did you?"

"No, I wasn't paying any attention to that," I said as I started up the car.

"You want us to help you go find it?" I saw Daphne through the rear-view mirror volunteer quickly. "Where do you think you last saw it?"

"Oh, would you please? He knocked it out of my hand in the park. Unless he ran off with it, it should still be there somewhere-"

Miss Ford started to open the door to look for her purse, but I kept the door locked.

"You better stay with us, Miss Ford. We'll help you look for your purse. I think it might be easier with me drivin' up in there and using my headlights-"

"Oh, would you please? My identification, cell phone, my money, everything's in that purse-"

We came up into the park and stopped near a tree that Miss Ford pointed out to us. She retraced her steps and we helped her until she spotted a big, long rectangle of black leather just off behind a dark green clump of bushes.

"That's it!" Miss Ford pointed to the ground, and then after taking a step, looked around hesitantly. "It was here that he first grabbed me-"

Daphne went over with Miss Ford and fished her purse out of a puddle next to the bushes.

"Thank you -" Miss Ford feverishly unclasped the purse and rummaged around for all her valuables. "Oh, this is a blessing!" Miss Ford looked into the night sky with relief. "Everything seems to still be here! My money, my driver's license, even this -"

Miss Ford held up a black case for what looked like a videotape cassette.

"What that?" Daphne said, flashing a quizzical smile my way. "A late rental or something?"

"Oh no, Mister Turner loaned this to me from his personal collection. "He made a copy for the library and we were viewing it at the party." Miss Ford looked away to one of the mansions they called homes that encircled the park. "Something called 'Cleopatra Jones' or something; I just can't understand why nobody from the house saw or heard me. Lord knows I screamed loud enough. Uh, look-" Miss Ford fished inside her purse again, "-it's getting late and I really don't feel like going down to the police station this late at night. Could you drive me back to my car and sort of escort me back to my friend's house so I can make a few calls? I'll call the police from there."

"Sure that's what you want to do, Miss Ford?"

"That's probably the safest thing to do at this ungodly hour, Alphonso," Daphne mumbled confidentially to me.

"I can get your names and numbers as eyewitnesses and have the authorities contact you should they catch that a-hole," Miss Ford went on as she re-clasped her purse, "but I'm too done in to do anything more right now, and I would rather just call it a night." Miss Ford took her key ring from her purse and nervously picked out the keys to her car. "The truth be told, I'm really a very private person, and since it seems nothing has been taken-"

"But are you sure you're okay, Miss Ford?" I interjected my concern, "You have any cuts or scrapes? Y'all was tusslin' pretty good, you might have bruises you don't even know about-"

Even under the street lights her grateful smile made her radiantly beautiful, and it was not hard to see why Samuel Turner would spend so much time jawing with her.

"That's real sweet of you, but from what I can tell I'm just shaken up, that's all. I'll have my doctor thoroughly check me out tomorrow, but at this moment, I just want to get someplace safe where I can sit down and be quiet. This was upsetting enough -"

Miss Ford looks like she's about to break down into tears again, so I do not press the point any further. Daphne sympathetically touched her on the shoulder

"I'll be all right once I can be to myself for a little bit. I just don't see the need to drag you and you lady friend any further into my trouble. Genner."

There was nothing more to say after that. We took Miss Ford back to her car and then followed her back to this colonial style white house, with its blue shutters and windows set far back from the street. When we got out, Daphne and I marveled at the rapidly returning sense of self-possession that Miss Ford communicated to us.

"I want to thank you again for just being there before anything bad could happen to me," Miss Ford told us as I shook her hand and patted her on the back. "I've got your numbers now, so I'll let you know what the police need from you; if anything. Just wait for me to go back inside. I'll give you a little wave, okay?"

"Are you sure you're okay?" Daphne begins again, "-wouldn't you rather-"

"Call me Christina," Miss Ford takes us both by the hands, "-the only thing I would rather do right now is get up out of this street. Goodnight, you all,"

Miss Ford dismissed us with hugs, and made her way wearily up the steps of this grand house, and I suppose to whatever remnants of a party there was left to receive her. Daphne and I went back to the Focus and watched and waited until a yellow square of light opened up before Miss Ford and she turned to us and gave us that little wave. I honked and we watched as the door closed behind her.

I was in the middle of moving the gearshift into drive when Daphne checked my hand.

"Alphonso?"

The way she looked at me, I knew she was working her looks to get what she wanted from me.

"What's the matter with you?"

"Nothing. I just want you to take me home, that's all. Please? Would you please?"

"I thought you were callin' Victor to come get you."

"Ohhh, you know he's probably still sleeping off his drunk and just snoring away!"

"Probably."

"So how about it?"

"When are you and him gettin' hitched, anyway?"

"Oh, I don't know. I'm sure my parents have masterminded all the particulars," Daphne pouted to the windshield, "- but for all they know, I just may decide to elope with you and break poor Victor's heart. What do you think about that?"

"Dream on, girl."

"What's the matter, Alphonso? Am I not a prize enough catch for the likes of you? You never know I might end up making you a very good wife."

"Now who's zoomin' who?" I put the car in park and turned to Daphne cynically. "Look me straight in the eye and tell me you want to have my babies, raise my kids and grow old with yours very truly, my Daphne."

When you want the truth, the eyes have it. Daphne and I lock gazes for a fully pregnant moment in eternity before her cheeks start to tremble and she flinches away.

"That's what I thought."

I put the Focus into drive and we roll away.

Daphne furtively glances at me and then tells the side window the real deal with lowered eye lashes.

"Alright, Alphonso. No, I don't think I would ever consider marrying you. When you get right down to it, you're far too glib about everything. Sometimes I feel like you're just sitting back and laughing at us all, we poor mere mortals with all our quirks and foibles. When we were having dinner tonight you even tried to make a joke out of the sacrifice of our Savior. There may have been a kernel of truth in much of what you were saying, but deep down, I couldn't help but feel you were working your way towards the next punch line. I just don't think the suffering of Christ can be encapsulated into some kind of intellectual joke. As far as I'm concerned, you were just as off base there as my father was with that reference to King Kong."

We were silent for a long while before Daphne spoke to the passenger window again.

"Besides, I wouldn't want you to be whispering sweet blasphemies into our little one's ear when it's your turn to burp the baby."

"What?"

"Nothing." Daphne says, turning to me with an exasperated sigh. "Are you taking me home or what?"

"No."

"I should have left in the same taxi we put Victor into," Daphne muttered, "Okay, let's put it this way; what do I have to do to get you to take me home instead of to my parents house?"

What I said next I have played back in my mind more times than I can count, but I still for the life of me do not know why I came up with the following bright idea.

"Hmmnn, I'll tell you what; you give me what you wrote down about Leonard Morris and the pencil you used and I'll consider taking you home."

"What do you need that for, Alphonso? All I wrote down was that I was going to talk to Daddy about him."

"I'm just thinkin' that if I show Morris that what you wrote down was harmless and was just a childish prank that couldn't possibly affect him in any way, I could then make sure that he never touches a hair on your head and close the deal that way."

"What?" Daphne exclaimed with consternation.

"You heard me. Hand over that sticky pad and the pencil, woman. I'm only doing this to see that no harm comes to you or yours on account of Morris or any of his posse."

Daphne folded her arms again and simmered with rage. She made little nods at me, sizing me up as she tapped her arm above her elbow with her fingers. She seemed to expel her breath in sibilant, fuming snorts, her gaze a narrowed cast of condemnation.

"My Christ, Alphonso! What is it that makes you so afraid of that man?"

The laser quality of her blue eyes were piercing enough to lay bare the marrow of my most inner intention.

"Mojo's out to take my life from me piece by piece," I confess with bowed head, "- he just wants to take pieces of me until there's nothing left; not even a hollow shell or a shadow or a mask to fill with the vapors of someone else's hopes, and ideas and dreams. You think you can get to that?"

"That's what you think, is it?"

"That's what I know."

"So I'm just a piece of your life you want to run away with and hide someplace where this Mojo can't reach. That how you figure it, Alphonso?" Daphne shakes her head with a contemptuous sigh. "I gave you credit for more backbone than that, Alphonso; you intending to run from this man your whole life? That's crazy! You've got to stand up to this fellow and fight for what's your own. You keep running like this, that man will run you to the ends of the earth; run you into a hole in the ground! Let me help you handle this guy once and for all, honey. I'll just call Daddy and-"

I run the Focus into an abandoned parking lot with a savage turn of the steering wheel. The recoil of the brakes and the shocks leaves Daphne shaken.

"There you go again! Just like the dumb white bitch I thought you were-"

"Don't you call me that! Don't you ever call me that again-"

"- thinkin' you can solve every problem with just a snap of your fingers-"

"Get your hand out of my face!"

"You ever think that maybe this goes beyond what you think your Daddy's money can do? Ever think maybe this goes way beyond all the millions of people who have to do without so that Daddy Warbucks can pile up all that wealth and privilege?"

"Whatever, Alphonso, whatever." Daphne fumbled inside her purse and produced the sticky pad and the eyeliner pencil. "Here. Go beg your boogie man for your pardon. Nooo problem. All I was trying to do was help you, but what kind of help can a daughter of the white oppressor give a down brother like you? Keep the faith, Alphonso, keep the faith. But just for your information, remember that we Wellingtons never ran from a fight! Let that be a lesson from your former hunkie girl friend. Now," Daphne slaps her thighs, "are you going to take me home or do I have to call a taxi?"

Whenever I reflect upon this moment, I have to ask myself would anything have turned out any differently just from hauling off and bitch slapping Daphne the way I know I should have. I'm hip that would have been a gross violation of Playa Policy, not to mention Gentle Protocol, but sometimes a babe is earning and burning for a spanking. As far as I was concerned, right about then, Daphne was bucking to be awarded the Bruise Badge of Courage, and I was having a hell of a time keeping my hand in my pocket.

I took the scribbled sticky pad and eyeliner and placed them in my wallet. I cursed myself for craving a cigarette about now, and opened the door to the car and got out. Daphne proceeded to exit from the other side and followed me.

"Aren't you going to take me home now, Alphonso?" Daphne asked, as her heels buckled in the gravel of the parking lot.

"Get back in the car, Daphne." I ordered her bluntly with a scowl.

"I will not!"

"Get back in the car." I repeated, then turned around to face her so she could see I wasn't playing.

Because I was standing in the shadow of the Laundromat next to the lot, Daphne couldn't see my face. I was just a hulking silhouette to her, and rather than step out of the light to continue quarreling with me, she instinctively shrank back and reluctantly returned to the car.

When I finally returned to the Focus she was sitting there looking up at me with a demure kind of resentfulness.

"What was that all about?" She asked me with a hint of apprehension in her gaze.

"You just don't understand, Daphne-"

"Yeah, I thought as much. You know, whatever, Alphonso. Why don't you take me home before we both do something we'll be sorry for, my good man."

"I still think you should stay with your parents for awhile."

"We've already discussed that, Alphonso. Don't you think we should be going now? I'll be sure to call Victor again once I'm safely locked inside my apartment."

"Suit yourself."

"Seems we've reached a parting of the ways, mate." Daphne evenly checked her makeup in the rear-view mirror. "Cheer up, Alphonso, I'll be sure to keep in touch."

There was nothing more to say after that. I put the car in drive and did a one eighty heading back to Daphne's place. When we got there, I made one last attempt to change her mind.

"Daphne, I-"

Daphne reached over and squeezed my cheeks between her fingers.

"There-there, Alphonsy-poo, mommy's all done in and doesn't want to philosophize about it anymore."

Daphne fought the impulse to kiss me goodnight and reached for the passenger door. I sat there in the car watching those admirable curves recede down the long walkway until she was inside the vestibule. When I saw the lights come on in her apartment and what looked like her silhouette looming in the window, I honked my horn and then drove away.

Anyway, deep down inside I knew Daphne was right. I would have to thrash this out with Morris sooner or later. I headed back to the Diamond Hut to have a powwow with the Mojo Man.

The crowd was beginning to thin inside and outside the Diamond Hut. When I came back to where Mojo had been sitting with Sheba Taylor, there was only Dougie Mack at the table and he was looking all morose with his head cupped in his hands.

"What happened to Maxine, Dougie?" I asked, and Dougie looked up at me. "Where'd she go now?"

"Ain't no thang, Alphonso," Dougie Shrugged, "I bitch slapped that cunt. Tole her to gon' bout her bizness."

"Why you do that, Dougie? What's wrong with you, fool?"

"She wasn't all in mah corner like I thought she was. She was talkin' all that whack junk and carryin' on, about how I would have my hands full with Mister Marine since he outweighed me, and outreached me and was breakin' ribs and jaws in his sparring practices. She was talkin' like that in front of Mojo and carryin' on, so I had to set her straight."

"What's the matter, man? You scared? You sound like this one is startin' to spook you."

Dougie grunts and then looks back at me with that soulful, mournful expression.

"I didn't think you was comin' back, Alphonso," Dougie continued, as I looked around to bum a cigarette off one of the busboys. "What's up with you and that Doctor No honey you been sportin'? Don't tell me she gave up the panties that fast."

"Thanks man," I tell an obliging busboy as he holds the light to the cigarette he gave me. "Nooo," I sit down across from Dougie and stretch out my legs, "you way off base there, my brother. I was just tryin' to do the right thing by her, that's all."

"Did you?"

"Did I what?"

"Do the right thing, fool! What you think I mean?"

"I don't know yet, Dougie. Have you seen Mojo around since I left?"

"Naw man, he booked. He didn't take too kindly to you dissin' him. He left you this note, though."

"Lemme see," I snatched the note from Dougie's outstretched hand and read quickly, "you saw him write this?"

"Yeah man, we was talkin' about the poker games you be havin' with the bloods nearly every Sunday. He tole me he would be stoppin' by one of these days to check out your stud poker technique and to teach you a little about respectin' yr elders."

"That's what he said?"

"Yeah, buddy-straight up."

I pull out my wallet and retrieve the sticky pad and eyeliner pencil. I'm about to tear up Daphne's note when I spot my nephew Antonio shaking hands at the far table with Samuel Turner and Theresa Cartwright. They wave at me as Antonio makes his way over to my table.

"Hey Uncle Alphonso-"

"What are you still doin' here?"

"Don't do me like that, Uncle Alphonso. We was kickin' it around with Mister Morris and he had me crackin' up about you." Antonio straddles a chair at the table. "Uncle Alphonso,"

"What?"

"Gelisa and me went up to your studio last night and I saw all these boxes stacked up against the wall. What you fixin' to do, anyway?"

"You'll find out. Where'd Gelisa go?"

"Oh, she went to the little girl's room, she'll be back," Antonio twists his neck in that direction and back. "Uncle Alphonso?"

"What man?"

"You get that 'Jungle Fever' out of your system yet? You ready to return to the land of the livin'?"

"Sure thing." I said to Antonio, hoping that would shut him up.

We kick it around a little bit more and then Antonio leaves with Gelisa and that's the last time I see him before the headlines come out in the Free Press.

I hand Robinson back the photograph of Theresa Loretta Cartwright.

"Whatever happened to that airline stewardess you was bonin', Rap, my man?"

"What? Oh, I had to fire that bitch! She kept callin' out Captain James T. Kirk's name every time she was cummin' and I got tired of that shit. I finally had to realize I was nowhere to be found on the Starship Enterprise. Ain't that a blip? Here I am doin' all the work, and that T.V. white man gets all the credit! That' fucked up, Alphonso."

"Yeah, well, it be's that way sometimes,"

Old man Rasmussen comes out into the lot where Rap and I are leaning against the jacked car set on the concrete blocks.

"Alphonso?" He waves a red handkerchief at me. "There's someone here to see yo' ass, young blood!"

Miguel Jimenez steps gingerly out into the lot and looks around warily as Rap Robinson stiffens with the initial symptoms of homophobia.

"Alphonso? Is that you?" Miguel sights with his hand over his eyes like a visor. "I came as soon as I could. It's a pity and a shame about Daphne, huh?"

"Come on over here, man. Meet my friend, Rap."

"Damn Alphonso, why you gotta go this way with the play," Rap mumbles and curses under his breath. "Who invited this fruit up here in this joint?"

"I did, man, it's tight - it's tight -"

"Make sure you take good care of what's in that cigar box, Alphonso," Rap fixed me with a steely gaze, "Now remember, Alphonso, don't make no move with this until Mojo draws first. He always does in situations like this, so just wait him out. When you see his heat then you move. You got it? You have to see him start to draw first."

I gave Robinson a stern nod.

"All right. This the only way you got to cover yo' ass later. Let him start to draw first..."

"I got it. Don't go no place, Rap. I want you to meet a friend of mine. I went to college with this dude, you know?"

Now there's just one more person I have to see, and after that, I ought to be able to run the table the way of the Gentle Man. At any rate, everything's just about in place, and it's going to be time soon to shuffle the cards and see who will be the chump who makes the champ.

Right about now, I'm just hoping it won't be me.

I reached for my cell phone but it was not to be found on my belt. I knew it was around here somewhere, but after scuffling with Victor, where it might be was anybody's guess. The truth is I was too dog-tired to pull the fire escape down and too sputtered out to scrounge around for that cell phone hopefully lying around in this alley someplace.

I leaned wearily against the wall between the dumpster and the dented garbage cans on the rack. My eyes welled up with tears of frustration and a deepening sense of futility. I took another look at Victor. He was still on his knees moaning about Daphne. I knew that if I did not find my cell phone, I would soon be joining him groaning about my missing nephew.

We would both be two scuffling and tusseling dogs, moaning and groaning about our lost loved ones in this alley behind Cadillac Square.

TONY GHETTO

"This is not a game..." Victor was still intoning as I started to cast about for something shiny on the alley floor. "This is not a game, I tell you..."

"Yeah, I think I understand that now," I told Victor.

"How could you understand anything? We should have never gotten mixed up with you and all your darkie friends from the slums!"

"Right!" I whirled about at Victor from my search. "White Privilege is a terrible thing to waste."

Victor silently mulled my last statement over for a while.

"What is that supposed to mean?" He asked me meekly.

"I thought you white boys from the suburbs understood everything. You figure it out and I'll let you show me how it's done."

Victor watched me as I keened my eyes around the alley.

Every once and awhile I would make a few steps in one direction and then a few steps in another. Now and then I would let out a sigh of exasperation.

"What are you doing now?" Victor asked as he swayed from side to side on his knees.

"Looking for my cell phone. Hey man, make yourself useful and help me find it, huh?"

"Ghetto Enterprises- can you hold, please -"

The time was finally at hand to have a skull session with Eugene Halloway, AKA Tony Ghetto. I knew Mojo wanted to put his Pimp Hand down in my business and use it as a front to make his own operations appear squeaky clean. He wanted to be my silent partner as bad as Tina Turner wished to be your private dancer, but I wasn't about to let any of that happen. Sooner or later Mojo would be applying the crowbar for leverage, but I wanted to make sure that should something happen to me, Tony Ghetto would be holding all of the cards.

"Mister Halloway will be with you in a minute," a copper toned secretary wearing her pinstriped jacket and skirt stood by the mahogany door to the inner sanctum, "why don't you have a seat, Mister Gentle?"

"Thank you, ma'am."

The plushness of the sofa was such that when I sank into the purple felt cushions, I was just about ready to turn over and go to sleep. Such were the troubles on my mind. I craned my neck and looked down through the wall window from my little perch in the Cadillac Square Building. I shook my head and spied at the traffic, unusually light for this time of the day. Eugene knew the score, I thought, as I shrugged to myself. There was nothing like looking down from a high place to make you feel you were moving up in the world.

"Ghetto Enterprises-may I ask whose calling-"

I surveyed the magazines on top of the glass-covered coffee table in front of me. There were copies of EBONY, BLACK ENTERPRISE, ROLLING STONE, NEWS WEEK, VOGUE, SPORTS ILLUSTRATED and TIME all fanned out across the surface. I picked up one of the copies of SPORTS ILLUSTRATED and started leafing through. Before long my thoughts were drifting over to Dougie Mack, and all the folks who were laying long odds against him winning this time.

"Yeah, now they think they done found the White Hope to beat me down, those hoo-jis want everybody to see it-"

"Slow down, Dougie, slow down-" I said, grunting every time he hit the heavy bag with me holding on.

"Yeah, what that man say back in the day? The revolution will not be televised, but Dougie Dogg's ass whoopin' most certainly will be from coast to coast!"

"Uhnn! Why you gotta inject race into everything, Dougie, man?"

"Hoo! Hunh! Why you gotta be such a Tom an' ack like it's not?" Dougie retorted, lunging into the heavy bag with thrusting uppercuts. "This supposed to be my last bout fore I turn Pro, and wouldn't you know but that they'd have to find some white boy somewhere to block my way thru the front do' somehow."

"Uh! Uhnh! Ain't studdin' you, Dougie. It's all about the money and you know that as well as I do."

"Hunh! Hah! Who you got your money on, Alphonso?"

"What kind of question is that? Why would I be standin' here helpin' train yo' ass if I didn't have my money on you?"

"Hah! Hee!" Dougie sends me and the heavy bag swaying back with hooks and crosses. "I see-said the blind man. Got to protect that investment, huh?"

"What you think, fool?"

Dougie rams the bag with jabs and uppercuts and begins to dance with a chuckle.

"One thing about you, Alphonso," Dougie feints and jabs-feints and jabs, "-you a businessman to the bone -hup! Hooo! I got to give that to you -hup! Hah!"

"Like the man said, 'business is business'."

Dougie comes in tight to hammer in the body shots.

"Uhnh! Uhnh! That what the man said? Damn! I woulda swore up and down you was in this cause we boon coon-hunh!"

"Time for you to grow up then, niggah!"

Dougie starts to circle and to aim high with his punches.

"That's more like it, man, keep it real- keep it real." Dougie said, mixing in a random pattern of combinations. "See -whoa! White people been kickin' ass for so long it's ancient history to them. Hah! Hah! The only way you can make them see the truth is to kick their ass with it. Whoa! Come on wid it -come on wid it! Here you go, money, here you go! Hunh! Whiteys see the light with love in their hearts once you bust that ass!"

"Maxine been missin' you, Dougie. Uhnh! You really oughta talk to her and get her back in your corner before the match, man."

"What I look like sniffin' up her skirt like some pussy whopped punk? Hah! What I'm supposed to say to her now? Whoa! Hah! Huh? 'Dear Maxine, you still gon' let me suck that titty should I get my ass kicked?' Hunh! I know what that hoe would say to that one. She would be out the door as soon as I hit the floor. Hah! Hunh! Hi-hoe-silver! Away! After that, it's 'Hang Em High with the next guy!"

"That's cold, Dougie."

"Just keepin'it real, Alphonso, just keepin' it real. Hoo! Hah! Hoo! Maxine ain't goin' no place. Everything will be copacetic once I beat me down some Marine ass. She'll come around and toe the mark after that. Hee! Hah! Hoo! Hunhhh!"

"What's wrong with you, Dougie? Everything ain't about kickin' ass. You need to do what you gotta do to get right with Maxine. Especially now, on the eve of this big fight."

"That's what's wrong with you, Alphonso! Everything is about kickin' ass! You just cain't accept that. Long as I'm kickin' ass, I'm Mister Big Time, the man of the hour and a real life hero to one and all. The second I get mah ass kicked, I'm just another niggah. Yeah, that's cold. The cold hard truth, money, I get mah ass whopped, and I'm back in the land of the lost, walking a livin' nightmare with the likes of Indigo Dunn. Flashin' my fight pictures to strangers on the street and anyone else who'll look. Besides, what Maxine got I don't need right now. Pussy tends to slow you down and make you weak in the knees."

Lawson, Dougie's trainer, comes over to unlace his gloves while I stand by the heavy bag and catch my breath.

"Win or lose, you still got to have somebody to love, Dougie. That's just straight up common sense."

"Hear that, Lawson?" Dougie gave me a derisive, gold-toothed smile. "Even when I lose, Alphonso will still love me!"

There is raucous laughter among the other boxers jumping rope and going through various aspects of their training routines.

"Awwww," Dougie joins in with the swelling, echoing chorus of his fellow colleagues in pugilism, "ain't that sweet!"

"Don't knock it till you done tried it," Lawson mumbled through a mouth full of chewing tobacco as he pulls the boxing glove off Dougie's taped hand. "Don't look now, but the Gentle Man might be on to something. Hey Alphonso, help me get this other glove off this pug!"

"Alphonso ain't shit!" Dougie scoffed to hoots and howls. "Can you kick my ass' is what it's all about. I ain't had to read that in no book. See -you done spent all that time in that arty-ass college with all them white folks makin' yo' mind weak. Now everything's got to be complicated. 'We should talk' and 'let's discuss this over lunch' and 'let's go over that last point before we forget to renegotiate the negotiation'. All that stuff is a waste of time and money when what it all boils down to in the end is 'Can you kick my ass?' "

"Sho' you rite!" Some fool answers up while Lawson and I pull the last glove off Dougie.

He starts stretching and flexing, but that don't stop his mouth from running full throttle.

"'Can you kick my ass?' Huh? You can do that, you got my respect; and I just might listen to what you got to say before I start to plan my revenge. You can't kick my ass then fuck you, cuz, cuz I can't be bothered. So how bout it, Alphonso?" Dougie paces up to me and pushes me back as he beats his chest with his taped hands. "Can you kick my ass? C'mon. That's what everybody in here wanna know and you cain't find that out lookin' in no book."

A deadly, primal silence wafts through the gym with the drafty, foul stench of sweat as Lawson steps between us.

"Whoa, soldier," Lawson cautions Dougie, "this here is a civilian!"

Now I know breaking up with Maxine has got to Dougie. He doesn't usually talk this much and I have never seen him this free with his emotions. He glances at Lawson like he's measuring him for a poke and then goes back to giving me the evil eye.

"I came here to help you, Dougie; but you keep this up, you gon' wind up kickin' your own ass."

Dougie squints like he's going to sweep Lawson aside. Let him come at me. I'm poised for the attack and the coldness is oozing out of me now at this point. That's when he starts to chuckle in little tremors until his shoulders are shaking and he claps his hands.

"Aww, mannn, I wuz jus fuckin' with you! Hey y'all, this here my teacher! He taught me how to read and rap and everything. I ain't about to put a hurtin' on this man, cause he sho' nufff has got that knowledge! He down with that Doctor No bitch came to Wilson's club the other night." The murmuring release of a relieved laughter fumigates the gym. "Yeahhh! C'mon man, I was jus fuckin' with you. I need you to train with me and be my sparrin' partner, cuz yo' reach about the same as Mister Machine Marine."

Dougie puts his arm, slick with sweat, over my shoulders as we move to the ring.

"I think the Marine done put the fear of God in you, Dougie. I never known you to be so loose with talk before a fight."

Dougie takes his arm away from my shoulders as Lawson gives him the rope. He regards me thoughtfully.

"That right, cuz? That what you think?"

"Hell yeah, that's what I think."

Dougie nodded calmly as he took the wooden handles of the jump rope in both hands.

"That's where you wrong, money." Dougie starts to dance and skip. "I got this loose mouth hangin' round the likes of you."

Dougie dances and skips away in time to the swinging rope and paces towards a giant poster on the wall of Tommy Hearns.

"Ghetto Enterprises-could you hold one moment, please-"

I leaf to an article about Barry Bonds and toss the SPORTS ILLUSTRATED issue back on the coffee table before checking my watch. I look around into the disinterested faces about me, and realize I am not the only one here to seek the special services of The

Ghetto Man. I decide to chill and pick up an issue of POPULAR MECHANICS this time. I flip through to this article on this new car that gives a hundred miles to the gallon and somehow Rap Robinson comes up in my thoughts.

"I know what you're talkin' bout," Rap nodded eagerly, as he let me take turns with him drilling in the lug nuts on the green Ford Contour Sport with a lug nut gun, "-it's like this here gas guzzler we're workin' on; how you got one energy system relaying and feeding power to another. See -it's all about energy, Alphonso. How do you get back plus what you done put in already. You figure that one out, you ready to see some big bucks and make a name for yourself. That's what Black Folks got to figure out how to do in the long run."

"What Black Folks got to do with it, Rap?"

"Here," Rap poured more lug nuts into my hand, "- work this gun some and I'll break it down to you. See - we been flowin' our energy into this whack-ass system for centuries too long and been gettin' nothing back. A lot of us been helpin' White Folks out for so long we don't even think about gettin' nothing back anymore. Just helpin' out is enough."

"What's wrong with that? You can help somebody, you should."

"Watch the gun, son, watch the gun," Rap scrutinizes my handling of the lug nut gun through narrowed eyes, "-what you don't understand, Alphonso, is that we were brought over here to help them. That's the part we play in the system. Everything we think, everything we feel, and everything we do is designed to be funneled and channeled into their inevitable well-being and ultimate benefit. That's the system White folks have created to oppress and exploit us. We put our energy into the system and it seems they the ones that get everything back. Anytime some black person makes the system give back more than what they've put in, well sir, they done beat the system and that's what it's all about. Here, let me check them lug nuts you done put on-"

"Let me get this straight," I said, as I pace around the Ford Contour, "what you're sayin' is that we have to always be comin' up with a system to beat the system. That what you're sayin'?"

"That's right. That one's pretty tight," Rap tells me through the whirr of the gun, "I'm gon' tighten up this one just a little more-" Rap moves the gun around to the right rear tire. "Square business, Alphonso, you got to make the system reward you instead of deny you. Who are our Black Heroes in the Hall of Fame?"

"Sounds like you still goin' after that Forty Acres and a Mule, man."

Pap! Pap! Pap! Pap! I can feel the leather of Dougie's boxing gloves slapping me in the face while we spar and it makes me dizzy!

"Forty Acres and a Mule?" Dougie grimaces as we take a break ringside. "Bump that! Rap don't know what he talkin' bout. Forty Acres and a Mule! That's too old school. The price done gone up, mellow. I want Forty Acres and a Mercedes! Forty Acres and a Mall! That's what I'm talkin' bout!"

"Don't knock it," Rap screws the lug nut gun off the hose, "Forty Acres and a Mule is at least a start, but how long ago was we promised that? What I'm really sayin' is let's be scientific about this and not rely on the White Man for nothing. If he comes through on his end so much the better, but let's not have any one monkey stop our show. See-we got to be like good ole J.C. and be the Master of our Disaster! Remember that scene where he fed the multitudes with just five fishes and two loaves? I sure would love to know how he made that work. That kind of knowledge would come in handy when times is tight. How do you think he worked that little number, Alphonso?"

"Hellifino. Got to ask your pastor about that. Got somethin' to do with Faith as far as I can tell."

"Yeah, I understand that part." Rap frowned as he cased the lug nut gun. "What I'm talkin' bout is the mechanics involved. I figure he was crankin' those loaves and fishes out of holes in space just the other side of the baskets that they was keepin' those five fish and two loaves inside of-"

"Don't let Smiley hear you talkin' like that. He's bound to call you a blasphemer."

"Smiley can kiss my ass! Ain't no commandment against speculatin' on how you make a miracle come about."

"Yeah, but who's to say he made more fish and bread in the first place, Rap? That's just the way you got it pictured. Maybe he fed them with something more than fish and bread and that is why they were satisfied."

"Hmmnnn, you got a point there, Alphonso. But I like my way better. My way everybody gets Free Lunch and there's some left over besides. Reminds me of the time I put fifty cents in the vending machine at Mack Stamping for a orange drink, and two cartons dropped down into the slot instead of one. That's what I'm talkin' bout. When what you put in comes back double you on the right track, my man!"

"No doubt about that, Rap."

"Come on, Man," Robinson patted me with the back of his hand as he moved over between the Contour Sport and the Thunderbird, "help me finish switchin' the engines on these rides 'fore Old man Rasmussen comes back in here with his mouth. Guess what though? I copped an issue of POPULAR MECHANICS the other day, and GM is working on a car that'll give you a hundred miles to the gallon-"

"Ghetto Enterprises-one moment, please-"

That's what Rap was talking about while we were switching engines. I don't mind telling you that GM Ultralite was a thing to behold, what with its gull-wing doors and carbon-fiber body shell. Reading about it and looking at the photographs, definitely made you want to get closer to it than the pages of a magazine.

I could see why Rap was so interested in the car. According to the magazine, you could plug in different types of engines, all the way from electric power to gas turbine. Rap was always ready to tinker with engines to any kind of machine.

I glanced up from my magazine at some dark skinned dude in a Du rag or maybe stocking cap reading a copy of the Detroit

News. The headlines on the back, 'HEIRESS AND TEEN STILL MISSING', made me feel cold and stiff up and down my spine. I thumbed through a little more of POPULAR MECHANICS, but the big, bold type on the back of that newspaper was souring my taste for light reading. At length I picked up a copy of ARCHITECTURAL DIGEST, to change the subject and pursue a different line of thought. While flipping through pictures of homes in styles as various as the Tudor, Dutch Colonial, Victorian and French Provincial, and coming across the obligatory reference to the homes of celebrities and stars, as well as architects like Le Corbusier and Frank Lloyd Wright, I thought about Pop. There were magazines like this all about my mother's house, many stacked against and falling off the numerous models my father made of nearly anything that could be replicated with toothpicks, dowel rods and balsa wood.

I would help my older brothers Willie and Earl bring Pop back from midnight benders at some local bar, where he would wallow in booze. He would eagerly explain to anyone who would listen how Benjamin Banneker finished designing Washington D.C. from memory. This after, of course, Pierre L'Enfant punked out and took his bat and ball, as well as the plans for designing our nation's capitol, back home to France with him.

I don't know how factually verifiable that particular anecdote was, but I'm sure Pop got it from my mother. She was always bringing these kind of 'fun facts' from the school where she was working in the cafeteria, and later from the African American Museum after Mayor Young passed away. Across a bar stool, I'm sure Pop made some fascinating listening. We could always hear Pop even before we walked in the door good.

"That Ben Banneker was somethin' else! He made the first workin' clock here in America! Kept the blueprint plans for Washington D.C. in his head! There's a black man behind the design of Washington D.C. and you can believe that!" He would turn his cylindrical head, greying at the temples, towards us like an African totemic sculpture and slam down his money on the counter after he saw us. "- and don't forget that! Thank you, barkeep, there will be no need to call a cab, I can see my boys have come to see about their old man -"

"C'mon Daddy," Willie would shake Pop by the shoulder, "come on home. You got moma worried sick about you -"

"What you doing in a place like this anyway?" Earl would crane his neck with distaste at the subdued lighting. "You don't need to be in no place like this."

"I was just giving," Pop would sway off his stool like he was going down for the third time, "our friends here, a lit-tle Black History lesson, that's all, son."

Willie and Earl would grab him by the shoulders, and I would be over in the corner sketching the way the lights glowed in the chandeliers above the wooden tables. Ever once in awhile I would quickly scribble a picture of some pretty girl I spied in those dives, but such events were rare even back in those days. Willie and Earl were always hollering at me to come help them carry Pop to the car. I was always happy to oblige, once my sketch book was safely tucked behind my back between my belt.

"- and did you know that Benjamin Banneker accurately predicted there would be an eclipse on October 18th, 1800? Did you, know that?"

Pop would look straight at me as though he were talking in his sleep.

"No Pop, how'd you find that out?"

"Aww, shutup, Alphonso!" Willie would raise his hand back like he was going to smack me. "Now you got him started when we just about got him through the door!"

I snickered to myself, because I had heard the answer to this one a million times before. I raised my finger to the ceiling in anticipation of what my father would say and how he would gesture when he said it.

"NO ONE," Pop would look around the bar to make sure he was holding everyone's attention, "no one, not one other astronomer agreed with him. But history speaks for itself! There was an eclipse on October 18th, 1800! Benjamin Banneker was correct, and all others, no matter how learned, proved to be wrong." Earl lifted Pop's legs into the car. "Think about that, y'all, I just want you to think about that -think about that -"

We got Pop home and stripped him down to his BVDs. Mom would be cussing up a white streak as she slipped his arms and legs through the sleeves and pants of his pajamas. Willie and Earl put his feet in his slippers while I buttoned up his pajama shirt. Meanwhile, Pop went on with enlightening us as mom guided him up the stairs to bed.

"- had no business going down there no way! What with three boys to look after, and a daughter away at college." Mom glared at us in annoyance. "Show's over. Y'all go to bed now."

But we were following right behind them to get to our room and you could hear my father all the way to the top of the stairs.

"Detroit is a broken wheel, with broken spokes - I could design a better city than this!"

"Yeah Daddy, in yo' dreams!" Earl would say out the side of his mouth.

"I could have been just like Benjamin Banneker. Just, like him!"

"Why can't you be like him now, Pop? You always tellin' us it's never too late." I said, just to see what he would say to that. "Ain't you black enough?"

Willie and Earl scowled at me with menacing eyes.

"Hush now, Alphonso, your father is going to bed-"

"Yeah, shut that stuff up, Alphonso," Earl slaps me upside my head, "before I knock all that play out of you!"

We made it with Pop to the top of the landing, and he seemed to wake up as though all of a sudden he was aware of his surroundings and knew where he was now. He put his arm around my mother's shoulders to steady himself. He looked back at us boys and pointed at us.

"That's right, Alphonso, I am black enough. You're right about that, son. I'm black enough to be the one black man who builds a city that will be the envy of the world!"

"Get down, Pop!" I duck as Willie reaches out to cuff me. "Black as you wanna be!"

"Shhh. Alphonso," Mom puts her fingers to her lips, "we're going to bed now, boys. Say good night to your father."

We said goodnight to Pop. I remember Willie and Earl threatening to end my life, once we were back in our rooms. They told me I would be buried in the backyard where the dogs could come and pee on me should I ever crack wise like that again.

Now I inwardly chuckle as I flip through the rest of ARCHITECTURAL DIGEST. No, I guess I didn't really believe my father could actually design and build a city like Detroit. Where would he find the time? He was down at the blueprint office all day and often long into the night. Besides that, where would he find the money? A city like Detroit must cost millions of dollars I thought back then to myself. Who was going to trust Pop with that much loot? No, it was best he just continue to work out the timeline of contributions Africans and African Americans have made to the history of Architecture. He seemed to be getting someplace with that, judging by all the models that were everywhere around the house.

"Ghetto Enterprises-yes, ma'am, I'll see if he is available-"

I replaced the ARCHITECTURAL DIGEST magazine on the coffee table and looked out the window. There was a heavier traffic of passerby on the streets below now, but nothing really interesting seemed to be going on outside. There was this lone yellow balloon floating above the tarred rooftops across from the Cadillac Square building that caught my eye for awhile, but even that got old after a minute. I checked my watch again and scouted the coffee table for another magazine to occupy my time. I found ARTIST'S magazine and picked that up. Something Danny said came to mind while I leafed through articles and pictures.

We were cruising down Woodward, scoping out the human parade on both sides of the street, heading downtown to check out his studio. Danny was at the wheel and felt the need to expound on the sights and sounds that reel past us as we accelerate towards that vanishing point always out of reach. Some people find the vast beauty of the real world too intense to grasp and assimilate, and they have to talk about it to try to relieve that pressure. Danny is one of those people like that. He has to talk, and I'll have to admit I am not unwilling to listen.

"- see my man at the bus stop; that one with the plaid shirt and corduroy jacket? Check out the way he was standin' there, one foot forward in his dingy dungarees and brown work boots? Check out how he was wearing his hat at an angle to cop that style? Standing strong against any foul wind that might blow against him. Unconquerable pride in the midst of all this urban blight and deep down dyed in wool poverty. Go 'head, my brother! Gone wid yo' bad self!"

"You trippin', Danny,"

"Naw I ain't! You want to be a painter, Alphonso? Do a Degas on that we just passed. The way Black folk look when they take off the clown face and nobody's lookin'. Capture the whole lot of informal hours and the residual dignity that oozes out when you see Black folks standin' up under the bone crusher and the meat grinder of this mechanized hoe culture! Capture the brother behind the frier at McDonalds and the sister taking a break behind the counter at the Burger King. The homeless old man sittin' on a milk crate, holdin' up a card board sign next to the curb beneath the overpass on the freeway for money he intends to smoke away on crack. That fine sister over there, pushing her brand new baby in a stroller for the first time and none too happy about it because the father left her with the bundle and run off -"

"You don't know that, Danny, just by lookin -"

"Chill, Alphonso. This a free country. I can use my imagination much as I wanna."

"Go 'head, man. I ain't about to stop you."

"Ghetto Enterprises-are you calling for an appointment? I'll check and see when Mister Halloway will be available-"

I put down the ARTIST'S magazine because there's not enough nudes in it for my taste. I check my watch again because I've got people to do and things to see. When I look up from my watch, Miss

Coppertone of the Year is standing in front of an open door, and nodding at me with a smug expression on her face. I have to admit it looks good on her.

"Mister Halloway will see you now."

"Thank you, ma'am."

I follow whom I later find out to be Miss Avery, into a large room surrounded by bay windows and covered with heavy, red velvet curtains only part way opened. There is a long, polished wooden conference table and a teen aged boy, no more than thirteen or fourteen, is sitting at the head of it. He has a notebook out, and is thumbing through what looks to be a textbook of some kind. Standing shoulder to shoulder with Miss Avery, I look straight ahead at a figure that is barely more than a silhouette, holding what appears to be a little girl in his arms behind a huge desk, stacked with papers and filled with drawers.

"Alphonso Gentle here to see you, Mister Halloway."

"Thank you, Miss Avery."

Miss Avery nods at Halloway and nods at me, and then turns on her heel to leave, the soul of propriety.

"Right. Thank you, Miss Avery." I mumble as the door closes gently behind her.

Eugene Halloway stands up with the baby girl in his arms, the sun to his back and fringing the top of his head and flaring down his shoulders and arms. He holds out an open hand to me. I look over at the little boy at the head of the conference table, tapping a ballpoint pen against the table's surface and eyeing me curiously. I grab Eugene by his gnarled hand with a hearty squeeze. "My man Alphonso! What it gon' be like? How can I help you, brother?"

"Everything is everything, Eugene. Just thought I might bring a little business your way,"

"Tony Ghetto can always use more business," Eugene halts with a smile as the little girl coos in his ear. "-oh, I'm sorry! This is my granddaughter, Kanesha." He takes her little hand into his own. "Say 'hi, Alphonso', Kanesha, 'hi, Alphonso'," he waves his little girl's hand at me.

"Hey there, little princess-" I stick out my finger and she grabs ahold of it.

"That's my youngest boy, Charles, over there," Eugene indicates with a testy jerk of his head. "You don't have to say nothing, man. Just make sure you get through that chemistry lesson so's I can check it."

"Hey man," I wave at Charles as he timidly waves back.

"Charles on the Bad List." Eugene tells me with wary sternness.

"How come, Eugene?"

"I'll tell you later, Alphonso. Right now, I just got him studying in my office before he becomes a menace to society. But you sit down, Alphonso, right there. What's the happenin's, my main man? You don't come around so often now that you have got all 'educated'!"

"You got to get that knowledge, Eugene."

"You hit the nail on the head there, my brother." Eugene carefully sat back down with his granddaughter in his arms. "Yeah, Kanesha, yeah, yeah, that's right-" He looked back at me, his face suffused with sunlight. "Now Alphonso, let's cut to the chase. What can Tony Ghetto do for you?"

"I'm feelin' frisky. I just thought you might be interested in a percentage of these increasing returns I'm bout to generate."

"Sho' you rite, my brother. Tony Ghetto is all ears."

I hand Eugene the note Mojo left Dougie to give me before I returned to the Diamond Hut. Eugene unfolds it and looks it over carefully, his little granddaughter playing her tiny fingers into his right ear. When Eugene looks up, I still can't tell what he is thinking and feeling, because the shadows cast by the strong sunlight through curtains mask his face in pools of blackness. I sit uncomfortably in the radiant silence while my friend taps the note on the table with a finger. He purses his lips and rubs his chin with rough knuckles.

"Willie and Earl know about this?" Eugene's voice is as grave as his expression.

"Naw, they -hey! How'd you know my brothers were in town?"

"I hear things, Alphonso, I hear things."

Eugene went to rocking Kanesha on his knee.

"Danny told me Morris was workin' on triangulatin' you down at the Shakers and the Takers. Why don't you alert the poh-lice about this, Alphonso?"

"The police ain't no good until something happens," I shrugged, "I'm tryin' to keep something from happenin'."

"That why you come to me?"

I remember him asking me that question, and how I couldn't see through the shadows that covered his eyes. I crossed my legs and sat back, trying to act nonchalant, but even the young boy Charles, over there at the head of the conference table was regarding me with curious interest. I reached for a cigarette in my lapel pocket that wasn't there.

"That's about the long and the short of it. No tellin' what might happen to me when Mojo comes to play poker with us this Sunday afternoon, but I got a body of work and a reputation to protect. I want you to help me do that."

"That all you want, Alphonso?"

"That will be enough for me. I have twentyfive pastel and charcoal drawings I'm having made into silk-screens for prints and T-shirts and sweatshirts, among other things. I'm having a hundred of my paintings made into prints and puzzles, and a dozen of my sculptures turned into plastic construction kits for kids. I'm mass producin' everything and I want to cut you in for a percentage because you know my stuff is gonna sell."

"Always has, Alphonso-"

"Always will, Eugene."

Eugene goes back to tapping on the note I gave him.

"I'm not too keen about the Art World," Eugene rubs his knuckles against his chin, "but it would seem to me some would say you sold out, went commercial of all things!"

"Those among the some can kiss my black ass! I'm going to take a page out of your book, Eugene. I'm going to work from the grass roots up, rather than from the top of the Ivory Tower down."

"That's been a successful business practice for the Ghetto Man."

"Should prove equally true for the Gentle Man."

We chuckled quietly to ourselves. Eugene takes the pacifier hanging from a necklace around his granddaughter's neck and replaces it in her mouth. He goes back to shaking her on his knee, and looking up at the ceiling for the words he wants to say to me.

"Willie and Earl tole me they had to remove that peacemaker you got from your grandma before you wound up hurtin' yourself."

"That's the way they tell it."

"What you up to, Alphonso? Let's hear your side of it."

"Nothin," I shrugged as I lied, "just tryin' to cut a deal with you that will make us both some ends."

"You sure you not tryin' to make a Jackson Pollock out of Mojo's brains?" Eugene asked the ceiling as he continued to rock Kanesha.

"I thought you said you weren't too keen on the Art World."

"I've seen a picture or two in my time, Alphonso."

"Well naw, then. 'Jack the Dripper' ain't my style."

"That so? What's this all about 'should something happen to me'? Sounds like you plannin' to get the drop on Mojo 'fore he do a 'double take' on you."

"Not really, I-"

"Come on, Alphonso!"

The sharpness of Eugene's tone made the young boy at the table look up from his textbook with renewed interest.

"What?" I snapped, "I just came up to offer you a business proposition, that's all."

"Alphonso, I'm your friend," Eugene turned his harsh shadow guarded gaze upon me, "If you not layin' for Mojo then 'grits ain't grocery, eggs ain't poultry, and Mona Lisa was a man!' Now tell me how you really got the situation sized up."

"I already told you everything, Eugene, plus showed you the note. Mojo wants to come down and see my studio, play a little poker and discuss a little business with me. He probably wants a slice of my business, but I would feel a whole lot safer if I could say I already cut a deal with you."

Eugene's little granddaughter has drifted off to sleep in his arms. Now he's softly swaying with her and humming a little tune.

"Uh huh. You sign on the dotted line with me, and then you feel free to go for your guns with Mojo should it get down to a showdown before sundown. Am I gettin' warm, Alphonso?"

"Look Eugene, I gotta protect me and mine."

"That's not what I'm hearin'. The way it comes across to me is I've gotta protect you and yours, while you book a ticket to that big Art Museum in the sky,"

"Might be someone else singin' the bordello blues on the night train to nowhere for all you know," I mumble under my breath.

"What's that, Alphonso? I didn't quite get that."

"Nothing, Eugene, nothing. No need to wake the baby up."

"Spoken like a champ, Alphonso. About time you started to consider somebody besides just yo'self."

The young kid at the conference table hid a titter with his hand.

"Charles! What you lookin' at, boy? Did I give you permission to scope on grown folks and they conversation?"

"No sir, granpa, I-"

"You finished figurin' up them chemical equations?"

"No sir, grandpa, I was just-"

"- then get to it! So we can get yo' behind back in class!"

"Yes sir, grandpa, I'm finishing up right now, I-"

"Don't tell me, boy, show me! I want results in black and white! Somethin' I can hold in my hands!"

"Yes sir, grandpa, yes sir," Charles hurriedly buried his head back in his book.

Eugene settles on me again with a grave expression. Kanesha stirs in his lap, as he bridges his fingertips together. I still cannot see his eyes through the shadows cast by the sunlight.

"Your application for martyrdom is denied, Alphonso."

"My what for WHAT is denied?"

"You heard me, man. Case closed."

"Case closed? Who you think you is, Eugene? Judge Joe Brown or somebody?"

"Hey, you came to me, Alphonso, 'case you forgettin' that. I know you was expectin' me to be your patron and everything with no questions asked, but dream on, brother. I'm not some European lookin' to make a killin' on some poor starvin' artist I done drove into the poor house; because I can make more bucks with him dead than alive. Why on earth would I want to represent you and your work when you're about to get yo'self kilt in a gunfight with some pimp? See what you done did? There-there, Kanesha, there-there-"

"What I done did? You the one raisin' the roof with all that hollerin'!"

"Lot you care! Look Alphonso, we don't need another martyr; not after that masterpiece of martyrdom Martin Luther King pulled off in Memphis, Tennessee. What we need now is for black men to live and get back to raisin' all these babies strong and straight. We damn sure don't need any more black men killin' other black men. Naw, Alphonso, you got me mixed up with one uh them white folks you done read about. I invest in Life, not Death; and why should I invest in you when you're about to make yo'self a statistic?"

"Just so Mojo doesn't end up with the whole hog."

"That's never gonna happen while I'm around. You give Mojo too much credit, Alphonso, he ain't that big. What you gotta do is come to a higher ground with Mojo, establish some kind of new understanding between the both of y'all without bleedin' each other. You show me you can do that, and I'll sign on any way you want."

I glance at my watch with a sigh of disgust. Daphne's missing and the Wellingtons want me held for questioning again. After all, I was the last one to see her before she disappeared. Alicia, my sister, went nuts when she found out Antonio was last seen at the Diamond Hut with me before he took Gelisa home. After smashing a vase over my head, she wanted me under the jail if I didn't produce Antonio in time for school Monday morning. At least I gathered that much as she was running me out of the house with a claw hammer. I come to the one brother I have always been able to depend upon in a clutch, and he ends up givin' me a spiel on brotherly love and the importance of being nonviolent with a sewer snake who would kill you as soon as look at you.

Moms was right. Sometimes the only person you can depend upon is yourself.

"Whatever, man, what -" I catch myself, because now I'm beginning to sound like Daphne! "Look, thanks for taking the time out your busy schedule to see me -" I reach out a hand to shake soul to soul with Eugene, "-naw man, don't get up. You might wake the baby."

"Be strong, Alphonso. You know that Japanese babe you introduced me to when you were graduating?"

"Who Stella?"

"Yeah, her. The one you said helped you find the mind you thought you lost. What was it you used to tease between each other?"

"'Mind by Yamamoto'."

"Yeah, that's it. It took me awhile to get it, but I got it."

"What about her?"

"Nothing really. Just that she sends me a post card every once and awhile, all friendly and polite and cordial. Somethin' you never do. She be askin' bout you, man."

"Oh, yeah?"

"Let her know everything is all right from time to time."

"I'm sure you'll have plenty of news for her in a few days, one way or another."

"Ms.Yamamoto gets a card from Tony Ghetto every Christmas."

"That's mighty black of you, Eugene." I said, as I turned to go.

"One more thing, Alphonso-"

"What?"

"If I were you, I would invite Samuel Socrates Turner over for a few hands this Sunday. It might give you some perspective on your present situation."

"I'll think about it." I start moving to the door, "He might not know how to play, Eugene."

"Oh, I'm bettin' he knows how to play. An if'n he don't, well, it'll just be your turn to give him some schoolin', Alphonso."

"There's just one more thing, Eugene," I said, as I twisted the doorknob and jerked my head over at Charles in Charge, "what's you grandson doin' here? Why isn't he in school?"

"Oh. I gave Charles a chemistry set for Christmas. He was doin' some experiments and made some acid in a beaker. He was gonna let it evaporate, so he put a book over the beaker and left it in the classroom where he has Science. When he came back the next day, the acid had burned a hole in the book and a hole in the roof of the school! He got suspended from school and his momma and his daddy grounded him. They took the chemistry set away from him and now they are blaming me for everything! Can you get to that? Anyway, I got him up here figurin' out what he mixed, so it won't happen again when his school takes him back. Say goodbye to Mister Gentle, Charlie."

Charles looks up at me with an abstracted look on his face.

"Take it easy, Mister Gentle, bye."

"Be safe, Charles, my man. Catch you later, Eugene."

"Peace out, Alphonso."

Peace out. I thought I would leave the Cadillac Square Building with an air of great power, but Tony Ghetto just gave me the air. There was nothing left to do now but rustle up Miguel Jimenez to help me set up for the party Sunday.

I was walking through the alley fixing to call Miguel when I ran into Victor Baseheart.

But you should know about all that because that's where you come in, isn't it?

"What happened to you, Alphonso?" Miguel exclaimed in horrified dismay.

"Just a little run-in with a disgruntled associate, Miguel. I'm all right..."

"No, you not. You a mess, honey!"

"I'll clean up later. Right now, help me move this poker table, you dig?"

"Anything you say, Alphonso."

Miguel and I flipped the poker table over on its back and started to attach the little wooden box with its slotted lid to the underside with tacks and staple guns. There was another box, however, that caught Miguel's attention propped up against the rest of our tools.

"What's in the cigar box, Alphonso?" asked Miguel, as he tested the little wooden box to see how securely it was nailed to the table. "You should tell me now."

"Never you mind, Miguel."

"Oh, I don't like the sound of that, Alphonso,"

"Come on, man, let's flip this table right side up-"

We got the table back on its legs, and I got a chair for myself and Miguel. I felt for the slotted lid in the little wooden box underneath. I pulled out the lid sideways and smiled with nodding satisfaction. I placed the cigar box inside and closed the slot. Later I knew I would have to be ready to remove its contents should this become necessary. I looked up at Miguel and folded my hands together as he began to apply his makeup from a compact.

"We better get started, Alphonso," Miguel checked his face in the mirror from his compact, "you said you wanted to see how I got the woman inside me out-"

"That's right, Miguel. We best get crackin'."

"- and I have always wanted to see how far you would go to cream every dream that walks, crawls or flies!"

"Help me get this table cloth back on, Miguel."

"Sure thing, Alphonso."

My cell phone rang and I unhooked it off the cuff of my blue jeans and clicked the receiver.

"Gentle here."

"King of Woodward."

"What up?"

"Black and white doves nested high. Cop these coordinates from your highness."

I gesture to Miguel quickly for pencil and paper.

"Miguel, I need some paper, man!" I whisper hurriedly as I snatch the pencil from his fingers. "C'mon, hurry up!"

"Alright, I hear you, Alphonso! Here, I just have this sticky pad-"

"That'll work-" I hastily scribble the address Rap gives me. "That everything?" I whisper at last into the receiver.

"Ipso facto."

"Gentle out."

"King of Woodward on the meter."

The click on the other end seals the deal.

"Who was that, Alphonso?" Miguel asks, standing with one foot on top of the other.

"King of Woodward."

"King of what? Who?"

"You still parked out back in the alley, right?"

"Yeah, but-"

"C'mon then, man! We gotta make ourselves presentable!"

I feel underneath the table and fumble for the cigar box.

Sunday afternoon and I'm closing the slot underneath the tablecloth. Nathan Eddie is at the window again, smoking Newports with that faraway look in his eye. The gang's all here with me; Smiley, Baldy, and Danny. Dougie Dogg Mack would be pullin' up a chair too, but this is the evening of his big fight. I call on Smiley, but I may be bluffing with a losing hand.

"Looks like you got company, Alphonso," Nathan Eddie tells me as he inhales the smoke from his Newport with narrowed eyes., "check this out, y'all."

Baldy drifts over to the window next to Nathan Eddie and blinks.

"Damn! Y'all better come and see this! Danny! Smiley! Look what Mojo done landed at the curb-"

"What -just when I'm holdin' a winnin' hand!" Smiley curses to himself through his gold tooth. "Let me see what you got, Alphonso. Just like I thought -"

"Rake 'em in, Smiley, rake 'em in-" Danny says as he rises from his chair. "Now let's see what Baldy's so excited about-"

Danny got up and sidled over behind Baldy. He turned to me from the window with an ashen expression on his face.

"Alphonso? I think you better check this out, man."

"Damn, Alphonso! It look like 'Independence Day' out there in nem streets!" Baldy exclaims and now I got to see what all the hoopla was about.

"Is it legal to have that many cars parked outside like that?" Danny asked as he turned to me. "Mojo acts like he's the President or something."

"Yeah, President of Pimp Nation -" Nathan Eddie says dryly and then inhales again on his Newport. "-he sure got a mean Presidential escort out there."

We peered down on the Boulevard and you would have thought it was Cadillac heaven. Why are we so into Cadillacs? There was an army of them out there on the street below. Big timers leaning bad and making the grand, glamorous exit out of nothing less than the Cadillac DeVille in Lincoln green, the Cadillac DTS in your basic white, the 2003 Cadillac Escalade EXT in grey, sky blue Cadillac Catera, Cadillac STS in aquamarine, 2001 Pearl Red Cadillac Seville, 1999 Bronze Cadillac Eldorado, lemon yellow 1993 Cadillac Fleetwood Brougham, 1998 White Diamond Cadillac DeVille Concourse, Rose White Cadillac Sedan DeVille D'Elegance 1999, and to spice it all up, a 2000 Mercedes Benz S500 in cream and that 1999 Mercury

Cougar I saw the other night, before Daphne disappeared, rounded out the list. Leonard Morris emerged from the Rose White Cadillac, fingering a pearl handled ivory cane and snapped his fingers for his honor guard to take their positions out on the street. He looked up at my building for a long time before he decided to sally forth.

"Wooo-oooo-weee! Damn Alphonso, what you do to make Mojo land on us like this? All them niggahs comin' up here?" Smiley asked, as he shuffled his hand nervously.

"I don't think so, Smiley," Nathan Eddie idly comments, "they're just for backup as a show of support. Naw, I would say it's only Mojo who grants us an audience up in here."

"Hey Danny, help me bring that big chair out, the one that looks like a throne. We'll sit Mojo across from me -"

We drag the big chair out into exactly the position where I want it. I sit back down, and pat the wooden box underneath the table cloth for assurance. The doorbell rings and a freeze seems to race throughout the apartment.

"Somebody get the door," I said as I put my elbows on the table and press my knuckles together. "Danny?"

Danny looks at me as though he's about to tell me to get it myself, and then reluctantly moves to answer the door.

"Ghetto Enterprises - is this the Gentle residence?"

Danny swings wide and there's a little uniformed girl, her pigtails jutting out of the kind of hat you used to see bellhops wear in hotels. She holds up a large box taped up in brown wrapping paper.

"Special delivery for Alphonso Gentle-"

Danny tips her and she curtseys before she turns for the stairs and skips her way back down. We hear the ding of the elevator and know that this time it will not be any little girl.

"You can put that package over on the shelf above the clay table, Danny," I tell him as Mojo enters with a swarthy gentleman in an open neck shirt and mohair suit. "Let's make our company comfortable."

Leonard Morris curls his lip, looks over at the window where Nathan Eddie is still standing and returns his nod. Everyone else just stands around and gawks, like they've been caught smoking weed in the Boy's Restroom. I rise up quickly, to make sure Mojo sits where I need him to be seated. The fellow accompanying him looks around at all the sculpture on the tables, and paces around sizing up the charcoal and pastel drawings and the paintings stacked, racked, and lining the walls. We're not even there, the way he moves around in his practiced disinterest.

"You were right, Leonard, the young man does have potential," I hear the man in the mohair suit tell a painting on the wall, "- oh! Excuse me, guys, Leonidas Orlando," he aims a hand in the direction of anyone nearest him, "I run a miniature golf course out in Sterling Heights. I'm an associate of Mister Morris here, and an interested party. I'm sorry, which one of you is called Alphonso Gentle around here?" The fellow asks with an ingratiating smile after pumping Smiley's hand.

"Over here, man, I be he," I gesture to him, "- come on, Mister Morris, You can sit right here-"

"I'll take your coat, Mojo," Baldy reaches for the fur lined garb, "how you doin' today?"

"Ump. That's more like it. How about a chair for my friend here?" Mojo snaps his fingers.

"Comin' up, Chief," Danny slides a chair next to the one with cushioned arm rests we set out for Morris, '-there! We're all set now."

Mojo and I shake hands with wary stares.

"Feel like talkin' now, young blood? You were in a mighty big hurry the last time we crossed paths with each other."

"You can't blame me, Mojo. I was workin' on a littlle sumpin'-sumpin' for the evening, I'm sure you know how that is-"

"Oh, I know how that is, young Gentle," Mojo turns and shares a derisive smile with his hawk-nosed 'associate', "-but I never had call to disrespect my elders just to cop me a piece. You better learn to slow down some, Gentle. You just might rush past the people who could do you the most good flaggin' down some tail! The pussy will be with us always -"

Smiley snickers, and then catches himself with embarrassment as he looks around. We all collect around the table to be seated as Mojo begins to hold court. I'm just waiting for him to sit down too, so I can see how he lines up with what I've got under the table.

"- but by now it should have finally dawned on you that a man's friends are a treasure beyond price. Now I heard you're a pretty good stud poker player, Alphonso , and I stopped by to see what kind of hand you can play. The time has come to see where you are on the Food Chain before I put my Pimp Hand down."

"Survival of the fittest-" I smile through gritted teeth as I gesture for Mojo to have a seat.

"Time you learned not to mess with the best, and Master Mojo is here to school you -what you got to drink around here, gentlemen?"

"We should be able to offer you something in the way of light refreshment -" I suggest, as I begin to wonder when this joker is ever going to sit down. "- what would you say to some fine red wine?"

Mojo sneers at me with a chuckle.

"You hear that, Orlando? Young blood here thinks I'm some kind of bitch! What would you say to some scotch and Jack Daniels?"

"We can hook you up."

We all at the table turn our heads in one sweep over to Nathan Eddie, still looking out the window. He turns to us with curious detachment and draws on his cigarette.

"Smiley, look in the fridge and get the gentlemen what they want," Nathan Eddie gestures idly as he returns to viewing the car show outside. "Mister Morris is a busy man and I'm sure he's worked up a considerable thirst."

"Sure thing. Something for yourself, Eddie?"

"I'll see later."

Smiley grabbed a tray and some coasters, as Danny reached across the table for the deck of cards and began to shuffle them.

"Shiver me timbers, bodda-bing!" Orlando's grin split his hawk-nosed face wide open. "It seems to me we've come into some real hospitality here, Morris."

"'Heaven must be like this', huh, straight shooter?" Mojo takes a filled shot glass off the tray when Smiley comes back. "This the scotch? Take it back then, gimme the scotch. Ahhh, now that's what I'm talkin' bout! Keep em comin', hoss-"

Mojo at last sits down with great ceremony.

"Deal a meal, Danny -" I tell him, and we got us a game.

"Gentlemen, are there any final requests before the Mojo Man takes all yo' money?"

"I'll take a little wine, Smiley," Baldy tugs on Smiley's sleeve, "naw, gon' head, Mojo. We is here to learn much as you-"

"We've had our eye on you for quite some time, Alphonso. Ain't that right, Orlando?"

"The kid's name has come up in a few of our conversations."

"I'm always tellin' Orlando how much potential you got; ain't that right, Orlando?"

"Everybody's got potential to you," Orlando pulls back his hole card.

"- some tricks," Mojo takes his face card, "all you gotta do is follow the money; but with you, Alphonso - all I gotta do is follow the pussy. I remember when you was just a teenaged kid, and you were helping Wilma sell Xeroxed copies of her poems for a nickel. You just don't know, Orlando, this little critter here used to be a super salesman!"

"That right?" Orlando slid his face card to him. "That could be useful information."

"Been about fifteen years ago. Yeah, that little hussy would write these little love poems and Alphonso would manage to charm his way into the Principal's office and sweet talk the secretary into printing him a hundred or so. After that, Wilma and my man here would walk the streets of downtown Woodward, hawkin' Wilma's poems for a nickel a sheet. After they made enough for milkshakes and hot dogs, Alphonso would take Wilma to the Quikee Doughnut Shop and they would eat all their earnings up in one afternoon."

Mojo sits there gazing fondly at his cards. Everybody looks around at each other and then back at me. What am I supposed to say?

"Uh, Mojo? You gonna raise or call?" Baldy timidly inquires.

"You jokin'?" Mojo snaps out of it and turns on the sternness. "I'm callin' yo' lame-ass bitch hand. There! See what I'm talkin' bout?"

Mojo rakes in his winnings with savage relish.

"-it wasn't long after that she let you inside and you lost your cherry, Alphonso-"

"What is all this? Who told you all that about me? How do you know about me and Wilma, anyway?" I protested, full of suspicion.

"Ain't much I don't know about you, sucker," Mojo sighted over his cards at me. "Deal!"

We play on for awhile and Smiley starts to win him a few pots, and you know what that is going to signify.

"Pieyah! Matthew Chapter 21, Verse 42," Smiley cracks jubilantly, "you said you were going to school us, Mojo. That may be, but I'm taking you all to Church!"

"When I'm finished with you, the Lord won't recognize you enough to help you, ain't that right, Orlando?" Mojo cackles, nodding at Orlando, who is busy nursing his bourbon. "What do you say, Alphonso? Finally dawnin' on you?'

"Whatchu talkin' bout, Mojo?"

"Fool! It's all about POWER! You kept tellin' that little Doctor No bitch that nobody knows what they really want, when it's just the opposite! Everybody knows what they really want, because what everybody really wants is power! The power to accept, the power to reject; the power to say yes, the power to say no; the power to give, and the power to take-" Mojo reaches into his vest pocket for a cigar, "-shame about that Wellington bitch, and your nephew too, when you get right down to it-"

"What's that got to do with you, Mojo-"

"Hold tight, young blood!" Mojo exclaims as Orlando matches Mojo's cigar and turns to me with a deadly gaze. "Did I say it had anything to do with me? All I know is what I read in the papers. I just said it was a damn shame, that's all."

Mojo takes a long pull on his cigar.

"I understand Miss Daphne's daddy is partial to this brand," Mojo narrows his eyes with a sly discernment, "you see, I was a young man back in the day, and you know what the pundits used to say?"

"Let me guess. Does it go something like this: 'POLITICS IS EVERYTHING'?"

Mojo brays and slaps Orlando on the shoulder.

"What I tell you, Orlando? What I tell you? The boy is sharp. I told you he was sharp! That is exactly what they would say, Alphonso, and you know what? While brothers were wearin' their black gloves at the Olympics and givin' the world the Black Power salute and bored suburban housewives were rallyin' to burn their bras and fight for women's liberation, guess what old Mojo was doin'?"

"I bet you was fightin' for the rights of sisters everywhere to raise themselves up out of poverty on behalf of the Pimp dollar, and launderin' money through Greenpeace and Habitat for Humanity."

Nathan Eddie raises his cocktail glass of red wine with an amused smile.

"You hear that, Orlando? What you make uh that?" Mojo blows cigar smoke at the lights in the ceiling. "You hear how 'intellectual' my boy talk and all? Damn, if'n that Jap broad didn't do him a whole world a good! What was in that bitch's pussy, anyway, Alphonso? The Encyclopedia Britannica?"

When Mojo said that about Stella, I slid the slot halfway out underneath the table. I was about to blow a hole in his stomach, but a chill went over me that told me I better wait until the time was right. I closed the slot again with reluctance and sat back with my cards.

"You see, young blood, while everybody was hollerin' about the Power they didn't have and was willin' to burn down the world to get, Master Mojo was askin' himself what made the planet really work. Naw, I wasn't buyin' into any easy answers or slogans that end up on T.V. and make everybody money but the folks who first coined them. I was askin' my own questions and gettin' my answers from the highest authority there is, Life itself."

"What kind of questions were you askin', Mojo?"

Mojo blew smoke in my face and I touched the wooden box under the table again, but I was startled to see that same soulful, mournful expression that used to possess Dougie's face come upon his own. He sat back and all the larger than Life clownishness that was his trademark seemed to vanish out of him. Mojo traced ash away from the crease in his pants and continued.

"All sorts of questions, young blood. Why some people go through their whole lives without anybody ever thinkin' enough of them to speak to them first. Why people would rather die than be told what to do by some, and yet follow blindly even off a cliff the directions of others. I used to wonder why this particular person was always being sought out by others for help and advice, while the opinions of another, perhaps even more knowledgeable, were always being criticized and shunned. There are many strange things goin' on in this world, young blood, and you can believe Master Mojo has seen them all. Yeah, I used to hear it be said that politics was everything, but it's less complicated than that. The people who talk like that are full of shit. You could say power relationships are everything, but it's less complicated than that. When you realize that power is everything," Mojo puffs on his cigar again, "you're finally in the ballpark where you can make things happen. People struggle for the power to make the little miracles happen that would turn their whole lives around. They -"

The doorbell rang again and the cowbell tinkled like mistletoe.

"Somebody's at the door, Alphonso," Nathan Eddie casually observes.

"I'll get it, my man," Danny touches my shoulder as he rises from his seat.

"Go head, Mojo," Smiley eyes his cards shrewdly, "- gon' finish your rap. I can't say that the Scriptures support your views, biblically speakin', but fresh insights are not things to be shunned when we're on the road to Truth-"

"Yeah," I nod to Smiley and then turn to eye Mojo cautiously, "go head and finish your rap, man."

"Like I was sayin'," Mojo flicks the ash from his cigar, "-people pray to a God they can't see somewhere up in the sky, or peak through their hands while they're on their knees and sometimes see me standin' there."

"That is, if they're lucky," Orlando cracks wise as he makes his call.

Danny comes back and stands next to me.

Who's at the door, Danny?" I ask, as I look at my hand.

"Samuel Turner wants to visit with you, man," Danny fingers his mustache and bows his head, "want me to tell him to come back some other time?"

Baldy looks at me with raised eyebrows, then wipes the sweat off his jowls with a handkerchief as Smiley raises. Mojo and Orlando trade confidential glances quickly.

"Naw, that's okay, Danny. Tell him to come on in here." I said, in as relaxed a tone as I could muster, noting the reactions around the table. "Maybe he'll prove to be lucky to someone at this table."

Mojo rears back and crosses his legs, his cigar held high and his cards in his hand on his lap.

"Finally beginning to dawn on you, Alphonso?"

"What's that, Mojo?"

"Why there will always be pimpin' in this world. Why the Pimp is like that Old Man River; he just keeps rollin' along-"

"I'll bite," I tell Mojo, "and I'll call too. Explain yourself. Pull up a chair, Socrates, where you been hidin'?"

Danny and the massive, Samuel Turner pull up chairs to the table.

"Gentlemen. Alphonso," Socrates nods as he lowers himself into a chair.

Samuel Socrates Turner was an impressive figure, and the second he sat down, the gravitic center in the room began to shift. Suddenly, Leonard Morris was not the sole focus of attention in the room. Something there was about Socrates' mere physical presence that made Mojo give him space. Samuel Turner was wearing that threadbare tweed jacket his students saw him in nearly everyday at the high school. Broad shouldered and muscular, the full shock of grey and black wooly hair combed back from his enormous brow almost made him resemble Frederick Douglass. What threw everything off were the thick lensed glasses wrapped around the prominent, bulbous nose to strengthen his weak eyes. The other thing was that simpleton smile he wore across his face like a bow tie, despite the sense of depression that exuded from him.

"I didn't mean to interrupt anything," Socrates looked around the table, "what's the topic for this afternoon?"

"We were discussin' how the Pimp will always be with us," Mojo sneered at Socrates, "you care to offer your input to the conversation, Professor?"

"Why don't I just listen and observe the proceedings for awhile?"

"Suit yourself," Mojo shrugged, "- now think back, Alphonso, to that night when you was hustlin' that Doctor No bitch into your ride. She was takin' notes on me for whatever reason and you was tryin' to get her to stop. Remember that? I don't know how she got so all fired interested in me all of a sudden. Right now I'm just tryin' to see things from your perspective, you know, walk a mile in your shoes and all that shit."

"Make your point, Mojo," I snap, checking out my cards.

"Hold tight, young blood, hold tight. I'm just sayin' that in your shoes I would have grabbed a hank of hair and bitch slapped that cunt until she did like I told her. See, it's a known fact that women don't respect a man who won't unhesitatingly exercise power over them when it's called for and necessary. Which is about a good ninety percent of the time. I think I'll call you on this hand, Mister Smiley. By the way, Turner, I saw the little lady you were rappin' to at the Diamond Hut. How're things goin' now between you two?"

Socrates seemed to darken and remained silent.

"What do you know about that?" Mojo exulted with a wolfish grin, "I appear to have the winning hand this time!" He raked in his cash. "Now you take my man Suckertease as a case in point. He easily falls in love with the concept of the unattainable and it takes a man like our hero Master Mojo to save his ass from the more disastrous consequences of Lust."

"What is Lust?" Socrates asks Mojo through shiny eyes.

"Hold on, Turner, hold on, lemme see who's gonna call this hand I got. Nobody? Well, all right then, Mojo gonna break it down for you, baby." Mojo raises and then continues. "What is this thing called Lust? Uh, this is the part where you can start takin' notes, Suckertease. Lust springs from and is generated by a desire for the unattainable. Therefore, to love what is unattainable is not love at all, but Lust. Whenever you make something unattainable that means it cannot be had at any cost. The unattainable by its very nature is excluded from the fair exchange and trade of interested parties. When people are denied access to that which is highly desirable and at times vital to survival, Lust will rear its ugly head. The individual regards the unattainable and asks 'How can I make this mine?' Depending on how strong the desire is for the unattainable object, the individual may find that he or she is willing to lie, cheat, steal, even murder for what they want to have. Suicides are committed and wars galore all break out for want of something made so scarce it may soon become unattainable. You gettin' all this down, Suckertease?"

"I'm listenin'-" Socrates acknowledges to Mojo.

"Good, cause this is where our hero the Pimp comes in," Mojo folds when Baldy calls his hand. "Ummm,"

"Actually, this is where I come in!" Baldy gratefully rakes in the dough. "Thank you, my brothers, thank you very much -don't let me stop you, Mojo-"

"The Pimp serves the social good by making the unattainable once more possible of attainment and possession through ordinary means. He strives to make that which has been deemed scarce once more an abundant commodity or property." Mojo pulls his face card to him and sets his cigar in an ash tray. "I defy y'all to find anyone in the world of today who will tell you anything is more scarce than Love."

"What is Love, Mister Morris, according to your definition?" asks Socrates with a wavering voice. "How does it seem to be to you?"

"You hear my man tryin' to wax me with that 'Socratic Method'?" Mojo reached for his cigar again. "I'll give you one thing, Suckertease, you know how to ask the right questions. That is one thing you got out of all that schoolin' that's runnin' out yo' ears. Make a mental note of this one, because Master Mojo does not dispense his wisdom to just anyone, ya hear what I'm sayin', Orlando?"

"I hear you, boss, I hear you," Orlando talks down at his cards.

"Hmph. One day I'm gonna publish my own little red book just like Chairman Mao. Anyway, fools will sell you anything under the gotdam Sun, but the one thing nobody will put a price tag on is the one thing people consider more valuable than anything else, or so I've heard it said." Mojo gazed at his cigar and savored its aroma. "That is why the Pimp will always be with us. I'm gonna say it again. There will always be pimpin'," I jolted when Mojo looked straight at Socrates, "because the Pimp will get you what you thought was unattainable and make abundant what you considered scarce at a price you can afford."

"You still haven't answered my question, Mister Morris," Socrates indicates quietly.

"No, actually, I have done just that, my friend. All you have to do is carefully review your recent relationships and you should have your answer. What you asked me for were good workin' definitions for Lust and Love, something you can verbalize like any good white man and write down on the blackboard for your students. That right, my main man?"

Socrates ran his fingers through his mane of wooly hair perplexed.

"Definitions of important terms are always useful in any subject,"

Mojo and Orlando eyed each other and shared a conspiratorial smile.

"What I tell you, Orlando?" Mojo nudged Orlando with a chuckle, "I bet that's word for word out of some book he read. Just for your information, my good Mister Turner, I'm gonna break down for you what Love is real quick, and then I'm going to go you one better and define YOU. How's that grab you, my main man?"

"We all would like to hear that one, Mojo," Nathan Eddie said by the window, as he sipped more of his red wine.

"Love, my friends, is the missing pea in the eternal shell game of Life. Now you see it," Mojo showed his hole card, "and now you don't. Thank you, gentlemen, I believe this shall be mine -the point being what you value the most is your Love. But when," Mojo looked straight at me this time, "you can't protect it from abuse or theft or get anybody else to respect your rights to it, well then, my friend, you become ripe pickin' for the sucker's game."

Mojo smugly raked in his winnings from the last hand.

"Hey, you got any beer nuts around this joint?" Orlando called out with a wave of his hand.

"We got Nachos-" Danny suggested with a hint of resentment.

"Oh? Yeah, that'll work-"

Mojo chews on his cigar as he fans out his cards.

"Now what do you love, Suckertease? I'll tell you what you love. You love the unattainable, and 'the unreachable star', and all that shit. Like that character Mister Magoo once played. You long for what's out of reach and just around the corner. You pine for what you can't have and worship with the spirit of the sacrifice of Christ the very thing you deny yourself." Mojo is glaring at me now. "Takin' notes, young blood? The truth is were Suckertease to have the very thing he most desperately desires, he wouldn't know what to do with it. He would be bound to be confounded and confused by it, fumble and abuse it, fail to appropriately take care of and use it, and in the end simply lose it. All so he can love it from afar where he can't sully it with his unworthy hands and the cycle begins all over again. Of course, the more he attempts to exercise a sense of Love, the more he experiences the consequences of his own Lust. Yeah, I know you wouldn't have thought someone with the smarts of a Samuel Turner, could think and figure himself into that kind of trick bag. But that's why we call him Suckertease. It's because he's the kind of sucker my bitches love to tease. Oh my Lord, how they do it with such ease! Every time he gets the itch, 'ol Mojo does the maneuver for the 'ol bait-and-switch.

You see, every once and awhile Master Mojo has to save Mister Turner from himself. I've been scopin' on the Turner life experience, and a trained observer such as myself soon came to appreciate the cyclical nature of the client's behavior; a behavior whose final outcome could be predicted with certainty. So just before Suckertease turned his collage of pictures from the girlie magazines into the inevitable nervous breakdown from the last straw of an unrequited love affair, the Love Doctor Mojo steps in with one of his assistants to provide therapy. Yes, the patient may recover fully now, nurse.

As you've probably surmised, lustin' for what in the client's mind is unattainable can be taxing on the health; even more so when it becomes obvious that the activity by its very nature must result in a dead end. My man Samuel Turner, for all his smarts, couldn't add that one up to rightly understand it. So Master Mojo wants you to consider this logical proposition; when you have already decided something can't be had, what sense do it make to start out after it?" Mojo holds his cigar like a teacher's pointer. "You catch my drift, baby? That's Samuel Socrates Turner in a nutshell. That's why when Mister Socrates comes to the realization of what he already knew deep down inside from the beginning, that there's not gon' be no happenings and he definitely won't be winnin', yeahhh, you guessed it, young blood! This has been another Mojo production in prime time live and all that jive. One ripe sucker among the many to go for the tease, please, come on here, bitches; let's shake 'em all down from the trees! Oh yeah, there will be a harvest for the world -and I betcha!"

We all turn our eyes to Socrates and wait for him to reply. He is moving his lips, but no speech seems to come out and there is spittle collecting at the corner of his mouth. Finally, he voices out his words with a croak.

"You –you -you mean Theresa Cartwright -!??"

Mojo and Orlando, each holding a cigar and a cigarette respectively, blow their smoke into the same air, and then gaze upon Socrates like ravenous sharks.

"Someone to watch over you, my main man, and pick that brain for the dope we need-"

"I-I wondered why she was so interested in my video collection-" Socrates snaps his fingers with sudden insight.

"We're gettin' ready to put one of your former principals in the Senate, and you and Miss Ford accidentally came across some educational tapes that don't belong in a high school library." We all grew silent again as Mojo let his last words sink in for awhile.

"Hey Alphonso," Orlando waved his hawk-nose my way, "it is Alphonso, right?"

"That's right."

"I know it's none of my business, but what's with all the boxes stacked up against the wall over there." Orlando gave Mojo a wink and a smile. "You might give people the wrong kind of impression that way. All those boxes make me think you're havin' a 'Going Out of Business' sale! You see what I mean?"

"Um," I look over my cards, "I hadn't thought of it that way-"

"No biggie," Orlando holds out the hand with the crooked index finger, "Just something to think about, that's all."

"I'll deal the cards again," Danny reaches out once more.

Mojo and Orlando are both looking at me now like I'm what's on the menu.

"Finally startin' to dawn on you, Alphonso?" Mojo digs at me again with the question.

"I'm not sure I know what you mean, Mojo-"

"Oh, I don't know," Mojo pulls his face card towards him, "I just thought you might be comin' to some conclusions as to how I copped a fly bitch like Sheba Taylor, when she was stone cold -heads up in love with you-"

Now being one of those individuals with an artistic temperament, it is easy for me to visualize just about anything. Right now, I can easily see Mojo sliding back from the blast and recoil of what I got under this table. I can see him biting down with gritting teeth on his cigar, as he holds on to his stomach bursting with red life giving juice like a wet balloon. I can see him falling back, chair and all and landing with a loud crash as I move around the table and take aim to finish off this sweating hog of a snake. I can see Danny trying to grab my arm and me having to pistol whip him away, as I give Mojo one more between the eyes and watch his head split open like a rotting watermelon. I can see myself putting my foot on his neck and watching and waiting for him to beg for his life while I put one more to grow on through that anus he's been using as a mouth and end all this verbal diarrhea. Every cell and fiber in my body is primed for the reckoning, but my mind tells me somehow this is not the time to be listening to anything that my body tells me. That inner voice inside my soul tells me to keep a cool head and my wits about me, and to play the game down to the last hand and just maybe I'll have Mojo right where I want him when the real deal goes down.

I bring my hand out from under the table and let out a long sigh.

"I don't know, Mojo," I shrug and scratch the back of my head as I look over my cards. "I would be lying not to admit I've kicked it around some. Why don't you enlighten me as to how you pulled it off?"

Mojo nodded at his man Orlando and put his hands behind his head.

"See, the trouble with you is you're always tryin' to palm yourself off as some kind of good guy, Alphonso. When you know in yo' heart of hearts you just a cock hound like me. You see, it takes one to know one. Sheba was truly in love with you, but she was just a chocolate doll, just a beautiful mannequin to you with moveable arms and legs and a head that could be repositioned any way you pleased. A lovely -what they call that thing, Orlando? Art de - Art de - Art de somethin' or another-"

"I think you mean Art de Object, boss man."

"That's what I'm talkin' bout!" Mojo put his finger on a spot in the air. "Sheba was just a lovely art de object to yo' ass. A piece of African sculpture with brownish black flesh you could run your hands all over without the security guard comin' over and tellin' you not to touch. All you really wanted to do was to savor her dimensions and proportions, and use that terrific physique as inspiration for further endeavors of the creative kind. That about right, Alphonso?"

"What's wrong with that?" I said, as I checked my hole card.

"Must have been a helluva drawback when you found out she could talk as well as walk. That she had a bitch's mind and emotions that went along with that package. That before you could have that body, you had to accept charges for the soul and sign for that too."

'What am I waiting for?'- I kept thinking to myself. Time to waste this niggah and be done with it! But that inner voice inside me keeps telling me to hold tight and just chill; wait and chill. Rap said wait for him to draw first so I must chill.

"So you're the cosigner on the loan Sheba made of her soul, huh?"

"Who told you that?" Mojo holds up his hands and shakes his head. "Naw, it ain't like that at all. I just helped the Queen of Sheba put her best assets to work, if you know what I be sayin'. Boy, she told me all about yo' ass!" Mojo chuckles to Orlando. "Most of the time you was gettin' high off her looks, you couldn't make up yo' mind whether you wanted screw her or sketch her. So you would either screw her before you sketched her or sketch her before you screwed her. I believe that's how she broke it down to Big Daddy here. Boy, you is one stone cold freak! Sheba was gettin' bored with the whole setup, but she was still willing to work it out with yo' ass until her grandmomma died and she came over to invite you to the funeral."

"She told you all that?" I said, as I raised on Baldy.

"Who else she gonna tell? She couldn't get a word in edgewise between you screwin' and sketchin', and sketchin' and screwin', and running off at the mouth about all those big ideas she could barely understand half the time. Who else would lend a kindly ear if not the 'bitch buster'?" Mojo's eyes narrowed as though he were reading me intently.

"Finally beginning to dawn on you, my main man? Is it all startin' to come back how you fouled the play with Sheba? Remember what happened when she needed a shoulder to cry on and someone to talk to who would listen? You beginning to see where your game went lame, my playa?"

That was her that time! No, that couldn't have been her, could it? That time after Rebecca Brooks finally earned her Black Belt, with a little help from yours truly. Now that I think of it, that must have been Sheba Taylor, ringing to come up to my apartment just moments after I had rode the white pony with Rebecca and racked her panties on my bed post. I told Rebecca to go answer the door, and she took the sheet with her, all wrapped up like some Oracle at Delphi. Now it's coming back to me! How Rebecca returned from the door and flopped back onto the bed. I remember how when I asked her who it was, she couldn't get the name straight.

"I don't know, Alphonso," Rebecca cradled herself back into my arms, "she bolted almost as soon as she got a load of me. Somebody named Sherry or Shirley, I don't remember which now. I asked her if she wanted to leave a message and a number where she could be reached, but after she nodded and I reached for the pad and pencil on the nightstand, soon as I looked up she was gone and running down the hallway! Can you imagine that?"

"I guess she wasn't expecting Xena: the Warrior Princess when she knocked on the door -"

"Now you stop all that stuff about Xena, Alphonso!" Rebecca tickled me in the ribs with her knuckles. "Before I noose you with my Black Belt! Amazon Warrior Princess indeed! I don't need that stuff. I am a newly minted expert in the Martial Arts and that will tide me over for the time being."

Now I remember the scene clearly. How I set everything up in my studio, half believing she would show up at all. There was a pastel drawing to finish up and a sculpture to paper mache', so I really wasn't on tenterhooks about seeing Rebecca arrive. I just remember how the light looked when she came around the corner and down the hallway. The self-reliant way she approached me in that long sleeved fitted black blouse and those tight hip-hugging black trousers. The way that black leather belt shone in the waning afternoon and was cinched about her waist with a C-clamp belt buckle. She treaded down the hallway and into the foreground of my mind with the confident strides of a warrior tigress. Each step she took towards me seemed to announce the coming out a princess of the Martial Arts. When she finally stopped those black Reboks in front of me, with the glare of the Sun casting a sheen along the edge of her waist length hair, I knew she passed her examinations for the coveted black belt with flying colors.

"Hi Alphonso," Rebecca nodded with cool self-possession, "what's up?"

We touched hands and squeezed fingers, as though we were facing off on a combat mat.

"Nothin' much. What's up with you? Welcome to my studio. Come on in here, woman-":

No sooner were we inside, then Rebecca slammed the door shut and pressed her back against it. She tossed the length of her brown hair over one shoulder, gratitude flooding the glinting blue eyes under those flat, bushy eyebrows. The warmth of a smile was working the corners of a prim, thin-lipped mouth, but she was trying to keep chill so that her emotions wouldn't spill out into a red-faced cry.

"I passed," Rebecca whispered to the floor in disbelief, "you were right, Alphonso! All that Creative Visualization and studying my katas on videotape for the floor exercises; it worked! I'm-I'm-I'm a first Dan Black Belt, Alphonso! Me! Rebecca Brooks!"

Rebecca's eyes were all swimming smiles. The thankful expression on her upturned face conveyed a radiant beauty that even her trembling cheeks and mouth could not work against. So I held out my arms to her.

"Come on, woman, show me some love-"

I took a step forward and Rebecca leapt into my arms! She wrapped all that excellent muscle tone around me like a catcher embracing her winning pitcher during the final and deciding game of the World Series. Those arms and hands tightened about my neck and under my arm around my back. Rebecca's powerful legs circled my waist in a scissors hold and I could not believe how strong she was! The power in those thighs nearly forced all the air out of me and it was all I could do to keep from toppling over.

"Thank you, Alphonso," Rebecca whispered in my ear as she pressed her head against my neck, "thank you-"

I wanted to say she was welcome, but for the way she nearly knocked all the wind out of me. I just hung on to keep from passing out. I expected she would run out of steam after awhile, but the vitality and strength in that woman's body was something else! Seconds turned into minutes and before I knew it, her tongue was teasing along the edge of my ear and I still couldn'tt ell whether her feet had touched the ground yet. She started to run her fingertips along the edges to my collar and unbutton my shirt. When she started to undo the buckle on my pants, I gently took her hand and patted it.

"Whoa-honey, let's do this right. This is my studio, Rebecca-" I cautioned as she pressed herself full against me and her mouth sought mine.

"Where can we go, Alphonso?" Rebecca asked with such solemnity between kisses, I almost thought we were in church. "Take me back to your apartment now, please? Please?"

The expression on Rebecca's face was mesmerizing. Suddenly she was Lois Chiles, Shirley Temple, Elizabeth Taylor and the Virgin Mary all rolled up into one. I was becoming weak in the knees when I realized that her feet were still in the air, and her ankles still locked around me as she reached for the zipper below my belt, her tongue still stuck in the corner of her mouth. "Here Rebecca," I said, as I zipped myself back up, "I'll tell you what we'll do. Here are my keys-" I held up the one to the Focus, "-go start the car and I'll be down once I turn out all the lights, okay?"

"Sounds like a plan, lover-"

Needless to say, we stayed in bed for the next three days. We were mixing licorice and hot chocolate with honey and ice cream when we heard drumming on the door and Rebecca snatched the covers to become the 'Livin' Large' babe. I sent her to the door to see who it was, but when she reported back, I was still in the dark.

Could that really have been Sheba at the door that day?

"Finally startin' to dawn on you, Alphonso?" Mojo read the question in my face despite myself. "You finally startin' to understand what it is you really want? If you got the balls to admit that, then you one in a million. But why keep everybody in suspense? Let me take a stab at it. What the Gentle Man really wants is to rule the beautiful bitches of the world. Dominate them cunts until they get with the program and do only like you tell em to do. That is, of course," Mojo lights up another stogie, 'with the full understanding that it's in they best interest and for they own good that they do so. Am I gettin' warm, my main man?"

Just keep talking, big man, I tell myself. I got something warm for you, all right.

"I'm just lookin' at things from where you stand, Alphonso. I bet you wished you'd left our Honey Rider at home with her parents. That way, she might have never gotten the idea to write up a big time operator like myself the way she did." Mojo flicked the ash from his cigar. "But then, you've always been kind of tender-hearted when it come to pullin' the reins on a bitch when she most needs it. You got to get over that, Alphonso-" Mojo picked up his cards and looked over his suit. "I'm not saying I really know what went on between y'all, but I suppose you would have been a damn sight happier, and Honey Rider a whole lot safer if she hadn't talked you out of takin' her back to her parent's crib. But that's always been the chink in yo' game, Alphonso. You couldn't just bitch slap the babe and lay down the law to her. Naw, you had to 'discuss' and to 'negotiate' and 'come to a compromise'. You let your bitch punk you out with a decision that did neither of you any good and got your nephew nabbed in the bargain. Now where is the sense in that?"

"How you know so much about what happened between me and Daphne, Mojo?"

Mojo chuckled in Orlando's direction and blew cigar smoke up at the ceiling lamp.

"All I know is what I read in the papers, man. The truth is I don't know shit about what happened between you and what her name? Daisy? Donna? What you call her?" Mojo snapped his fingers. "C'mon Alphonso, help me out here-"

"Daphne."

"Daphne? You said 'Daphne'? Naw, I don't know the bitch. Any more than I know why your nephew took such a liking to me when we was rappin'. I'm just usin' my imagination same as you would to get at the truth. Professor Turner would know what I'm talkin' bout. He quoted somethin' off a bookmark he got from Border's Bookstore one time. Hey man, what was that you said Einstein used to say?"

Socrates looked up and closed his hands into fists around his cards, without ever losing the little smile pasted across his face.

"C'mon, man," Mojo snapped his fingers at him, "what was that you told me he said?"

"'Imagination is more important than knowledge'. "

"That's it!" Mojo snaps his fingers again. "I told you Suckertease would know. I don't believe he said that, myself, but you know how it is. You gotta sell bookmarks to go with them books. Naw, I don't believe he said that at all. Once I know how to make a bitch put out for all that dough-re-mi that's a damn sight more important than anything I could imagine about her." Mojo turned with a sharp look to Socrates. "What you say to that, Hoss?"

"What I think Einstein was referring to -" Socrates began with hesitation as he examined his cards carefully.

"What? I can't hear you. Whatcha say, Hoss?"

"I said, I think what Einstein was suggesting was that -that inner truth is more to be valued than external physical fact."

Mojo and Orlando shared with each other another confidential smile, before they burst out laughing in Socrates face.

"Hee -yeah. Well, that sounds real good comin' from a trick who couldn't get himself laid to save his life." Mojo said, throwing down his hand and looking at me. "Hee -see what I got to deal with, my main man? The Pimp will always be with us and there will always be pimpin' in this world, because after the average Joe gets his fill of nice, polite, 'discussions', and 'ne-goat-she-atin'" with his woman for that pussy, and 'comin' to a compromise' about who should wear the pants in the family, he gets down on his knees to pray to his God with a hole in his soul where his manhood done leaked out. One of those times he peeks through his fingers and he sees me standing there. I'm everything he hates, holdin' on to everything he secretly desires because he hasn't got the balls to reach out and take it himself."

"I - I think I won that hand, Mister Morris," Socrates indicates timidly.

"What's that?" Mojo asks as though he's hard of hearing. "What's that you say, Hoss?"

"I won that round, Mister Morris. See?"

Mojo chews on his cigar, and nods down at Socrates' straight flush.

Socrates rakes in the coins and adjusts that little smile on his face.

"That's all right. Chump change for the chump, eh, Orlando? But back to what I was tellin' you, Alphonso. I'm just lookin' at things the way I imagine you see 'em. I can just see how while you were discussin', and negotiatin', and comin' to a compromise with that Honey Rider bitch, the thought probably crossed your mind a fleetin' moment how much easier everything would be if you just put the Pimp Hand down on your woman. Making her toe the line with no lip the iron clad rule. But of course you couldn't put the Pimp Hand down on her because you ain't no Pimp." Mojo inhaled on his cigar and then held it, regarding it and savoring it's aroma. "Let me put it the way brother Socrates would put it in the intellectual's terms. The dream of every man is to be the sole authority defining the terms and the conditions of his relationship with his woman. You find even in the Bible it says that woman shall be subject to and ruled over by the man."

"Mojo got a point there, Alphonso," Smiley observes, wincing at his cards, "that's Genesis, Chapter 3, Verse 16-"

"Shutup Smiley!" Danny sighs in disgust. "Who asked you anything?"

"What's wrong with you, man? All I said was that it's in the Good Book."

"What I tell you?" Mojo snatches up his hole card. "All my bitches do what I tell 'em or else I put my Pimp Hand down. Why? Because I reserve for myself the power to define the terms and conditions of the relationship with all my women. Any real man finds this a tremendously attractive proposition. Think about it, Alphonso. How great and wonderful a thing it is to have a bitch so strung out on you that you can finally say 'these are my conditions', with complete confidence that she will comply with whatever rules you lay down! Think about it! Instead of beggin' for pussy and apologizing for being a man, you take the power and responsibility and make that bitch toe the line every time. That would make being a man a worthwhile enterprise, wouldn't you agree, my main man?"

Everyone looks around at me to see how I am taking to all this wisdom Mojo is putting down. But I'm not one of Mojo's bitches to be twisted, and the time has come to pull out the slot and get busy. But what Rap said about making sure Mojo drew first stays my hand now.

"You know what else I been hearin' bout you, Alphonso?" Mojo comments idly.

"What have you been hearin', Mojo?"

"I been hearin' you been keepin' snakes up in this joint? That true or false?"

Where has Mojo been getting all this inside information about me? Could it be he's been stalking me from Jumpstreet? Learning my ways until I'm bagged game and meat on the table? Why all of a sudden has my life become an open book to him?

This is starting to creep me out.

"I've been breedin' a few garter snakes for household pests and such. What's it to you?"

Mojo and Orlando share knowing winks again.

"Face it, Alphonso, you the best show in town right now. You love pussy so much you've gone international with yo' game! I heard you took the Wellington snake down to that there local Animal Shelter when you found out Honey Rider and your nephew were missing in action. Seems you were so upset you ended up coppin' some full-blooded Pocahontas nookey -"

Mojo pulled his face card towards him and regarded me to see how his words were registering with me.

"Where did you hear something like that?" I said, frowning at my cards.

"Boy! When you gonna learn you can't hide nothing from Master Mojo?" Mojo showed his hole card to one and all and started sliding the cash his way. "Yeah, from what I understand she was a full-blooded Potawatomi Indian with straight black hair, and that fresh college look without makeup you love so much. She gave you some tips on how to talk to the animals, and you took her to the Happy Hunting Grounds and back. Am I right, Alphonso?"

Pauline Little Fox was a veterinary assistant at the Mercy Academy of Veterinary Medicine. The Jewish people are eternally vigilant with regards to any renewed interest in ethnic cleansing, and rightfully so, but when was the last time you ran into an Indian? The event is so rare, for me at least, that it always sticks out in my mind. I have always believed the term genocide applies more accurately to Native Americans than to any other people on the planet. Look around and pick one out. The truth is they are simply not there.

Where did all the Indians you see on T.V. go?

Their names are on street signs and our language is peppered with all sorts of words and terms derived from the cultural life of Native Americans. But where are they now? I can't help feeling they were tossed aside onto the scrap heap of History, and I don't care what anybody tells you!

Pauline was a revelation to anybody singing '-where have all the Indians gone?'. She wore a bright smile and was as beautiful as any wildflower streaming with the wind in the field. There was something in her physical appearance that radiated health, seemingly untouched and unspoiled by centuries of oppression. There was something about being in her presence that made you feel that Native Americans were coming through all this just fine and were vitally alive and intact.

She took my injured garter snake through an open door and down this flight of stairs. I stood on top of the landing and she was halfway down when she turned to me with curiosity and raised eyebrows.

"Come on, it's okay-" Pauline smiled invitingly, and waved me down.

We made our way down the steps and through a maze of wire cages. The cages lined the tiled floor and the light green walls. There was hooting, barking, cawing and purring going on all around us as Pauline brought my jar to a little lighted room way in the back.

"This where you have your office?" I asked, straining my voice to rise above the din of all those noisy animals. "How can you hear yourself think down here?"

"Oh, I can always close the door," Pauline said, as she took me into her office, "besides, I like being down here with all my little friends. Why don't you have a seat, Alphonso, while I fill out some of these forms?"

I slumped down into the couch and watched my garter snake writhe around inside the jar that was filled with grass and dirt. Pauline had it sitting at the edge of her desk, and the mask of her face was set in a businesslike scowl that seemed almost cruel in nature. The scrabble of her pen over the necessary papers I would have to sign was counterpoint to the muffled animal sounds beyond the closed door.

I will have to admit I liked the way the highlights bounced and shone in her black hair.

"What do you intend to do with friend snake once he is properly healed?"

"Oh, I don't know. Probably throw him back into the Wellington's backyard. Have you heard of the Wellington family?"

"I have. Putting on the Ritz there, aren't you, bro?" Pauline put the retractable tip of her pen in her mouth and looked up at me, noticeably blanching in my evident admiration. "Here." She tapped the top form with her pen. "You sign here, Alphonso. Are you upset?"

"Upset?"

I got up to sign the form.

"Well, yeah, it's been in all the papers. You must be upset with all the alarm that has been raised in the media about this." Pauline got up and came around to sit on the edge of her desk as she dangled her legs over the side. "There are a lot of fingers pointing your way. As I understand it, by all accounts you were the last one to see her missing. That, beside the fact that your nephew appears to have disappeared along with her. I know something like that would keep me up at night-"

Looking down into that round brown, orangey face with its high cheekbones, I felt something rise in the dank air of that basement between Pauline and myself. She tossed and ruffled her shining black hair behind the collar of her lab coat and down her back. I stood there regarding her beauty, and she returned my gaze with a hint of cool defiance. I placed the palms of my hands against her soft shoulders to steady myself, and she grasped me sympathetically by the elbows.

"Yes Alphonso, I think we should now," Pauline whispered, as her hands went about my neck.

I saw myself reflected in those probing, black eyes and the expression on Pauline's face made what we were about to do seem almost religious. I picked up her stocky, busty, frame and as she flicked out the lights set her gently upon the couch.

"Daphne Wellington was engaged to someone else," I confessed to Pauline.

"That doesn't matter now, Alphonso," Pauline said, with consoling kisses about my nose and eyebrows.

"What happens when we're caught down here?"

"Doctor Montgomery is away on a house call." Pauline placed my hand over her heart and ran my warm fingers through her hair and down to the hollow in her neck. "Someone's German shepherd got his paw caught in a fence. There's no one here to disturb us. This was meant to be, Alphonso-"

'How do you know that, Pauline?"

I watched my reflection dance in those dark, questing eyes.

"I felt my womb stir as soon as I beheld you, Alphonso. That has never happened to me before. I sensed you felt the same. My heart quickened and made me glad."

"Don't worry, Pauline, I won't hurt you-"

"That doesn't matter now, Alphonso," said Pauline, running her hands inside my shirt and down my back, "this was meant to be-"

Mojo nodded grimly in concert with Orlando as I drew my hole card towards me.

"Finally dawnin' on you, young blood? You can't hide nothing from the Master!"

"Damn! I'm out, Alphonso!" Baldy threw down his cards in disgust. "This is gettin' too deep for me. Say, it's almost time for Dougie's fight to come on! Mind if I watch, Alphonso?"

"Naw Baldy," I said, liking the hand I have now, "go knock -"

There was a red dot of light tracing its way down the back wall, over the radiator and making its way crawling across the floor. Mojo's eyes glowed with malice between puffs of his cigar. Orlando nonchalantly looked at his wristwatch and checked his cufflinks.

"There's nothing you can hide from me, Alphonso," Mojo began between puffs again, "you are just a fly on the wall that I watch buzzin' by while I eat my supper. When the time comes to swat you, I'll swat you! Whatever there is left of you, I'll just wipe up off my shoe."

Time swells as though it were a seed in Pauline Little Fox's womb and everything seems to come together. The red dot disappears and nobody seems aware that it was even there. Now I am wondering to myself, was that red dot just some kind of optical illusion, or did I just imagine that I saw a spot of red light appear out of nowhere?

I have a strange sensation, almost identical to the way I felt when I came down the hallway to my apartment after leaving my snake with Pauline.

"Lay your money down, Mojo, you so big and I'm so insignificant," I tell him as I call his hand. "Let's see what the real deal gonna be about."

I remember putting the key into the lock, and having that odd feeling that somehow Pauline had done me instead of me doing her. I couldn't shake this picture of her sitting triumphantly nude on her office desk. She crossed her tawny honey legs as she combed out her straight black hair and hummed a little song to herself.

"Don't worry about your little friend, Alphonso," Pauline looked over at the jar still perched on her desk with affection, "you come back near the end of the week and he should be feeling much better. Hopefully, I will have a mate for him by that time."

Pauline straightened out the collar to my shirt, and patted me on the back as I buttoned it up the front. When I turned my face to thank her, she clutched my shoulder and kissed me. When I began to return the kiss, she went back to humming and combing her hair.

"Ahhh, I think we've had enough sexual congress for one afternoon, Alphonso," Pauline said, giggling when I tickled her, "let's not wear out our welcome with each other so soon. I hope we have a chance to know each other better during your next appointment."

"At least we've gotten the introductions out of the way," I remarked, as I kissed her on the shoulder again.

"I should say we have! We should have these discussions on a regular basis. There's no telling what we may discover about each other at this rate!"

"Pauline?"

"Oooouuu! You say my name so sweetly! Yes, my wonderful Alphonso?"

"I was wondering about something-"

"No, my dear Alphonso, let me guess! Are you afraid you may be in danger of becoming a father before your time?"

"What I'm saying is I didn't bring any protection-"

"Protection from what, Alphonso?" Pauline exclaimed with flashing black eyes and a joking snort. "Do you really think you can protect yourself from Life?" Pauline reached out playfully and touched my hand with mocking concern. "Oh no! It's something else, isn't it? You want to know my sexual history to be sure you won't wind up dying of AIDS!" Pauline tossed her head again with mirthful insouciance, and went back to combing out her hair, the long black strands as fine as any you find on a horse's mane. "Uh-oh! I better watch out before you throw this poor red trash back in the dumpster from whence she came!"

Pauline slapped me on the hip, as I reached out to finger the wonderful texture of her hair.

"No, that ain't what I mean! I just didn't expect-" I murmured almost indistinctly as Pauline playfully slapped me on the hip again.

"That 'isn't' what you mean, Alphonso. Speak good English! You can save the slang for your homeys when you get back to them. However, for your information, you are my very first time and you can consider yourself most fortunate."

"You're a virgin, Pauline?"

Pauline gave me an ironic smile.

"I think we just successfully went beyond that phase in my development, Alphonso," She tenderly placed her hand along my cheek, "and I must say I feel most thoroughly touched. Thank you again for a most amazing inauguration into the joys of the birds and the bees!"

Pauline touched my chin and turned my face so she could read my expression, "Oh, cheer up, Alphonso!" Pauline pulled out a drawer in her desk and reached for a small mirror. "I would be honored to bear you a child."

Pauline checked herself in the mirror, and went back to combing out her hair.

"I just don't want you to think I took advantage of you or nothing like that-"

Pauline looked askance at me as I plunked down on the couch to put my socks back on.

"No, I would hardly put it like that. You came in here looking so down in the mouth and then I recognized you from the papers. I just sensed what was going on inside you, Alphonso. The devastation you felt was just stifling. Even the creatures we keep here were aware of it. Engaged or not, I could tell you cared very much for that Wellington girl, and of course your nephew's mom must be terrified with worry and not too well disposed to viewing you kindly these days."

Pauline put a bobby pin between her teeth as she gathered her hair at the nape of her neck. "Besides, something in my heart told me you needed to know me, and that I needed to know you now before your sense of loss became too great." Pauline gave me a coy smile, as she kept her hands placed behind her back and began to plait her hair into one long braid. "I read somewhere in the papers that you were a painter, Alphonso. How about it?" Pauline took a deep breath as she pinned back her hair and her plump breasts swelled under the florescent lights. "Do you think you might want to paint my portrait one day?"

"I would be honored to capture your beauty on canvas, Pauline."

"I know, Alphonso. I felt you mentally undressing me the moment you laid eyes on me. Do you have a studio of your own?"

"Yeah. I could invite you over sometime, if you like."

"Um, I think I would like that."

Pauline's nimble fingers went down her back as she braided her hair into a long, black rope that rested in the hollow of her spine. I'll have to admit I was getting the itch to sketch her just as she was right now in the altogether. Somehow Pauline sensed this and glanced at me with a laugh.

"No time for that now, my black Picasso. I'll do Life Drawing Class with you another time. Better help me get dressed just in case the good Doctor comes a calling." I kissed her bra and panties back on her, and helped her shimmy back into her dress. "Besides," Pauline caught my eye with a brazen smirk, "you got to get back to your buds and brag how you ran into Pocahontas and popped that coochie, man!"

"Get out of here, Pauline!"

I slapped her a smart crack on the rear end.

"Sha-pow!" Mojo flipped his hole card when I called his bluff and then smugly slid the cash his way. "Yeah! Mojo got a brand new bag! You know," Mojo caught a glimpse of Dougie on the T.V. mounted overhead, "I was all ready to hook Mack boy up with some people I know who would help him turn Pro, but he told me I should talk to you first-"

"You made a wise decision," I told him as I checked out my hand.

"I'm willin' to do the same for you, Alphonso-" Mojo looked up from his cards to see how his remark registered with me.

"Pop Quiz time, my friend," Orlando held up a quarter and looked to his left. "Smiley, am I right?"

"You called it, my man." Smiley answered up. "What's on your mind?"

"I was just wondering if you could name the face on this coin for me."

"That's George Washington on the quarter, my friend," Socrates told Orlando.

Orlando frowned at Socrates as though his answer didn't count.

"How bout it, Smiley?" Orlando held up the coin high. "Think you can name me a verse that has something to do with a coin like this?"

Smiley considered for awhile and then his face lit up.

"Hah! You ain't slick, man. You signifyin' about the Book of Matthew, Chapter 22, Verse 20-22. Ain't I right, now?"

"You're on the button, pal." Orlando flicked the coin rolling my way. "Check it out, my good friend, Alphonso. I think the time has come to give to Caesar, just like the Good Book tells you to do."

I opened the door to my apartment and Wilma came running up the stairway.

"Alphonso! I heard, baby, I heard!" Wilma said, running over to me, shaking her copy of the Detroit News in her fist. "I liked to died when I heard someone snatched Antonio last night, and now that Wellington girl is gone too!" She gave me a consoling hug, and came close to just about breaking down into tears in my arms. "What can we do, Alphonso? We gots to do something fore it's too late!"

Strange, the things you think about when you're standing deep down in someone else's grief and tribulation. I could feel Wilma drying her wet eyes against my shirt, but at the same time I couldn't help but think about what Pauline was telling me while we cuddled naked on that huge Naugahyde couch.

"Empires come and go, Alphonso," Pauline mused while she played footsie with me, "we Native Americans were fortunate enough to have our heyday in the Sun. The part inside me that is Indian senses and knows we will rise to the top once more. The part inside me that is more than Indian senses and knows it's all a game of shadows and masks. Who knows what cloak of darkness I may wear tomorrow? Who knows what mask I may choose in the hereafter to hide behind? I am content to let Time spin the wheel of my being and to have it stop here where I can rest with you."

Pauline nuzzled against my cheek and I held her tight as I kissed her fingertips.

"I'm glad we could have this discussion," Pauline said. She squealed as I blew in her ear. "You have got to admit, Alphonso, this sure beats any Platonic relationship you might have been considering having with me!"

"Where did you hear about Platonic relationships?"

"Oh, I've held my nose more than once while some well-meaning teacher force fed large helpings of Western Philosophy down my gullet. After which were ladled in huge doses of Christianity for good measure. Open me up and you'll find I'm a veritable pinata of assimilated Western answers and solutions!"

"Yeah, I'll bet! I'll bet you don't even know what "Platonic' means!"

"You would lose your money, Alphonso. Pauline Little Fox knows more than you imagine. The word 'Platonic' refers to Plato who was a pupil of – of – of - I know-don't tell me-"

"See I told you."

Mojo pulled in his dough with a sneer and laid his cigar to rest in an ashtray.

"Yeah, my main man, time to give to Caesar what is Caesar's. Now you take our client Suckertease over there; that fine representative of the supremacy of Western Thought. Once upon a time, he thought he would deny Caesar his due, he even plotted and planned to blow the whistle on ole Mojo and his game awhile back. Now you can see what happened to him. We pulled the plug on Mister Turner way back when; and ever since he's been runnin' into signs that read 'NO OUTLET' and 'DEAD END'. Every once in awhile I'll flex my connections and throw the poor dog a bone. Suckertease is smart enough to know the score by now. He knows it's 'switch that bait' and 'bait-and-switch' everlasting for his ass until the end of time." Mojo put his elbows up on the card table and cracking his knuckles, glared at me. "An' guess what? Ain't a got damn thing Mister Ph.D with all his 'Socratic Method' can do about it!"

"Hush up, y'all, it's about to come on now!" Baldy whistles softly to himself. "That Marine Billy Gordon is shore a big 'un. I don't know about this, Alphonso. That's a tough lookin' chunk uh white boy Dougie Dogg is facin' up against." Baldy turns around with edgy concern. "I hope you didn't bet the store on this one, my man."

"Nothing more I can do now, Baldy," I flip my hole card and take the cash, "it's all on the Dogg now."

The sound of the fight bell goes through my heart like an icicle. I didn't think I would react this way, but I'm worried about Dougie. I know he's squaring off against a hot dog Marine who out reaches him by half a foot, and outweighs him by a good forty pounds. Now I am finding myself second-guessing everything we did while we trained together. Did we watch the fight video on Gordon enough?

Did we spar enough? Did Dougie find the weakness with Gordon he was looking to find? I can feel the fear in the pit of Dougie's soul so strong, it comes right through television set. I have to put down my cards for a second just to compose myself. When I raise my head again, Mojo and Orlando are peering at me keenly

"Now, if I were in your shoes," Mojo took up his stogie from the ash tray, "and one of my relatives was missing along with the lady who was my date for the night, I would be hoping to hear word about a ransom note or something. Anything just to know that they was still alive and kicking. I would be rackin' my brains to know how I could get them back safe and sound. I would be prayin' to the Lord that the Wellington broad wasn't gettin' a train run through her end to end an'that my nephew wasn't bein' held by his big toe out some fourth story window somewheres. Ain't that right, Orlando?"

"Been known to happen, Boss Man."

There's that red dot again, buzzing across the ceiling like some crimson insect. Nobody at the table really seems to notice, and only Danny glances down when the cellular phone clipped to my belt goes off.

"I better answer that," I excuse myself as I unclip the phone, "Hello, who is this? What? Just a minute." I reach over with the phone towards Mojo, "- it's for you, man -"

Mojo and Orlando attempt to stifle it, but I see genuine surprise register on both their faces now. Mojo reluctantly reaches for the phone.

"Hello? Who the hell is this callin'?" Mojo locks me in a deadly gaze. "What kinda mess is this you think you puttin' down? Whatchu mean, you 'got' my bitches? You say Sherry there with you? Yeah, niggah, what you think? Put that hoe on the phone! Quick!"

Now right about now, Rap Robinson has a ski mask pulled over his head, and is clicking the chambers of a .44 Magnum against the temple of a whore named Sherry McCall. He and a few of his crew are taking turns playing Russian Roulette with a half dozen of Mojo's most lucrative call girls. I can see Mojo tense up every time he hears a chamber click off. I can imagine Sherry McCall telling Mojo how they're all blindfolded and in some undisclosed place and not to do anything rash.

But then, I'm just imagining all that.

There's a wild look in Mojo's eye and he nearly chews off the end his cigar.

Now! Draw, sucker, draw! Go for your piece!

"What you puttin' down, Alphonso? You tryin' to get yo' nephew and that little Wellington girl kilt?"

This ought to make him draw, I thought to myself. He's got to draw after this.

"Naw, I don't want that. I would do anything to have them here by my side right now. Just like I know you would like to have all your women that got snatched returned to you as soon as possible."

Now I watch as Mojo and Orlando's mouths open even wider as Daphne Wellington, my nephew Antonio Gentle and Sheba Taylor emerge from behind the black curtain that partitions the dressing room up that stairway where my models change.

"Hello, Mister Morris-" Daphne waves as she sits down next to Baldy to watch Dougie in his fight, "- don't let Alphonso cheat you with any marked cards."

"Hey baby," Sheba sits on the other side of Baldy, "them shore were some nice things you said about me. You know what? I may have me enough loot for college now."

Never let it be said that Mojo was a man to be left speechless. But what's he waiting for now? Go for your gun, sucker!

"Bitch! Get yo' ass over here!" Mojo spat out as he threw his cigar thudding against the wall.

He was about to rise when I finally pulled out the slot and placed my .38 on the table. I could not wait for him to draw first any longer.

"Now who you callin' 'bitch', Mojo?" I asked as the room rustled with the activity of folks ducking for cover. "Sit back down, sucker, before I give you some lead to digest - sit back down!"

Mojo replaced himself in the seat across from me. Danny, Socrates and Smiley were in freeze frame around the table with me. Nathan Eddie was looking up at the skylight.

"Dog, Uncle Alphonso, I didn't know you was like that!" Antonio cried from a safe hiding place behind the sofa with Daphne and Sheba. "You gon' git us all killed tryin' to deal like a thug with Mister Morris there!"

"Rats usually get washed overboard on the Good Ship Lollipop." Orlando observed coolly, but his voice was barely a whisper.

"Better listen to your nephew, Alphonso," Mojo reached for another cigar in his vest pocket, but I could tell by the trembling in his hand that he was shaken to the core. "- in case you did not notice there's a high powered rifle aimed at your head even as we speak."

The red dot skipped and skittered its way down the wall and then over my sleeve to rest somewhere on my body. Needless to say, I could flash to a bunch of other places I would rather be, but I was here now, and I would have to call the play out to the end. I held on to the .38 and kept a steady aim on Mojo.

"He's right, Alphonso," Nathan Eddie observed carefully, "there's somebody up in the skylight drawing a bead on you-"

"Damn Alphonso," Danny looks at me through reddening eyes, "Got damn-"

"Better call him off, Mojo, better call him off," I warn menacingly, "-cause one thing you can count on, if anything happens to me, you can write off all them bitches been makin' you so much cash and start from square one. I get smoked, they get choked and that's all she wrote!"

"Alphonso! Nooo!" Daphne cried out.

"Baby, don't do iiiiiit-" Sheba wailed in anxious earnestness.

"Don't move! Baldy, make them stay where they are!"

"Y'all heard the man!" Baldy took the women both by the arms. "Y'all do like Alphonso say do! You can see the score now. Got dog-it, Alphonso, I hope you satisified now. You done put yo' head in the lion's mouth for sure this time!"

Mojo snapped his fingers but the sound was fainter this time as Orlando reached to light him up. He sucked in on a fresh cigar and tried to look casual as he considered this last remark made by Baldy.

"Yeah - his dickhead-"

Dougie was taking quite a pounding, but was getting in a few licks of his own from what I could hear on the televison set. My breath was coming out slow and regular, the way it did when I would meditate with Stella. I kept the .38 aimed on Mojo, but still the way it stood at this point, we both were no more than lined up in each other's sights. Damn! I thought I could get him to draw on me first!

"That piece getting kind of heavy, son?" Orlando inquired solicitously.

"I can deal with it."

Mojo appeared to have regained himself again. He blew a jet of cigar smoke my way before he made a little cough into his fist.

"All I have to do is adjust my tie, young blood, and you're dead meat." Mojo explained to me evenly.

"- as we go hand in hand to hell-" I assured him.

"What you got to say about all this, Suckertease?" Mojo glanced at Turner sneering with an acid contempt. "You been mighty quiet of late."

"My middle name is Socrates, Leonard," Socrates spoke in a voice clear as a bell, "I say let the young man slide. He may not appreciate the consequences of what he's doing, but at least he has the balls to stand up to the likes of you."

Mojo and Orlando curled their lips and nodded to each other with mock approval.

"Nothin' like starin' death in the face to make a man give you the straight truth, huh, my man Orlando? Sounds like that 'Socratic Method' is kickin' up again with Turner."

"Sounds like it to me. You know, when you've got more than one pig squealing it's time to reach for the spare rifle."

Mojo looks at me curiously as I start to feel beads of sweat roll down my neck.

"How did you get your personnel back with you safe and sound, Alphonso?"

"That's for you to wonder about while you're spending those sleepless nights biting the devil's ass!"

"Watch your mouth, boy," Mojo points at me with his cigar, "you better pray to God I don't find I need to adjust my tie, because from where I sit, you've got somethin' red between yo' eyes."

I did not reckon on this. I have drawn first while Mojo plans to take me out by remote control.

"Yeah, well, I got a full course meal for you too, Mister Mojo Man."

Mojo cackles and elbows Orlando gleefully.

"That's what I like to hear! Now that we got each other at gunpoint, it's time to nail down some of the finer points in our discourse on Truth, Justice and the American Way!"

"Sounds like a winner." Socrates chimes in again, "What is death to the human soul that is true to itself?"

"Don't tell me you got more of that "Socratic Method' to bring to the table," Mojo seemed noticeably irritated that Socrates would have anything to say, "-I bet you don't really know where that 'Socratic Method' really comes from, do you, Turner? I'll tell you where it comes from. The real Socrates had a naggin' wife who was always stickin' logical pins into everything he said whenever he invited his friends over for dinner and a rap session. Instead of bitch slapping the cunt and sending her to bed without any supper, he devised a way of manueverin' her into a position where she could look at her ideas and be forced to admit how big a fool and how ignorant she was before all of Socrates' friends. This proved so successful that Socrates then decided to take his show to the marketplace and that's how Western Philosophy was sold to the whole world!"

"What's your point?" Socrates asked tensely, flitting up his eyes at the skylight.

Mojo snickered with Orlando and made a little nervous tap on the table

"See if you can get to this, Suckertease. This great system of thought, which is part and parcel of the Western Philosophical Tradition, actually began because a henpecked husband was tryin' to figure out how to put his naggin' wife back in her place. Even back in the day, white men were tryin' to put the Pimp Hand down on the bitches they had in they stable! Now I betcha my man Smiley can quote me a verse that supports my claim. What about it, Smiley?"

"I-I don't know, Mojo," Smiley said, beads of sweat forming on his forehead, "it's kind of hard to remember Scripture when you is 'under the gun'. You get what I'm sayin'?"

"Why you so down on Socrates?" I asked, my voice getting hoarse. This is all backwards, I think to myself. I drew first!

"That's another misconception you got, young blood. I'm Samuel Turner's last resort and salvation."

"How you figure that, Mojo?" I said, my grip on the .38 getting slippery.

Nathan Eddie starts to slip silently away from the window into a corner of the room where the afternoon shadows deepen.

"The simple fact being that Sam the Man actually believes in Thought and Reason as the way to success. No doubt he ran across the idea in some book he was readin' and fell in love with it; and you gotta respect a man who can love an idea more than pussy. The trouble is most of us buy our ideas 'under the gun' like Smiley was signifyin', and at face value. A trick can be suckered into buyin' an idea because the wrappin' is pretty and it has lots of sex appeal. But when he gets it home and opens the box, he'll find that there's little or nothing inside. Now you take the 'Socratic Method'. Nobody ever questions what sense it makes to learn how to convince people that they're hypocrites and are stupid and ignorant. Look what happened to Socrates after a lifetime of doing that! Now you gotta decide, Alphonso, before I straighten out my tie and book from this scene, whether you gon' throw in with me and get over like a fat cat or throw in with our old Suckertease and fall in love with all those big ideas that keep you fuckin' yourself and sleepin' in garages like yo' brother Bobbie." Mojo took a long drag on his cigar, and viewed me through narrowed eyes as Orlando fussed with the cuff link on his shirt. "Now I done put my cards on the table. You got a lot of potential and your own way of lookin' at things. I ain't got to tell you that there's money to be made on a sweet setup like that. But you can bet yo' bottom dollar on one thing; nobody puts the Pimp Hand down on Master Mojo and lives to tell it! It's on you now, my young blood-"

Strange the things you think about when somebody from on high is set to make a murder burger out of your brains. There's a red dot right between my eyes and I'm figuring that should it come down to me having a third eye, my grip around the butt of this .38 and my finger pressed against the trigger should make the thing go off as my hands tighten in the reflex of the first death throes. Mojo's got a big pot belly, so it going to be hard to miss that.

Before I pull the trigger to find out whether or not my application for martyrdom will be accepted, my thoughts go to Dougie. I can hear how he's spinning off the ropes and feinting and jabbing and mixing in those combinations. I remember all that trash talk he was giving me when I was sparring with him.

"That's it, Alphonso!" Dougie pushes me back with a jab and tags me on the nose with a right cross. "I think I got it now!" Dougie starts taunting me like I'm Billy Gordon in the flesh. "Come on, Creeper! Come on now!" I use my reach to jab Dougie back. "That's it, Alphonso! Come on, hoo-ji, do like the Terminator an' see where that gets you! Time to find out why you will NOT be back!"

I take an angle on Dougie and throw a left hook which he blocks with ease before I force him against the ropes in a clinch with a series of uppercuts.

"That's it, Alphonso, that's it! Harder, man, harder! Just like Mister Machine Marine would do! That's it!" Dougie tags me on the nose again and draws blood. "That's it! Don't hold back now!"

Dougie dances away circling to the left with half a dozen jabs.

"Come on with it! Ain't no pussy in here with you now, Alphonso!" Dougie feints to the right like Lawson schooled him before coming in with the combinations.

"Huah-hupt!" I block a hook and catch Dougie in the ribs with an uppercut before he dances away with a flurry of punches.

"That's better! Now you thinkin' with your dukes instead of yo' dick! Come on now, show me what you got!"

I hold Dougie back with my reach and swing at him wildly with hooks and crosses.

"That's it! That's how that yahoo from Hickeyville gon' do it! Do it, Alphonso, do it! Do it, man!"

Dougie's voice merges and transforms into Wilma's the night she brought me the news in the papers about Antonio and Daphne and we wound up between the sheets.

"Oooo! Alphonso! Do it! Yeah! Yeahhh! That's what I like! Do it! Do it! Doooo it!"

Now the red dot between my eyes winks out. Mojo and Orlando look up at the skylight startled. Finally, I have made up my mind to give Mojo a bullet when Willie and Earl burst through the door!

Mojo turns towards the sound of the banging-crashing my brothers make as they rush into the room and I fire off the first round with a whining roar!

"ALPHONSO!" Willie shouted with an angry Halloween grimace, "-what the FUCK you call yo'self doin'-"

Daphne and Sheba screamed repeatedly as they ran hand in hand to the busted door.

Mojo reached for his piece, but the time is all wrong and fucked up. Smiley and Danny and Baldy were all over him and Orlando. Nathan Eddie sprung out of the shadow in the corner and twisted the gun out of Mojo's hand. Willie was all over me for what reason I don't know and threw me to the ground. He kept banging my gun hand against the wooden slatted floor, but the only thing that ran through my mind was how big a fool I was to draw first.

Damn that hurt!

Even my nephew Antonio was trying to pry the .38 out of my grasp! Damn! All because I drew first!

"Come on, Uncle Alphonso," Antonio wheeezed, "come on! You don't need to be doin' none of this! Let it go, Uncle Alphonso, let it go!"

But I wouldn't let go. I couldn't let go. Suddenly Daphne and Sheba were back in the room helping Willie and Antonio to wrest the gun out of my hands, and those honeys were supposed to be on my side! Now I hear Earl's mouth as he rushes breathlessly into the room.

"Got him, Willie! Snuck up on the roof where the sucker was layin' and got 'em!" Earl is starting to catch his breath now as the room whirls with all this tussling and Earl is banging my head against the floor. "You ain't shit, Alphonso," Earl puffs as he bends over and clutches his knees, "you -you ain't shit! Knew you was –was -was up to no good!"

"Alphonso, honey, let go-" Daphne is pleading with me.

"Come on, baby, come on! Baby, let go now, let go!" Sheba urged along with Daphne.

What is this? You would think I was the felon or something! The way everybody is down on me and grabbing and reaching for the piece in my hand. What about Mojo and his partner in crime? I might as well tell you I lost it right there and then and I don't care who knows it!

Damn! I knew good and well not to draw first!

"Let me go!" I hollered at the top of my lungs. "Fuck you, Earl, fuck you! You don't know nothing! I sent for you and Willie to help me out, and you wouldn't do shit! Fuck you!" I turned this way and that to shake them off of me, and kicked my feet against the floor. "Whatchu lookin'at? I said fuck you! Fuck you! Why ain't you holdin' on to Mojo and his 'associate' the way you manhandlin' me? Fuck you! Fuck you! You wouldn't do shit about what had to be did! I said fuck you! Fuck you all!"

"Damn, Alphonso!" Willie measured me for a chop to the chin, "-me and Earl should have buried you that time in the backyard where the dogs could go pee on you -"

"Fuck you, Willie! You and whose army? You ain't shit! I said fuck -"

Willie crossed my neck with his arm and came down with the chop. Everything was all spinning lights with the urge to throw up engulfed in blackness after that.

That's mostly how the Thug-O-Rama went down.

Now I've been here in the pen these last ten months because my conviction is on appeal. Mojo's lawyers have me in here for wrongful injury, possessing an unregistered weapon and half a dozen counts of attempted kidnapping since I'm the alleged 'mastermind' behind the snatching of Morris' whores. I just managed to nick that Mojo in the stomach and even then the bullet didn't really go all the way through. I should have taken target practice before Mojo invited himself over.

There are nights when I lay awake in my cell wondering whether or not it was worth it all. Socrates comes over and leaves me these reading lists, but reading without right of way into Stella's pussy is like soup without a sandwich. Besides, I've never been that partial to sharing my most intimate thoughts with hard legs. Socrates confides in me sometimes about his life and tries to get me to confide in him, but I already have a father. Most of the time I tell him he really ought to be sharing some of that True Confession stuff with someone as well read as himself. Someone like Miss Ford.

Sometimes people come to visit me who ask what I would change if I could do it all over again. I suppose there are those who would like to see me break down and cry and admit the error of my ways and confess my sins. Smiley comes here all the time with his friends and quotes me Bible verses, comparing my situation to what people have gone through in the Good Book. I will have to admit I have a hard time likening myself to Jonah or somebody like that, even though I am in a whale of trouble so to speak. When it comes to regrets, as I said before, I just wish I'd been a better shot when Mojo finally came around. I also wish I could have figured on Mojo not depending solely on his piece. I never did reckon on that Orlando dude posting a sniper above my skylight. That little maneuver was somewhat beyond my power to consider and calculate.

All I can say is you live and you learn.

Even though I fouled the play somewhat with the Mojo Man, I found to my most profound surprise, that I was shooting somewhat straighter than I intended to with Stella, Wilma, Pauline and even Daphne. I cannot tell you exactly how it happened, but I'm in the midst of a little baby boom of my own right now, and am a little mystified as to how I got here.

That time I took Stella to the airport, there was something subdued in her mood that I could not for the life of me get her to talk about. I kept probing, asking if anything was wrong and she just kept shaking her head and keeping mum with that little smile on her beautiful face. I knew she was sitting on something, but I figured she would tell me all in her own good sweet time. I have found there is no need to pressure women when they don't want you to know something, You can hold their feet to the fire, and find out everything but what you really want to know.

Anyway, I checked into this place and not long afterwards, Eugene Halloway sends his grandson Charles with a package from TONY GHETTO ENTERPRISES. I find out lil' bow wow worked out all the chemistry and is marketing his own candy bar. I have him sign me up for a couple of cases, and while I'm emptying out the box and checking out the goods, I spy this photo album underneath all those Charlie Bars.

"What's all this, Charlie, my man?"

"Search me, Mister Alphonso," Charles shrugs his shoulders, "Grandpa said just to make sure you got it."

"Tell him for me, then, I got it."

"Good."

"We straight then?"

"Yes sir, Mister Alphonso. Would you like to order a year's supply of Charlie Bars now or on a monthly basis?"

"Let's do it on a monthly basis. You may not always be able to reach me at this address."

"That'll work. Monthly basis it will be. I'll see you in a few weeks, Mister Alphonso."

"I'll be here."

I took the box filled with candy and the photo album back to my cell. The Charlie Bars weren't bad with the creamy date filling and the flaked almond chocolate covering. I opened the photo album and found a note from Eugene Halloway:

> Dear Alphonso:
>
> Your application for Fatherhood has been accepted. Welcome to the club!
>
> Stella sends you tidings of love from the Source of the Sun. I knew you would reject Master Mojo's sophisticated program for spaying and neutering the present generation of men, women and pets.
>
> Take advantage of the time you have at your disposal to acquire valuable skills. Now that I have invested in your products, you need to consider how best to manage your revenues and assets!
>
> Best Regards and Success,
Eugene Halloway
Tony Ghetto Enterprises

When I opened the photo album, I found out I was the father of a little boy by the name of Eisaku Yamamoto! He was barely four years old and I wondered why Stella waited until my incarceration to share with me this stunning news. The photographs of mother and child were really inspiring and now I would have something to sketch while I was in here, and someone to send all these Charlie Bars to as gifts.

When I opened up Stella's letters and read how much she missed me and how determined she was to raise little Eisaku with proper Japanese values, well, I found it necessary to turn around in my bunk and face the wall for awhile. I wrote Stella and sent her preliminary sketches from the album she had given me.

I promised to visit as soon as I was able and to start learning how to speak fluent Japanese. Daphne would show up often after the first year. How she came to bear me Dwight Rockwell is one for Ripley's Believe it or Not. You may or may not remember seeing the item in the society papers, but she was all set to be the proud wife of Victor Baseheart after Miguel and I sprung her out of Mojo's trap. I was packing up all my stuff in boxes, getting ready for my little vacation in prison when I heard the buzzer ring to my apartment. When I opened the door there was Daphne, all decked out in her wedding dress complete with train! She jumped into my arms and as I swung her around in her excitement, she kicked the door closed with her high-heeled shoes.

"Alphonso! Oh, my Alphonso! I have never been happier!" Daphne literally danced around my apartment, holding out the glittering rock on her ring finger. "See?"

"Impressive," I said, as I held her at arms length admiringly, "you make a beautiful bride, Daphne. I think marriage becomes you."

"Do you, Alphonso? Do you really?" Daphne asked with an earnestness that was at once touching and disarming. "Victor and I are to be married in June with the blessings of our parents. We're going to honeymoon in Europe and visit all the Capital cities there. Everything's turning out splendidly perfect. I feel so lucky! Look, I came to give you an invitation to our wedding. I do so want you to come, Alphonso. The whole thing is going to be such a grand affair."

"Sounds like a Hollywood Movie, Daphne," I took the envelope with the invitation from her, "I wouldn't miss it for the world," I lied carefully.

"I have you to thank for all this, Alphonso," Daphne reached over and grabbed me by the ears and kissed me flush on the mouth, "-the way you and Miguel went about in disguise and searched and searched until you found us! Nobody," Daphne's gaiety starts to wither right before my eyes, "Nobody, has ever," Daphne's lower lip begins to tremble, "gone to such lengths for me ever-ever-ever-" Daphne sniffed and removed a doily from the cuff of her sleeve to dab at the corner of her eyes, "ever -ever-ever-"

"Aww, Daphne, you just wait until Victor gets through with you, I'm-"

"WHERE are you going, Alphonso?" Daphne turned slowly around once more in deepening dismay. "Why do you have everything you own packed and ready to go?"

"Didn't I tell you? I'm going on a trip too, Daphne. First to Paris, France and the Louvre, and after that, why-"

"Stop it, Alphonso! You just stop it!" Daphne breaks down into a cataract of sobs and tears. "You've never been a very good liar-"

"I beg your pardon! I can lie with the best of them, I-"

"Oh, stop it, stop it!" Daphne stamped her foot. "You just shut-up, Alphonso!" Daphne flung off her bridal bonnet and veil. "You're being sent to do time for what you did to that Morris character! Here, help me out of this bridal gown, will you? Hurry up!"

"Daphne! What are you doing?" I say as I hesitantly help her undo the buttons on the back of her dress.

Daphne flashes me an angry, red faced, teary scowl.

"What you wanted me to do all along, Alphonso! Here, help me undo the hooks to my bra! Don't play with me and pretend this isn't what you want, Alphonso-"

"But Daphne, you're -you're about to be married!"

"- and you're about to go to prison so I'll do what's best for all concerned. But nobody ever thought to consult me about what I think is for the best! What do you want, Alphonso? You want I should beg you on bended knee? Careful with my stockings, I don't want to get any runs in them if you don't mind-"

"But Daphne, what about Victor?"

"What about me, Alphonso? What about you? Are you going to stand there and tell me you are not burning up with love for me at this very moment?" Daphne stands there fully unclothed, waiting for me to embrace her, and once again on the verge of breaking down into sobbing tears. "I love you, Alphonso, I've always wanted you. I'll do anything you want me to do. There. I've said it!" Daphne slaps her thigh with resolve. "Now will you take me to bed and make love to me?" "Daphne, I-" I put my arms around her to soothe and dry her tears, "- are you sure you want to do this?"

"Oh yes, Alphonso, yes!" Daphne put her arms around my neck and pressed her wet face against my chest. "Whatever the consequences are, I will bear them. I just can't live this lie anymore and pretend I don't want you as much as you want me. Now you take off the rest of your clothes and you love me." Daphne gave a little laugh, and wiped her nose. "I don't want to be the only naked person standing in the middle of this room." Daphne kissed my bare shoulders and my chest as I took off my shirt. "Is that your bedroom back there, Alphonso?"

I stepped out of my clothes and swept Daphne up into my arms. We entered my bedroom and began to weave a dream. Nine months later, Dwight Rockwell was born.

Wilma would show up with Sheldon Ray and ask to take pictures of us together.

"When you think you'll be gettin' out, baby?" Wilma would ask and it pained me I could never give her a definite answer.

"Just hold the fort, hon, it can't be much longer. Do you need money for the baby?" I would ask as I tickled Sheldon Ray. "Have you got everything you need?"

"Eugene set up an account for us," Wilma smiled confidentially, "all yo' stuff is selling on the Internet like hotcakes, Alphonso. Everything is paid for including Sheldon's college education. We just want you outta here, baby."

Pauline Little Fox would just sit there on Visitor's Day, her little papoose strapped to her back or set carefully in her lap while she read about the Great Speeches By Native Americans or some other tome by Jamake Highwater or Dee Brown. Phillip Gentle Fox was a very agreeable child, who neither laughed or cried much, but loved to move his arms and legs with great bursts of abundant energy.

Pauline always asked me how I was doing and never seemed to desire to make any demands on me whatsoever.

"I went to your studio as you asked me do, Alphonso."

"Did you find the snakes, Pauline?"

"Yes, I did, my love,"

"So how are they doing?"

"They're doing fine. Phillip loves to play with them. Don't you, Phillip? Don't you?"

Phillip made a face and a little giggle.

"Some of them I took with me and released into a habitat where they could thrive. I think it was best for them, Alphonso."

"I can always trust you to do the right thing, Pauline. Do you need anything? I would feel a whole lot better if you would let me set up an account for you and Phillip."

"I didn't come here to get anything from you, Alphonso. I just thought you would like to see your son from time to time." Pauline's merry expression was tinged with irony. "As you see now, Alphonso, I saved your seed for posterity. I figured it might be worth something one day." Pauline wrapped her shawl about her shoulders. "Here, let me sit in your lap and give you a big goodbye kiss, so Phillip slowly gets some idea of how he got here. Soon you won't be living here anymore, and you will have to come and visit us from time to time." Pauline kissed me and rubbed her nose against my cheek. "Eh? Is that right, Phillip? That's right, isn't it, Phillip?"

Daphne would hold Dwight Rockwell in her arms and talk about the private schools she was choosing from for little Dwight. This particular day, however, he was having a bad case of the hiccups and after patting him on the back for quite some time, Daphne at the end of her patience handed him to me.

"Here," Daphne said brusquely, "it's your turn to burp him, Alphonso."

We searched around for what seemed like forever. Victor and I wound up retracing all the steps of our little stomping match. He looked behind the garbage cans and I looked under the dumpster. I made a careful survey of the cracks between all the paving stones. I'll have to admit I was glad we only covered the ground where we were thumping each other. We both took a good look at exactly where we entered the alley. Finally, it occurred to me there was only one thing left to do.

"Let's take the rack out from against the wall and look underneath there," I suggested to Victor.

"I looked under there," Victor shrugged while wincing in pain. "I didn't see anything."

"I know, but some of that space is in shadow. We move the rack, we can see everything without the shadows in the way."

Victor shrugged again.

We moved the rack and even took the garbage cans off.

"Nothing." Victor looked down and around and over at me.

We sat on the garbage can rack and thought about it for a minute.

"Let's try the dumpster. I know, I know. If I don't find it under there, we'll call the whole search off. How about it?"

"Yeah, then I can go back to kicking you ass, Gentle."

"I would have thought you'd had enough of me for one afternoon, Baseheart."

Moving the dumpster was a whole other matter entirely. It was lucky for us it was on wheels.

"Hold on a moment." Victor's gloomy countenance brightened briefly with the pinprick of a new idea. "Before we give ourselves hernias moving this dumpster, why don't we call your number and see if we can't locate it that way.?"

"Yeah, that sounds like a plan." I admitted to Victor.

"Here's my cell phone. Knock yourself out."

I tapped in Miguel Jimenez's number.

We walked and looked around. Nothing. Not even a reasonable facsimile of a ring tone. Victor looked down and then up at me with a wry frown.

"Still want to move that dumpster to look for it?" Victor asked me.

"Hold tight." I halted him as he started to move over there. "I think..."

I saw it wedged between the curb and the adjacent flagstone at the entrance to the alley.

"I found it!" I exclaimed as a frown slowly formed on my face. "Ain't that a blip! The battery's gone dead."

"My! My! That was really something, Alphonso..." The old lady remarked as she grasped her husband's hand. "We're so glad you invited us to visit you."

"Come on now, dear," the old man said as he patted his wife's arm. "Mister Gentle is probably tired now having us talk his ear off all this time."

"No," I attempted to assure them, "it's all right. It was kinda cool, really."

"Now you take care of yourself in here, young man," the old fellow said as he rose to go and helped his wife up.

"Sure thing." I said looking down at the sketches I had been doodling of them as we talked. "Stop by again any time."

The old couple moved to go when the lady appeared to have an afterthought.

"I'll tell you what. When do you get out? We'll come and visit you."

"Keep in touch. I'll let you know."

I watched them go with just one thought on my mind.

THE END

CPSIA information can be obtained
at www.ICGtesting.com
Printed in the USA
BVHW031938280619
552133BV00017B/64/P

9 781646 067343